CSA

KT-461-623

Susanna Gregory was a police officer in Leeds before taking up an academic career. She has served as an environmental consultant during seventeen field seasons in the polar regions, and has taught comparative anatomy and biological anthropology.

She is the creator of the Matthew Bartholomew series of mysteries set in medieval Cambridge as well as the Thomas Chaloner books, and now lives in Wales with her husband, who is also a writer.

Also by Susanna Gregory

MURDER ON HIGH HOLBORN

Susanna Gregory

SPHERE

First published in Great Britain in 2013 by Sphere

A CIP catalogue record for this book
is available from the British Library.

ISBN 978-1-84744-433-2

Typeset in Baskerville MT by Palimpsest Book Production Limited,
Falkirk, Stirlingshire

Printed and bound in Great Britain by Clays Ltd, St Ives plc

Papers used by Sphere are from well-managed forests
and other responsible sources.

MIX
Paper from
responsible sources
FSC
www.fsc.org FSC® C104740

Sphere
An imprint of
Little, Brown Book Group
100 Victoria Embankment
London EC4Y 0DY

An Hachette UK Company
www.hachette.co.uk

www.littlebrown.co.uk

For Eileen and Paul French

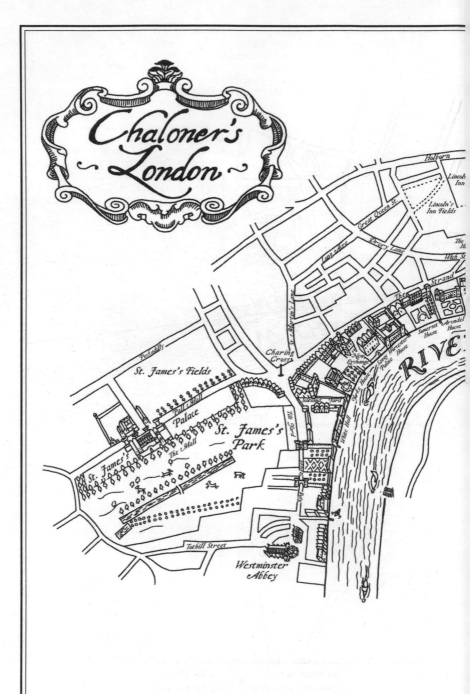

Chaloner's London

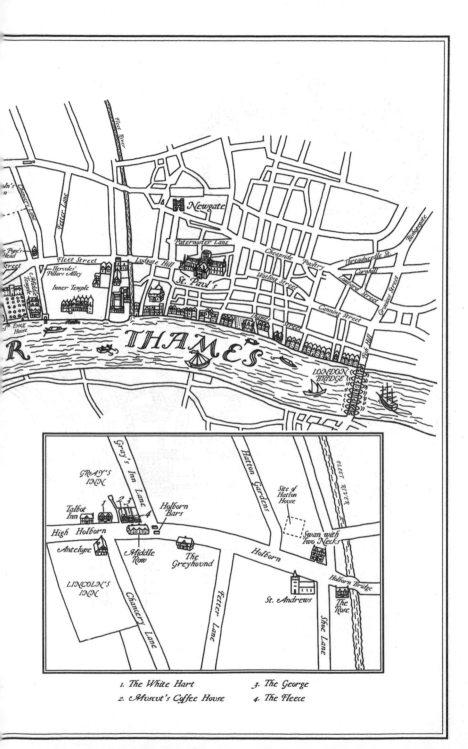

1. The White Hart
2. Moscut's Coffee House
3. The George
4. The Fleece

Prologue

His Majesty's Ship *London* was a magnificent sight as she sailed down the Medway from the Royal Dockyard at Chatham. Carrying some eighty guns, she was one of the largest ships in the navy, and the Admiralty expected her to play a crucial role in fighting the Dutch – war had been declared two weeks before. She was the flagship of Admiral Sir John Lawson, and would sail up the Thames to collect him from Queenhithe, after which she would join the rest of his fleet in the Channel.

HMS *London* had always enjoyed a special relationship with the city after which she was named, so the crew was looking forward to taking her there, relishing the opportunity to show off her exquisitely painted woodwork, bright new sails and gleaming brass cannon. There were three hundred seamen aboard, and those not on watch had contrived to be out on deck, proud and trim in their best embroidered jackets and snowy white trousers.

There was also a smattering of passengers – a few

1

of the Admiral's relations making the journey between Chatham and Queenhithe as a treat. They would disembark in the city, after which the ship would revert to a fighting machine. The festive ribbons that fluttered from her masts would be taken down, her crew would exchange their smart, shore-going rigs for working clothes, and all would be battened down ready for combat.

Captain Jeffrey Dare, in command until the Admiral boarded, ordered the mainsails set and *London* heeled over as the wind caught her, a sharp bow-wave hissing down her sides. He was glad to be away at last, although he was concerned about the failing light. He had intended to get under way at dawn, but there had been some wrangling over paperwork with the dockyard's commissioner, and it was noon before the matter had been resolved.

Wind sang in the rigging as *London* picked up speed, a joyful sound that drove the petty frustrations of the refit from Dare's mind. He smiled. It was good to feel the deck alive under his feet again, and although he thought the King and his Privy Council were insane to declare war on a powerful maritime nation like the Dutch, he was eager to do his duty. And at least they had had the sense to put the Channel Fleet under Lawson, not some clueless aristocrat who had never been to sea. The Admiral might be a rough-mannered, salty-tongued braggart, but at least he knew his way around a ship.

Thoughts of Lawson reminded Dare of the two large chests that had been brought aboard earlier that day. Did they really contain the Admiral's bass viols, as Commissioner Pett had claimed? Dare had been astonished to learn that Lawson was interested in music: no matter how hard he tried, he could not imagine that gruff old seadog engaging in anything so cultured.

He had challenged Pett about the weight, too. The boxes were extremely heavy, and he was unconvinced by the explanation that Lawson had purchased a new kind of instrument made of metal, so they would not lose their tone in the damp sea-air. But the Admiral's luggage was none of Dare's business, especially now, when the ship was under way and he had duties to attend.

He bellowed a complex stream of orders that changed *London*'s course as she flew out of the mouth of the Medway and into the Thames Estuary. She responded immediately, like the good ship she was, and he was pleased with both her and her crew – the Dutch would not know what had hit them when HMS *London* met them in battle!

Her motion was different once she was in less sheltered waters, and she began to pitch and roll; Dare grinned when several passengers made a dash for the rail. Normally, he would have tacked immediately, but the wind was capricious that day, and to the east lay the Nore, the hidden, shifting sandbanks that had brought many an unwary ship to an ignominious end. Wisely, he deferred until he was certain the danger was past.

He happened to glance landwards as they passed the little village of Prittlewell, a low huddle of cottages strewn along a bleak, muddy shore. Fishermen and their families had gathered on the beach, tiny figures who brandished their hats and waved joyously. Some of the crew waved back, as did those passengers who were not retching. Dare felt a surge of pride, knowing what a noble sight *London* must be, with her great press of canvas billowing white against the dark pebble-grey of the sky.

3

The delay in leaving meant they had missed the tide, so Dare climbed up to the crosstrees – the beams that attached the rigging to the mast – wanting the better view that height would provide. From that elevated perch he could really *read* the water – interpret the ripples and changing colours that warned of currents, shoals and contrary breezes. It was an undignified thing for a captain to do, but Lawson did it, and what was good enough for that staunch old mariner was good enough for Dare.

He fixed his eyes on the course ahead, and shouted directions that would alter their bearing a fraction. It was not really necessary, but there was no harm in working the crew after so many weeks in dock. The wind made his eyes water; it was much colder aloft than it was below, with a brisk south-westerly blowing.

Suddenly, there was a tremendous crack, followed by an explosion, and the ship heeled violently to one side. The lurch was so great that it almost dislodged him from his precarious perch, and for a moment he could do nothing but flail about in a desperate attempt to regain his balance. He glanced down as soon as he was able, and was horrified to see clouds of billowing smoke and bodies in the sea, bobbing and lifeless.

With a tearing groan the mainmast behind him began to topple, taking with it a mass of sail and several shrieking sailors. Dare did not understand what was happening! They could not have run aground, because they were in the middle of a wide, deep channel. Had the powder magazine exploded then? But how? No one should have been down there, and it was locked anyway. With a shriek of protesting timbers, *London* listed farther to starboard. Dare swung in the air for a moment, then lost his grip

4

to cartwheel sickeningly towards the churning brown water below.

On shore, the villagers of Prittlewell watched in stunned disbelief. One moment, *London* was ploughing with silent grace up the river, her sails full and fat, and the next she was tilting heavily to one side, belching smoke. Corpses littered the water around her, while tiny splashes of white showed where the occasional survivor was frantically struggling to stay afloat.

'Launch the boats!' bellowed Jeremiah Westcliff, Prittlewell's oldest and most experienced fisherman, the first to recover his wits. 'Hurry!'

He had to shove some of his shocked neighbours to bring them to their senses, but then all was action and urgency as brawny arms heaved the little crafts into the waves. Once away, the villagers rowed for all they were worth, sinews cracking and breath coming in agonised gasps. Terrified screams and a gushing fountain of water told them that *London* was going down fast. They intensified their efforts, summoning every last ounce of strength to send their boats skimming across the grey-brown water.

But their labours were in vain: by the time they arrived, the ship had gone. The fishermen leaned on their oars, panting hard as they gazed helplessly at the bodies that floated everywhere they looked. The dead would not stay long, of course: the tide was never still, and Father Thames was already tugging some of his gruesome cargo away from the scene of the disaster.

Yet there were survivors. Several clung to a mat of cordage and spars, while a few more flailed in the water. The villagers began to pull them out, but their number was pitifully small.

'Twenty-four,' Westcliff eventually reported to the only

5

officer they had found, identifiable by his fine blue coat. 'How many were aboard?'

'More than three hundred.' Dare's face was grey with shock. He had no idea how he had survived his fall, although the lower half of his body was numb and he wondered whether death might claim him yet. When his eyes were drawn back to the horrible swirling wreckage and the bodies of his sailors, he hoped it would. 'What happened?'

Westcliff shook his head uncomprehendingly. 'One moment the ship was going along as proud as Lucifer, and the next she was blown to pieces. Were you carrying much powder?'

'One magazine was full,' Dale replied hoarsely. 'But we were going to load the others in Queenhithe.'

'Then it was an accident,' surmised Westcliff. 'A tragic, dreadful accident.'

'No,' whispered Dale. 'It was not.'

'Of course it was,' said Westcliff, briskly but kindly. 'What else could it have been?'

Chapter 1

London, Monday 13 March 1665

It was an undignified way to die. The corpse was lying on its back with its mouth open, wearing nothing but a pair of bucket-topped riding boots and a Cavalier hat. The quality of the apparel indicated that its owner had been a man of wealth, and so did the fact that he had been enjoying the 'gentleman's club' at Hercules' Pillars Alley in the first place. It was an establishment that catered only to the extremely rich, and he would not have been allowed inside had he not belonged to the very highest echelons of society.

'You can see why I asked you to come,' said Temperance North, the club's owner, in an unsteady voice. 'This is Paul Ferine from High Holborn, and he has been murdered.'

Thomas Chaloner, intelligencer to the Lord Chancellor, regarded her in surprise. 'What makes you think that?'

There was nothing he could see to suggest foul play, and it appeared to him that Ferine had simply expired on being entertained by one of the club's vivacious and extremely energetic ladies. It would not be the first time it had happened, and Temperance was usually adept at handling such situations – her discretion was one of the reasons why the place was so popular. Thus he was bemused as to why he had been dragged from his bed in the small hours of the morning to 'help'.

'Because he was full of the joys of life an hour ago,' she replied. 'And now look at him. We cannot afford to be stained with the taint of murder, Tom. Business might never recover.'

'It sounds healthy enough to me,' said Chaloner.

The ornate clock on the bedside table showed it was well past one o'clock, but the parlour downstairs was full of customers enjoying the atmosphere of debauched jollity, while every bedroom on the upper floor was in use. Maude, the formidable matron who kept order among the guests – no easy matter with men who were more used to issuing orders than obeying them – had been too busy to do more than nod at Chaloner as he had walked past.

'Yes, but it is very easy to lose favour. And as I said, this is Paul Ferine from High Holborn.'

The way she spoke told Chaloner that he should know Ferine, yet there was nothing remotely familiar about the fleshy, middle-aged face with its sagging jowls. However, he was the first to admit that his knowledge of London and its luminaries was lacking. After the civil wars, he had been recruited by Cromwell's intelligence services, and had spent the next twelve years overseas. He had returned home when the Commonwealth had collapsed, and had been fortunate that the Earl of Clarendon, currently Lord Chancellor, had been willing to employ him, because opportunities for ex-Parliamentarian spies were few and far between in Restoration Britain.

'I never met him,' he hedged, loath for anyone, even Temperance, a friend, to know that Ferine's name meant nothing to him. 'Did he spend much time at White Hall?'

Temperance regarded him askance, and he could see there was a tart remark on the tip of her tongue. Then she seemed to recollect that she had summoned him to help her, and that disparaging remarks about his ignorance were not in her best interests.

'Yes, he was Groom of the Robes.' She shot him a sidelong glance. 'Which means he performed the odd ceremonial duty at Court in return for a handsome salary. Obviously, the King is fond of him – His Majesty does not confer that sort of favour on just anyone.'

Chaloner gave her an irritable look. His knowledge of individuals might be lacking, but he was familiar with the Court's workings, because he was part of it – his official title was Gentleman Usher to the Lord Chancellor. Unfortunately, his Earl kept sending him on errands overseas, never giving him the opportunity to settle down and become better acquainted with his fellow courtiers. The most recent jaunt had been to Russia, and he had only been back three days.

'What shall I do?' whispered Temperance tearfully, and he caught a glimpse of the vulnerable, innocent girl he had once befriended, a wholly different creature from the worldly woman she had become since an inheritance had allowed her to purchase a house and set herself up in the brothel business.

'The first step is to find out whether you are right,' he replied practically. 'Neither you nor I are qualified to determine causes of death, so send for Wiseman.'

Richard Wiseman was Surgeon to the King, and was also Temperance's lover. If there had been foul play, then

9

Wiseman would know how to spot it. But Temperance shook her head.

'No, Tom. He has just been elected Master of the Company of Barber-Surgeons, and cannot afford to be associated with scandal.'

'And I can?'

'You are a spy; it is different. Besides, you have dealt with far nastier matters in the past. Why do you think I sent for you now?'

'He will be hurt if you exclude him.' Chaloner spoke a little stiffly. He knew her affection for him had cooled since she had turned from Puritan maid to brothel-keeper, but did she have to make her disregard quite so obvious? 'And we cannot make any decisions until we understand exactly what has happened. Or do you know another discreet *medicus*?'

Temperance was silent for a moment, then left the bedchamber without another word. He heard her ordering one of the servants in the corridor outside to fetch Wiseman, and when she returned, her face was grey with worry.

'So what happens when Richard tells you that Ferine *has* been murdered?'

'You tell Spymaster Williamson.' Chaloner referred to the man who currently ran the country's intelligence network and dealt with untoward happenings involving members of government and the Court. 'And he will investigate.'

Temperance was horrified. 'Then I am ruined for certain! My patrons will never visit me again if they think *he* might be here.'

'I am afraid you have no choice. But Williamson will be discreet – the King and his cronies have never been

10

as unpopular with the people as they are now, and he will not want to advertise the fact that courtiers haunt brothels.'

Temperance eyed him beadily. 'This is not a brothel, Thomas. It is a gentleman's club.'

Chaloner inclined his head in apology. 'But my point remains: Ferine is an important man, and his death will need to be investigated by the proper authorities.'

'Damn!' Temperance rubbed a hand across her face. 'Why did his killer have to choose here to ply his nasty skills?'

Chaloner regarded her curiously. 'You seem very sure that something untoward has happened, yet there is no evidence to say that you are right.'

'Yes there is. You see, poor Ferine had been saying for weeks that something bad would happen to him two days before the Ides of March. Well, it has.'

Chaloner frowned at the archaic way of referring to the date, and glanced at the clock. 'I suppose it did become the thirteenth at midnight . . .'

'Yes, and I saw him alive shortly before twelve, which means he died today – exactly when he predicted a calamity for himself.'

'Predicted how?' asked Chaloner, bemused.

'He had calculated his own horoscope,' explained Temperance. 'And he was quite clear about what he read in the stars. They foretold a "grave misfortune" for him – and you do not get a graver misfortune than death.'

Solicitously, Chaloner took Temperance's arm and led her downstairs to wait for Wiseman. She pulled away as they passed the parlour, and went to check that all was well. The parlour was a large chamber with judiciously

11

dimmed lamps and dark red decor. Pipe smoke swirled thickly, mixing with the sweet, sickly perfume he always associated with bordellos. A game was under way between the clients and some of the girls, and it took a far less vivid imagination than his to guess that the manly cheers meant someone was divesting herself of her clothes.

Several patrons scampered towards Temperance when they saw her at the door, clamouring for her attention like fractious children. She listened to the ribald poem they had composed with every semblance of enjoyment, making Chaloner marvel at her patience. He folded his arms and leaned against the wall to wait for them to finish, and a glance towards the riotous fun at the far end of the room allowed him to recognise five Members of Parliament, three churchmen, four barons, two influential businessmen and an admiral.

The most boisterous participant was the Duke of Buckingham, the King's oldest friend and the implacable enemy of Chaloner's employer. He was a tall, athletic man in his thirties, whose licentious ways had rendered his once-handsome face lined and puffy. He possessed a brilliant intelligence, and might have been an asset to his country if he had given as much care to affairs of state as he did to his pleasures.

Next to him was Prince Rupert, who had fought valiantly, if somewhat mercurially, in the civil wars. Now in his forties, he was a petulant dandy, displeased with everything and everyone around him. Chaloner was surprised to see him with Buckingham, as it was common knowledge that they detested each other. This was a problem: both were on the Privy Council – the body that advised the King – and as neither could bring himself to agree with the other, meetings tended to be long, bad-tempered and alarmingly lacking in sound counsel.

'Enough!' Rupert was snapping irritably. 'It is late, and we should all be in bed.'

'Yes, we should,' leered Buckingham. 'Which whore do you—'

'I am going home,' interrupted Rupert, stalking towards the door and shoving past anyone who stood in his way. Being sober, Chaloner was able to step aside, but others found themselves shunted very roughly.

'Ignore him, Lawson,' said Buckingham to the stout, barrel-chested fellow whose wine had been knocked from his hand. 'He has been in a foul mood all day.'

Lawson was in his fifties, and spurned the current fashion for wigs, allowing his own yellow-grey hair to flow freely over his shoulders. He spoke with the distinctive inflection of the Yorkshireman, and replied to Buckingham's words with a string of obscenities that had even the jaded Duke's eyebrows shooting up in astonishment.

'Language, Admiral,' said another patron mildly. 'There are ladies present, and you are not at sea now, sir.'

The speaker was tall and lean, with a face like a wax mask that had been grabbed by the nose while still molten and pulled. He wore a long black coat sewn with silver stars – an exotic garment, even by London standards – and his voice had been soft yet commanding. His hands and neck were adorned with symbols, a permanent marking with ink that Chaloner had never seen in England – and certainly not among the kind of men who frequented the club.

'That blackguard spilled my wine,' shouted Lawson

13

angrily. 'Wine should be poured down the throat, not on to the floor.'

'Then let me refill your cup,' said the stranger, taking the enraged mariner's arm and thus preventing him from storming after Rupert and demanding satisfaction at dawn.

The poets finished regaling Temperance with their verses and rushed away to rejoin the undressing game – the club's patrons tended to be easily bored, and rarely stuck with one activity for very long. She went to stand next to Chaloner, and when she saw who he was watching, she began whispering in his ear.

'Poor Admiral Lawson suffered a terrible tragedy last week. His ship *London* blew up in the Thames Estuary.'

'Did it?' Chaloner was doubtful. While warships were certainly packed to the gills with guns, powder and ammunition, they did not usually explode unless under attack.

'It was the talk of the city. Did you not hear?' Temperance raised her hand. 'I forgot – you have only just come home. Well, it was a dreadful business, and more than three hundred men were killed. I imagine he came here to put it out of his mind for a few hours.'

Lawson did not look particularly grief-stricken, and began to regale the gathering with a raunchy song favoured by sailors. It had jaws dropping all over the parlour, and these were men used to a bit of bawdiness.

'Who is the fellow with him?' asked Chaloner. 'The one wearing the peculiar coat?'

'Dr Lambe,' replied Temperance disapprovingly. 'He is a sorcerer and a physician, and is the newest member of Buckingham's household.'

'Buckingham's father had a sorcerer-physician named

14

Dr Lambe,' recalled Chaloner. 'He was accused of making his enemies impotent and summoning whirlwinds, although I suspect he had no such skills and was just a trickster. He was murdered forty years ago by an angry mob.'

'This is his son, apparently. He can divine the future, and it is rumoured that his unusually accurate predictions come courtesy of the devil, who helps him with them.'

'He did not predict Ferine's "grave misfortune", did he?' asked Chaloner, thinking that if so, Lambe would probably be arrested if the courtier did transpire to be murdered. It would not be the first time a seer had manipulated events to ensure that a 'prophecy' came true.

'Ferine was quite capable of calculating his own horoscope. Indeed, he was better at it than Lambe – he told me only tonight that three black cats had walked in front of him on his way to the club, while a jackdaw had cawed thirteen times from a chimney. He said there were no surer warnings that something dire was going to happen.'

'Then why did he not go home – keep himself safe until the thirteenth was over?'

Temperance sighed unhappily. 'I do not know, Tom. And we can hardly ask him now.'

Chaloner followed her out of the parlour and along a hallway to the private quarters at the back of the house. Near the kitchens was a cosy sitting room where she usually sat to count her nightly takings. It was a testament to her unhappiness that she barely glanced at the heaps of coins on the table. He poured her a cup of wine to steady her nerves but she waved it away and reached for her pipe instead. He studied her as she tamped it with tobacco.

15

She was still in her early twenties, but the decadent lifestyle she enjoyed with her clients was taking its toll. She had always been large, but access to extravagant foods had doubled her size, and her complexion had suffered from never seeing the sun. She had once owned luxuriant chestnut hair, but she had shaved it off to wear a wig. Her teeth were tobacco-stained, and too much time listening to the opinions of men like Buckingham and Rupert had turned her acerbic and petty-minded.

'How was Russia?' she asked as she puffed. 'I cannot imagine you enjoyed it. It is said to be very desolate – bitterly cold, with filthy streets and superstitious citizens.'

Wryly, Chaloner thought her description applied equally well to London: the weather had been foul since he had returned; every road was a quagmire; and she had just finished telling him about one man who was a sorcerer and another who put faith in black cats and jackdaws. He saw she was waiting for a reply, but good spies did not talk about themselves and he was a master of his trade. He made an innocuous remark about the amount of snow he had seen, then changed the subject by asking whether anything interesting had happened while he had been away, knowing that she, like most people, preferred to talk than to listen anyway.

'Well, we are now officially at war with the Dutch,' she replied. 'Hostilities were declared three weeks ago, and both navies are already at sea. We shall win, of course. The butter-eaters cannot defeat our brave seamen.'

Chaloner disagreed, and thought that fighting the United Provinces was a very bad idea. He had tried very hard, within his limited sphere of influence, to prevent it, but the hawks on the Privy Council had itched to flex their muscles, and so that was that.

16

'We shall soon have all the best trading routes,' Temperance went on. 'Routes that Buckingham says should be ours anyway, because we deserve them.'

And there was the nub of the matter, thought Chaloner sadly: there was not enough room on the high seas for two powerful maritime nations. It was a war of commerce, not politics.

'Yet I cannot imagine how it will be funded,' she sighed. 'Not with taxes – there is already a ridiculously high duty on coal, which means the poor cannot heat their homes or cook. The government would not dare introduce another levy – not unless they want more civil wars.' But her expression was distant, and before he could comment, she burst out with, 'Who would want Ferine dead? He had his detractors, but who does not?'

'What detractors?'

Her expression was unhappy. 'Those who hated the fact that he had stopped being a Christian and put his faith in superstition instead. He took his horoscopes and omens very seriously.'

Chaloner was about to ask more but the door opened and Richard Wiseman walked in. The surgeon was a large man in many senses of the word. He was tall, broad and added to his bulk by lifting heavy stones each morning. He wore no colour except red, which served to make him even more imposing, and his character was arrogant, haughty and proud. He was not someone Chaloner would normally have chosen as a friend, but circumstances had thrown them together, and the spy was slowly beginning to appreciate Wiseman's few but significant virtues – loyalty to those he liked, an ability to keep a secret and a strong sense of justice.

17

'I understand you have a corpse for me,' he boomed cheerfully. 'Good! Lead me to it.'

Upstairs again, Chaloner sat on a chair that would have cost him a month's pay, and watched Wiseman examine Ferine. The sounds of dissipated rumpus still emanated from the parlour below, while girlish shrieks and manly guffaws from the bedrooms indicated that business was continuing as usual upstairs as well – so far, at least.

'Well?' he asked, when Wiseman had finished. 'I assume his heart gave out?'

'Then you would assume wrong. He has been smothered.'

Chaloner blinked. 'I saw no evidence of—'

'Of course not – *you* are not a surgeon. However, he inhaled two feathers from the pillow that was pressed over his face, there is a cut on the inside of his lip, and his eyes are bloodshot. Ferine was definitely murdered.'

Chaloner's duty was clear: he had to send word to Spymaster Williamson, then distance himself from the entire affair. Ferine's death was not his concern, and the Earl would be aghast if he ever learned that his spy had visited a brothel, regardless of the fact that he had done so to help a friend and not to avail himself of its delights. But years in espionage had imbued Chaloner with a keen sense of curiosity, and his interest was piqued.

'I know the wine flows very freely here, but surely the lady who was with Ferine would have noticed someone shoving a cushion over his face?'

'Snowflake,' said Wiseman, naming one of Temperance's more popular employees, a small, vivacious blonde with a sensuous body and world-weary eyes. 'Shall I fetch her?'

18

He returned a few moments later with both the lady in question and Temperance. The two women entered the bedchamber reluctantly, and Snowflake would only explain what had happened after Chaloner had covered Ferine's body with a sheet.

'He always liked to frolic in nothing but his hat and boots.' She shrugged at Chaloner's raised eyebrows. 'Such antics are not unusual, and we aim to please. Afterwards, I slipped out for a moment, and when I returned, he was lying on the bed . . . I thought he was asleep.'

'They do nod off on occasion,' put in Temperance. Her voice was hoarse – she took no pleasure in hearing her suspicions confirmed. 'Running the nation, managing dioceses or directing large commercial ventures is very tiring, and our guests are often weary.'

Chaloner thought it best not to comment. 'Did you see anyone in the hall outside when you left?' he asked of Snowflake.

She considered the question carefully, pulling a silken shift more tightly around her slender shoulders. 'No, it was empty.' She turned apologetically to Temperance. 'I was only gone for a minute – just long enough to run down to the kitchens for a jug of wine.'

Temperance frowned. 'Wine? But that is why we hire Ann – to fill the decanters between clients. You should not have had to fetch it yourself.'

'Bring Ann up here,' suggested Wiseman. 'Then we can ask why she forgot.'

'She is usually very reliable,' said Snowflake when Temperance had gone. She shuddered. 'I cannot believe this is happening! Men do die here, of course – we make them feel like youths, and their hearts

19

sometimes cannot take it – but no one has never been murdered before.'

'How did Ferine behave this evening?' asked Chaloner. 'Was he nervous? Fearful?'

'Drunk,' replied Snowflake. 'Although he did mention the unfavourable horoscope for the thirteenth. After he had finished here, he planned to go home and not stir all day, in the hope that the bad fortune could be averted. He meant to leave before midnight, but we lost track of time. I imagine he did not expect disaster to strike quite so soon.'

'Clearly,' said Wiseman drily.

'Yet I do not believe he thought he would *die*,' Snowflake went on. 'I think he envisaged losing some money or tripping over a rug.' She looked sadly at the sheeted body. 'He was a lovely man, and generous, too. He gave me a dried toad only last week, and said that licking it three times before going to church would bring me good luck.'

Chaloner winced. 'And has it?'

'No, not yet – my stepfather's perfume business still founders, and I have not won at cards.'

'Did you notice anyone watching him with undue interest tonight?'

'Well, he made a dreadful fuss about losing his wood-lice. That attracted the "undue interest" of the whole club – guests and staff.'

'His woodlice?' queried Chaloner warily.

'He liked to keep three of them in a box around his neck, as they are thought to bestow good health on the wearer. The box fell off, and he had us all in an uproar until he found it.'

The object in question was on the bedside table. Chaloner liberated the creatures through the window, at the same time checking to see whether a killer had entered that way. The catch was so stiff that he was certain it had not been opened in weeks.

'Prince Rupert was not very nice about the commotion,' Snowflake was saying. 'He refused to join the hunt, and sat looking sour the whole time.'

'If he let me drill a hole in his skull, these wicked moods would be a thing of the past,' said Wiseman. 'And if any man is in need of such a procedure, it is him. The rest of the Privy Council would love me to do it, especially Buckingham. They are all weary of his nasty temper.'

While he and Snowflake discussed whether Rupert should submit himself to such a drastic procedure for the convenience of others, Chaloner examined the hallway. There were plenty of alcoves, and the windows had been fitted with heavy curtains to ensure that no one in the street outside should be able to see in. Scuff marks on the floor suggested that the killer had hidden behind one, waiting until Ferine was alone. Chaloner inspected the area closely, but there were no clues that he could see.

Eventually, Temperance arrived with a tearful white-haired woman in tow. Ann's clothes were cheap but clean, and it was clear from her nervous demeanour that she was terrified of losing her job. 'I *did* fill the flagon!' she declared before anyone could speak. 'I know I did.'

Temperance began to remonstrate with her, but Chaloner opened an ornate chest and was not surprised to discover a lot of claret-soaked blankets.

'The culprit dumped it here after Ann had been,' he explained, to the woman's obviously profound relief. 'Then he concealed himself behind the curtains in the hall until Snowflake left to fetch more.'

'How did he know that Ferine would want some?' Wiseman asked doubtfully.

'They all do,' replied Temperance, pale at the notion that such a determined and resourceful villain should have been in her house. 'Being with a lady is thirsty work.'

'A fact of which the killer was obviously aware,' surmised Chaloner, 'which suggests he is familiar with the club and its ways.'

'My guests are not murderers,' said Temperance firmly, although her eyes were fearful. Her patrons were powerful men, who would not take kindly to accusations that might be used to ruin them.

'A member of staff then,' suggested Chaloner. Temperance opened her mouth to disagree, so he hastened to explain. 'Your club has two doors: the front one, which is guarded by the porter; and the kitchen one, which means passing the cook and his assistants. The only people who can enter this building without exciting attention are patrons and staff.'

'My people are beyond reproach,' stated Temperance. 'I chose them myself.'

'The staff would never kill anyone,' agreed Snowflake, while Ann nodded at her side. 'We all make a good living here, and no one is stupid enough to risk it.'

Chaloner was tempted to point out that if the staff were innocent then the culprit *had* to be a guest, but he did not want to argue. Feeling he had indulged his curiosity quite long enough, and that it was time to put the matter into official hands, he told Temperance to contact the Spymaster.

Once a note to Williamson had been sent off with a fleet-footed servant, Chaloner settled down to wait. He would rather have gone home, but he did not want to annoy a dangerously powerful spymaster by leaving the scene of the crime without permission. Unfortunately, it was not Williamson who appeared an hour or so later, but one of his agents, a slow, ponderous man named Doines, who was better at intimidation and coercion than conducting politically sensitive investigations. He refused to hear the statements of witnesses, preferring instead to drink wine and leer at the girls, which he claimed was background research.

It was nearing dawn before Doines finally deigned to speak to Chaloner and Wiseman, but his note-taking was perfunctory, and they were soon dismissed. Chaloner was glad to be away. He had to be at Clarendon House at eight, and his Earl was unlikely to be impressed if he arrived late with the excuse of being interrogated about a murder in a brothel. However, he had not taken many steps along the hallway before he heard a sudden exclamation.

'Tom Chaloner! Good God! I thought you would be dead by now.'

It took a moment for Chaloner to place the speaker, a handsome fellow with shiny black hair, bright brown eyes and a confident swagger. The voice carried a colonial drawl.

'John Scott,' he said, as the face clicked into place in his mind. They had met some years ago in New Amsterdam, where he had been tracking a dangerous spy and Scott had been paid to help him. They had shared a number of adventures, and he had never met anyone, before or since, who could lie with such effortless ease.

'The very same,' grinned Scott. 'From Scott Hall in Kent.'

Chaloner nodded politely, although the family who lived there vigorously denied all knowledge of this particular 'kinsman'. 'What are you doing here?' he asked. 'You once told me that you could never return to England, because you had been convicted of insurgency.'

Scott's dismissive wave told Chaloner that the 'confession' had been one of his stories, an invention designed to make himself sound more interesting. 'I came to tell our King that the time was ripe to snatch New Amsterdam from the Dutch. It is because of *me* that it is no longer ruled by Hollanders, but is now the British-owned Province of New York.'

The Dutch *had* recently been ousted from their American territories, but Chaloner doubted Scott had had anything to do with it – the man was spinning him yarns already. He recalled conversations they had had in the past, and repeated them rather wickedly. 'You often said that you admire Holland more than any other country in the world. Have you visited it yet?'

'You remember falsely.' Scott cast a furtive glance around him, to ensure no one had heard. 'I have never been there and I never will.'

He turned abruptly, leaving Chaloner to note his stylishly expensive clothes as he flashed a wide but insincere smile at the women who were waiting to escort him out. This was a courtesy rarely extended to other guests, and meant he had charmed them, no mean feat with Temperance's prematurely cynical lasses.

Chaloner reached the door where the porter, Preacher Hill, was alert and bristling with anger that murder should have been committed in the building he was paid to protect. Hill did not like Chaloner, because the spy made no effort to disguise the fact that he considered him a hypocrite of the first order – Hill was a nonconformist fanatic, whose night work at the club left him free to spout sermons about the perils of sin during the day; he genuinely failed to see that earning his bread in a bordello sat poorly with his moralising.

'The Kingdom of Christ will be here soon,' he said tightly. 'I shall stand at Jesus's side, naturally, but the rogue who killed Mr Ferine will be cast into hell.'

Chaloner was not surprised to hear Hill expounding millenarian views. A small but vocal minority had been predicting the end of the world for as long as he could remember, its beliefs fuelled by the upheaval of the civil wars and the execution of King Charles I. Before he could reply, Hill was addressing the patron behind him.

'Mr Jones! How did *you* get in? You know you are not welcome here.'

Jones was a small, dark-featured man with pale, unblinking eyes. He did not look like the kind of fellow who belonged in the club – his clothes were too plain, and a lack of aristocratic swagger suggested he was not rich enough to pay its exorbitant prices.

'I should not have bothered,' said Jones coolly. 'I was bored. You do not even provide newsbooks to help visitors while away the time.'

'If you want to read, go to a coffee house.' Hill glowered as Jones walked away without responding, then turned back to Chaloner. 'One of the girls must have sneaked him in. She should not have done, because we do not want his type in here. The same might be said for your Mr Scott. I did not take to him, but that is not surprising – not if he is *your* friend.'

'What do you know about Scott?' asked Chaloner, electing to ignore the insult.

'Nothing,' replied Hill sullenly. 'Other than that he is the new Cartographer Royal. Good evening, Admiral Lawson. Shall I summon your coach? Where did you leave it?'

'He does not have one,' sneered Buckingham, who was behind the mariner. 'He prefers to ride about in hackney carriages.' The last two words were pronounced in a fastidious hiss.

'I do not hold with fancy nonsense,' retorted Lawson shortly. 'There is no room for it at sea, and there should be no room for it on land either.'

'A private coach is a necessity, not a nonsense,' declared Buckingham. 'And every man of breeding would agree.'

'Breeding!' jeered Lawson. 'Any cur can sire a litter. I judge a man by his mettle, not by his damned ancestors.'

Hill interposed himself between them, spouting some tale about the latest addition to Temperance's stables. The skill with which he did so led Chaloner to surmise that it was something he did on a regular basis, when clients had had too much to drink and old animosities surfaced. Keeping up a steady monologue that gave neither the chance to take issue, Hill escorted them off the premises.

Chaloner stepped back smartly as the remaining customers trooped out in a noisy rabble. They would snatch a few hours' sleep before arriving at their places of work – government offices, consulates, White Hall, episcopal palaces. Or perhaps, he thought sourly, they would go to them straight away, and make wine-muddled decisions that would plunge the country into even greater chaos.

He began to walk up the lane, but had not gone far before someone grabbed his arm. It was Wiseman, who suggested a restorative draught in the Hercules' Pillars tavern, a place famous for all-night card games and gargantuan portions of roasted meat. There was still time before Chaloner was expected at Clarendon House, so he followed the surgeon inside, where they were met by a powerful aroma of spilled ale and burned fat.

'I know you have no authority to investigate Ferine's death,' Wiseman said, once they were seated. 'But you cannot abandon Temperance to Doines. He is a bumbling fool who will not be discreet, and the incident may be used to close the club and force her to leave London – which I should not like at all. Besides, she has been a good friend to you in the past.'

'What can I do?' Chaloner raised his hands in a shrug. 'Government officials, churchmen and wealthy merchants will not talk to me without a warrant. Indeed, I imagine most will deny even being in Hercules' Pillars Alley.'

'The villain will not be a patron,' averred Wiseman. 'So they are irrelevant.'

'On the contrary, they are potential witnesses and probably the only way the culprit will ever be caught, given that there are no other leads to follow. But I cannot meddle, Wiseman. You will have to put your trust in Doines.'

'Lord!' breathed Wiseman, appalled. 'Poor Temperance! I think I had better visit Williamson to see what can be done. He is improving as Spymaster, because he has learned

27

to heed suggestions. Unfortunately, he is still nowhere near as efficient as the one Cromwell had.'

Chaloner said nothing, because Wiseman was a committed Royalist, and he did not want to draw attention to the fact that they had been on opposite sides during the wars. However, Wiseman was right: Cromwell's Spymaster had been the talented John Thurloe, a man who was now Chaloner's closest friend.

Wiseman peered at him in the flickering firelight. 'You are very pale. Is anything amiss?'

'Nothing sleep will not cure. Unfortunately, I seem destined not to have any – my wife kept me talking the first night I was back; Clarendon wanted some letters written in Dutch during the second; and Temperance's summons came in the early hours of this morning.'

'You will survive,' said Wiseman unsympathetically. 'Incidentally, did I tell you that I have been appointed Master of the Company of Barber-Surgeons? It is a great honour, you know.'

He had mentioned it at least three times in as many days. Unfortunately, Chaloner knew that Wiseman had been elected not because he was popular, but because he was the only senior member of the Guild who had not had a stab at the post. The truth was that his colleagues were dreading what he might do during his incumbency.

'I shall make changes that will make them sit up,' he vowed, a determined gleam in his eye. 'I am tired of surgeons being a poor second to physicians, and I intend to put matters right. By this time next year we shall be as respected as any other medical profession.'

Chaloner eyed the tattered, bloodstained bag of

28

implements that sat at Wiseman's side, and thought his friend would have his work cut out for him.

It was not far from Hercules' Pillars Alley to Clarendon House, but Chaloner took a hackney anyway. It was drizzling, and London was never pleasant in the wet. Its major streets were said to be cobbled, although he had never seen evidence of it, overlain as they were by a thick carpet of filth. Moreover, it had been raining for days, and the roads had degenerated into refuse-laden rivers of mud and liquid manure.

Despite the darkness and the early hour, the city was busy. It was a Monday, so businesses were opening after the enforced break – theoretically, at least. In reality, Sunday was much like any other day, with shops open and traders doing business. It was a bone of contention with the fanatics, who thought the Sabbath should be as it had been under Cromwell's Puritans, where even wearing lace, singing or playing musical instruments was deemed anathema.

Along the Strand, the wheels of carts and carriages sprayed up thick deluges of reeking mud, horses skidded, and pedestrians swore as they tried to keep their balance in the gloom. Alehouses and taverns were open for pre-work tipples, and many were already full. Bakeries and cook-shops were doing a brisk trade, and the streets rang with the calls of vendors hawking lily-white vinegar, pale-hearted cabbages and fresh asses' milk.

The city was also packed with visitors, because it was less than two weeks until Lady Day – one of four dates in the year when taxes and tithes were settled. People poured into London to pay or be paid, and many took the opportunity to conduct other business or buy supplies while they were there. Every bed in every inn was taken; lawyers and clerks were working to capacity; and farmers and tenants from the provinces explored the capital with open mouths, putting themselves and others in danger with their reckless disregard for London's traffic.

Chaloner's carriage rolled to a halt when it reached the New Exchange – the stately but soot-stained building that housed dozens of expensive shops – and he leaned out of the window to see that a coach had overturned not far ahead. It was a large one with six horses, and he could tell that the resulting 'stop' would take an age to clear, especially when the driver began a series of violent arguments with other road users. Loath to be late for his appointment with the Earl, Chaloner paid his hackney-man and continued on foot.

He almost fell as he traversed the open space of Charing Cross, when one foot sank into mud so deep that he staggered trying to pull it free. Street cleaners were doing their best to create paths for pedestrians by laying down bundles of straw, but their efforts were hampered by horsemen and carters, who careened across them with selfish disregard.

The Earl's mansion stood on the semi-rural lane known as Piccadilly, and Chaloner was relieved to leave the noisy chaos of London behind as he splashed along it. The track was just as deeply rutted with mud, but it was good to be away from the worst of the traffic. He inhaled air that smelled of wet earth and soggy leaves, and the rumble of wheels and hoofs gradually gave way to the chirrup of sparrows and the caw of crows.

Clarendon House was a sprawling, showy monstrosity that had only been finished in the last few weeks. Chaloner hated it, feeling its glittering ostentation would

30

do his Earl no favours. Unfortunately, the Earl did not agree, and nothing delighted him more than showing it off to visitors, especially if they happened to be people he wanted to lord it over.

However, while the house was ready, its grounds were not, and comprised a sea of wet dirt and discarded building supplies. Trees had been planted, but it would be years before they grew to maturity, and their slender, leafless limbs lent the house a rather temporary air. The scrawny shrubs by the gate did not help either, dwarfed as they were by a pair of soaring pillars that were topped by sculptures that looked like flying pigs.

Chaloner was halfway up the drive when a coach arrived, spraying muck in all directions as it clattered towards him. He tried to jump out of the way, but the ground was far too treacherous for such a manoeuvre, so not only did he end up drenched in mud, but he also stepped in a pothole that slopped water over the top of his left boot. The carriage rolled to a standstill not far ahead, and he was about to give its driver a piece of his mind when the curtain was pulled aside and a familiar face looked out.

It was Joseph Williamson. Gushing apologies, the Spymaster insisted on giving Chaloner a ride to the house. The distance was hardly worth the bother, but Williamson refused to take no for an answer, and Chaloner was too tired to argue.

Williamson was a haughty, aloof man who had been an Oxford academic before deciding to try his hand at politics. He and Chaloner had fallen foul of each other almost immediately, which was unfortunate, because Chaloner would have liked to continue his work spying in foreign countries; Williamson had refused to hire him,

31

and Chaloner's situation had been desperate until the Earl had stepped in with an offer. The antagonism between them had eased slightly since, although wariness and distrust persisted on both sides.

'I have an appointment with your master,' said Williamson, to explain his presence at Clarendon House. He took care to sit well away, so his own finery would not be soiled by Chaloner's splattered coat. 'It is unconscionably early, but he works very hard.'

Chaloner agreed. 'Does your meeting concern the Dutch situation? I know he still hopes to broker a peaceful solution before blood is spilled.'

'Unfortunately, there are too many warmongers on the Privy Council, so he will not succeed. Incidentally, I hear you were summoned to Hercules' Pillars Alley this morning.'

So the offer of a lift had been to elicit information, thought Chaloner, not to make amends for the coachman's inconsiderate driving. Moreover, it had not escaped his notice that the Spymaster had failed to reveal why he was meeting Clarendon. The two did not usually do business together.

'Only because Temperance was unsure of the protocol,' he explained. 'She sent for you as soon as Wiseman deemed Ferine's death suspicious.'

The Spymaster smiled. 'Wiseman told me as much when our paths crossed just now. But as it happens, I am glad you were there, because it will give you an edge when you investigate.'

Chaloner blinked. 'The Earl would never allow me to explore a death in a brothel. Besides, such matters come under *your* remit, and—'

'I should like to pursue the matter myself, believe me,

but my budget has been cut to raise money for this foolish Dutch war,' interrupted Williamson. He grimaced. 'Although the Privy Council still expects me to provide the intelligence that will help us win, of course. However, the upshot is that I have no one available to explore Ferine's death. Except Doines, and he is hardly the thing.'

'No, but—'

'It is your patriotic duty,' Williamson went on. 'Have you not heard the news? The Dutch have taken three of our ships and killed one of our captains in a sea battle. The war has started, and I cannot afford to be distracted by courtiers getting themselves dispatched. Help me, and you help your country.'

It was not Chaloner's idea of patriotic service, but he nodded acquiescence.

Chapter 2

Chaloner entered Clarendon House through the back door, although his position as a gentleman usher meant he could have used the front one had he wanted. He aimed for the poky chamber that served as an informal common room for the Earl's senior staff, where the first person he met was Thomas Kipps, the Lord Chancellor's Seal Bearer. Kipps was an amiable, friendly fellow, who was never less than perfectly attired. He winced when he saw Chaloner's coat, and advanced purposefully with a damp cloth.

'How was Russia?' he asked as he set about the mess with determined vigour.

Before Chaloner could reply, they were joined by Humphrey Leigh, the Earl's Sergeant at Arms, a small, truculent martinet with a massive moustache.

'I have heard it is nothing but windswept plains and bogs,' Leigh said. 'And its people are brutish and stupid.'

'Worse, there is not a single inn in the entire country.' Kipps spoke in a shocked whisper. 'I cannot imagine life without ale. Indeed, I am surprised it is possible.'

'Were you right about Archangel, Chaloner?' asked Leigh. 'I recall you saying before you left that the port would be closed by ice, and that no ship would be able to get through.'

'Like the Thames,' mused Kipps, pausing in his scrubbing. 'It froze clean over this winter. Indeed, I have never known a more bitter few months.'

They chatted on, neither giving Chaloner the opportunity to answer the questions they asked, which bothered him not a jot. Eventually, damp from Kipps' ministrations, he escaped and made his way to the cavernous vestibule known as My Lord's Lobby, where the Earl conducted business when not at White Hall. He was glad to discover that Williamson had gone – he had no wish to encounter the Spymaster a second time that day. He opened the door and entered.

The Earl of Clarendon had lived in some dismal places when he had followed the King into exile during the Commonwealth, and was busily making up for his years of privation by stuffing his home to the gills with works of art. Personally, Chaloner thought such extravagance was vulgar, and wrinkled his nose in distaste when he saw four Rembrandts and three Brueghels crammed together without regard to subject or size.

The Earl, short, fat and fussy, was sitting at a massive Venetian desk with his gouty foot propped on a stool in front of him. He was wearing a casual gown called a mantua, which was so richly embroidered that it was twice as thick as anyone else's, further accentuating his princely girth. His wig rested on a specially made stand nearby, ready for donning, but in the meantime a quilted nightcap protected his shaven pate from the chill of the great marble room.

'There you are, Chaloner,' he said crossly. 'I thought I told you to be here at eight.'

Chaloner glanced towards the window, to gauge the hour. There was no point in relying on the many clocks that graced the room, as they had been purchased for their fine cases, not their mechanics, and none were good at telling the time. Even so, he was fairly sure the hour had not yet officially struck, and that he was early rather than late.

'I asked you to come because I have a task for you,' the Earl went on. 'There will be another rebellion in the next two weeks, so you must infiltrate the plotters' inner circle and thwart it.'

Not everyone had been pleased to see King Charles II restored to his throne four years earlier, and there had been a number of uprisings since. A few had been serious, but most comprised small bands of badly organised fanatics who were more nuisance than menace. Chaloner was not surprised to hear there was yet another in the offing. However, he would not foil it by following the Earl's instructions, and started to explain why.

'If these insurgents are within days of their objective, they are unlikely to trust anyone new now, sir. It would be better to—'

The Earl cut across him. 'Luckily for us, their gunpowder expert blew himself up, and they are in urgent need of another. I am sure you know enough about the subject to pass muster.'

Chaloner knew as much as anyone else who had operated artillery during the civil wars, but was a long way from being an authority on it. The Earl read the doubt in his face.

'Do not worry about setting explosions. If you do your job properly, there will not be any – the villains will be under lock and key.'

36

'I will try, sir,' said Chaloner, wishing the Earl would let him decide how best to go about such matters. Unfortunately, he knew from experience that suggesting a wiser plan would not be well received, and that he would have to do what he was told. 'Who are they this time?'

'Fifth Monarchists. A very dangerous sect.'

Chaloner was taken aback. 'I thought they had been disbanded after their leaders were executed three years ago.'

The Earl pursed his lips. 'It will take more than a few beheadings to silence that gaggle of fanatics. They are very much alive and represent a serious threat.'

'Do they?' Chaloner sincerely doubted it. 'I cannot imagine there are many of them – the notion of a "Fifth Monarchy" is very peculiar.'

'That Christ will reign on Earth after the rise and fall of four kingdoms,' mused the Earl. 'Babylonia, Persia, Macedonia and Rome. They expected Him after the last king's execution, and pestered Cromwell relentlessly about getting ready. They see the current regime as a hindrance to their designs, and Williamson says they aim to rebel against us in the very near future.'

'Then why does he not send one of his own men to infiltrate them?'

'All his spies are busy with the war,' explained the Earl. 'Besides, it will be easy for you – you can use your uncle's name to ensure that you are accepted into their bosom.'

Chaloner winced. His father's brother had signed the old king's death warrant, and fanatics and republicans of all denominations tended to revere his memory.

'That will not work, sir. Too many people know I am employed by you.'

'Then I shall dismiss you, and you can say you have been ill-used with a clear conscience. Do not look alarmed – you will be reinstated when you have put an end to their uprising. I shall say I ousted you because you lost the jewels and dispatches intended for the Tsar of Russia.'

Chaloner was dismayed. 'But I explained that, sir! They were locked in the forward hold, which was the first part of the ship to flood when she struck ice and sank. I did my best to rescue them, but it was impossible.'

'Yes,' said the Earl with exaggerated patience. 'Your account has been verified in all its details by her captain. But we need some excuse to fall out, and this fits the bill perfectly. So do not mention to anyone else your herculean efforts to recover my property, or people will think me unreasonable.'

'And we cannot have that,' muttered Chaloner.

'It will only be for a few days,' said the Earl, cocking his head as he tried to hear what his intelligencer was mumbling. 'After which we shall say there was a misunderstanding, and your reputation will be restored. And you will not have to fight these villains by yourself – you will have help from William Leving.'

'Who is he?' Chaloner was becoming increasingly alarmed. He liked working alone, and did not want assistance from someone he had never met.

'A rebel who has seen the error of his ways. You see, a few months ago, a band of insurgents hatched what became known as the Northern Plot – a major uprising in Yorkshire and Cumberland. Leving was among them, and was captured when the venture failed. He was sentenced to hang, but Williamson "turned" him. Have you come across the expression?'

Chaloner regarded him askance, wondering how the Earl could ask such a question of a man who had spent his entire adult life in intelligence. 'It means he was allowed to "escape" and return to his old ways. In return for his life, he will betray his fellow conspirators.'

'Precisely. But Williamson does not trust him, which is why he wants you involved. Leving will introduce you to the Fifth Monarchists as a man who knows gunpowder. You are to meet him tomorrow at noon in Muscut's Coffee House on High Holborn.'

It was a reckless plan, and Chaloner heartily wished he had been at their meeting to suggest some sensible alternatives. 'Williamson told me to investigate the murder of a courtier, too,' he said, in the hope that the Earl would be annoyed by the presumption and would withdraw the offer of help in tackling the Fifth Monarchists. His heart sank when Clarendon nodded.

'Yes, he did mention it. I told him you would be delighted to oblige.'

Chaloner tried again. 'It seems unfair that you will be paying me while he reaps the benefit.'

'But I will not be paying you,' said the Earl with a seraphic smile. 'You are dismissed, remember? There will be no salary until the matter is resolved – we must be convincing, as your life may depend on it.'

Chaloner shot him a sour look, not such a fool as to believe that the decision derived from concern for his welfare: the Earl was notoriously mean. 'Very well. But if I am no longer in your employ, how am I to visit White Hall, to ask questions about this murder?'

The Earl's smile turned rueful. 'You will be far more popular as my enemy than as my retainer – most of the Court will welcome you with open arms. But Williamson

39

neglected to tell me who has been killed. Was it anyone I know?'

'Paul Ferine.'

'Well, well! In that case you certainly must probe the matter. I did not like Ferine. I invited him to dine not long ago, and he made a terrible fuss because three candles were lit – he said it was a bad omen, and that someone in the room would die. It unsettled my other guests, I can tell you! However, he was a royal favourite, so we must have a culprit.'

'It may transpire that he was killed by another courtier,' warned Chaloner. 'Are you sure you want me to investigate, sir?'

'Oh, yes,' replied the Earl airily. 'None of my friends are murderers, so the killer will be among my enemies. How can I refuse an opportunity to strike a blow at one of them?'

A muted roar woke Chaloner that night. He started up in alarm, but it was only rain drumming on the roof. He lay back down again and forced himself to relax. It was pitch dark, but an innate sense of time told him it was nearer dawn than dusk, and that he should get up and begin his enquiries. Yet he was loath to leave his warm bed for the foul weather outside, so he decided to reflect on what he had been charged to do instead.

He was not surprised to hear that there was another rebellion in the making, because the King had not endeared himself to his subjects during his four-year reign, thanks to his dissipated lifestyle and wanton companions. Folk who had been happy to see him return were having second thoughts, while those who had opposed him were defiantly open in their dissatisfaction.

Chaloner winced when he thought about the Earl's plan. The Fifth Monarchists were unlikely to welcome a conveniently available 'gunpowder expert' into their midst, and any effort to win their trust on such terms would almost certainly fail. But then he brightened: he had spent the last decade and more prising information from those who did not want to part with it, so even if the rebels did reject his offer to blow things up, there were other ways to learn their intentions. He would look on it as a challenge to his talents.

He turned his mind to Ferine. He had passed the previous afternoon loitering in White Hall, listening to gossip about the dead courtier, most of which revolved around Ferine's ability to produce uncannily accurate horoscopes. Chaloner decided to visit the man's parish priest later, to find out whether Ferine had been a real heathen, or just a man whose life was ruled by superstition.

The Earl had been right about the Court's reaction to his 'dismissal': he had lost count of the number of people who had congratulated him on his escape. Yet he wished Clarendon had devised a different tale. Several high-ranking barons had offered to buy the dispatches he had 'lost' and were openly incredulous when he told them the documents really were under fifty fathoms of water; while every dubious character in the palace had advice about how to dispose of hot jewels.

In the evening, he had visited Ferine's lodgings on High Holborn, which transpired to be two rooms so cheerless that he could only assume the courtier had spent very little time in them. A few books on the

41

occult were lined up on the windowsill, and both chambers were liberally scattered with smelly pouches that he supposed were charms against evil, but there was nothing else of a personal nature, and he had learned little about Ferine as a man.

He turned over, feeling Hannah warm and soft at his side, and a range of emotions surged through him, none of which he understood. They had married before they had really known each other, learning too late that each had habits the other deplored. She loved the company of the Court debauchees she met in the course of her duties as lady-in-waiting to the Queen, and was prone to appalling morning tempers; he was taciturn and solitary, and his chief passion was playing the bass viol, a pastime she decried as dull in the extreme.

On his return from Russia, he had discovered another aspect of her character that was cause for concern: extravagance. He was used to her hiring too many servants and renting a house that was larger than they needed, but in his absence she had discovered the joys of lavish entertaining. He had arrived home to a mountain of unpaid bills.

He lit a candle and studied her in its flickering light. Not even her best friends would call her pretty, yet there was a pleasing determination to the jut of her jaw. She made him laugh, too, and her humour was rarely cruel. He wondered how she would react to the news of his 'dismissal' – whether she would be angrier about the indignity of it or the economies that would have to be made until he was reinstated. It did not occur to him to confide that it was a ruse.

When he heard the bellman call five o'clock, he decided to visit the club – it seldom closed before dawn

– to see what its patrons could tell him about Ferine. He had tried cornering a few at White Hall the previous day, but they had been guarded and wary, and he knew he needed to catch them when they were drunk and more inclined to chatter.

Reluctantly, he forced himself from under the covers. The bedroom was bitterly cold, and the rain that battered the windows sounded as though it was well laced with ice. He dressed in a smart grey long-coat, new black breeches, thick boots and a hat that was still new enough to repel water, clothes that were suitable both for visiting the club and for meeting Fifth Monarchists in coffee houses later. He buckled a sword around his waist, tucked a dagger in his waistband, another in his boot, and a third, much smaller one, in his sleeve.

'Where is your periwig?' came a sleepy but admonishing voice as he aimed for the door. 'Surely you are not going out without it?'

When the King had started to go grey, he had elected to conceal the fact with a wig, and most courtiers and a growing number of Londoners had promptly followed suit. Chaloner baulked, though. He had a perfectly serviceable head of thick brown hair, while wigs were expensive, uncomfortable to wear and prone to lice. However, it was only a matter of time before he would have to bow to the trend, or he would stand out as unusual, something no spy liked to do.

'It is raining,' he explained tersely. 'I do not want to ruin the thing.'

'Then why go out?' she demanded peevishly. 'It is the middle of the night.'

He knew better than to remark that five in the morning

was hardly 'the middle of the night'. 'Close your eyes,' he whispered. 'I am sorry I woke you.'

'I suppose you are sneaking off on an errand for Old Misery Guts.' The Earl was fond of Hannah, but his affection was not reciprocated. 'You should leave him and find employment elsewhere.'

'I am glad you think so,' said Chaloner, supposing he should break the news before she heard it from someone else. 'Because he has dismissed me.'

Hannah gaped at him, then struggled to sit up. '*What?* But why?'

'Because I lost the Tsar's jewels.'

Hannah was fully awake now. 'The wretched, mean, spiteful old *goat*! You did not mislay them on purpose and he knows it. I shall have words when I see him today. How *dare* he!'

'Please do not,' begged Chaloner, afraid she might say something that would prompt the Earl not to reinstate him. Yet there was a silver lining to the situation. 'I am afraid we shall have to curtail our spending until I get another post.'

'Lord! We had better find you something fast then. Perhaps the Duke will hire you.'

She referred to Buckingham, for whom she had formed a rather unfathomable attachment. Chaloner deplored the association, but there was not much he could do about it, except let her discover for herself what a scheming, treacherous, unsteady fellow the Duke could be.

'I doubt he will want me,' he said wryly.

'Someone else, then. We cannot have you thrown in debtors' gaol.'

'No,' agreed Chaloner, who had harboured a pathological hatred of prisons ever since he had been

44

incarcerated in one for spying in France. He could not help shuddering at the notion.

'But perhaps we worry unduly,' Hannah went on thoughtfully. 'There is plague in Holland. Maybe it will come here, and our creditors will die.'

Chaloner had lost his first wife and child to plague, and was disinclined to view it as a convenient way to cheat tradesmen. 'Go back to sleep,' he said curtly. 'I will see you tonight.'

'Very well, but do not be late. I plan to bake a pickled ling pie.'

Chaloner struggled not to gulp. Hannah was an awful cook, and pickled ling pie was one of her more deadly creations – a case of rock-hard pastry filled with vinegary fish that she declined to debone or behead. He had forced down one or two to win her good graces while they had been courting, but now he wished he had been honest from the outset.

'I doubt I will be back in time,' he said rather desperately. 'Give it to the servants.'

'Oh, they shall certainly have some,' she vowed grimly. It sounded like a threat. 'But I shall set your half aside. Incidentally, there was talk at Court yesterday that Paul Ferine was murdered in Temperance's club. Is it true?'

One of Hannah's virtues was that she was liberal-minded, and did not object to her husband's friendship with a brothel-owner. She would never visit the place herself – at least, not to partake in the revelries – but she liked Temperance, and had always treated her with friendly respect.

Chaloner nodded. 'Did you know him?'

'Yes. I caught him bowing to a new moon once,

bobbing up and down like a demented pigeon. For luck, apparently. And he knew some very unpleasant people.'

'Courtiers?' asked Chaloner, when she paused.

She shot him a disagreeable glance. 'Courtiers are not unpleasant, Thomas. I refer to dubious types from High Holborn. But ask Ferine's particular friend Duncombe about them. I expect he will be at White Hall today.'

Chaloner went to the kitchen for something to eat before he left, and found it in the grip of frenzied activity, as if there were a houseful of demanding residents to tend, rather than two people who would be out for most of the day. One servant cleaned shoes, two sliced carrots, one washed pots and a fifth tended the fire. All worked under the beadily malevolent eye of Housekeeper Joan, who had served Hannah's family for years, and was smug in the knowledge that her position in her mistress's household was unassailable. She and Chaloner had been at loggerheads ever since their first encounter.

'May I help you?' she asked icily. 'If so, perhaps you would wait in the drawing room. I shall send Gram to tend you.'

'Gram?' queried Chaloner. 'I thought the footman was Robert.'

'I dismissed Robert for smoking, and we have Jacob now. However, he is polishing the mistress's shoes, so you will have to make do with our page.'

The page, who appeared to be at least seventy and whose chief qualification for the post seemed to be his diminutive size, hobbled forward. 'I can see to you here,' he offered. 'What do you want?'

It was hardly the most deferential of approaches, but that was not what enraged Joan. 'See to him in the

46

drawing room,' she snapped. 'It is inappropriate for an employer to enter our domain.'

As Hannah was made welcome in there when she was 'cooking', Chaloner could only suppose the stricture applied to him alone. But he liked the kitchen with its blazing fire and comforting smell of bread and spices, and he objected to being told there were areas he could not go in his own home. He ignored Joan, and went to the pantry, aiming to take what he wanted to eat, not what Joan thought she could spare.

There were plates of raw meat, several live eels in a bucket, and jars of pickled fruit that had been laid up the previous autumn, although as Hannah had been in charge of the operation, a number had already exploded while others released a foul smell. Nothing was suitable for an early morning snack, and the oatmeal for the servants' breakfast was not yet ready. Then his eye lit on a jug of milk. He drank some, aware of Joan's quiet pleasure – cold milk was generally deemed to be poisonous. Chaloner, raised on a country estate, always associated it with the happy, carefree days of his childhood, although the kind Joan bought was thin and watery. He set the empty cup on the table, and left the house with relief.

A steady drizzle rendered the streets soggier than ever, and the filth was so deep that he wondered whether the city would ever be rid of it – or if Londoners would be doomed to wade through calf-deep muck for eternity. It reeked, too, comprising as it did a noxious mix of sewage, vegetable parings, butchers' waste and rotting straw. City folk were used to it, so could easily be distinguished from Lady Day visitors, who wrinkled their noses and tried to preserve their shoes by placing each foot with care.

Chaloner was just raising his hand to knock on the club's front door when it was whipped open and he found himself facing Preacher Hill. He braced himself for the usual exchange of insults, but the porter only smiled thinly at him.

'Temperance told me that you are going to catch the villain who murdered Mr Ferine,' he said, although it was clearly an effort to be cordial to a man he disliked. 'And that I should answer any questions you might have. Well, I can tell you right now that the culprit was an intruder. It will not have been a guest, because they are not killers.'

As Hill's compliance was unlikely to last, Chaloner hastened to make use of it. 'Temperance said Ferine had detractors. Do you know who they are?'

'Folk who disapprove of the fact that he was not a Christian, probably. I should not have let him in here, I suppose, but he was generous with tips. Or perhaps he was killed by someone from the Swan with Two Necks or the Antelope on High Holborn. Both are dens of iniquity, which I know, because I sermonise outside them, and its patrons never listen to me.'

The only people who did listen to Hill were either lunatics or people with too much time on their hands, so Chaloner did not think a refusal to heed his rants proved anything.

'The Swan is especially disreputable,' Hill went on. 'And everyone who visits wears a disguise. I might not have recognised Mr Ferine, but his bucket-topped boots are distinctive.'

Chaloner was thoughtful. So Ferine had been involved in business that had necessitated hiding his identity. 'What do you think he was doing there?'

Hill's voice dropped to a whisper. 'Being seduced by the devil. Satan likes High Holborn, which is why I preach there: to remind him that there *are* godly men in this wicked city.'

Chaloner decided to visit High Holborn later, to see if he could learn what Ferine had really been doing. 'Will you tell me what happened last night?'

'Ferine came at nine, the same time as Dr Lambe, who is the Duke of Buckingham's physician. Or should I say his *sorcerer*?' Hill hissed the last word, giving it a sinister timbre.

'Ferine and Lambe were friends?'

'They knew each other. After all, a pagan and a warlock are likely bedfellows.'

'How did Ferine seem to you?'

'Cheerful, noisy, drunk. He played two games of Blind-Man's Buff and one of Chase the Lady before retiring upstairs with Snowflake. Earlier, he had told me that a personal disaster was in the offing for the thirteenth, and said that he intended to be home before midnight in the hope of avoiding it. He must have lost track of time.'

'I need a list of everyone who was here – staff and guests.'

'I cannot,' said Hill shortly. 'Our guests' privacy must be respected. But you will be wasting your time if you pester them anyway. I told you, the villain is an intruder, a stranger who broke in for mischief. I will stake my soul on it.'

Chaloner entered the club cautiously – on previous occasions he had narrowly escaped being hit with lobbed food, not all of it removed from its serving dishes. But there was nothing to fear that morning, because the place was unusually quiet. Maude nodded a greeting from her desk at the foot of the stairs, and made a gesture with her hand to say that business was slow. He stood in the hall and looked into the parlour. Four patrons were playing a card game called lanterloo, while half a dozen more were enjoying desultory conversation with some of the girls. He had never seen the club so empty. Temperance came to greet him, grey smudges of worry under her eyes.

'Williamson sent us a note saying that you will be looking into what happened to Ferine. Thank God! I was afraid he might use Doines, and that would have been the end of us for certain. As it is, rumours have started to circulate, and precious few of our regulars came last night.'

'Courtiers have short memories,' said Chaloner comfortingly. 'They will soon forget.'

Temperance's expression was bleak. 'Will they? Reputation is everything, and ours has been compromised. You *must* find the killer, Tom. We shall not recover until you do.'

'Then tell Hill to give me a list of everyone who was here when Ferine died. Your patrons are potential witnesses, and might have seen something useful.'

'We cannot.' Temperance handed him a piece of paper. 'This explains why.'

It was the letter from Williamson, informing her that Chaloner would be investigating Ferine's murder, and going on to say that there would be dire consequences if members of the government, Court, the Church or the mercantile community were harassed in any way. Its tone was darkly menacing, and Chaloner was not

50

surprised that Temperance was keen to comply. He was irked, though. How was he supposed to solve the case when he was forbidden to speak to witnesses?

'May I interview your staff, or are they off limits, too?' he asked coolly.

Temperance patted his arm. 'I shall assemble them for you now. Wait in the parlour until they are ready and help yourself to a glass of wine.'

It was far too early in the day for drinking, so Chaloner studied the guests instead. The four men at lanterloo were Admiral Lawson, Dr Lambe, Prince Rupert and John Scott. Scott's face was aglow with triumph – he was on a winning streak. However, it did not take long for Chaloner to determine that his success owed more to sleights of hand than to skill.

'I should pull out if I were you, Lawson,' advised Rupert, as more of the Admiral's money went across the table. 'Or Scott will make a pauper of you.'

'I shall be rich again when I take Dutch prizes at sea,' growled Lawson, indicating with a nod that Scott was to deal another hand. 'God will give them to me, because He likes me smiting His enemies. Besides, no landlubber is going to bring *me* to a lee shore at cards.'

Chaloner suspected that Scott had already done it, and it was sheer bloody-mindedness that drove Lawson to persist.

'Are you calling *me* a landlubber?' demanded Rupert. The Prince was notoriously quick to take offence, so was something of a liability in normal conversations.

'The *London*'s sinking was a sad business.' Scott quickly changed the subject, clearly afraid that a row might stop him from winning the rest of Lawson's cash. 'I understand you had family on board, Admiral.'

51

'I did,' growled Lawson. 'It was meant to be a pleasant jaunt from Chatham to Queenhithe, but they ended up with an experience they are unlikely to forget, poor devils. Fortunately, they can swim, so they survived. Unlike my poor mariners. Three hundred souls . . .'

'I teach all my soldiers how to swim,' said Rupert provocatively. 'You should have done the same with your sailors, then they might still be alive.'

'I understand you want the vessel raised from the seabed,' said Lambe, as Lawson's expression went from haunted to angry. The sorcerer was a figure who commanded attention, partly because he possessed charisma in abundance, and partly because of his height and striking attire – he was wearing his star-spangled coat again, and the inked symbols on his skin were dark and mysterious in the half-light. His entry into the discussion meant Lawson ignored the Prince's shrewish remark.

'*Weighed*, not raised,' corrected Lawson. 'And yes, I do. We cannot afford to lose a ship of *London*'s calibre, not to mention the fact that she carried eighty brass cannon.'

'Brass!' scoffed Rupert. 'An antiquated metal for artillery. Iron is much better.'

'Nonsense,' countered Lawson. 'They explode after two rounds, because they overheat.'

'Not if they are turned and annealed,' argued the Prince with lofty condescension. 'I would never allow brass guns on *my* ships.'

'*Your* ships?' spluttered Lawson indignantly. 'You do not have any. And what is this "turning" and "annealing"? Describe how it—'

'I shall soon command a fleet,' interrupted Rupert smugly. 'The King promised. And I will be senior to you, so take *that*, you coarse northern upstart!'

52

Lawson responded in language so ripe that even Chaloner was taken aback. Rupert's reaction was more vigorous. He sprang to his feet and whipped out his sword. Lawson did likewise and they circled each other like jackals. Lambe and Scott hastily scrambled to a safe distance, although Scott swept his winnings into his purse first. The sound of rapiers whistling through the air alerted Maude to the trouble; she raced in from the hall and began imploring them to disarm.

'Help me!' she cried, appealing to the onlookers.

Chaloner was about to oblige but Lambe was there before him.

'Stop,' he ordered in a voice that held considerable authority. 'The stars are not right for a skirmish today. You will bring bad luck on yourselves if you persist.'

'Stars!' sneered Lawson, although he lowered his weapon. 'The only stars I hold in faith are the ones you can navigate by. The rest is hocus-pocus, and only fools are led by such nonsense.'

'They are a potent force,' argued Lambe. 'And if you do not believe me, look at Ferine. If he had followed the advice they offered, he would still be alive.'

'That bastard!' spat Lawson. 'Do you know what he said to my crew? That *London* was an unlucky ship. What sort of blackguard does that on the eve of a war?'

'But she *was* an unlucky ship,' Lambe pointed out. 'Three hundred corpses prove it.'

Lawson opened his mouth to argue, but could apparently think of nothing to say, so he closed it again. Contempt in his every move, Rupert sheathed his sword, collected his cloak and stalked out, slamming the door behind him.

'No wonder he lost the Battle of Naseby,' said Lawson

sullenly. 'What soldier would obey orders from a coxcomb like him?'

'He should learn from you, Admiral,' said Scott fawningly. His purse was so heavy that it threatened to tear off his belt. 'I imagine your men would follow you anywhere.'

'Into hell itself,' agreed Lawson. 'Not that *I* shall ever see such a place, of course, being favoured by God. Did I tell you that He likes me to smite His enemies?'

'Once or twice,' replied Scott. 'But I am not averse to boastful remarks where they are justified. I also like to—'

'I do not boast; I speak the truth.' Lawson jabbed a thick forefinger at the door, scowling as he did so. 'Seafaring men will never fight under that foreign peacock, and if *he* is put in charge of a fleet, we may as well start learning Dutch. He is not fit to command a barge.'

'That will not stop the Privy Council from appointing him, though,' said Lambe softly. 'It is as inevitable as Clarendon's new mansion being renamed Dunkirk House by the masses.'

'The sale of Dunkirk *was* a wicked affair,' said one patron sourly. 'We should have been able to get double the price paid by those thieving French, and it is obvious that some corrupt hand was at work. And Clarendon was in charge of the negotiations . . .'

The port of Dunkirk had been British ever since Cromwell had bought it during the Commonwealth, but the Restoration government had hawked it in order to raise some quick cash. Unfortunately, Clarendon had agreed on a price that was far too low, giving rise to rumours that the French had bribed him. The sale had been unpopular at the time, but now people were livid – it could have

54

been a haven for British warships, but instead the Dutch were using it as a base.

'Dunkirk House,' intoned Lambe. 'Clarendon's home will soon be known by no other name. I predict it, and my prophecies are never wrong.'

Chaloner rolled his eyes. People had been using 'Dunkirk House' for months, and if it did pass into common usage, it would be because the likes of Lambe kept harping on it. Others were impressed by the sorcerer's declaration, however.

'Lord!' breathed Scott. 'What else do you know about the future? Can you predict the outcome of the war?'

'Of course,' replied Lambe sibilantly. 'Yet the matter is complex and—'

'Nonsense,' spat Lawson. 'No one can. And anyone who claims otherwise is a liar.'

Lambe's eyes narrowed to angry slits. 'My Lord Buckingham says—'

'Another idle bugger,' interrupted Lawson scornfully. 'I do not care to hear his opinions. Now get out of my way. I am going home.'

'Would you like a ride in my coach?' asked Scott pleasantly. 'I know you do not have one of your own. Neither do I actually, despite being Cartographer Royal, so I decided to hire one for a few days in the hope that the King will see my sad predicament and arrange for me to have one at government expense.'

'God gave me two feet,' said Lawson, shoving past him. 'I do not need wheels.'

Scott scurried after him, his persistence in the face of such rank discourtesy giving the impression that he was loath to let the Admiral go while there was still money

55

in his pockets. As Lambe was alone, Chaloner took the opportunity to corner him.

'Temperance says you are kin to the Dr Lambe who served Buckingham's father,' he began, aiming to see what he could learn about a man who clearly meant Clarendon harm.

Lambe smiled serenely. 'Yes, my sire served his sire, and now I serve the son.' He made a sudden gesture with his hand and for one shocking instant Chaloner thought he saw sparks on Lambe's fingertips. 'But dawn approaches, and I am a creature of the night. I must be away.'

He spun around so abruptly that his coat billowed behind him, accentuating his height and commanding mien. Chaloner stared after him for a moment, then followed, aiming to finish the discussion, but when he reached the door, the courtyard and the lane beyond were empty. He turned to see Hill lounging nearby, smoking a pipe.

'Did Lambe just come out?' he asked.

'No,' replied the preacher. 'Only Admiral Lawson and John Scott. Why?'

Supposing the sorcerer must possess a very stealthy tread if he could slip past Hill, Chaloner returned to the parlour, where Temperance was waiting for him.

'Lambe is a sinister fellow,' she whispered. 'Especially given that so many of his predictions come true. However, I hope he is right about Dunkirk House. It will serve that fat old villain right for taking bribes from the French.'

Chaloner knew there was no point in telling her that Clarendon was innocent, and they stood in silence until she nodded towards a bald, bony, middle-aged man who was enjoying a final paw at the ladies.

56

'That is John Duncombe, Ferine's particular friend. You can question him if you like. He will not remember any impertinences later, because he is too drunk.'

Chaloner recalled Hannah's remark about Ferine and Duncombe's friendship. 'Who is the man with him?' he asked. 'The fat, grave fellow.'

'Edward Manning, who says it is his chilblains that make him limp so badly. I hope he is telling the truth – that he does not have some nasty disease he will pass to my girls.'

Chaloner blinked. 'Why on Earth would you think that? And why let him stay if you fear—'

'Because we had so few guests tonight that I told Hill to admit anyone, just to make the place look less empty. Not that it worked. But you can see why I dislike Manning. He is a sly, slovenly creature, not the kind of person who should keep company with admirals and princes.'

From what Chaloner had seen of Lawson and Rupert, he suspected it was Manning who had lowered his standards. He took her at her word and went to sit with Duncombe.

'You knew Ferine,' he said, taking one look at the courtier and deciding that the man was far too inebriated for a subtler approach.

Duncombe promptly burst into tears. 'He was the best friend who ever lived! He said something vile would happen to him on the thirteenth, but neither of us imagined it would be his murder. If only he had watched the time!'

'It would have made no difference,' said Manning, laying a kindly hand on the courtier's shoulder. His fingers were fat, dimpled and not very clean. 'Not if it was ordained.'

'That is not what Ferine believed,' sobbed Duncombe. 'He calculated horoscopes so that people could *avoid* trouble – he always said that nothing was inevitable. But he thought his own bad luck would be minor. A stumble, perhaps, or a loss of money. Neither of us imagined . . .'

'So who killed him?' asked Chaloner baldly.

'Some beastly robber who wanted his purse,' wept Duncombe. 'There are a lot of strange people in London at the moment. They flock here from the provinces, for Lady Day.'

'Ferine made a horoscope for me,' put in Manning. 'It cost me a pretty penny.'

'Money well spent,' sniffed Duncombe. 'Lambe is good, but Ferine was better.'

'I hope you are right,' said Manning. 'He told me that a certain business venture I intend to pursue will be successful, and I have invested everything I own on his advice.'

Chaloner would have liked to question Duncombe further, but the man chose that moment to pass out. With the assistance of Temperance and Hill, he manoeuvred the courtier into his coach, and by the time they had finished, the club was empty. With a weary sigh, Temperance indicated that Chaloner was to accompany her to the kitchen, where she had assembled the staff.

'Interview the girls first,' she directed. 'Then they can go to bed. I do not want them yawning and heavy-eyed when they start work tonight.'

Chaloner obliged, although the prostitutes were young, fit and vivacious, and he doubted they would be troubled by the loss of an hour's sleep. They were all shapes and sizes, so as to accommodate any particular preference among the guests, and were in a state of careless undress, which made it difficult for Chaloner to concentrate on his questions.

'We saw nothing unusual,' said one named Belle, taking the role of spokeswoman. 'It was busy but it always is on Sundays. Our gentlemen are forced to spend hours in church, you see, so they cannot wait to come here and make up for all the tedium.'

'Especially the clergymen,' interposed Snowflake.

'Did any of them do anything unusual?' asked Chaloner.

'We cannot reveal that,' declared Belle indignantly. 'It would be a betrayal of trust.'

'I meant when they were in the parlour,' explained Chaloner. 'Other than the woodlice incident, did anyone pay Ferine particular attention? Did he say or do anything to annoy someone? Was there a disagreement or a squabble? Perhaps over Snowflake – I know she is popular.'

'I am,' agreed Snowflake proudly. 'But no. Our guests behaved exactly as they always do – with relief to be away from the strictures of high society.'

'All the men I allowed upstairs were clients who had been here many times before,' added Maude. 'None would have hurt Ferine.'

'How can you be so sure?' asked Chaloner. 'Some of them fought in the wars, which means they are no strangers to violence. And all are wealthy enough to hire assassins.'

'Oh, fie!' cried Belle. 'You read too many salacious broadsheets! Our patrons are gentle, peaceable men, and there is not a malicious bone among them.'

Chaloner struggled not to gape, given that their members included such feisty individuals as Buckingham,

59

Rupert and Lawson, two of whom had drawn their swords that very night.

'It is true,' insisted Snowflake. 'We see a different side of them. Take Rupert, for example. One of his favourite places is Hackney Marsh, which is where I am from, and he loves to chat about the ducks on the River Lea. He has even met my father.'

Chaloner seriously doubted that Rupert had done any such thing, and strongly suspected that the Prince had lied in order to make her more willing to do what he wanted in bed.

'Perhaps you would tell me where you all were at the time of the murder,' he said.

There was some consternation at this request, as most had been with clients and Temperance had forbidden them to mention names, but he eventually managed to establish that they all had alibis for the salient time. Except Snowflake.

'Well, *I* did not kill him,' she said crossly. 'He was one of my favourites – especially when he gave me presents.'

'Like dried toads,' recalled Chaloner.

Snowflake nodded. 'And wood from a gibbet to protect me from agues. He also gave me something valuable, something he said that a lot of people will want in time, so I am to keep it safe. Show him, Maude.'

Maude unlocked the heavy chest where Temperance stored her money, and produced two metal cylinders about the length of her hand. One fitted inside the other, and they looked ancient.

'What are they?' asked Chaloner, regarding them blankly.

'I do not know,' confessed Snowflake. 'But he said they will make me rich one day.'

60

There was no more to be learned, and Snowflake seemed an unlikely killer, so he nodded to say he had finished, and watched the girls troop off to bed. Then he questioned the cooks and the servants who cleaned the rooms, but none had anything of substance to add.

Next, he explored the house. There was a storage room on the first floor, which overlooked the back yard and was easily accessible by climbing the ivy outside. There were scratches on the sill, a muddy footprint on the floor, and the latch had been forced.

'I was in here on Sunday afternoon, looking for a mousetrap,' said Maude. 'The latch was not broken then, and there was no mark on the rug. And Ferine was murdered a few hours later . . .'

'Thank God!' breathed Temperance. 'Hill was right: the culprit *is* an intruder.'

'I do not see that as cause for relief,' remarked Chaloner. 'Your guests will not feel very safe in a place that can be readily accessed by murderers.'

'We can remedy that with new windows and additional guards,' said Temperance, giving the first genuine smile he had seen since he had been summoned to inspect Ferine's body. 'Our guests will *flock* back now we can assert that none of them is under suspicion.'

Chaloner doubted it would be that simple.

Chapter 3

Holborn was a long, wide thoroughfare, dipping down to the grubby Fleet River in the east and narrowing to pass St Giles's Fields in the west. It was the usual combination of elegant houses and tenements of shocking dilapidation. Several Inns of Chancery were there, too – preparatory schools for those wishing to be called to the Bar.

About halfway along was a line of cottages called Middle Row, which had been built smack in its centre, where they and two sturdy gates combined to cause a considerable impediment to the flow of traffic. The road to the west was known as 'High' Holborn, and Muscut's Coffee House stood just off it, on a narrow lane that afforded so little light that lamps were needed even on the brightest of days. Its windows were filmed with greasy soot from the roasting beans, and its floor was so thickly coated with filth that it was impossible to tell if it was made of wood or stone.

Chaloner did not particularly like coffee, although he suspected that he might find it more palatable if he added sugar, which he avoided as a silent and largely futile objection to slave-operated plantations. Still, it was an improvement on tea, with its complex rituals for preparation and pouring, and infinitely better than chocolate, which was an oily, bitter brew generally only taken as a tonic by those who wanted to feel they were doing something healthy.

The owner arrived with the traditional long-spouted jug, and poured his new customer a dish of coffee. While Chaloner sipped it, he studied the other patrons, trying to determine who looked like the kind of man to accept the traitor's shilling. He had just settled on a dour, shifty rogue near the back, when someone tapped him on the shoulder. He turned quickly, hand on the hilt of his sword. Standing next to him was a youngish man with a wide grin and a Cavalier moustache. The fellow's clothes were showy rather than fine, and there was something about his eager amiability and wide-set eyes that suggested he was not the sharpest sword in the armoury.

'Thomas Chaloner?' he asked brightly, louder than the spy would have liked. 'I am Will Leving. Come outside with me. I know it is raining, but we shall not be disturbed in the garden, and we need to talk.'

Warily, Chaloner followed him into a tiny yard, a dismal, unkempt place so dank that nothing grew except patches of slime. It reeked of urine and rotting coffee grounds.

'As we have never met, I shall tell you the story of my life,' Leving announced with a smile that was unnervingly vacant. 'We should know a bit about each other if we are to work together.'

Chaloner nodded cautiously, his heart sinking lower with every word the man spoke. His first assessment had

63

been right: Leving was a dimwit, and no intelligencer liked working with those.

'I fought for Parliament during the wars,' Leving began, 'and I did well when Cromwell was in power. But he died, and along came the King, so I decided to leave London and head north, where false friends encouraged me to join a bit of an uprising . . .'

'The Northern Plot,' recalled Chaloner, 'which was more than a "bit of an uprising". It had the makings of a full-blown rebellion.'

Leving shrugged carelessly. 'Well, I was caught and sentenced to hang, even though my heart was never really in it. It was grossly unjust, actually.'

'Right,' said Chaloner, wondering if there was a way to dump Leving and investigate the Fifth Monarchists by himself.

'But I convinced Spymaster Williamson that I would be of more use alive. He let me "escape" to come here, where I shall help him snare those insurgents who evaded his clutches in York.'

Chaloner was confused. 'Your remit is to track down Northern Plot rebels? I thought we were supposed to be chasing Fifth Monarchists.'

'We shall do both,' declared Leving, all childish delight. 'Because two of the Northern Plot's leaders are also Fifth Monarchists. This was news to Williamson, and he was very grateful to me for pointing it out. He has not said so, but I know he considers me his most valuable asset.'

'Christ,' muttered Chaloner.

'Their names are Jones and Strange,' Leving chattered on. 'Both very desperate villains.'

'Jones?' asked Chaloner, recalling the man outside Temperance's club. Yet it was a common name and he imagined there must be dozens of them in London alone.

'Roger Jones,' elaborated Leving. 'And Nat Strange.'

Chaloner had never met Nat Strange or Roger Jones, but he had certainly heard of them, because they had rebelled against Cromwell, too. Like most fanatics, they did not know what they wanted from a government, only what they did *not* want, which meant no regime could ever win their approval and they were doomed to perpetual discontent.

'I could have bested them by myself,' Leving went on when Chaloner made no reply. 'But Williamson insisted on appointing you to help me. For the glory, I imagine – he wants an excuse to claim some of the credit when they are caught.'

Or to ensure they were actually thwarted, thought Chaloner acidly, which was unlikely if Leving was left to his own devices.

'Strange and Jones are dangerous,' he said. 'Why does Williamson not arrest them at once?'

'He wants to know what they are planning first. Besides, they have so many minions that apprehending them now will not stop what has been set in motion. I call it the High Holborn Plot, because most meetings take place up here. It runs off the tongue much more readily than "the Scheme that Involves Fifth Monarchy Men Making a Nuisance of Themselves in London".'

Chaloner listened with growing alarm, thinking Williamson must be short-handed indeed to have recruited Leving, because it was folly to set someone like him against seasoned dissidents like Strange and Jones. 'Do you know the names of these minions?'

'Yes, I have learned seven so far. Williamson wants me

65

to compile a complete list, although it will not be easy when there are so many.' Leving recited the ones he had, but none meant anything to Chaloner.

'Have you attended their meetings?' When Leving nodded, Chaloner asked, 'So what are they proposing to do?'

'Put King Jesus on the throne instead of King Charles.'

'Yes,' said Chaloner, striving for patience. 'That is the stated aim of all Fifth Monarchists. But how will they do it?'

'I have no idea, but it will involve explosions, because their gunpowder man blew himself up recently, and they have been desperate to find another. They will be delighted when I arrive with you in tow – an old Parliamentarian soldier with a regicide uncle.' Leving winked conspiratorially. 'Williamson told me all about you.'

'Did he?' Chaloner was unimpressed; it was hardly professional.

'He did, and I think you will be *much* better than old Scarface Roberts.' Leving chuckled. 'He earned that nickname by discovering the hard way that explosives are unpredictable. He should have taken heed of the mishap and learned another trade – then he would still be alive. But time is passing and we have work to do. Are you ready?'

'Ready for what?' asked Chaloner suspiciously.

'Jones gave me some documents to deliver to a fellow named Edward Manning at the Fleece tavern.' Leving pulled a package from his coat. 'You can come with me.'

Chaloner frowned. 'Manning? Is he a fat, grave man with chilblains?'

Leving started. 'Yes, why? Do you know him?'

'Our paths crossed earlier today.' Chaloner was unwilling to tell the gabbling Leving that it had been in Temperance's club. 'Is he a Fifth Monarchist?'

Leving nodded. 'Yes – a very unsavoury one.'

'Most rebels are unsavoury,' muttered Chaloner. 'Present company *not* excepted.'

Beaming in a way that made Chaloner sure he should be in Bedlam, Leving led the way out on to High Holborn. But Chaloner still had questions to ask, and grabbed his arm rather roughly, preventing the man from skipping off down the road.

'What is in these documents?' he demanded.

'Jones did not tell me. He just said to meet Manning in the Fleece, and pass them to him.'

'But you have opened them, naturally,' pressed Chaloner.

'Open letters addressed to someone else? No, of course not! It would be ungentlemanly.'

Chaloner assumed he was joking until he saw the earnest expression. He regarded Leving in disbelief. 'You are in possession of messages from one conspirator to another, and you have not analysed them? What kind of spy are you?'

'No kind at all,' declared Leving indignantly. 'I am a patriot, using my unique position to foil a misguided attempt to cause trouble for the government. Spies are low, treacherous creatures with no scruples. I am not one of those. My calling is a *noble* one.'

Chaloner was tempted to point out that there was nothing noble about befriending people and betraying their secrets to the Spymaster, but he did not want a debate on the matter.

67

'Your remit is to foil the High Holborn Plot,' he pointed out shortly, 'not to deliver messages that will help it succeed. So give them to me. I will open them.'

'You will not!' cried Leving, clutching them to his chest. 'Manning will notice and tell Jones. And I would rather not cross *him* if it can be avoided. He has a bit of a temper, you see.'

'Manning will not suspect a thing. I promise.'

'It is too risky,' said Leving firmly. 'Everything depends on me being friends with these men, and it would be a pity if I am ousted, just because you want to pry into letters not intended for your eyes. Now follow me before Manning begins to wonder whether we are coming.'

He was off before Chaloner could argue, capering down High Holborn like a carefree boy. It was not far to the Fleece, and he had opened the door before Chaloner had caught up with him. Resignedly, the spy followed him inside. The Fleece was a pleasant tavern, which smelled of woodsmoke, sweet ale and roasted meat. As it was the time when most people ate dinner, it was crowded, and its atmosphere one of noisy jollity. Many folk were dressed in the comfortable smocks and woollen cloaks of the country, indicating that they were Lady Day visitors.

Leving led the way to a cosy chamber at the back where a number of farmers discussed how war might affect the price of wheat. Tucked into a corner behind them was Manning, along with a man whose red nose and purple cheeks suggested he was a habitual drinker – an unprepossessing individual with oily hair, dirty clothes and thick red hands that were covered in old burn scars; he was fast asleep.

Manning frowned when he saw Chaloner. 'You were

68

in the club this morning – you helped Temperance stuff poor Duncombe into his coach.'

'He is Thomas Chaloner,' supplied Leving. 'Nephew of the regicide, and recently dismissed from his post at Court. He is no lover of the current regime, so you can trust him.'

Manning regarded Chaloner suspiciously, clearly thinking he would make up his own mind about that, while Chaloner winced. Leving's voice had been loud, and London was full of Royalists eager to vent their spleen on anyone even remotely connected to the old king's execution. With a flourish, Leving handed over the letters, although not before Chaloner had seen that they had been addressed in an elegant cursive with a distinctive flourish to each capital letter.

'He thinks we should have opened them,' Leving said, indicating Chaloner with a smile that made the spy wonder afresh whether he was sane. 'But I refused. However, perhaps you will repay my honesty by reading them aloud now. I confess I am curious as to their content.'

Manning's eyebrows shot up into his sparse hair. 'Then I am afraid you will have to stay curious, because they are none of your affair.'

'Is this Sherwin?' Unperturbed by the snub, Leving turned his attention to the dozing man. 'He does not look up to much. Are you sure he—'

'You are not seeing him at his best,' interrupted Manning. 'But he knows his business, I assure you. Lord, my chilblains hurt! It is this wet weather: my feet are never dry, and these shoes pinch something cruel. That ointment you sold me was useless.'

'Well, well,' came a voice from behind them. It was

noisy in the tavern and Chaloner had not heard the approach of John Scott. Chaloner frowned: his old associate was appearing in some unexpected places. 'This is an interesting gathering – Manning, Sherwin, Chaloner and Leving.'

'You had my note, then,' said Manning with a patently false smile. 'Telling you to meet me here? You were supposed to arrive before Leving, so that I could explain certain developments.'

'Funnily enough, it never arrived,' said Scott flatly. 'However, I saw you and Sherwin on High Holborn, so I decided to follow. And what do I find? Negotiations under way without me.'

'Nonsense!' cried Manning, rather too vehemently. 'Nothing would have been discussed without you, as you know perfectly well.'

'Do I?' Scott turned to Chaloner, who was wondering what was going on. 'I am surprised to see you here. I thought you had secured yourself a nice post with the Earl of Clarendon – one that pays enough to let you enjoy Temperance North's costly brothel.'

'He was dismissed,' said Leving before Chaloner could answer for himself. 'And he has other interests now. Such as protecting me from danger.'

This was news to Chaloner, although Scott did look dangerous at that particular moment, and he could see why Leving and Manning were nervous of him.

'A bodyguard?' Scott regarded Chaloner with rank disdain. 'Well, I suppose a man must eke a living where he can.'

Before Chaloner could ask questions that might tell him what was happening, Sherwin woke with a noisy snort.

'Ale,' he slurred. 'I need ale.'

'I had better take you home,' said Scott. 'And it might be wise not to venture out again unless I am with you. As I have told you before, Manning is unequal to protecting you, should you fall foul of *certain people.*'

'Home to the Pope's Head?' asked Sherwin brightening. 'Good! They have ale there.'

'He *is* safe with me,' objected Manning, stung. 'I have a sword and I know how to use it.'

'With your chilblains?' asked Scott archly. 'You can barely walk, let alone fence.'

They were still squabbling as they bundled Sherwin outside, neither casting so much as a glance at the two men they were leaving behind. When they had gone, Chaloner turned to Leving.

'I think you had better explain what that was about.'

'I wish I could,' said Leving ruefully. 'But I have no idea.'

He might have done, if he had read the letters, thought Chaloner sourly. 'Then tell me who they are. And do not say Fifth Monarchists, because Scott is no religious fanatic.'

'All I know is that Sherwin has some valuable information – information that Jones is keen to acquire and that Scott and Manning are keen to sell him.' Leving lowered his voice. 'But a few of the Fifth Monarchy leaders are due to meet in a private house in a few moments. Shall we join them? I can introduce you as our new gunpowder expert, and you can ask them these questions.'

As Leving led the way back on to High Holborn, Chaloner was tempted to drag him down an alley and interrogate him vigorously. Unfortunately, he suspected it would be a waste of time – that Leving had nothing much to tell. Indeed, he could not help but wonder whether Williamson had been duped, and that while Leving had no doubt leapt at the chance to save himself from the noose, he had exaggerated his importance in the rebels' fraternity.

Suddenly, Leving turned to face him, his expression serious. 'Do not mention the letters at this meeting, by the way. Jones told me to deliver them secretly, and I suspect his cronies know nothing about them.'

'You mean there are rifts within the leadership?'

'Oh, yes! The Fifth Monarchists are a very argumentative crowd: Atkinson is a romantic dreamer with his head in the clouds, while Strange and Quelch have *their* heads in the sewers. No one disagrees with Jones, though. You will understand why when you meet him.'

He began walking again, and approached the curious island of cottages called Middle Row. He aimed for the largest, an attractive brick-built affair with unusually clean paintwork, polished windows and decorative pots in the porch. It looked like the home of a respectable maiden aunt, and was certainly not the kind of place Chaloner would have associated with rebels.

'They use this for small meetings,' explained Leving in an undertone as he knocked on the door. 'But they hire a hall in the Talbot for bigger ones, which can attract two or three hundred people. Of course, that is only a fraction of their total. I heard Jones tell Strange only yesterday that the movement has at least ten thousand supporters.'

'Ten thousand people represents a serious uprising,' said Chaloner worriedly. 'The Northern Plot did not involve a quarter as many.'

Leving nodded sombrely before opening the door and stepping inside. Chaloner followed, entering a pretty parlour with a virginals in one corner and a flute on the windowsill. There were embroidered cushions on the benches, half-finished knitting by the hearth, and an impressive arrangement of dried flowers. Then four men trooped in carrying an assortment of plates and jugs. A woman walked behind them, herding them along like sheep.

'Leving,' blurted the first, stopping so abruptly that the others careened into the back of him, leaving a smear of cream on his coat and a dusting of cinnamon down his breeches. 'And you have brought a guest, I see.'

'I told you I would find a gunpowder expert,' said Leving with a happy grin. 'So here is Tom Chaloner, nephew of the regicide.' He turned to the spy. 'Allow me to present Roger Jones, our esteemed leader.'

Chaloner was surprised to note that Jones *was* the man who had complained to Hill about the lack of reading material at the club – fanatical religious sects tended to frown on brothels.

'I knew your uncle, Chaloner,' said Jones, eyeing him intently. 'He would have liked the merry debauchery at Hercules' Pillars Alley. Is that why you frequent the place?'

'No,' replied Chaloner, although Jones was right: his fun-loving uncle would have adored the club. 'It is owned by a friend of mine. What drew you to it?'

Jones smiled, an expression that made his eyes seem colder than ever. 'I went there for the Cause. I met a man who supports us – an influential person.'

Chaloner wondered who among Temperance's clientele was a Fifth Monarchist, and supposed he had better find out. It was one thing for tradesmen and labourers to hold lunatic views, but another altogether for powerful politicians, churchmen or military commanders to do it.

'You know each other?' asked Leving. 'Good! It saves the need for more of an introduction, although I must tell you that Jones is a great writer of revolutionary tracts. He penned *Mene Tekel*, but is too modest to mention it himself. Have you heard of it? It has caused quite a stir.'

Mene Tekel, or The Downfall of Tyranny was an incendiary underground pamphlet that had been published a few months earlier. It was a bald attack on the monarchy, and was thus popular with the more extreme kind of republican. Chaloner had tried to read it, but had given up halfway through, exasperated by its contorted logic and flowery language.

'It has,' agreed Jones, pleased. 'However, it is nothing compared to the ones I shall compose when the Last Millennium is here. I have much to say about politics and religion.'

Chaloner was sure he did.

'Yet thou didst not cause stir enough,' said the large man behind him, setting his plate of cakes carefully on the table. 'Or the King would have abdicated in favour of Jesus.'

'This is Nat Strange,' supplied Leving helpfully. 'A leading Fifth Monarchist.'

Chaloner thought that Strange looked like a man with madcap beliefs – huge, red-faced, yellow-haired and wild-eyed.

Strange scowled, and indicated the remaining two men. 'Since thou makest free with my name, let me do the same for these: Richard Quelch, watchmaker, and John Atkinson, stockinger.'

Quelch was a bald, bristling man with bad teeth, while

Atkinson looked more like a scholar than a rebel; there was ink on his fingers, and he had a shy, almost diffident air.

'And Ursula Adman,' added Leving, bowing to the woman who stood behind the men. 'Her sister is Anna Trapnel, who was arrested for writing accounts of her visions.'

Chaloner was familiar with Mrs Trapnel, who was hailed as a seer by her followers – and a woman with crackpot opinions by everyone else. He regarded Ursula uneasily, wondering if *she* was the type to fall on the floor and start railing about the Apocalypse. Ursula, however, was the picture of normality. Her clothes were of decent quality, although she was a little too plump for them, and her hair was curled into fashionable ringlets.

'Anna would love to be here,' she told Chaloner quietly. 'But her gaolers refuse to release her, so she asked me to take her place.'

'It is good of thee.' Strange's rough features softened into a smile. 'Brave, too.'

'And you make *excellent* cakes,' added Quelch, taking one to prove it. 'Your gingerbread-men . . . well, suffice to say that Jesus will certainly want a few when He comes.'

'Yes, He will,' agreed Ursula, without a flicker of humour. 'They are the best in London.'

'Chaloner would like to replace Scarface Roberts,' said Leving to Jones with one of his vacant beams. 'He has recently been dismissed by his employer, the Earl of Clarendon, for losing a lot of valuable jewels, and so he finds himself with time on his hands.'

'*Lost* them?' asked Quelch suspiciously. 'How?'

'On a ship,' replied Chaloner. 'When it sank.'

75

'You mean you were careless?' asked Ursula uneasily. 'And you want to work with gunpowder?'

'I was not careless,' said Chaloner with unfeigned irritation. 'I warned Clarendon that winter is not the best time to be delivering jewels and dispatches to Russia, but he refused to listen. The ship struck ice and went down before I could rescue them, although I tried.'

'An unfair dismissal,' said Jones softly. 'It is certainly enough to make a man rebel.'

Chaloner had no idea if he was serious.

The Middle Row meeting was like no conspiracy that Chaloner had ever known. It was conducted around a large polished table loaded with Ursula's cakes, all served on dainty plates. She supplied little silver forks to prevent savage use of fingers; Quelch, Strange and Leving struggled to ply them, but Atkinson and Jones were adept. Despite his unease, Chaloner was forced to concede that Ursula's culinary skills were impressive, and wished Hannah's were half as good.

'How did you gain your knowledge of gunpowder?' Atkinson asked conversationally, passing the platter of knot biscuits to Jones before taking one himself. Jones had eaten three already, but it did not stop him from having a fourth, devouring it with quick, nervous bites, like a squirrel. Or a rat, thought Chaloner, who had not taken to Jones.

'In the wars,' he replied. An exploding cannon had almost killed him at the Battle of Naseby, so he could say with perfect honesty that he had acquired first-hand experience of how deadly ordnance could be. 'And then in Holland.'

'What do you want him to blow up?' Leving asked

Jones. 'You have never said, but the sooner he knows, the sooner he can go about making plans. Is there any more fruit pie?'

'We shall tell him in time,' said Jones shortly. 'When we know each other a little better.'

'He hates the Court,' began Leving, then yelped when Chaloner kicked him under the table. 'What did you do that for? It hurt!'

'You have a big mouth,' said Jones, smirking as Leving leaned down to rub his ankle. 'He is warning you to keep it shut.'

'Or we shall shut it for you,' growled Quelch.

'Leave him be,' snapped Strange. 'He does not need to hear thy threats.'

'I do not,' agreed Leving, hurt. 'I am only trying to expedite matters. You want to know about Chaloner, so I am telling you.'

'We shall ask our own questions, thank you,' said Quelch curtly. 'However, *I* think it is suspicious that he should appear with such fine credentials in our hour of need.'

Jones bared his teeth at Chaloner in the parody of a smile. 'You must forgive our caution, but we have learned to be wary of fanatics. Their unpredictability makes them dangerous allies.'

Chaloner joined the general murmur of agreement, and had he not been so tense, he might have laughed at the notion that the Fifth Monarchists did not consider themselves extremists. The author of *Mene Tekel* was hardly a rational being, while Strange and Quelch were clearly hotheads. He wondered what had possessed Atkinson and Ursula, who seemed sensible, to join their ranks.

'My sister dislikes fanatics, too,' said Ursula. Then she sighed. 'I wish she were here instead of me. She would be much more of an asset.'

'Yes, but she cannot cook,' said Strange, rather fervently. 'We are happy with thee.'

'Strange is led by his stomach,' sneered Quelch, looking pointedly at his companion's ample paunch, while Ursula preened at the praise. 'But *I* am here for my conscience.'

'Liar!' spat Strange, nettled. 'Thou hast no conscience, except that it serves thyself. Thou art naught but a low-born watchmaker whose timepieces are never accurate.'

'Yes, they are!' cried Quelch, stung. He addressed Ursula. '*He* thinks that being a Baptist pastor makes him better than the rest of us. Well, when King Jesus comes to reign it will not be *Strange* who stands at God's right hand.'

'It will not be thee, either,' Strange snarled back. 'The worst sins are swearing, pride, drunkenness, Sabbath-breaking, whoredom, lasciviousness, stage-plays, popery and superstition. And thou didst commit every one of them in Hercules' Pillars Alley on Sunday night.'

Chaloner regarded Quelch with interest. The feisty watchmaker was certainly the kind of man to dispatch a fellow patron for some misguided religious principle. Could he have killed Ferine for devising horoscopes?

Quelch paled with anger. 'I went there to do God's work. Ask Jones.'

'Neither of us enjoyed our time in that den of iniquity,' stated Jones loftily. 'There were no newsbooks or political pamphlets to read, and it was not easy to repel the attentions of those rapacious females. But duty called, so we had no choice but to endure.'

'Was it worth the sacrifice?' asked Ursula, humour dancing in her eyes.

'We made contact with the necessary individual,' replied Jones, so coldly that it extinguished the merry twinkle. 'Now we must wait to see whether our labours bear fruit.'

'Were you there when that courtier was murdered?' asked Atkinson, in the uncomfortable silence that followed. Even Chaloner was unsettled by Jones's icy tone, and it certainly stopped the sparring between Strange and Quelch. 'My stepsister told me about it yesterday.'

'I hope she does not think *we* were responsible,' said Jones, narrowing his eyes. 'And regrets distracting the porter to let us slip in through the front door.'

'No, no,' said Atkinson quickly. 'She is quite committed to the Cause, I assure you.'

'I cannot imagine why thou acknowledgeth her, Atkinson,' said Strange unpleasantly. 'If a member of *my* family turned to whoredom, I would disown her.'

'Snowflake is not a whore!' cried Atkinson. 'She is a simple country girl who has lost her way. I tried to help her when she first arrived in the city, but she did not want to be a stockinger.'

Chaloner struggled not to laugh. There was nothing of the 'simple country girl' about Snowflake, and he knew for a fact that she had marched up to Temperance and given a résumé of her talents that would have impressed even the most particular of brothel-keepers. However, he had not known that she had connections to the Fifth Monarchists, and supposed he would have to find out how many other men she had sneaked into the club behind Hill's back – including, perhaps, Ferine's killer.

'You called this meeting,' Jones was saying to Atkinson. 'Do you have something to report? If so, I am sure Leving and Chaloner will excuse us while we talk privately.'

'There is no need,' said Atkinson, as Chaloner started to rise. Leving stayed where he was, evidently prepared to argue for his inclusion. 'It was only to tell you that the Dutch Smyrna fleet has been seen near Scotland. Word is that an invasion is imminent.'

'Good,' said Quelch. 'While the Dutch attack from the sea, we shall strike from within.'

'The Dutch,' mused Leving. 'They will certainly benefit from a weakened Britain. Have you made contact with them, to ask for weapons and money to assist our revolt?'

Chaloner cringed: Leving would not live long if that was his idea of discreet intelligence gathering.

'No, we have not,' said Atkinson crossly. 'We may not like the King and his corrupt government, but we will never side with the Dutch against our fellow countrymen. Never!'

'But we will be doing it for King Jesus,' objected Quelch. 'That makes it all right.'

'Pass me another knot biscuit,' said Jones loudly, thus ending the discussion. He smiled at Ursula. 'Is it my imagination or is there more nutmeg in these than in previous batches?'

While Ursula regaled him with the recipe, her fellow conspirators ate their fill, and when Jones declared the meeting ended, all nodded eagerly when she offered to wrap parcels of goodies for later. They had discussed nothing of import, but Chaloner suspected it was not because he and Leving were there – the conference had been called because Atkinson had wanted to sample

80

Ursula's baking, and the others had not minded an excuse to do likewise.

'You see?' asked Leving, as he and Chaloner walked away together, each with a neat package under his arm. 'They trust you already.'

'Hardly! And your gabbling did not help. Please do not do it again.'

'I did not gabble,' declared Leving indignantly. 'What a horrible thing to say!'

The day was drawing to a close, yet Chaloner felt as though he had made scant progress on either investigation. However, there was one thing he could do before going home to Hannah's pickled ling pie – ask the parish priest about Ferine's religious opinions. Unfortunately, a visit to the vicar told Chaloner that Ferine had never set foot inside his church. Instead, he was directed to St Dunstan-in-the-West, which tended to attract courtier types, being generally regarded as a fashionable sort of place. Chaloner was pleased. Its minister was Joseph Thompson, whom he knew well, and he knew exactly where to find him at such an hour: in the Rainbow Coffee House on Fleet Street.

The Rainbow was one of Chaloner's favourite haunts, although he was not sure why, given that he liked neither its coffee nor most of its clientele. He supposed it was because there was something comfortingly familiar about its smuggy warmth and worn benches, and as his own life was disturbingly unpredictable, he appreciated the fact that nothing in the Rainbow ever changed.

It was the first time he had visited it since arriving home, but the scene that greeted him was exactly as he had left it weeks before. The same people sat cradling dishes of the usual foul brew, and the dog-eared government newsbooks lay ready for them to peruse. The customary reek of burning beans assailed his nostrils, and the resident cat was in her regular place by the fire. He knew he would shortly learn that the bigoted and ill-informed opinions of its patrons had not changed either, and that it would not be long before he was annoyed by them.

'What news?' called James Farr the owner, voicing the traditional coffee-house greeting. He beamed when he saw Chaloner. 'Hah! We were beginning to think you were lost in the icy wastes of the north. Now we shall have some decent conversation!'

'We had plenty while he was away,' objected a young printer named Fabian Stedman, who spent his every waking moment in the Rainbow; Chaloner often wondered if he had a home. 'Especially once war was declared on the butter-eaters.'

'I did my best to turn public opinion against hostilities,' sighed Rector Thompson, coming to his feet to grasp Chaloner's hand in a warm gesture of friendship. 'But to no avail.'

'Well, I am glad our government took a stand,' declared Stedman. 'There is only enough room for one nation to rule the waves, and that is us.'

'It will be costly in blood and money,' warned Thompson.

'I do not care about the blood, as long as it is not mine,' said Farr. 'But I am worried about the money. Who will pay?'

'We will,' declared Stedman stoutly, ever the staunch Royalist. 'It is our patriotic duty to provide funds for this noble venture.'

82

'Not me,' said Farr. 'My taxes are too high already. Still, at least my hard-earned shillings are not being used to fund the intelligence services – I heard yesterday that Williamson's budget has been cut yet again.'

He sounded gleeful: coffee houses were places where patrons spoke their minds, and no spymaster worth his salt failed to monitor them. Needless to say their owners did not like Williamson or his insidious agents.

'It has,' nodded Thompson. 'And he has his hands full with the Dutch war, so if anyone fancies staging a rebellion, now is the time to do it.'

'Have you heard that one might be brewing?' fished Chaloner.

'Not recently,' replied Farr, while the others shrugged to say they had not either. Chaloner could only suppose that either the Fifth Monarchy uprising was not as serious as the Earl had led him to believe, or its leaders had managed to keep their plans secret.

'Tell us about Russia,' said Thompson pleasantly. 'Was it as terrible as depicted in that doom-laden book you bought before you left?'

Stedman interrupted to say that Olearius's *Travels* was a very accurate account of the Tsardom, and Farr found it incumbent to disagree. By the time they had finished quarrelling, Thompson's question had been forgotten, which Chaloner did not mind at all.

'Three suns were seen over Hamburg last week,' said Farr, launching off on an entirely new subject, as was often the wont in the Rainbow. 'There is a new comet, too – different from the one we had in January.'

'And there is plague in Venice,' added Stedman darkly, 'while the devil appeared at a Quaker meeting in York. All are signs of looming disaster.'

83

'Nonsense,' said Thompson. 'Superstition is an insult to God. You should all know better.'

'But He might be the one sending the signs,' Stedman pointed out. 'Moreover, next year will be sixteen-sixty-six – and we all know what three sixes means.'

'We do?' asked Farr, frowning.

'It is the sign of evil,' explained Stedman. 'Of the beast. The Antichrist, if you will.'

'Then you had better repent before it is too late,' said Thompson tartly. 'You can begin by *listening* to my Sunday sermons instead of chatting through them, as you usually do.'

'Coal is terribly expensive these days,' said Farr, after a sheepish silence. 'Poor folk cannot afford it now, because the government has imposed such enormous taxes.'

'To raise money for the war,' explained Stedman. 'We will not win it on air – funds are needed for ships, crews and provisions.'

'I would not mind so much if the King spent what we give him wisely,' grumbled Farr. 'But he squanders it on frivolities. Look at the Lady Day firework display. It is costing a fortune, and who will foot the bill? We will!'

Then another argument was under way. Thompson threw up his hands in despair and left, so Chaloner followed him outside.

'Is there a member of your congregation named Paul Ferine?' he began. 'A courtier who—'

'Yes, a man who took superstition to new heights,' interrupted Thompson disapprovingly. 'He lost three teeth to decay last year, and carried them around in his pocket.'

Chaloner blinked. 'What for?'

84

'So he could rise up whole on the Day of Judgement – he did not want to face eternity bereft of incisors. I suppose we should be grateful it was only teeth, not a foot or an arm.'

'He was not a Fifth Monarchist, was he?'

'No. Fifth Monarchists are Christians, for all their eccentricity. Ferine stopped attending church when his wife died, and he was a self-confessed heathen. Afterwards, grief drove him out of his fine townhouse and into rented rooms on High Holborn.'

'Did you know him well?'

'He was Groom of the Robes, Thomas. Such men consider mere rectors beneath their notice. Thankfully! I would not have wanted a heretic in my circle of friends.'

Darkness had fallen while Chaloner had been in the Rainbow. Lanterns were lit in the wealthier houses, and linkmen – youths with pitch torches – were out in force, ready to light the way for anyone willing to pay them. The golden gleams glittered in the wet mud as feet, hoofs, wheels and paws squelched through it, churning it into an ever more foul soup that not even the chill of the day could prevent from reeking.

As Chaloner was full of cake, he decided to postpone the ordeal of Hannah's pie until he was hungry. To pass the time, he turned up Chancery Lane, a handsome street dominated by Lincoln's Inn, one of four foundations in London that licensed lawyers. He had been a pupil there briefly, where he had met John Thurloe, who had later become Cromwell's Secretary of State and Spymaster General. Thurloe had retired from politics at the Restoration and now lived quietly, dividing his time between London and his estate in Oxfordshire.

Lincoln's Inn was a haven of peace after the noisy streets and Chaloner walked through it slowly, enjoying the timeless tranquillity of its buildings and its elegantly manicured gardens. He reached Dial Court and climbed the stairs to Chamber XIII, aware of the warm, comfortable scent of wax polish, wood-smoke and old books.

Thurloe did not look like someone who had been one of the most powerful men in the country. He was slightly built with shoulder-length hair and large blue eyes. His modest, unassuming manner led some people to believe he was weak, but he possessed a core of steel, as many enemies of the republic had learned to their cost. He had inspired deep loyalty among those he employed, and many continued to send him snippets of information, so he was almost as well informed now as when he had been Spymaster. He did not smile often, but he beamed when he saw Chaloner, an open, delighted grin full of pleasure and affection.

'Tom! I had no idea you were home. When did you return? Come, sit by the fire and tell me all about it. Cromwell's ambassadors always claimed that Russia is dreadfully squalid. Is it?'

'I did not see enough of it to judge.' Chaloner allowed himself to be ushered into a chair and provided with a cup of something warm. He sipped it cautiously. Thurloe imagined himself to be in fragile health and swallowed all manner of potions that promised to restore the vigour he had enjoyed at twenty. He was not above foisting them on his guests, so Chaloner was always wary of anything he could not immediately identify.

'It was a dangerous mission,' Thurloe went on, 'carrying dispatches begging for the Tsar's help in the event of us losing the Dutch war. Clarendon was right

86

to send them, of course: France and Spain might well attack us while we are weak, in which case we shall need a powerful ally.'

'Yes,' agreed Chaloner.

'But the Privy Council will denounce him as a traitor if they ever find out. We cannot win the war, but they consider it treason for one of their number to say so. What did the Tsar say? Was he amenable to Clarendon's proposal?'

'I never delivered it. All Russia's ports are closed by ice in winter, and the so-called expert who told the Earl that this year is an exception was wrong. A storm blew us against a great sheet of it, which sliced through the hull like a knife through butter. We sank within minutes, and the dispatches were lost, along with the jewels the Earl had included as a bribe.'

'Lost?' asked Thurloe, puzzled. 'How? Surely you carried them on your person?'

'Clarendon insisted that they would be safer in the forward hold. Unfortunately, that was the first place to flood, at which point I learned that I am not very good at picking locks underwater in the pitch dark.'

'You were reckless to have tried. What happened next?'

'We abandoned ship and swam to the ice edge. Fortunately, it was not far to the coast, and we were able to reach a village.'

'And its people lent you a boat to return home?'

'They offered, but I thought I should at least try to deliver Clarendon's message. I continued the journey on horseback, and Captain Lester came with me. But when we reached the Russian border we were told that we would not have been allowed in even *with* the dispatches, as we had not been issued with the necessary passes. We were accused of spying and put in prison.'

'That cannot have been easy for you,' said Thurloe sympathetically. He was the only person who fully understood Chaloner's aversion to such places. 'But you escaped?'

'Yes. And then we came home.'

That had not been easy either, given that a pack of angry Russian guards had been hot on their heels, and Chaloner did not think he had ever spent so many hours in the saddle in so short a space of time. He liked travelling, but that had been an ordeal he was keen to forget.

'Shall we talk of other matters?' asked Thurloe kindly. 'You can start by telling me what scheme compels you to be "dismissed" from Clarendon's service.'

Chaloner hoped no one else would see through the Earl's ploy so readily. 'He thinks it will allow me to infiltrate a band of malcontents – with the help of a turncoat named William Leving.'

'Leving,' mused Thurloe. 'He fought for Parliament during the wars, but was dismissed from the army for siding with trouble-makers. He is a very silly man.'

'What else do you know about him?'

'He was part of the Northern Plot a few months ago, and was imprisoned in York. I doubt his escape was genuine, so I can only assume that he offered to spy on his erstwhile colleagues in exchange for his life.'

Chaloner groaned: if the Fifth Monarchists thought likewise, then he and Leving were living on borrowed time. 'Have you heard rumours of another rebellion in the offing?'

'No. London is unusually peaceful at the moment.'

'Then what about any inexplicable movements of horses and guns? You cannot have an uprising without those, and someone must have seen or heard something.'

'No, nothing, Tom. All has been very quiet. Who is behind this mischief?'

'Fifth Monarchists. Roger Jones, to be precise.'

Thurloe frowned. 'Jones has joined the Fifth Monarchists? I suppose I should not be surprised – he is a vociferous dissident, and their wild ideas will certainly appeal to him.'

'His cronies include a stockinger named Atkinson, a watchmaker named Quelch, a Baptist pastor named Strange, a fat, grave man named Manning and a lady who bakes – Ursula Adman.'

'She is sister to the infamous Mrs Trapnel, hailed as a visionary, but in reality just another lunatic. Mrs Trapnel is currently in Bristol gaol, and I am sorry if Ursula feels obliged to carry the family torch while her sibling is indisposed, as she seems a decent, God-fearing woman.'

'And the others?'

'Atkinson is a naive dreamer; Strange is a rash, heady person who thinks our King is the Antichrist; Manning is nobody much; and Quelch is an incurable thief with a string of convictions as long as your arm.'

'Really?' Chaloner was amused. 'Then he will be in for a shock if the Kingdom of Christ does come to pass. Even if his dishonesty is overlooked, his hypocrisy will not be.'

Thurloe eyed him beadily. 'I hope you are not being irreligious, Thomas. But to return to your malcontents, Jones and Strange are uncompromising militants who should be under lock and key, while Quelch is a

89

malcontent who likes to spread trouble. They have chosen a good time to make a nuisance of themselves – Williamson is distracted by the war.'

'There was some suggestion that the Dutch might finance their Cause . . .'

'The Dutch will not waste money on Fifth Monarchists. I once described them as worms who think they can thresh mountains, and I have learned nothing to make me change my mind.'

'Clarendon has also ordered me to investigate Paul Ferine's murder. I do not suppose you have heard anything about that, have you?'

'I am afraid not, but I shall listen for rumours. Would you like a sip of Sydenham's Laudanum or a Goddard's Drop? You are very pale. Clearly you are not yet recovered from Russia.'

'Actually, it is the prospect of eating Hannah's pickled ling pie,' said Chaloner gloomily.

Feeling like the worst kind of coward, Chaloner delayed going home yet again when he walked through Charing Cross and saw St Martin's Lane stretching away into darkness on his right. He walked up it, aiming for a shabby shop with a battered sign outside saying it belonged to the Trulocke Brothers, gunsmiths. It was guarded by a fierce dog, which leapt to its feet snarling as he approached. Then it wagged its tail, remembering past bribes of bones. Chaloner had no bones that day, but one of Ursula's biscuits worked just as well.

Inside, he approached the largest of the hulking, shaven-headed trio who stood behind the counter, and laid down several coins. Edmund Trulocke stared at them, licking his lips.

'I want some information,' said Chaloner in a low voice, although the shop was so often used for illegal transactions that none of the browsing clientele made any effort to listen. 'Have you heard rumours of a large shipment of arms recently?'

Trulocke's glistening eyes snapped up from the coins, full of indignation. 'No, why? Is someone planning an uprising without telling us?'

'So you have heard nothing?'

'No,' said Trulocke, aggrieved. 'But keep them coins, and if *you* hear anything I will give you double if you tell me the name of the villain who provided the guns. This is *our* patch, and we don't take kindly to trespassers.'

Chaloner supposed it was as firm an indication as any that the High Holborn Plotters were not buying weapons to support whatever was in the offing.

Chapter 4

Chaloner was guiltily relieved when he went home to find a note from Hannah, telling him that she would be late and that the pickled ling pie was to be postponed until the following evening. Apparently, there was to be a service in St Paul's Cathedral to commemorate the loss of HMS *London*, and the Queen wanted her there. Chaloner understood why: Her Majesty had failed to produce a royal heir, and there were rumours that she was barren. The Court shunned her, and she was naturally keen to have a friendly face on hand at such a public occasion.

There was a second letter, too, this one from Leving, informing Chaloner that he was to be at the Talbot tavern at three o'clock the following afternoon. Chaloner was unimpressed that messages should be sent to his home; it was an unwritten rule of espionage that fellow intelligencers' families were to be kept away from such dealings.

He gave the servants the rest of the evening off on condition that they all went out, and when he had the house to himself he settled by the drawing room fire with his viol. He played airs by Lawes until well past midnight, relishing the instrument's rich tones as he lost himself in the joy of music. Then he heard Hannah struggling to insert her key in the front door. Hastily, he stowed his viol in the cupboard under the stairs, and was standing innocently in the hallway when she finally managed to stagger inside.

'Tom,' she slurred tipsily. 'What are you doing here?'

'It is where I live,' he replied, making a dive to catch the delicate clock on the hallstand as she jostled against it. 'Well, some of the time, at least.'

'Silly!' she cried, giving him a playful thump. 'I mean why are you in the corridor in the dark? Have you forgotten your way upstairs?'

She began to laugh, leaning against the wall while tears of mirth streamed down her cheeks. Chaloner watched her warily, wondering how she had contrived to get drunk at a memorial. Then he recalled that it had been at White Hall, and the King's merry courtiers had an uncanny knack of introducing wine at any occasion, no matter how inappropriate.

'I met Clarendon,' she said, once she had gained some semblance of control. 'I told him.'

'Told him what?' asked Chaloner uneasily.

'That he was an arse for dismissing you.' Hannah giggled. 'But he thought he had misheard.'

Chaloner sincerely hoped so: the Earl deplored bad language, and would certainly object to being called names. Such an incident might lead to Chaloner losing his post permanently.

'Oh, and we have a problem,' said Hannah airily, attempting a twirl. She stumbled and would have fallen had he not caught her.

'What manner of problem?' he asked, under the powerful impression that it was something she would not have dared mention had she been sober.

'Debt,' she replied crisply. 'We owe lots of people lots of money. A hundred pounds or more.'

'*What?*' Chaloner was horrified. 'How have you—'

'These things happen, and it is not my fault that you do not earn a decent salary.'

Chaloner's salary had been perfectly respectable, and he could not conceive how she had contrived to spend so much. But there was no point debating the matter while she was drunk – it was a discussion that needed both of them sober.

'Your coat is wet,' he said instead, the tone of his voice cool. 'Give it to me. I will hang it in the kitchen to dry.'

She tossed it at him playfully. He caught it without a word, and took several deep breaths as he draped it over a chair, struggling to control his temper. However, by the time he returned to her she had slumped on one of the drawing room settles and was snoring softly. He carried her upstairs, and it was a testament to how much she had imbibed that she did not stir as he removed enough of her clothing to let her sleep comfortably.

She was still dead to the world the following dawn, and knowing she was unlikely to rise feeling amiable, he dressed and left the house before she woke. It was raining, but he barely noticed the weather as he trudged towards King Street, bowed down by concerns about money.

He had always felt his employment with the Earl was precarious, so he had set aside a certain amount each month for emergencies; it was hidden behind a skirting board in the bedroom. However, he resented the fact that it would have to be used to pay bills that could have

94

been avoided, and he determined that Hannah would never put him in such a position again – they would have a serious discussion that evening, and she would keep within their means or she would find herself living with his family in rural Buckinghamshire, well away from London and its expensive charms. In the meantime, he needed to thwart the Fifth Monarchists as quickly as possible, so that the Earl would start paying him again. He thought about what he had learned thus far.

Jones and Strange were fanatics who needed the services of a gunpowder expert, and Leving thought their followers numbered ten thousand. Atkinson was a misty-eyed idealist who would probably baulk if bloody rebellion did come to pass; Quelch was a thief; and Ursula should have left insurrection to her fiery sister. Leving was an unreliable helpmeet, and Chaloner did not like the notion that John Scott was somehow involved. What was in the letters that Leving had delivered to Manning, and what secret did his associate Sherwin have that Jones wanted?

And the murder of Ferine? The man had been deeply superstitious, which had earned him enemies; he had visited taverns in disguise; and he had predicted a mishap for himself, although he had not anticipated that it would be a fatal one.

Chaloner took a deep breath and moved from reviewing evidence to making plans. First, he would visit the Pope's Head, as Manning had mentioned taking Sherwin 'home' there. Sherwin would almost certainly be in bed, and sleep-befuddled men were easier to interrogate than alert ones, so it was a good time to ask him what was going on.

Next, he would follow up on Hill's intelligence – that

Ferine had visited the Antelope and the Swan with Two Necks. He would have liked to monitor Jones or Strange, but he did not know where they lived, so his best option was to loiter outside Ursula's home in the hope that one of them would visit her to scrounge cakes. Then he would follow them and see where they went and whom they met. Finally, he would attend the meeting in the Talbot at three o'clock.

He sloshed along the Strand and Fleet Street, then picked his way up the tiny alley that led to the Pope's Head.

The inn was a coaching tavern, so people were preparing for journeys that would begin at dawn. The place smelled of pipe smoke and warm soot, and folk stood in sleepy gaggles, sipping jugs of breakfast ale. Chaloner waylaid a pot-boy, and a penny bribe earned him the knowledge that Sherwin had spent the night drinking with an acquaintance in one of the back rooms. Both were still there.

'Sherwin is probably our last paying tenant,' said the lad gloomily. 'We can't pay the Lady Day rent, see, so we are to be evicted Saturday week.' A sly smile crossed his face. 'But the owners won't benefit from making us homeless – a legal wrangle means this place will lie empty for weeks before all can be settled.'

Chaloner was not surprised to see that Sherwin's 'acquaintance' was Scott, spinning some yarn about New Amsterdam when he had single-handedly foiled a raid by Dutch colonists. To give credence to his tale, Scott had sketched a map, although Chaloner thought it bore no resemblance to reality. It was prettily done, though, with attractive flourishes in the corners, and each feature painstakingly labelled.

96

'I wondered how long it would be before you appeared,' said Scott, putting his artwork away hurriedly when he saw Chaloner looking at it. 'What do you want? Sherwin is too tired to talk to anyone, and will soon be going to bed.'

'But not too tired to hear your stories?' asked Chaloner, although a glance at Sherwin's half-closed, bleary eyes did suggest that getting answers from him would be hard work.

Scott regarded him angrily, then forced a laugh, revealing white, even teeth. 'Why are we arguing? Here we are, two friends from another world, and we snipe at each other like fishwives. Let me buy you an ale, and we can talk about old times.'

Chaloner was not in the habit of giving his past a romantic slant, and suspected his memories and Scott's would differ so widely that there would be scant common ground. However, it was a chance to draw him and Sherwin into conversation.

'How is your wife?' he asked, sitting down. 'Dorothea? Was that her name?'

'She divorced me for desertion actually,' said Scott tightly. 'But I am well rid of her. My home is here now, and the King told me only yesterday that he cannot manage without my services as Cartographer Royal. He is grateful for my other advice, too.'

'What other advice?' asked Sherwin, snapping awake as the pot-boy brought more ale.

'It was I who suggested that New Amsterdam should be renamed New *York*, in honour of the King's brother.'

Chaloner stared at him, thinking that time had not changed Scott one bit: he was the same smoothly inveterate liar. The New Englander wore an exquisite silk suit

97

with plenty of lace, and anyone meeting him at White Hall would believe he had every right to be there. He might even become Cartographer Royal by virtue of putting it so firmly in people's minds.

'And you, Sherwin?' asked Chaloner. 'What brings you to London?'

'The ale,' chuckled Sherwin, raising his jug. 'I was kept away from it in Tem—'

'In Dorset,' interposed Scott quickly. 'Where he lived before coming here.'

Sherwin blinked dully for a moment, then nodded. 'Yes. I lived in Yeovil. Ale was banned in my particular line of work, but that John Browne is a sanctimonious fool and I hate him.'

'What kind of work?' asked Chaloner, offended that they should consider him stupid enough to believe such poorly crafted lies – and that he might think Yeovil was in Dorset.

'Cabinet making,' said Scott, speaking over whatever Sherwin started to say. 'Drinking ale is discouraged, as chisels are sharp.'

Chaloner was about to suggest they answer his questions honestly when a shadow fell across the table. It was fat, grave Manning. The Fifth Monarchist's eyes narrowed when he saw Chaloner, and Scott hastened to explain.

'Chaloner and I are old friends, and we have been recounting our past adventures together, but he is just leaving, and Sherwin is ready to retire to his room.'

'You mean he has not been to bed yet?' cried Manning, dismayed. 'But he will need his wits about him later, and we cannot have him fuddled from lack of sleep.'

'I told Scott what I shall tell you,' said Sherwin, suddenly sharp. 'I sleep when I feel like it, not when you

98

decide I should. And I am not going anywhere until I have another ale.'

'One more,' said Manning irritably. 'But it had better not affect your performance. We have a lot resting on your skills.' He turned to Chaloner. 'Good day to you.'

There was not much Chaloner could do once he had been so summarily dismissed, but he did not go far. The confusion with Dorset and Yeovil was one mistake, but choosing cabinet making as an occupation for Sherwin was another. Chaloner had noticed before that Sherwin's hands were flecked with old burns, and woodwork necessitated using sharp tools, but not hot ones.

He found a shadowy corner and settled down to monitor them. Scott and Manning were arguing, but in voices too low to hear, while Sherwin drank steadily. Eventually, he passed out, so they carried him to a chamber on the first floor where they put him to bed with a tenderness that underlined his importance to them. When he was settled, they fell asleep, too. Clearly, nothing else was going to happen, so Chaloner gave up his vigil and turned to his other enquiries.

It was fully light when he reached High Holborn – or as light as it was going to be with thick clouds slouching overhead and drizzle in the air. He aimed for the Antelope first, a large, rambling inn with a reputation for clean beds, wholesome food and honest staff. He bought an ale, and engaged the taverner in conversation. Unfortunately, the man was obsessed with the coal tax, and only remembered those patrons willing to discuss it with him. As Ferine had not ventured an opinion on the matter, the landlord could not say whether he had visited or not.

Chaloner turned to the customers, buying ale liberally

in exchange for information, although he worried at the expense. Noon came and went, and he ate a fine venison pastry with a sad-faced man from Islington, who claimed to have seen Ferine with several companions.

'An odd crowd,' he recalled. 'They huddled together in a back room, all wrapped in cloaks and big hats, and stopped talking if anyone went near. At one point I heard them chanting.'

'Chanting?'

'Incantations,' whispered the man ominously. 'That particular chamber has always attracted strange people. Go and look at it. The moment you step inside, you will know what I mean.'

Chaloner followed his directions to a small room that was conspicuously empty, although he imagined patrons might use it if the landlord lit a fire – the place was freezing. The tabletops and all four walls had been etched with runic symbols identical to the ones inked on Lambe's neck and hands. There were three dried toads on the windowsill, the desiccated body of a crow in the hearth, and several strategically placed pouches that smelled of pungent herbs.

'You should not be in here alone,' said the landlord as he passed the door. 'It is haunted. We paid a vicar to say some prayers last month, but they did not work, so we hired a sorcerer instead.'

'Dr Lambe?' predicted Chaloner. 'Who works for the Duke of Buckingham?'

The landlord nodded. 'He is said to be the best, and I do not like having a room that I cannot use. However, it is still here.'

'What is?'

'The ghost,' came the reply, voice lowered. 'This room

100

stands on the exact spot where three Catholics were betrayed during the reign of Good Queen Bess. It is cursed. You must have noticed that it is colder than the rest of the building.'

'Yes – because it has no fire.'

The landlord pursed his lips. 'You can think what you like, but I know my tavern, and there is something badly amiss with this bit of it.'

Feeling he had wasted his time, Chaloner walked to the Swan with Two Necks, which was near the Fleet River. It was smaller than the Pope's Head, although it had a sizeable yard and an impressive row of stables. The sign that swung over its door portrayed a double-necked bird, the faces of which had been rendered distinctly malevolent by the inclusion of teeth. Every Londoner knew, of course, that 'two necks' actually meant 'two nicks', and referred to the practice of annually notching swans' beaks to identify their ownership.

He entered and immediately sensed an atmosphere. There had been a comfortable buzz of conversation as he had opened the door, but it stopped when he closed it, and he was aware of hats being pulled low to hide faces. He took a seat at an empty table.

'We are closed,' said the landlord shortly. 'Try the Rose instead.'

'I was told to come here,' lied Chaloner. 'By Paul Ferine.'

The landlord stared at him for a moment, then walked away without a word. Discussions resumed, although more softly than before. A quick glance around told Chaloner that most patrons were respectably dressed, some in plain country clothes and others with the lace

101

and ribbons of high fashion. They included women as well as men, old people and young. They seemed as disparate a group as it was possible to get, but they had one thing in common: all kept their faces averted and had thick cloaks that would conceal their clothes when they left. Preacher Hill had been right to say that the folk who frequented the Swan wore disguises.

A sharp thump made him start. It sounded as though it had come from under his table, but when he looked beneath it, there was nothing to see. Others heard it, too, and there were knowing nods. He leaned back and folded his arms. Ferine might have been duped by such antics, but *he* did not believe in ghosts and was not about to be unsettled by tricks. However, it was clear that the other customers had taken the bump seriously, and understanding came in a flash: it was a belief in witchery that drew these folk together. It explained their hidden faces and their unease with strangers – such gatherings were illegal and dangerous.

A few moments later, a woman stood and glided towards him. She pushed back her hood to reveal black hair, startling blue eyes and the whitest skin he had ever seen. She was beautiful, but it was a cold loveliness, more like a statue rather than a thing of flesh and blood. As she sat, a chill breeze wafted around her, carrying with it a dank, musty scent that reminded him of a tomb.

'What do you want?' Her voice was deep and soft.

Chaloner was acutely aware that everyone was listening. He feigned nonchalance, although every fibre in his body was tense, and the dagger he carried in his sleeve was already in his hand. He was an experienced warrior, and doubted any individual in the Swan could best him, but there were at least forty patrons, and some might have guns. The hair on the back of his neck stood up, as it always did when he was in danger.

'The same as Paul Ferine,' he replied evenly.

The woman nodded slowly. 'Very well. How many?'

While he struggled for a reply that would not reveal he had no idea what she was talking about, it occurred to Chaloner that he had spent much of that day in conversations he did not understand. 'It depends on the price.'

'That is non-negotiable, as we told Ferine. So are you buying or not?'

'How long will it take to get them?' Chaloner hoped he did not sound as baffled as he felt.

The woman's eyes narrowed. 'The same as always. Are you sure you are Ferine's friend?'

'I was,' replied Chaloner. 'Unfortunately, he is dead.'

'Yes,' breathed the woman. 'It was predicted, so of course it came to pass.'

'*He* did not think he would die.' Chaloner seized the opportunity to discuss the murder. 'He believed he would lose at cards or catch a cold. Are you saying that you knew differently?'

'Give me your hand,' ordered the woman abruptly.

Chaloner eyed her suspiciously. 'Why?'

Her eyebrows shot up. 'Why do you think? Come on, do not be shy.'

Nerves jangling, Chaloner held out his left hand – he was not about to offer up the right one when the dagger was in it. Her fingers were corpse-cold as they traced the lines on his palm, and the smell of old graves seemed suddenly stronger. She released him abruptly, for which he was inordinately grateful.

103

'There is violence in your future,' she hissed. 'Along with uncertainty and fear.'

Chaloner did not doubt it, given his occupation. 'Well? Are we in business or not?'

She smiled, although it was a nasty expression, and the hair went up on the back of his neck again. Irritably, he tried to pull himself together.

'Yes, if you tell us how many,' she replied.

'Three,' he replied promptly, prepared to add zeros if necessary.

'Good!' The smile became predatory as she held out her hand. 'Give me the pertinent information and we will begin at once.'

'I do not have it with me.'

The smile faded. 'Then why did you come? You know we cannot do anything without it.'

'I had to be sure. Ferine trusted you, but we do not know each other.'

She stared at him, eyes as hard and blue as old ice, then stood and stalked out, moving so smoothly that she appeared to be floating. Perhaps it was his imagination, but the moment she had gone the temperature around him seemed to rise.

There was no more he could do in the Swan, especially when he was on the receiving end of some very hostile, wary and fearful glances from the other patrons, whose unease made it obvious that there was no point in asking questions. Outside, he slipped into a shadowy doorway and settled down to wait. After a while, someone else arrived. He seemed familiar, but Chaloner was not sure why until he saw a hand covered in inked symbols: Lambe.

Chaloner rubbed his chin. The sorcerer had been at the club the night Ferine was murdered, and now he was visiting the same tavern. Of course, there were not many places where witches and their disciples could gather together safely, so perhaps it was no surprise that both frequented the Swan. Regardless, Chaloner would have to find out if anyone could verify where in the club Lambe had been when Ferine had been suffocated.

The sorcerer did not stay long, and was out again in moments. Chaloner tried to follow, but Lambe flagged down a hackney, which set off at a cracking pace – too fast for Chaloner to chase on foot. He returned to his shadowy doorway and waited again.

Eventually, the woman emerged. She wore a hooded cloak, but her peculiarly flowing gait gave her away. She attracted some odd glances as she glided along Holborn, and everyone gave her a wide berth, as if they sensed something amiss and did not want to be too close.

North of High Holborn was a mansion named Hatton House, which had once been inhabited by an ambitious Elizabethan courtier. It was now ruinous and due to be demolished. The woman walked up a path fringed with brambles to a lichen-dappled door, which swung open with a groan that was audible even from a distance. She stepped inside and disappeared into the gloom.

Chaloner followed, and found himself in what had once been a grand hall; now weeds grew through the floor and the walls were green with mould. The remains of a staircase stood in front of him, which had ascended in an elegant sweep to the upper floors.

There was no sign of the woman, but there was a door to his right. It opened into a dim passageway that stank of rotting wood. She was not there either, but there was another door at its far end. He went through that, but the next chamber was also empty, and so he continued, tiptoeing through a succession of sadly derelict rooms.

Eventually, he reached a chapel. It had once been exquisite – there were traces of gold leaf on what remained of the ceiling, and rails where curtains had hung. It was unmistakably Catholic, which perhaps explained why it had been so thoroughly despoiled. The woman was kneeling there, hands clasped as she prayed to the non-existent altar. A shaft of light came through the shattered roof and illuminated her face. Had it been a real church, he might have been struck with religious awe, but in the decommissioned chapel it was decidedly sinister.

'Why are you following me?' she asked, coming to her feet in one easy, sinuous movement.

There was no point hiding any longer, although Chaloner was surprised she had detected him – he was good at tailing people without their knowledge. 'I wanted to talk.'

'About what?'

'Ferine. I would like to know more about his business if I am to engage in it.'

She regarded him oddly. 'Why? You gave the impression that you understood and approved of what he was doing.'

Chaloner shrugged. 'A man cannot be too careful.'

'So what do you want to know?'

'Your name would be a start.'

'Eliza Hatton.'

'Hatton? Do you hail from the family who used to live here?'

'This house was built by my grandsire, but its foundations are steeped in blood.' Her words were hissed, and set up a disconcerting echo. 'Five monks were executed on this very spot, and a priest was hanged here forty years later. There have been others, too. Murdered for their faith.'

'Ferine was not murdered for his faith,' said Chaloner. 'And I wanted to ask—'

'No? Can you be certain of that?'

Chaloner was not sure what happened next, only that there was a loud crack, and he only just managed to throw himself to one side as a ceiling beam fell, bringing with it a shower of plaster. He picked himself up and hurried to where Eliza had been standing, but there was no sign of her. He looked around wildly. She was not under the rafter, and she had not passed him to reach the door, yet there was no other way out – except the windows, and they were too high.

Had he been talking to a ghost? Such a notion would not usually have crossed his mind, but he had been in a 'haunted' tavern that day, and the chapel was dark and shadowy. Or was it just another trick? Yet despite as careful a search as he was able to make in the gloom, he could not discover how Eliza had disappeared or why the beam had fallen.

Confused and full of questions, he took his leave.

It was nearing three o'clock, the time when Chaloner was due to meet Leving in the Talbot. He trudged along Holborn, feeling new mud seep inside his boots with every step. The clouds were thick and black, and they depressed his spirits. Moreover, he was disturbed by what had happened in Hatton House – he had always disliked cases that involved the inexplicable.

He had been in the Talbot before. It was near Gray's

Inn, so was always full of lawyers, and invariably rang with loud, argumentative voices. There was no sign of Leving, so he found a table and settled down to wait. A pot-boy brought him ale that was weak and sour, of the kind that was often served in large, impersonal taverns. He was hungry, but the pickled ling pie would be waiting, so he decided he had better reserve his appetite. Eventually, a shadow fell across him.

'The next time you contact me, leave a message at the Golden Lion on Fetter Lane,' he said without looking up. 'Do not visit my home.'

Leving sat down. 'You are as bad as Williamson. He told me never to darken *his* doors again, too. Where lies the problem? Your wife was out, and there was no danger.'

'But she does not *stay* out, does she, and you are not to go there again. Now tell me why you asked me to meet you here.'

Leving grinned. 'Because the Fifth Monarchists are having an assembly soon, in the hall at the back. They have been rather clever, actually. This tavern is full of lawyers, all in professional garb with wigs and falling bands, so the conspirators have decided to wear the same, and thus be indistinguishable from them.'

'You are not wearing a disguise,' Chaloner pointed out. 'Neither am I.'

'Yes, but *we* are not being hunted by Williamson. We do not need to bother.'

Chaloner did not hide his exasperation. 'The Fifth Monarchists do not know that, and failing to conform may arouse their suspicions.'

Leving was crestfallen. 'Lord! I suppose it might. What shall we do, then? Ask a couple of these clerks to lend

108

us their costumes? I am sure we can find a pair who will not mind.'

'Perhaps you should just stand on a table and announce that we have been charged to infiltrate some rebels but have neglected to effect a disguise,' suggested Chaloner acidly.

'There is no need to be facetious! I made a mistake; it will not happen again. But look – people are making their way to the hall. It is time to join them.'

Chaloner regarded him balefully, giving serious thought to knocking him over the head and continuing the investigation alone. Or perhaps Williamson would return him to gaol until the rebellion was over. Regardless, something had to be done or they were both going to be killed.

The hall the Fifth Monarchists had hired was enormous and already crammed with people. Chaloner did a quick count and estimated that there were at least two hundred. All had donned wigs and robes, but as few had access to genuine legal regalia, they had improvised, with the result that most were very bizarrely attired. Many had the ruddy faces and thick hands of farmers or labourers, while others looked to be the more lowly kind of tradesmen – tanners, tallow-makers, cobblers and weavers. Conversations were about the iniquitous coal tax, the late start of the lambing season and the dreadful price of imported cloth.

About thirty men had gathered at the front of the hall, and these were another matter entirely. They were dour, grim-faced individuals who spoke in strident voices about the Kingdom of Christ and 'smiting work'; several brayed prayers in a way that suggested they thought the Almighty might be deaf. Among them were Strange and Quelch.

109

'Where are your disguises?' hissed Jones angrily, when he spotted Leving and Chaloner. 'If you are recognised by the Spymaster's men, it could mean the end of our plans.'

'What plans?' asked Leving keenly. 'You have not told me yet, and—'

'Go and stand where no one can see you,' snapped Jones. He caught Chaloner's arm as the spy passed. 'You are wiser than him. Keep him in check, or I will hold you accountable.'

'I am not his keeper,' said Chaloner, freeing himself with more vigour than was necessary. He disliked being manhandled.

Jones's pale eyes bored into him. 'You are now.'

Chaloner did not think his opinion of the Fifth Monarchists' operation could sink much lower, but it did. A number of genuine lawyers were intrigued by the peculiarly clad 'colleagues' and were asking what was going on. Atkinson explained that it was a meeting of people who had invested in a certain type of government bond. Clearly, he thought he had chosen a subject too dull to warrant further enquiry, but lawyers were immune to tedium. Their interest was piqued, and they hovered until Strange appeared and threatened to run them through unless they shifted.

'Really, Strange,' chided Atkinson. 'There was no need to be rude.'

'Thou art a milksop,' retorted Strange. 'And rudeness will be as nothing when we sweep away the vile corruption of their iniquitous legal system.'

'They *are* corrupt, but that does not give us licence to be unmannerly,' said Ursula coolly, so quick to support Atkinson that Chaloner wondered at it.

Strange relented, revealing that he had a soft spot for Mrs Adman – or for her baking. 'My apologies, lady. I am so eager to see the New Kingdom that I forget myself. I ask thee to forgive my intemperate words.'

Ursula inclined her head and changed the subject. 'I do not think we have enough seedcake. Shall I run out and buy some? It will not be as good as my own, but it is better than nothing.'

'I shall go with thee,' declared Strange. A flash of disappointment in Atkinson's eyes told Chaloner that the shy stockinger would have liked to the opportunity to be alone with her himself.

When they had gone, Chaloner watched the remaining Fifth Monarchists in growing disbelief. The atmosphere was more like that of a wedding party than a plot to overthrow the government, and he wondered how many of them really knew what they were doing. He spotted someone he recognised, and made his way through the throng towards her.

'Lord!' gulped Snowflake in alarm when she saw him. 'Please do not tell Temperance what I do in my spare time. She would not approve.'

'Nor would your customers,' remarked Chaloner. 'They belong to the established order, and will not appreciate you consorting with those who aim to bring it down.'

Snowflake waved a dismissive hand. 'If they are ousted other wealthy men will take their places, and *they* will hire my services – it is a fact of life. But Temperance is a nice lady, and I do not want to upset her. Besides, I am only here because my stepbrother John invited me.'

She pointed to Atkinson, who waved gaily. Chaloner tried to imagine the bookish stockinger and the worldly

111

prostitute plotting in darkened rooms to topple the monarchy together. The image would not come.

'I wanted to speak to you anyway,' he said. 'To ask why you smuggled Jones and Quelch into the club on Sunday night.'

Snowflake gaped in dismay. 'How did you find out? They promised not to tell anyone.'

'Why did you do it?'

'Because John said they needed to speak to one of our patrons, and they did not know how else to do it. They did not fit in very well, though – Jones is a cold fish, while Quelch was vulgar.'

'Which patron?'

'Well, they both spent a while with Admiral Lawson, but Quelch nattered to a number of other guests, including the Duke, Rupert, Scott, Dr Lambe and Duncombe. Jones concentrated on the girls – he asked them questions and made a note of their answers. He probably intends to quote them in one of his nasty pamphlets.'

'You should have told me,' said Chaloner irritably. 'Jones and Quelch are violent men and one of them might have murdered Ferine.'

Snowflake favoured him with a haughty glance. 'Do you think I let them wander around unsupervised? All the girls watched them, and neither Jones nor Quelch left the parlour all night. Would you like me to swear it on a Bible?'

As Chaloner doubted the Good Book held much significance for her, he shook his head. Yet he believed her tale. Reluctantly, because a Fifth Monarchist as Ferine's killer would have been a tidy solution, he mentally crossed Jones and Quelch off his list of suspects.

112

'Who else did you let in?' he asked.

'No one! It is not very easy to do, and I only arranged it as a special favour to John. It will not happen again, though. I do not want Temperance to find out and send me packing.'

Again, Chaloner believed her. 'Have you heard any rumours about Ferine's death?' he asked.

'No, because no one is coming to the club any more. Well, that handsome John Scott visited, and brought a drunken sot named Sherwin with him. He told me to make the fellow happy. I did my best, but Sherwin was more interested in the wine than me, and he was very drunk. He kept mumbling about something being turned.'

'Could he have said some*one* being turned?' asked Chaloner, hoping Sherwin had not been referring to Leving.

'Possibly, but he was slurring so much that he was difficult to understand.'

Atkinson arrived then, bringing her an especially large piece of cake, and the smile they gave each other made it clear there was genuine affection between them.

'We are not really related,' Snowflake told Chaloner. 'Our widowed mothers married our current stepfather, although not at the same time, obviously. John has always been good to me. He wanted to train me to be a stock-inger, but I had grander plans.'

'You may *have* to work in my shop when the Last Millennium dawns,' warned Atkinson. 'I doubt brothels will be allowed then.'

Snowflake pushed him playfully. 'Of course they will, silly! Men will not stop being men just because of a new ruler. Besides, I imagine King Jesus will be too busy

113

smiting lawyers to bother with the likes of us. They are where the *real* source of corruption lies.'

'True,' agreed Atkinson. 'That is why I became a Fifth Monarchist – to abolish corruption in the courts, and introduce a system that will deliver equal justice for rich and poor. We also expound equality for women and gainful employment for all.'

'Here is Ursula, back with the cakes,' said Snowflake, clearly bored with the discussion. 'The meeting can start now.'

Once the door had been barred to prevent several very interested lawyers from coming in, Jones walked to the front of the hall and began to address the throng. There was an immediate hush, which was just as well, as Jones spoke in a sibilant hiss that was difficult to hear from the back.

'Brothers and sisters in Christ – thank you for coming. We shall start by reciting the oath.'

'Oath?' whispered Chaloner to Atkinson. 'I thought Fifth Monarchists refused to take them, on the grounds that it is a misuse of God's name.'

'We do,' replied the stockinger. 'Usually. But Jones insists.'

Chaloner was puzzled: Did it mean that Jones was not a true Fifth Monarchist, and had simply hijacked the movement when his Northern Plot had failed? While he pondered, the audience held their right hands aloft, and chanted a promise never to reveal the Cause's secrets. When it was done, the thirty dour fanatics took seats at a long table at the front, while everyone else stood in the body of the hall, shuffling their feet until they were comfortable.

114

'Our day draws near,' whispered Jones once the fidgeting had stopped. It sounded like a snake speaking. 'We shall soon have what we have striven for all these years.'

'About time,' declared Quelch loudly. 'Jesus will not wait for ever.'

'He might,' countered Strange. 'Eternity is nothing to the Supreme Authority.'

'Plans have been laid, and you will soon be allotted specific tasks,' Jones continued. 'Our operation will begin two Sundays hence – an auspicious time, as I think you will agree.'

'Easter Day!' whooped Strange with a wild grin that made him look deranged. 'King Jesus will oust the Stuart usurper on the anniversary of His glorious Resurrection, and will take up His rightful throne in White Hall.'

'What happens if the throne is dirty?' asked Ursula. She flushed when everyone turned to look at her, but persisted with her point. 'That Court has disgusting habits, and I should not like to think of Him faced with a soiled seat.'

'He will not use the one in White Hall,' asserted Quelch. 'He will bring His own.'

Chaloner was struggling to keep a straight face, although Quelch's proclamation had the grim men at the front nodding earnest agreement. But Ursula had other concerns, too.

'Then what about St Paul's Cathedral? It is falling to pieces, and I should not like it to collapse just as He steps through its doors.'

'Unless you can devise a way to rebuild it in ten days, we shall just have to trust Him to keep it standing,' said Jones, a little impatiently. 'But you are right about the Court. It is full of profligate villains who squander public money. I could cite a dozen instances of their selfish greed, starting with the Lady Day fireworks, which are a wicked waste of taxpayers' money.'

'Perhaps we should strike sooner then,' suggested one of the men at the front. 'Today, before our enemies have wind of what we intend to do, and try to stop us.'

'They cannot – not now,' stated Jones. 'We have the support of the entire country – honest, decent folk who are tired of the dissipated libertines in White Hall. The wicked coal tax has brought them flocking to us, while there have been omens . . .'

'Comets, a profusion of ghosts, Mrs Trapnel's visions,' listed Strange. 'All signs that King Jesus is coming. One only needs to glance at the Bible to see it is all ordained.'

'I would publish a pamphlet explaining it all, but the printing presses are too closely watched by the forces of tyranny,' said Jones. 'But that will not be a problem in the Last Millennium, when I shall write dozens of tracts for your edification and enjoyment.'

Snowflake chose that moment to give a bored sigh, which made a number of people turn to look at her. Atkinson shot her a warning glance, but she only grinned engagingly at him.

'She always could wrap me around her little finger,' he whispered ruefully to Chaloner. 'No wonder I could not persuade her to settle for the staid life of a stockinger. I am far too dull!'

'You are not dull,' whispered Ursula warmly. 'Unlike this meeting. I fear that rather too many people have been promised an opportunity to rant.'

She was right: at least a dozen men were pulling notes from their pockets, ready to treat the gathering to their religious and political reflections. Strange was

116

first, stepping forward to aver that Easter Day would see heavenly hosts marching down High Holborn and seraphim taking over the Banqueting House; Quelch interrupted to say it would be the other way around. It was tedious stuff, and by the sixth speaker, Chaloner had had enough. So had most of the audience, which began to shuffle and fuss.

The speeches finished eventually, and Jones asked if anyone had questions. There was a tense silence, lest someone did, thus causing the pontificating to start again. After a closing prayer and a piece of cake, the rebels drifted away, sidling past the curious lawyers who still milled outside the door. Chaloner lingered, watching the people he knew – Strange and Quelch, quarrelling as usual; Ursula pressing extra cake on hungry apprentices; Atkinson laughing with Snowflake; and Leving, who had taken out pen and paper and was brazenly making notes for Williamson. Then he became aware of someone standing at his side. It was Jones.

'Leving has been different since the Northern Plot,' he said. 'If it were anyone else, I would suspect he had been turned, but not even Williamson would stoop to using such a low creature.'

'If you think there is a spy in your midst, you will have to manage without me,' said Chaloner quickly, lest the remark was a test. 'There are plenty of other ways to avenge myself on Clarendon – ones that will not see me on a scaffold.'

Jones's reptilian eyes glittered. 'Leving knows nothing. Even if he is a traitor – and I cannot see him having the courage or the wits, to be frank – he cannot harm us.'

He indicated that Chaloner was to accompany him

to the front of the hall, where the thirty dour men still sat around the table. Atkinson joined them there after bidding an affectionate farewell to Snowflake.

'We are the Sanhedrin,' Atkinson explained. 'The leaders of the Fifth Monarchy movement.'

'We named ourselves after the courts of ancient Israel,' added Jones. 'We are men of choicest light and spirit, imbued with judgement, righteousness and understanding – men of truth and integrity, fearing God and hating covetousness, being filled with the fruits of righteousness, full of mercy and good works, without partiality or hypocrisy.'

'Oh,' said Chaloner, thinking they did not look like paragons of virtue to him, and that the Last Millennium would be in trouble if they were allowed to run it. He glanced at Jones, and thought he saw a glimmer of amusement in the cold eyes, which again made him wonder whether the man was as committed to the Cause as he would have everyone believe.

'I made enquiries about thee, Chaloner,' said Strange. 'About thy service in the wars and in Holland. And I have decided that thou wouldst make an excellent gunpowder man.'

'No,' snapped Quelch immediately. 'I do not trust him.'

'I care nothing for what thou thinkest – thou art a fool.' Strange turned back to Chaloner and gave one of his wild grins. 'Welcome. Thou art now our brother.'

'Thank you,' said Chaloner before Quelch could argue. 'However, I shall need time to prepare, so advance notice of the target will—'

'No,' snapped Quelch. 'We will tell you when it suits us.'

118

'Welcome to the fold, Chaloner,' said Atkinson with a friendly smile. 'But do not be too hopeful of supplying us with a blast. If all goes well, there will be no need for explosions.'

'Oh, yes, there will,' countered Jones. 'You cannot have a revolt without a bang or two.'

'We can and will,' countered Atkinson. 'I do not want a needless effusion of blood, and neither do most others. There has been too much of it already.'

'Hear, hear,' said Quelch. 'A gentle revolution is the thing. We are all weary of civil war.'

'I am not,' declared Strange. 'The Bible sayeth: "out of his mouth goeth a sharp sword; with it he shall smite the nation, and he shall rule them with a rod of iron". That is what I intend to do.'

The Sanhedrin launched into a debate on the matter, and it was some time before Jones was able to regain control. When he did, he addressed Chaloner.

'Manning did not appear today, and I need something delivered.' He handed over three letters and a box the size of a large book. 'Take these to him at the White Hind in Cripplegate.'

'Let me do it,' cried Quelch in alarm. 'Or another of the Sanhedrin. You cannot trust—'

'A stranger is better,' interrupted Jones. 'One not known to Williamson's spies.'

Chaloner opened the box to discover it full of grey powder. He made a show of inspecting it, picking some up between his fingers. The entire Sanhedrin flinched backwards when he rubbed it between them. It was like the softest sand, more akin to talc than explosives.

'My fingers are not metal,' he explained. 'They will not produce the spark needed to ignite it.'

'Do not be so sure,' said Jones, easing further away. 'This particular compound is the most volatile substance that has ever been created, and its manufacturers tell us that even the merest hint of abrasion will set it off. It is deadly stuff, and not to be poked.'

'If you were any good at your trade, you would have known that,' said Quelch accusingly.

Chaloner met his eyes. 'I could rub this all day and nothing would happen. And even if it did ignite, it would not explode – it would burn. You need a confined space for an explosion.'

'Perhaps,' said Jones, clearly a long way from being convinced. 'But run along now. It was only a loan, and Manning wants it back.'

'What—' began Chaloner.

'No questions. You have been told all you need to know. For now.'

Frustrated, Chaloner took his leave, and found himself walking along High Holborn with Atkinson and Ursula. She was heading for the market at Leadenhall, hoping to catch some bargains before it closed, and Atkinson had offered to accompany her.

'I make delicious soup for needy parishioners,' she explained as they went. 'I buy leftover provisions most evenings.'

'I would not mind tasting your soup,' sighed Atkinson, 'if it is anything like your cakes.'

It was a clumsy compliment, but Ursula accepted it as her due. 'The coal tax is hard on the poor, but it will not be a problem much longer, not with the New Kingdom at hand.'

Atkinson frowned. 'I accept that there might have to be a *little* bloodshed to win our equitable society, but I hope there will not be too much. I argued against hiring Scarface Roberts, and I argued against replacing him when he died. I am sorry if I offend, Chaloner, but I speak as I find.'

'Mr Chaloner is not the kind of man to blow things up unnecessarily,' said Ursula, with more confidence than Chaloner felt was warranted given that they barely knew each other. It told him again that she, like Atkinson, was foolishly naive and hopelessly out of her depth.

'I shall do my best to ensure that his expertise is not needed,' vowed the stockinger.

'Good,' said Ursula. 'I saw some bodies from the ship that exploded last week – *London* – dragged from the river a few days ago, and I should hate to think that we might be responsible for something similar.'

She shuddered, so Atkinson changed the subject, talking about a service he had attended at St Paul's Cathedral, where the choir had sung like angels. As he spoke, Chaloner wondered why the stockinger had embroiled himself with hotheads like the Fifth Monarchists. Was it just because he was enamoured of Ursula? If so, it might transpire to be a costly courtship.

Chaloner had no intention of giving anything to Manning without examining it first – he, unlike Leving, had no compunction about opening other people's letters – but he had known from the moment he had left the Talbot that he was being followed. He ducked into the Fleet Rookery, a dangerous, crime-ridden area of filthy tenements, seedy ale-houses and close-packed slums, and threaded through a complex maze of alleys before hiding in a doorway.

His tail was Jones, who swore under his breath when

he saw that his quarry had disappeared. He stopped a gang of slouching villains to ask whether they had seen a man wearing a grey long-coat, but the answer he received made him back away quickly and aim for the safety of Holborn. Chaloner went in the opposite direction, emerging on Fleet Street and then running as hard as he could to Lincoln's Inn, where he bounded up the stairs to Chamber XIII.

'Quickly,' he said, flinging the three letters on to the table. 'Help me read these. I have to deliver them to a tavern in Cripplegate, and I cannot take too long or Jones will be suspicious.'

As Spymaster, Thurloe had opened thousands of missives without their senders' or recipients' knowledge, and it did not take him long to slit the seals in such a way that they could be closed again without revealing what had happened.

'They are in cipher,' he said, scanning them quickly. 'We shall make copies and translate them at our leisure. Read them aloud while I write.'

His pen was soon flying across the paper, while Chaloner struggled to interpret a spidery hand that was not always very clear. Fortunately, none of the documents was very long, and they soon finished. Thurloe resealed them expertly.

'What do you make of this?' asked Chaloner, passing him the box of powder.

'Nothing,' replied Thurloe, after a brief inspection. 'Other than that it seems to be unusually fine. You know far more about such matters than me.'

Chaloner emptied it into the coal-scuttle and replaced it with soot from the chimney. Smiling enigmatically, Thurloe added something from his medicine chest – some of his remedies verged on the toxic, so Chaloner did not like to imagine what he was about to pass to Manning.

'Have you heard of an explosives expert named Scarface Roberts?' he asked.

Thurloe nodded. 'I used him during the Commonwealth – a very skilled man. Why?'

'He blew himself up, which made me assume he was not very competent. However, if you say he was, perhaps he died experimenting with this stuff.'

Thurloe regarded it uneasily. 'I had better dispose of it carefully then. I do not want to be responsible for the destruction of Lincoln's Inn.'

Chaloner left at a run, and soon reached the White Hind, a ramshackle tavern that sent the enticing aroma of roasted meat into the cold night air. It was busy, being popular with Lady Day visitors as well as locals. Manning was sitting on his own so Chaloner took the seat opposite.

'Oh, it is you,' said Manning with an unfriendly scowl. 'What do you want this time?'

'Jones asked me to come,' replied Chaloner.

Manning's eyes narrowed. 'Why? Where is Leving? He is the one who usually brings me messages from the Sanhedrin.'

Chaloner shrugged. 'I am just following orders. Why did you miss the meeting today? Are you not interested in our plans for the future?'

'I could not face the walk with my chilblains.'

'What about Sherwin? Where is he?'

'Safe,' replied Manning. 'Not that he is any of your business. And speaking of business, what do you have for me?'

Chaloner handed over the letters. Manning peered at

123

the seals and Chaloner held his breath, hoping Thurloe's skills were up to scratch, but Manning soon nodded his satisfaction and slipped them inside his coat. As he did, Chaloner became aware that they were being watched.

'Well, well,' said Scott, sauntering up to them. 'What are you two doing? Did I just see documents changing hands?'

'No, you did not,' said Manning furtively. He nodded to the box. 'He came to return that.'

Scott made a grab for it, which encouraged Manning to do the same, and there followed an unseemly tussle. Not surprisingly, the lid came off, scattering the contents over them both. Scott leapt up and brushed himself down frantically, although Manning only smirked.

'You had better watch how you light your pipe from now on. I, of course, do not smoke.'

Chaloner lingered at the White Hind, drinking ale with the ill-matched duo, and trying every ploy he knew to learn what was afoot. Unfortunately, Scott was too clever to be caught out, and was adept at preventing Manning from making incriminating remarks, too. Eventually, seeing he was wasting his time, Chaloner made his farewells and left.

It was bitterly cold, and the rain had turned to sleet. He turned up his collar, and was about to begin the long trudge to Tothill Street when he heard someone behind him. He turned quickly to see that Scott had followed him.

'I strongly advise you not to deal with Manning,' Scott said. 'He is a liar.'

'And you are not?' asked Chaloner archly.

Scott looked pained. 'I was a different man when you

124

knew me in New Amsterdam. Now I am a pillar of respectability – Cartographer Royal, and one of His Majesty's chief advisers.'

Suddenly, Chaloner had had enough of tiptoeing around for answers, and decided it was time for a more direct approach. He moved fast, and had Scott pinned against the wall with a knife at his throat before the man knew what was happening.

'Who is Sherwin? And do not say a cabinet maker, because we both know he is not.'

Scott began to struggle, but stopped when Chaloner poked his neck with the blade. 'I know nothing about him,' he replied sullenly. 'My orders are just to make sure that Manning does not spirit him out of the city.'

'Who issued these orders?'

'Spymaster Williamson,' came the unexpected response. 'Manning is a dangerous dissident – a Fifth Monarchist, no less – and my remit is to protect Sherwin from him at all costs. More than that I do not know.'

Chaloner did not believe him. 'Why is Sherwin so important?'

'I did not ask.' Scott became haughty. 'My goal is simply to serve my country.'

Chaloner did not believe that either. 'What do you know about the gunpowder?'

'Only that it is unusually fine, and that Manning has masses of it stashed away somewhere. He refuses to tell me where.'

'If Williamson is so concerned about Sherwin, why does he not place him in protective custody? Or arrest Manning to put an end to his machinations?'

'You will have to ask him. And when you do, you will learn that I am telling the truth.'

125

It was a claim that could be verified, so perhaps he was being honest for a change. Yet Scott was such a slippery character that Chaloner remained wary and suspicious. However, he could see there was no point in pressing the man further. He stepped back and indicated that he could leave. Scott slithered away, turning to speak only when he thought he was at a safe distance.

'Manhandle me again and Williamson will hear of it,' he snapped. 'Then you will be sorry.' He held Chaloner's gaze for a moment, then spun around and stamped away.

Chaloner headed for home, thinking gloomily that it had not been a good day for either of his enquiries. He was just walking past Chyrurgeons' Hall when he remembered that Surgeon Wiseman had recently moved there, to take up his new appointment. He knocked on the gate and was conducted to the Masters' Lodgings, where Wiseman received him with pleasure, delighted with an opportunity to show off his new domain.

'It is only mine for a year,' he said, 'but I mean to enjoy it. I have already brought my anatomical specimens from Fleet Street. Would you like to see how they look on the shelves?'

Chaloner flailed around for an excuse to avoid it. 'Hannah wants me home early tonight – she is making pickled ling pie.'

Wiseman shot him a sympathetic look. 'That is something no man should have to endure, and you were right to come to me for help. We shall give her my professional medical opinion: that you cannot consume such a foul creation so soon after your arduous experiences in Russia.'

'No!' exclaimed Chaloner, horrified that the surgeon

should think he would beg such a favour. 'She will never forgive us if we tell her that.'

Wiseman nodded slowly. 'True. Then we shall send an apprentice to say that your humours are awry, and that you are under my care for the evening. She cannot argue with a surgeon.'

Chaloner was sure she could. However, even viewing Wiseman's collection of grisly objects was preferable to the pie, so he nodded assent. Thrilled to have company, the surgeon showed him around. Chaloner averted his eyes when Wiseman took down one of his jars, but not before he had seen that it contained severed noses.

'I really should go,' he said, as Wiseman began to explain why its contents were of such great scientific value. 'I have work to do.'

'Stay,' urged Wiseman. 'I feel like entertaining, and I cannot think of anyone else to invite. All my colleagues are scoundrels and Temperance is working.'

Wiseman's arrogance and abrasive manners meant he was loathed by his fellow *medici* and feared by his patients, and it was common knowledge that he had no friends. Chaloner feigned dizziness when Wiseman resumed his ghoulish narrative, although the ploy backfired when the surgeon made him swallow a foul-tasting potion to restore his wits.

Afterwards, they sat by the fire in the parlour, listening to rain tapping against the windows. Wiseman embarked on a rambling monologue that ranged from the falling numbers at the club, to Prince Rupert's unpopularity at Court. As he listened, it occurred to Chaloner that the surgeon was well placed to listen to gossip, given that he was often at White Hall.

'Yes, people talk about Ferine,' Wiseman said. 'He

127

knew some very dubious people, apparently. His friend Duncombe denied it when I mentioned it to him, but he was lying. Have you interviewed him yet?'

Chaloner nodded. 'But I will speak to him again if you think he is hiding something.'

'He is – I could tell by the way his pupils contracted. You might try speaking to Richard Hubbert and Thomas Odowde, too. They were also Ferine's cronies.'

'Has a Cartographer Royal been appointed recently?' asked Chaloner, moving to another subject.

'There is no such office. However, I heard Williamson say something about buying maps from a resident of New Amster—New *York*. They will be used to oust the Dutch from other areas that the Privy Council thinks should be ours. If Rupert and Buckingham can agree on a plan of attack, of course.'

'Did Williamson mention John Scott?'

'Yes, I think he did. Why? Do you know him?'

Chaloner nodded, thinking it was typical of Scott that he should equate selling a few charts with being granted a royal appointment.

'But most chat is about HMS *London*,' Wiseman went on. 'Admiral Lawson is pressing for her to be weighed, although she was a massive ship, and I cannot see such a venture succeeding. I dislike that man. He fought for Parliament during the wars, and there is some suggestion that he is a Fifth Monarchist.'

Chaloner stared at him. Was Lawson the guest who Jones and Quelch had wanted to corner at the club? Was he to play a role in their uprising? If so, then the situation was serious indeed, because Lawson commanded the entire Channel Fleet.

'Prince Rupert told me about Lawson's peculiar

religious beliefs,' said Wiseman, seeing his friend's alarm. 'It is very worrying. The Admiral is charged with protecting us from the Dutch, but if he is a secret fanatic . . . There are disquieting rumours about the ship *London*, too.'

'What are they?'

'At first it was said that she exploded because someone was in her powder magazine with a naked flame, but now there are doubts. Her loss weakens our navy considerably, to the advantage of the Hollanders.'

Chaloner frowned. 'What are you saying? That she was destroyed deliberately?'

'There are certainly concerns to that effect. And with Lawson being a Fifth Monarchist . . .'

Chapter 5

Chaloner woke the next morning in the same chair with a blanket tossed over him, and could hear Wiseman snoring in the room next door. His first thought was a guilt-ridden one: he had missed Hannah's pickled ling pie. His second was that he had a great deal to do that day, and should grab the opportunity to make an early start.

He stood and stretched, easing the stiffness from his limbs. Someone had cleaned his coat and boots while he had been asleep, so he put them on, walked to the window and opened the shutter. It was just growing light, and the streets were already echoing with the low roar of traffic – trundling wheels, clattering feet and the sounds of cattle being driven to market. It was still raining, but only lightly.

Being on the top floor, Wiseman's rooms afforded a fine view of the surrounding rooftops, close-packed and glistening wet. Chief among them was the unusual shape of the Anatomy Theatre. Students gathered by its door – one of the masters was about to give a demonstration. Chaloner watched idly, most of his mind on making plans for the day ahead.

First, he would see whether Thurloe had decoded the cipher. Next, he would report to the Earl, hoping that Hannah had not been too offensive to him the night before last, after which he would hunt down Duncombe, Odowde and Hubbert. Then he needed to explore Lawson's link to the Fifth Monarchists. He decided to ask his friend Captain Lester about it – Lester would certainly have an opinion on a fellow sea-officer.

He was about to leave Chyrurgeons' Hall when Wiseman appeared wearing a billowing nightgown. The surgeon bellowed for his breakfast, then began the peculiar ritual of stone-lifting that he performed each day. Some of the rocks he hefted were enormous, and explained why his muscles bulged like those of a prize fighter.

'You should do it,' he panted. 'A trim physique would be useful in your line of work.'

Chaloner looked down at himself. 'I *am* trim.'

Wiseman sniffed dismissively and turned his attention to the procession of servants who began to bring plate after plate of food. 'Excellent! There is nothing like red meat to set a man up for the day. And nothing like six raw eggs whisked with wine and cream either, while shredded cabbage does wonders for the digestion. Come on, Chaloner. Do not be shy.'

It was curious fare for so early in the morning, but Chaloner ate it anyway. His day promised to be busy, and he did not know when the next opportunity to dine would arise. He sat in the window as he struggled with the slippery egg mixture, staring into the yard below.

The students had disappeared inside the Anatomy Theatre, and a queue of people was forming by the gate. Some were paying patients with appointments, but the bulk were London's poor, who came to be treated free of charge in exchange for letting the *medici* practise on them. He watched sympathetically, thinking they must be desperate indeed to resort to surgeons, when it was common knowledge that most did more harm than good.

He snapped into alertness when he saw Eliza Hatton among them, her pale beauty visible even in the dim light of dawn. The porter noticed it, too, and fawningly indicated that she was to advance to the front of the line, much to the disgust of those who had arrived before her.

'That is Alice Fanshaw,' said Wiseman. 'I am treating her for a pathological coldness of the limbs. Damn! She is coming up to me now, and I am not dressed.'

'She told me that her name is Eliza Hatton.'

'Then you misheard,' said Wiseman, grabbing his red coat and tugging it over his nightgown. 'She is definitely Alice Fanshaw – I knew her mother. Besides, Eliza Hatton is dead.'

A cold shiver ran down Chaloner's spine. 'Dead?'

'Torn limb from limb – literally, by all accounts.' Wiseman grinned rather diabolically as he donned a pair of scarlet breeches, tucking the nightgown in to hide it and adding six inches to his waistline. 'And when she was found, blood was still pumping from her body, thus proving that the illustrious William Harvey was correct in his theory about the heart's role in venous circulation.'

Chaloner could have done without that detail. 'When did this happen?'

'Forty years ago,' replied Wiseman, as he knelt to put on his shoes – smart black ones with crimson heels. 'So do not worry, I doubt you will be asked to solve the case.

Of course, I doubt there is any truth in it: it is a tale to titivate the gullible.'

'So why did she lie to me?'

'She is a mysterious lady.' Wiseman went to the mirror to fluff up his auburn curls. 'But I shall ask her if you like. She will not regale *me* with falsehoods.'

'Thank you. She knew Paul Ferine, you see, and her answers may help Temperance. I will hide behind the curtains and listen.'

'You will not!' declared the surgeon. 'She will want to discuss personal medical details, and it would be unethical to let you eavesdrop. So shut yourself in my bedchamber and stay there until I tell you to come out. How do I look? Is there any meat between my teeth?'

Before Chaloner could reply, footsteps heralded the arrival of Eliza – he could not think of her as Alice – so he stepped into the room that Wiseman indicated. There was a knock and she was in, entering while the surgeon was still busy with a tooth-brush. She closed the door in the admiring porter's face, and held out a limp white hand for Wiseman to kiss. The surgeon obliged with a courtly flourish, although he scowled and made an irritable gesture behind her back when he saw the bedroom door was ajar. When Chaloner did not close it, Wiseman took her to his laboratory instead. Chaloner tiptoed towards it and put his ear to the door.

Eliza was complaining about an inability to sleep, and she and Wiseman discussed several remedies before settling on a draught of poppy juice and mandrake. These were potent herbs, but Chaloner supposed the surgeon knew what he was doing. She emerged from the consultation so abruptly that he was not sure he had managed to duck fully out of sight. Wiseman

133

accompanied her to the gate, his eyes fixed appreciatively on her behind as she preceded him across the yard. Chaloner slipped back to the bedroom, where he waited until the surgeon returned.

'She has gone,' Wiseman reported with a wistful sigh. 'And do not ask what she wanted, because it was personal. Nothing to do with Eliza Hatton or Ferine.'

'Did you ask her about them?'

'Lord, I forgot!' Wiseman became defensive when he saw Chaloner's irritation. 'My first responsibility is to *my* profession, not yours, so you will have to question her yourself. But do it gently: she is a sensitive woman.'

'So is Temperance,' said Chaloner pointedly.

Sensitive or not, Chaloner needed answers from Eliza, so he hurried out of Chyrurgeons' Hall, aiming to speak to her. He caught up with her on Aldersgate Street, but before he could hail her she had flagged down a hackney and clambered in. Had she seen him, and was escaping before he could ask questions? Or was she just a woman in a hurry? He decided to find out, and jumped on the back of the carriage, landing lightly enough not to warn the driver that he was carrying a non-paying passenger. It was something done as a dare by small boys, not by grown men, so more than a few people stared at him as the carriage rattled along.

The driver slowed as they reached High Holborn, and stopped opposite the Talbot. Chaloner jumped off, swearing under his breath when mud caused him to land with an ungainly stagger. He hid behind a stationary cart, and watched her approach a nearby house. The amount of time it took her to undo the door told him it was unlikely to be her own. He waited until she was inside, then followed. The door was locked, but that was no obstacle to a man who made his living out of entering places that wanted to keep him out. He took two metal probes from his pocket, and had the satisfaction of hearing the mechanism snap open almost immediately.

Inside was a long, gloomy corridor that smelled of dust and stale air. There was no one in sight, and a glance into the rooms he passed showed furniture swathed in sheets, and windows and chimneys boarded up – the owners were away, and intended to be so for some time. He crept on, noting cobwebs hanging in gossamer strands across the stairs: Eliza had not gone up there, or they would have broken. He reached a kitchen that smelled of old fat and mouse droppings, but she was not there either. The back door had been barred from the inside, and a layer of dust along it told him that it had not been moved for some time.

He retraced his steps and searched the entire ground floor, but found no Eliza. Puzzled, he climbed the stairs, feeling the cobwebs brush his face. He was almost at the top when he stumbled – two of the last three steps were of radically different heights. He had seen similar devices in castles, designed to wrong-foot invaders, but he had never before encountered them in a private house. He explored the upper floor as carefully as he had the bottom, but Eliza had disappeared without a trace for the second time in as many days.

It was not far to Lincoln's Inn, and Chaloner walked there briskly, baffled by what had happened. He had been trained to locate secret passages and hidey-holes, but the house had none that he could find. Moreover, it had had a peculiarly desolate feel, and he could not escape the conviction that something terrible had happened there.

He arrived to find Thurloe in the garden, although he was vexed to see that the ex-Spymaster had company in the form of one William Prynne, another Lincoln's Inn 'bencher'. Prynne held some of the most odious views in the city, which he liked to make public by means of pamphlets. He despised everything about the age in which he lived, and decried Catholics, theatres, Quakers, maypoles, mince pies, bowls and horse racing with equal fervour. Thurloe liked him no more than Chaloner did, so the spy was surprised to see them together.

'Long hair offends me,' Prynne was braying. He was a bustling, elderly little man who wore a felted cap to hide the fact that his ears had been chopped off as punishment for writing scurrilous nonsense about the King's mother. 'I consider it sinful, effeminate, vainglorious, evil, immodest, indecent, lascivious, wanton, dissolute, whorish, ungodly, pernicious, offensive, ridiculous, foolish, childish, unchristian, hateful, unmanly, depraving and unseemly.'

Thurloe's own flowing locks were tucked under his hat, which seemed to have been enough to make Prynne forget them. 'You do not approve then,' the ex-Spymaster said mildly.

Prynne had worked himself into a frenzy. 'I do not, and—'

'Tom!' exclaimed Thurloe, when he saw Chaloner. 'What a nice surprise. Have you come for that book I offered to lend you? You must be in a hurry, so let us fetch it now.'

'But I have not finished telling you about my latest

136

pamphlet,' cried Prynne. 'And I rose early to catch you, as I knew you would want an exclusive preview.'

'How kind.' Thurloe fixed Prynne with a baleful eye. 'But such tracts must surely be expensive to produce? Perhaps you should curtail your opinions and save some money.'

'It is expensive,' agreed Prynne. 'But I have nothing else to spend it on. Personally, I am glad the process is costly, as we would be inundated with all manner of rubbish if everyone could afford it. My latest piece on Court fashions is—'

'I would not rail against long hair if I were you,' interrupted Chaloner. 'The King has some, and if you lose his favour, he will dismiss you as Keeper of Records at the Tower.'

'Tom has a point, Prynne,' said Thurloe. 'You know how much you love that work.'

'I do love it,' acknowledged Prynne. 'But His Majesty has *short* hair. He shaved it off when he started to go grey, and now he wears a periwig. I have nothing against those.'

'You do not mind wigs, yet you object to hair?' asked Chaloner, mystified. 'Surely wigs are far more vain? They—'

'Good gracious, is that the time?' interrupted Thurloe, shooting Chaloner an irritable glance for effectively inviting Prynne to hold forth. 'I must take my daily tonic at once.'

'Invest in a horoscope instead,' advised Prynne. 'It is all the rage at Court, and will save you a mint in medicine. After all, no remedy will work if one's stars are unfavourable.'

'I do not hold with fortune-telling,' said Thurloe coolly. 'It is an insult to God.'

Prynne sensed he was on dangerous ground and hastened to justify his remark. 'I was only telling you what is popular. There are a lot of superstitious folk at White Hall.'

'Like Paul Ferine?' fished Chaloner.

Prynne nodded. 'And his friends Odowde and Hubbert. They have been telling tales about the city's haunted places – a certain room in the Antelope tavern, the ruins of Hatton House . . .'

'Hatton House is not haunted,' stated Thurloe firmly. 'The wailing sound one hears is only wind whistling through its broken windows.'

'You are doubtless right,' said Prynne, unwilling to take issue with a man whose good opinion was important to him. He changed the subject hastily. 'Have either of you heard of a man named John Browne? I keep hearing him discussed, and I am curious. He has been mentioned by Prince Rupert, John Scott—'

'You should not eavesdrop,' interrupted Thurloe sternly, while Chaloner recalled that Sherwin had mentioned a 'sanctimonious fool' named John Browne, who held opinions on drunkenness. Could it be the same man? 'It is unbecoming.'

'You did it,' said Prynne flashed back, nettled at last. 'It kept Cromwell in power for years.'

'But you are not a spymaster,' retorted Thurloe tartly. 'Nor a secretary of state. There is a world of difference between official intelligencing and repeating gossip.'

Chaloner almost laughed, knowing Thurloe would never have made such a foolish remark had Prynne been less annoying. 'What did these folk say about John Browne?' he asked the old man.

'Nothing that made sense,' admitted Prynne. 'It just sounded as though he was important.'

Chaloner ignored Thurloe's irritable gesture telling him to walk away. 'You referred to Hatton House a moment ago. Do you know Eliza Hatton?'

Prynne's vindictive face hardened. 'I *did*. She seduced the Spanish ambassador, who was then accused of her murder. Of course, that was forty years ago now . . .'

'So she *was* killed? It is not some ghoulish tale?'

'It is a fable,' said Thurloe shortly, before Prynne could speak. 'Put about to explain how Bleeding-Heart Yard came by its name. But the reality is that there was a church dedicated to St Mary nearby, and in it was a statue of her being pierced by swords.'

'Popery,' spat Prynne. 'I might have known.'

'I wish you would not encourage him, Thomas,' said Thurloe crossly, once Prynne had been persuaded that London was eager for his views on courtly fashions and had gone to put poisonous pen to paper. 'Never, *never* ask him questions. Especially when it forces me to hear his answers.'

'I am sorry. I thought he might know something useful.'

'He might, but you would never separate it from his loathsome opinions.'

They walked in silence for a while, then Chaloner furnished the ex-Spymaster with an account of his discoveries the previous day.

'Easter is ten days hence,' he concluded glumly. 'And the Earl may not rehire me if I do not thwart whatever the Fifth Monarchists are planning.'

Thurloe was dismissive. 'A few hundred fools baying their lunatic beliefs around London will make people laugh, not race to join them. Nothing will happen on Easter Day.'

'I am not so sure,' said Chaloner worriedly. 'They want equal justice for rich and poor, an abolition of unfair taxes, and gainful employment for all. These are attractive notions.'

'Fifth Monarchists are worms who believe they can thresh mountains,' said Thurloe, voicing what he had claimed before. 'No sane person can believe that Jesus intends to take up residence in White Hall. Or that He will share power with a Sanhedrin that comprises a lot of spiritually arrogant, humourless, vociferous fanatics.'

'Leving heard Jones say that they have ten thousand supporters,' argued Chaloner.

'Then Jones was exaggerating. This so-called uprising is more nuisance than threat, and Williamson is a fool to waste your time on it. He should use you to spy on the Dutch.'

'But Admiral Lawson may share their convictions, and he commands the Channel Fleet,' persisted Chaloner. 'You should not underestimate them.'

'Lawson has more sense than to throw in his lot with lunatics,' said Thurloe firmly, and the note of finality in his voice told Chaloner that the subject was closed.

Usually, Chaloner trusted his friend's views on such matters, sometimes more than his own, but this time he was sure Thurloe was wrong. He said no more, though, and Thurloe was also silent, so the only sound was the squelching of soggy leaves underfoot.

'So have you been accepted into the Fifth Monarchists' cabal?' asked Thurloe eventually.

Chaloner nodded. 'Theoretically, at least. However, Quelch is suspicious, and the others must be, too, no

140

matter what they say to my face. Meanwhile, I do not trust Leving, and I am not sure what is going on with Manning and Scott . . .'

'Scott's arrival does bode ill,' Thurloe agreed. 'And this business with "Eliza" is curious.'

'She is definitely involved in something peculiar, given that she feels the need to disappear all the time. It is almost as if she is a ghost . . .'

Thurloe shot him a weary glance and declined to acknowledge the remark. 'I have asked my contacts to listen for rumours about Ferine, but they have reported nothing yet. And I sent the letters we copied yesterday to Wallis the mathematician. If he cannot decode them, no one can. I wish I could do more, but I am busy with my own work at the moment.'

Chaloner hoped Wallis would not take long.

White Hall was the King's main London residence, a sprawling palace said to contain more than two thousand rooms, ranging from the elegant apartments occupied by His Majesty, his family and his ministers, to the squalid, cramped quarters allocated to the army of cooks, cleaners, scullions, grooms and porters needed to keep the place running. Chaloner walked through the Great Gate and aimed for the Earl's offices, hunched into his coat against the sheeting rain. He saw the Earl's Seal Bearer in the Privy Garden, and changed direction to intercept him.

'*I* do not believe that you made no effort to save the Tsar's jewels when your ship went down, no matter what the scandal-mongers say,' declared Kipps, speaking without preamble. 'And nor do I believe that you are bankrupt. Hannah's debts cannot be that serious.'

Chaloner was horrified that his personal finances should be the subject of gossip, but Kipps blustered on before he could reply.

'Have you come here to look for another post? If so, loiter in the Privy Gallery. It is next to the Great Hall, as you know, which has just been converted to a permanent theatre. Its first performance is due to start at noon, but there are not many seats, so folk will hover in the Privy Gallery, ready to make a dash for them when the doors open.'

As the residents of White Hall had a penchant for lewd dramas, Chaloner suspected that the construction of a place where they could be viewed more frequently would do nothing to enhance the Court's reputation among the people. Sourly he thought it no wonder that the radical sects who denounced them, like the Fifth Monarchists, attracted popular support.

'*The Parson's Dream*,' continued Kipps, tight lipped. 'I am no prude, but that goes well beyond my limits. Anyway, the King intends to see it, so every courtier and hanger-on in London will be there. One of them will want a good intelligencer, so do not worry.'

Chaloner changed the subject by gesturing to the garden, where several servants were toiling among the winter-brown shrubs. 'What are they doing?'

'Preparing for the Lady Day fireworks,' replied Kipps disapprovingly. 'Come and look at what they have done. It is all very, very wrong.'

The labourers had dug a long, waist-deep trench at the far end of the grounds, their workings carefully concealed behind a knee-high hedge of privet. Chaloner regarded it, then Kipps, blankly, not sure why this should have earned his disapprobation.

142

'It is dangerous,' the Seal Bearer explained crossly. 'I fell in on my way home last night, and ended up covered in mud.'

'Why do fireworks need a ditch?'

'So that they and the fellow who ignites them – the so-called "Green Man" – can remain invisible to spectators. All we shall see is rockets blasting into the sky.'

'Who is the Green Man this year?' asked Chaloner conversationally.

'The Master of Ordnance,' replied Kipps. 'It is a good choice, as it takes considerable skill if the event is to pass off without incident. The last fellow who did it managed to set himself alight, while the one before him killed two servants and one of the King's dogs.'

'I would have thought the Master of Ordnance had more important matters to consider – like organising armaments for the Dutch war.'

Kipps nodded. 'The fireworks are an unnecessary expense, especially when the poor clamour for us to reduce taxes. Indeed, the whole thing is wicked – Lady Day is the Saturday before Easter this year, and it is inappropriate to celebrate with such extravagance while we are still in Lent.'

Chaloner raised his eyebrows. Kipps had never struck him as religious before.

The Seal Bearer shrugged. 'Call me superstitious if you will, but it is asking for bad luck. There have been more than the usual number of omens of late, *and* ghosts along High Holborn.'

That reminded Chaloner of his investigations. 'I have been asked to look into the murder of Paul Ferine. Did you know him?'

'Yes. It is a pity he got himself murdered in

Temperance's club, because no man likes to take his ease in a house where assassins might lurk. Worse, the attention has divested it of its anonymity, and wives are paying attention . . .'

'Was Ferine married?'

'He was, but she died a few months ago in their house on High Holborn. Wild with grief, Ferine ordered the doors locked and the windows shuttered. No one has set foot in it since.'

'How did she die?' asked Chaloner, his mind racing.

'Fell down the stairs and broke her neck. Personally, I think it was the shock of losing Grace that turned Ferine superstitious. Afterwards, he started to find comfort in odd rituals, such as not starting journeys on a Friday, and spitting whenever he saw a white horse.'

The house Eliza had visited *had* to be Ferine's, thought Chaloner. High Holborn was a desirable location, and there could not be many buildings on it that were closed up. Moreover, the steps were definitely a tripping hazard, because he had stumbled on them himself.

'The rector of St Dunstan's told me that Ferine was a widower,' he said. 'But no one has mentioned Grace's curious death. Not even Duncombe, Ferine's particular friend.'

'That is not surprising – Grace was Catholic, so Ferine tended to keep her quiet. Moreover, Duncombe has been drunk ever since the murder, and no one can get any sense from him. I only know about Grace because one of Ferine's servants was the sister of one of mine.'

'What else do you know about him?'

'He was superb at horoscopes.' Kipps's expression was troubled. 'He did one for me, and predicted a grave mishap. Sure enough, the next day I was "uninvited"

144

from Lady Castlemaine's Shrove Tuesday party, which I had been looking forward to for weeks.'

As Lady Castlemaine – the King's mistress – was one of the Earl's most bitter enemies, Chaloner thought Kipps had no business attending her soirées anyway, but there was no point in saying so: Kipps was a great admirer of her thighs, and thought the rest of her could do no wrong.

'Perhaps Ferine knew beforehand that she had revised her guest list,' he suggested.

'No – her decision was prompted by the King telling her that he was cutting back on her allowance, which happened *after* Ferine and I spoke.' Kipps sighed. 'That prediction was accurate, so I hastened to comply when he later suggested that I purchase a human skull to keep witches at bay. It is on the mantelpiece in my bedroom, next to my spare teeth.'

'*Spare* teeth?'

'Lest I lose any of my own. There are rumours that the Last Millennium is nigh, and I should not like to face eternity bereft of fangs. How would I manage at heavenly feasts?'

As Lord Chancellor, the Earl of Clarendon was entitled to rooms in White Hall, and had secured himself a pleasant suite overlooking the Privy Garden. Chaloner hid behind an oversized ornamental vase in the lobby until he was sure his master was alone, then opened the door and slipped inside. The Earl was at his desk, while an inferno roared in the hearth. The fire was so loud that Chaloner approached unheard, and was obliged to cough to attract attention.

'I wish you would not do that,' snapped the Earl, one

plump hand to his chest. 'And you should not be here anyway. No one will believe we have fallen out if you visit me.'

'I was careful, sir.'

The Earl regarded him with pursed lips. 'I met your wife the night before last, at a ceremony to commemorate HMS *London*'s dead. And I am afraid to report that she was intoxicated.'

Chaloner's heart sank. 'Was she?'

'I could not understand a word she said, although she was clearly trying to convey something of import. Perhaps you would ask her to visit me here, so she can try again when she is sober.'

Chaloner did not think that would be a very good idea. 'She was very distressed about *London*, sir. I am sure that was all she was trying to say.'

The Earl frowned. 'She sounded more angry than sad to me. But no matter. Why did you come here today? Do you have something to tell me?'

'I thought you might like to know what I have learned about the Fifth Monarchists. They are led by a Sanhedrin, and two of them – Jones and Strange – were involved in the Northern Plot. The uprising is scheduled for Easter Day.'

'Then you have ten days to stop it,' said the Earl, calculating on his fingers. 'But I am expecting visitors in a few moments, and their business concerns you, so you might as well wait here and meet them.'

Before Chaloner could point out that his cover would certainly be compromised if he attended conferences in the Earl's chambers, there was a rap on the door, and he had only just ducked behind the curtain when Kipps entered.

146

'A Mr Lee and a Mr Smith, sir,' the Seal Bearer announced. 'I will tell them to return later if you are busy.'

'You will do no such thing.' It was Rupert, who did not understand that it took more than a cloak and a false name to conceal his identity. He was with Williamson, whose disguise was not much better, although he had at least covered his face with a scarf.

Chaloner was bemused. Rupert and the Earl hated each other, while neither had much time for Williamson, so what was happening that necessitated a secret meeting between the three of them?

'Thank you, Kipps,' said the Earl crisply. 'Ensure we are not disturbed, if you please.'

'Must you keep the fire so high?' grumbled Rupert, flinging off his cloak and going to douse it. A selfish individual, it did not occur to him that someone else might be cold.

'Chaloner is here,' said the Earl, pursing his lips at the Prince's presumption, but making no effort to check him. 'You can hear his report for yourselves.'

'Good,' said Rupert, as Chaloner stepped out of the shadows. 'The Fifth Monarchists are causing the government considerable concern, so I hope you have something useful to tell us.'

Chaloner's confusion intensified. He understood why Williamson would want to be kept informed, but why should the matter concern Rupert? He decided to be economical with the facts until they told him what was going on. 'Not really.'

'Why not?' demanded Williamson waspishly. 'You have had three days now.'

'He has discovered that there will be trouble on Easter

147

Day,' said the Earl, shooting Chaloner an irritable glance for his caginess. 'And they have a Sanhedrin that includes Jones and Strange.'

'We knew that already,' snapped Rupert. Williamson nodded, but Chaloner could tell from the Earl's raised eyebrows that they had not shared the information with him. 'What have you learned that is *new*?'

Chaloner regarded him levelly. 'If you tell me what you have discovered to date, I will not waste your time by regaling you with details that you already have.'

'Don't you take that tone with me,' snarled Rupert. 'How dare you!'

'He cannot help himself,' explained the Earl tiredly. 'He is even insolent to me on occasion – the man who pays his wages.'

Or not, thought Chaloner acidly. He addressed Williamson, hoping the Spymaster would listen to reason. 'You need to allocate more men to monitor these rebels. You are right to be concerned: Jones and Strange in particular are unpredictable zealots.'

Williamson sighed. 'I wish I could, but all my people are busy with the war.'

'Besides, this is a sensitive business, and we cannot have half of London knowing about it,' interposed Rupert. 'They might decide to join these villains, and then where would we be?'

'But half of London probably *does* know,' argued Chaloner. 'I counted two hundred people at a meeting yesterday, while there are reports of ten thousand more waiting for orders. You cannot have that many folk enrolled and expect to keep it quiet.'

'But it *is* being kept quiet,' said Williamson worriedly. 'There has not been so much as a whisper of it in

148

the coffee houses. And believe me, I listen for such tales.'

Chaloner turned to the Earl, although his remarks were intended for all three. 'There is clearly more to this case than you have revealed, sir. If you were to give me the whole story, I am far more likely to find the answers you—'

'No,' interrupted Rupert firmly. 'What you do not know, you cannot reveal, should you fall into the wrong hands. You must work within the limits we set.'

That instruction told Chaloner for certain that they were hiding something. Moreover, it had to be something unusually troublesome, or the three men would not have formed an alliance – especially one that necessitated donning disguises when they met. However, Chaloner could tell from the Earl's baffled expression that he did not know the full particulars either. He was being used, and Chaloner suspected it would not be Rupert or Williamson who would pay the price should anything go wrong.

'I am likely to discover it anyway,' he persisted. 'Telling me now will save time, which we cannot afford to waste if we are to prevent—'

'I said no,' repeated Rupert harshly. 'All we want from you is a list of every filthy rebel who meets in these sordid taverns, and a rough idea of what they plan to do. Personally, I do not see why Leving could not have managed on his own, but Williamson said we should recruit you.'

'I have never trusted turncoats,' explained the Spymaster. 'And Leving is low on wits. This affair is too important to entrust to him alone.'

'Important?' pounced Chaloner. 'Surely, it is just

149

another rebellion? The same as the dozens of others that have rumbled since the Restoration.'

'This one is more pressing,' said Rupert tightly. 'But that is all we are prepared to tell you. Now get out there and learn what we need to know.'

He turned on his heel and stalked out, leaving Williamson to run after him with the cloak that would provide his disguise. Wordlessly, the Earl went to stoke up the fire that Rupert had savaged, but his inept prodding threatened to extinguish it altogether, so Chaloner went to help him.

'I am not sure I can manage this investigation on my own, sir,' he said quietly, once the blaze had been restored. 'Not without understanding what is really going on.'

'You will cope,' replied the Earl, not looking at him. 'And I cannot afford to cross Rupert or Williamson. I stand a better chance of staying in power if they are on my side.'

'They will not support you if I fail,' warned Chaloner. 'And I have a bad feeling about the whole affair. Rupert's interest makes no sense.'

'Not to me, either,' admitted the Earl. 'But we had better do as he says. I will almost certainly lose my position on the Privy Council without his backing, while you will be unemployed if I am ousted. It is a wretched situation, but it cannot be helped.'

Chaloner left the Earl's offices as stealthily as he had arrived, but had not gone far before he saw two cloaked figures huddled behind a buttress. It was not a good place for a private discussion, because it was absurdly easy for anyone to approach unseen and eavesdrop. Williamson kept his voice to a discreet murmur, but Rupert was more

150

used to bawling orders on battlefields, so although Chaloner had to strain to catch everything the Spymaster said, he had no trouble at all with the Prince's side of the conversation.

'. . . would be a catastrophe if that happened,' Rupert was hissing. 'A disaster.'

'More financial than tactical, though,' said Williamson. 'And I cannot help but wonder whether you place too much value on it.'

'Nonsense! It will turn the tide of this war and all wars in the future.' The Prince lowered his voice, and Chaloner heard the greed in it. 'Although the money is no small concern, of course.'

'In that case, your people should have been more careful. Especially John Browne. This is a distraction I could do without – I should be concentrating on the Dutch.'

'It is a distraction *I* could do without, too,' snapped Rupert. 'I wish to God you trusted more of your people, because Clarendon's spy is right – we *should* allocate more men to this matter.'

'Then use your influence on the Privy Council to win me more funding,' Williamson flashed. 'You cannot expect men to stay loyal for the pittance I am able to pay.'

'Then are you sure Chaloner can be trusted? I doubt Clarendon is a generous paymaster.'

'He is a bizarre exception to the rule.'

'He will have his price,' said Rupert bitterly. 'Just like the men who put me in this situation in the first place. But can he stop these villains before it is too late? He did not seem to understand the urgency of the matter.'

'Because you refused to tell him.'

151

'I could not bring myself to do it – I hate spies. Still, if he fails, it will not be us who bear the blame. That will be Clarendon's prerogative, and I shall delight in watching his fall from grace.'

'You promised to protect him,' said Williamson, startled. 'That was the agreement.'

'What agreement?' asked Rupert slyly. 'I signed nothing. And Privy Council meetings will be a lot more fun without him whining for peace at every turn. I cannot abide pacifists.'

'You do surprise me,' said Williamson drily.

When they had gone, Chaloner mulled over what he had heard. Who was John Browne, and how was he associated with whatever was unfolding? Should the Earl be warned that Rupert had no intention of honouring whatever arrangement had been made, or was he politician enough to know it? Chaloner certainly hoped so, because it would not be easy to say that the King's cousin was a duplicitous scoundrel with no honour.

Because so many people wanted to see *The Parson's Dream*, the Privy Gallery was crowded, and virtually everyone was gossiping. Much of the talk was about HMS *London* – Catholics were to blame, of course, as they always were when something exploded. There was chat about Ferine, too, and amused whispers about Lambe's new name for Clarendon House. There was, however, nothing about thirty fanatics forming a Sanhedrin and planning something nasty for Easter Day.

Kipps was there, so Chaloner asked him to point out Odowde and Hubbert. The Seal Bearer directed him to two unexceptional men in brown wigs and dowdy clothes. The only thing that made them distinct was that Hubbert

152

had a black eye. They were with several people who had gathered near the window, and Chaloner saw they were listening in rapt attention to Dr Lambe. The sorcerer was wearing his star-spangled coat, and was speaking in a low hiss that had his audience straining forward to hear.

'. . . of Venus. And that is always a bad sign.'

'Oh,' breathed silly Lady Muskerry, her eyes huge in her bovine face. 'That is worrisome. The last time you mentioned Venus, the ship *London* sank.'

'Yes, I predicted it,' said Lambe smugly. 'And I predict that the engineers will fail when they try to pull her from the seabed next week. Lawson is wrong to say the venture will succeed.'

His voice assumed an eerie timbre as he pronounced these words, and a frisson of fear rippled through his audience. He seemed to grow in size as he spoke, and although Chaloner knew it was a trick, he had to admit that Lambe did it very well.

'I intend to watch,' said Buckingham, who was standing next to his protégé in a slightly possessive manner. 'No matter what happens, it promises to be a spectacle.'

'Because of the bodies?' asked Lady Muskerry ghoulishly. 'They will have been in the water for nigh on a fortnight by then, and will not be a pretty sight.'

A wave of excitement ran through the listeners, and Chaloner was hard-pressed to stay in the shadows and not surge forward to tell them what he thought of their unseemly fascination with the disaster. He was glad when the discussion moved to other matters.

'What does the new comet mean, Lambe?' asked Will Chiffinch, a man whose main function at Court was to furnish the King with whores when his mistress was unavailable. 'What disasters loom for us in the future?'

'Perhaps the war,' said Lambe, making a sudden peculiar motion with his hand that had Lady Muskerry scooting back with a shriek of alarm. Giggling at herself, she edged closer again.

'What about the war?' pressed Chiffinch. 'Will we win?'

'Possibly.' Lambe folded his hands inside his sleeves and bent his head in a curious and disconcerting imitation of a medieval monk. 'Or we will lose.'

Chaloner smothered a smirk as the listeners exchanged awed glances, thinking even the dimmest halfwit should know that it would be one or the other. But Lambe possessed charisma in abundance, and it was this that made people accept his pronouncements without stopping to analyse them first. At that moment Odowde stepped forward.

'I do not believe in fortune telling,' he declared. 'Why should we accept what you say?'

Lambe looked up slowly, an expression on his face that unnerved even Chaloner. Those standing near Odowde eased away. Then the sorcerer raised a finger and pointed.

'An ill will soon befall *you*,' he intoned. The finger dropped to touch Odowde's arm. 'A tumble perhaps, or an assault. Regardless, it will be broken.'

Hubbert lifted a tentative hand to his bruised eye. 'Take heed, Odowde. I ignored Dr Lambe's prophecy and look what happened to me – punched by my own footman in a dispute over pay.'

Lambe inclined his head in acknowledgement, then spun on his heel and stalked away, his coat billowing behind him. It was a dramatic exit, and Chaloner was impressed by his skilful use of the theatrical.

'He is quite a man,' said Buckingham, gazing after him proudly. 'The son of the fellow my father hired, who was viciously murdered by a mob some forty years ago. I am lucky to have him helping me.'

'Helping you do what?' asked Lady Muskerry in a hoarse whisper.

'Discover the Philosopher's Stone,' replied Buckingham grandly. Chaloner looked for some indication that he was joking, but there was none.

'What is the Philosopher's Stone?' breathed Lady Muskerry, agog.

'The thing that turns base metal into gold,' explained Buckingham. He spoke a little impatiently, as it was not something most people needed explaining. 'I hired him to assist me with my experiments, but his ability to foresee the future is an added bonus. There are those who say that Ferine was better, but they are wrong. Lambe is by far the superior of the two.'

Lady Muskerry gulped. 'Dr Lambe predicted that I would be with child by the end of the month, but I thought he was joking. Perhaps I should take heed, because my husband is away at the moment, and awkward questions would be asked . . .'

'He forecast that *I* would die of plague,' whispered Chiffinch. 'Then he recommended a course of potions to make me immune. I have not missed a single dose, I can tell you! But we should move nearer the door or we shall be at a disadvantage in the race for seats.'

Most of the party hastened to do as he suggested, although Odowde and Hubbert were too lowly to claim a place at the front of the queue, so held back

155

deferentially. Chaloner was about to approach them when someone else arrived. It was Duncombe, well on the way to being drunk despite the early hour. Even better, thought Chaloner, advancing with purpose.

'We have met before,' said Duncombe, peering at him. He craned forward too far, and Chaloner was obliged to catch him before he toppled over. 'Now where was it?'

'Here, I expect,' replied Chaloner, unwilling to mention the club.

'We were just talking about Ferine,' said Hubbert conversationally. 'The poor man who predicted his own death.'

'Actually, he just forecast something unpleasant,' corrected Duncombe. 'Not murder. Yet there are a lot of dangerous people around these days. Perhaps they will kill me, too.'

'Come, Duncombe,' said Hubbert briskly. 'You let grief interfere with your reason.'

'I *do* grieve,' said Duncombe tearfully. 'So did Ferine, because he was never the same after that ghost pushed Grace down the stairs. He locked up his house and forbade anyone to enter it ever again. He said it is infested with evil spirits, and he was right.'

'Nonsense,' said Odowde shortly. 'She probably fell when she was drunk.'

'Then how do you explain the fact that there are at least three other haunted buildings on High Holborn?' demanded Duncombe. 'Wickedness *is* unfolding up there, and nasty people inhabit that road and the surrounding area.'

'What nasty people?' asked Chaloner keenly. 'Fifth Monarchists?'

Duncombe blinked, while Odowde and Hubbert seemed equally bemused.

'Fifth Monarchists?' echoed Odowde, frowning. 'Do they still exist? I thought they had either been executed or locked in Bedlam as lunatics.'

Chaloner questioned the trio a little longer, but learned nothing useful, and was on his way out when his attention was caught by Rupert. This time, the Prince was engaged in conversation with Buckingham, who was entitled to at least a veneer of civility when they were in public, despite their mutual and very obvious antipathy towards each other. Buckingham was holding forth, so Chaloner loitered nearby to listen.

'. . . new comet,' Buckingham was saying enthusiastically. 'Lambe thinks it presages the downfall of an unpopular politician. Clarendon, with any luck.'

'I hope the thing has not appeared to tell us that we will lose the war,' said Rupert gloomily. 'I know I encouraged an opening of hostilities, but Clarendon is right as it happens – the Dutch navy *is* better than ours.'

'Rubbish,' said Buckingham, safe in the knowledge that he would not be called upon to fight it. 'We shall win handily.'

Chaloner started to edge away. Nothing was being said that he did not know already.

'How is your candle factory?' asked the Duke, and there was something in the sly tone of his voice that made Chaloner stop. 'Have you managed to invent one that is less prone to exploding?'

Chaloner frowned. Candles were not prone to exploding at all, so was it a euphemism for something else?

'The project is coming along nicely, thank you,' replied

Rupert stiffly. 'Although I wish we were further ahead. I wanted them installed on all our ships, to give us an edge.'

'There were none on HMS *London*, were there?' asked Buckingham snidely. 'Because something made her ignite with the loss of three hundred lives.'

'Not *my* candles,' said Rupert sharply. 'They are safer than any others. But since you mention *London*, can you verify the whereabouts of your sorcerer when she exploded? He did predict the disaster, and I have always been wary of seers whose prophecies come true.'

'I can, actually,' said Buckingham icily. 'He was with me in Wallingford House, working on the Philosopher's Stone. He is no charlatan. Like his father, he is a man of extraordinary power.'

'Can he *prove* he is kin to the first Lambe?' Rupert did not bother to conceal his scepticism.

'I have a painting of his sire, and the likeness is unmistakeable,' replied Buckingham frostily. 'However, what convinced me most is his skill with alchemy.'

The King arrived at that point, mistress on his arm. He aimed straight for the theatre, and his courtiers rushed to follow. Those who failed to secure seats inside soon disappeared on other business, and the Privy Gallery emptied rapidly. It was not long before only a handful of people remained, along with a few members of the Tangier Committee, which was meeting that morning. Chaloner was on his way out when he saw Sir Alan Brodrick, the Earl's favourite cousin.

'I dined with Prince Rupert last night,' Brodrick whispered, hand to his head. Unlike his prim kinsman, he liked nothing better than a wild party. 'He told me there would be music, but it transpired to be marches played

158

on flageolets.' He shuddered and so did Chaloner – they shared a love of good music, which allowed each to forgive a good deal in the other. 'Afterwards, I felt so low that I went to Temperance's club.'

'It is back in fashion again?'

'Alas, no. It was as dead as a tomb, so I took it upon myself to cheer her up. It was hard work, and I swallowed too much wine in the process. Ah, Mr Pepys! Congratulations on your election to the Royal Society! Is it true that it boasts the finest minds in the country?'

Samuel Pepys was a navy clerk and a member of the Tangier Committee – probably the only one who understood the complex issues discussed. He nodded earnestly at Brodrick's question.

'Indeed it does. The King is a member, and so are the Duke of York and Prince Rupert.'

Chaloner would not have said the King possessed a fine mind, while York was reputed to be actively stupid. However, he was interested to know that Rupert had been elected, especially after the discussion concerning non-exploding candles. The Royal Society was famous for its experiments and inventions, so had the Prince been accepted as a member on the basis of something he had done with explosions that had impressed them? Or had he, like York, simply been able to afford the entrance fee?

'Rupert likes to dabble in alchemy,' said Brodrick, diplomatically not commenting on the other two. 'Have you seen his glass beads that blow up when the tail is broken? Very entertaining, although I should not like to wear a necklace of them.'

Chaloner excused himself and left but did not get far:

159

someone stepped out of the shadows by the door to intercept him.

'Why are you here?' asked Williamson irritably. 'You should be investigating Fifth Monarchists.'

Chaloner did not bother to remind him that he had Ferine's murder to solve, too, which necessitated time spent in White Hall.

'I would investigate them far more efficiently if you told me what is really happening,' he said, equally tart. 'There is more to it than mere rebellion.'

'Jones and Strange's last "mere rebellion" damn near succeeded,' growled Williamson.

'Rupert is making candles,' Chaloner persisted. 'Does that have anything to do with it?'

'Do not be ridiculous,' said Williamson scornfully. 'Now go and thwart these conspirators before they have London awash with blood.'

'I will try, but it would be easier if you removed Leving. Jones and his cronies will see through him soon, at which point they will kill him. And possibly me, too.'

'Then you will just have to be careful,' said Williamson, unmoved.

Chapter 6

Chaloner's first port of call after leaving White Hall was the Talbot, to ask questions about the meetings and those who attended them, so he was disconcerted to discover some fifteen or so of the Sanhedrin already there. They had taken over one of the smaller and more private chambers, where Jones held forth in a sibilant whisper. His words were received with eager appreciation by the others, except Atkinson and Ursula, who sat apart, knees touching under the table. She was showing him a pair of hose she had knitted, paying no attention at all to the hissing, treasonous talk at her side. Also present was Manning, ridiculous in a large hat and oversized cloak.

As he had been eavesdropping all morning, Chaloner decided a little more would not go amiss. He walked outside and identified the window of the conspirators' room. A cart stood nearby, and no one took any notice as he rolled it forward to provide a crude but effective screen while he crouched down to listen. The Sanhedrin really were rank amateurs, he thought in disgust, unimpressed that they should plot next to a window with badly fitting panes. Not only was he able to hear with perfect clarity, but he could see them, too.

'. . . almost ready,' Manning was saying. 'And then we shall strike.'

'I hope thou art right.' Strange sounded angry and sullen. 'Or thou shalt pay the price. It is imperative that Sherwin does what hath been promised.'

'He will,' averred Manning. 'He is too interested in money to let us down.'

'Such delicate cross-stitching,' murmured Atkinson. 'Much finer than mine.'

'I wish Scott were not involved, though,' said Quelch disagreeably. 'I distrust him intensely.'

'You are wise to be suspicious,' said Manning, nodding vehemently. 'I hate the way he has imposed himself on me. Sherwin is *mine*, and he had no right to insinuate himself into my plans.'

'So why did you let him?' asked Jones.

'I had no choice. We were both staying in the Pope's Head, which is cheap now that the taverner will be evicted on Lady Day, and he noticed how solicitous I was of Sherwin. One night, when I was out, he bought Sherwin enough ale to make him garrulous and got the whole story out of him. When I returned, Scott said I could either go into business with him as a partner or he would take the matter to Spymaster Williamson.'

And he was in a position to do it, thought Chaloner. Assuming he had been telling the truth about being in Williamson's pay, of course.

'I prefer to work in silk,' Ursula confided to Atkinson. 'But it is expensive now that war has been declared, like all foreign imports.'

162

'Why did you not kill him?' Quelch asked of Manning. 'I would have done.'

'Kill the Cartographer Royal? I hardly think that would have been sensible, even if he is a sly, manipulative charlatan who would cheat his own mother. I urge you again – do not deal with Scott for any reason. Send all your correspondence to me.'

'Very well,' said Jones. 'But are you *sure* he is not in secret negotiations with the French? Or even the Dutch?'

Manning made a dismissive sound at the back of his throat. 'Even he would not dare to collaborate with enemy states. But I must be off. I dare not leave him with Sherwin for long, lest he poisons him against me – which would be disastrous for the Cause.'

He pulled his hat over his eyes, wrapped his cloak around him, and left by the back door. Chaloner held his breath as the fellow tiptoed past the cart, but Manning did not so much as glance in its direction. When he had gone, Chaloner edged closer to the window, confident now that the Sanhedrin were so inept that they had not even considered the possibility that someone might be watching them. Indeed, he could not recall ever monitoring anyone who paid less heed to security.

'I have penned another pamphlet,' Jones was saying with palpable pride. 'It is about the huge sums of money that were squandered in creating a permanent theatre in White Hall. The Court will watch lewd dramas in it, and it is an abomination.'

'I shall enjoy reading thy thoughts,' declared Strange. He sounded sincere.

'You should not have wasted your time,' countered Quelch. 'This playhouse will not exist after Easter Day, so your thoughts will never be known.'

163

'Of course they will,' said Jones testily. 'I shall publish them in the Last Millennium.'

'Then you will be squandering good money,' flashed Quelch. 'Pamphlets will be costly, even in the Kingdom of Christ, and there is no point wasting funds on issues that will be redundant.'

Jones's voice was icy. 'It will be necessary to remind people that the Stuart usurper spent a fortune on his pleasures while his subjects were crippled by taxes. My tract *will* be published, and decent, God-fearing folk will remember exactly why we ousted him and his profligate Court.'

'Thou speakest the truth,' averred Strange loyally. 'That theatre and those fireworks are a wicked extravagance, and a pamphlet is certainly needed to point it out.'

'More than one,' said Jones crisply. 'I have plenty of thoughts on the matter.'

'I am sure you do,' sneered Quelch nastily.

'Perhaps you will postpone this domestic talk until later,' snapped Jones, venting his pique with Quelch on Atkinson, who was telling Ursula the best way to hem a curtain. 'Tell us what *you* think of Manning's scheme. Or perhaps you will oblige, Mrs Adman? Atkinson claims you are an asset to the Sanhedrin, so let us hear your opinion on the matter.'

The couple's stammered replies suggested that they had paid no attention to the debate, although Atkinson concluded with, 'Manning is a scoundrel, and dealing with him may bring our movement into disrepute. I recommend we have no more to do with him, Sherwin *or* Scott.'

'I agree,' said Ursula. 'None of them are very nice.'

'We should kidnap Sherwin and get him to reveal his

164

secrets to us directly,' said Quelch. 'Cut out Manning and Scott altogether.'

'How?' asked Jones archly. '*You* signed a legally binding agreement with one of them. I advised against it, but you forged ahead anyway, just to further some spat between yourself and Strange.'

'It was more complicated than that,' objected Quelch stiffly. 'But I have no problem breaking my agreement with Manning. He claims to be a Fifth Monarchist, but he is more interested in money than the Glorious Design, and such men do not deserve fair play.'

'Then thou art a villain,' declared Strange. 'King Jesus will not approve that sort of thing.'

'It is you who is the villain,' snarled Quelch. 'And while we are on the subject of villains, Chaloner is one, too. I know his uncle was an admirable man, and the tale about being dismissed by Clarendon is true – I checked it myself – but the younger Chaloner's timely appearance is suspicious. I vote we kill him before he betrays us.'

'He will not betray us,' said Atkinson. 'He seems a decent soul.'

'Besides, he knows nothing to our detriment,' said Jones. 'But treachery is a particularly loathsome vice, and I shall write a pamphlet on it in the Last Millennium.'

'I should go.' Strange stood, looming over the others. 'Art thou sure thou must burden me with thy company, Quelch? I would far rather go alone.'

'I imagine so,' growled Quelch. 'But I trust you even less than Manning and Chaloner.'

When the meeting broke up, Chaloner was faced with a dilemma. Which of the Sanhedrin might be persuaded to confide in him? He doubted the fanatical Jones or

165

Strange would oblige, while Atkinson and Ursula seemed more interested in each other than insurrection and probably knew little of import. He decided to pick whichever of the others set off alone.

Unfortunately, Jones announced that he was going to read aloud from one of his pamphlets, and everyone except Quelch, Strange, Atkinson and Ursula went to listen. Chaloner followed the smaller group, in the hope that Quelch would eventually be on his own – the watchmaker might provide answers if Chaloner threatened to expose his criminal past. Again, the conspirators revealed their lack of professionalism by not looking behind them once to ensure they were not being followed, which allowed Chaloner to come so close that he was almost within touching distance.

They passed Gray's Inn, and Atkinson stopped outside a shop. The swinging sign above the door said it was his own, the place where he made stockings.

'Here is a quince cake,' said Ursula, handing him a parcel with a sweet smile that revealed the depth of her affection for him. 'For your assistant, Old Ned.'

'It will be wasted on him,' declared Quelch, eyeing it greedily. 'We had better eat it instead. Then you can be assured that it will be used to fuel the Almighty's work.'

'For once, he speaketh the truth,' said Strange. 'It should not be wasted on the ungodly.'

Ursula glowed at the praise, and all four trooped inside to cut it up. Chaloner went in, too, pulling his hat low as he pretended to admire a display of stockings. No one gave him a second glance, because Old Ned immediately began to wail that he had never been so busy in his life – Lady Day was generating a lot of extra business, and orders were coming in faster than they could be filled.

166

Even as he spoke, more customers arrived, including a wealthy merchant who was irked when told that his twelve pairs of woollen hose were not yet ready.

'You shall have them tomorrow,' promised Atkinson. 'Even if it means me working all night.'

Mollified, the merchant left, at which point Old Ned began to bleat that the task was impossible. He faltered into silence when Ursula shrugged out of her coat.

'I am as talented with a needle as I am at baking,' she declared, sitting at the table. 'Your merchant will be fortunate to have stockings stitched by me. Now hand me some thread.'

'I suppose we might manage if you help,' Old Ned conceded. 'Especially if we send for Snowflake as well.' He glanced hopefully at Strange and Quelch. 'Can you two sew?'

'Not me,' said Quelch hastily. 'And I have more important work to do.'

Strange could not reply because his mouth was full of quince cake. So was Quelch's the moment they were outside, and both were so intent on eating that Chaloner felt he could have trodden on their heels and they would not have noticed. They passed St Giles-in-the-Fields, and his heart sank when he saw where they were heading – to Tyburn, a field west of the city where a permanent gibbet had been erected. The road was busy, and there was an atmosphere of excited anticipation. There was going to be an execution, and Strange and Quelch intended to watch.

Hoping that Quelch might follow the 'entertainment' with a session in a tavern, where he could be plied with drink and questions, Chaloner followed the pair through the throng, learning from snippets of overheard conversation that eight unfortunates were to die that day – four thieves, a witch and three traitors. The witch was unusual, and scuffles broke out as people vied for places that would afford them the best view of her death.

Chaloner had never seen Tyburn so busy, the crowds swollen by Lady Day visitors. Vendors were out in force to provide them with anything they might need – cushions to sit on, ale, pies and oranges. There was even a 'Gentleman of Ease' – a man with a bucket and a voluminous cloak that acted as a screen when his arms were outstretched – who provided a service for those who did not want the inconvenience of finding a bush.

Pickpockets abounded, although none bothered Chaloner, perhaps because he wore a sword and looked as though he knew how to use it. That did not stop the whores, though, who had arrived in droves, distinctive in their scanty clothing and rouged cheeks. Repelling their advances, he watched Strange and Quelch fight forward until they were at the scaffold itself, although he had no desire to be so close to it and did not follow. A distant cheer told him that the carts bearing the prisoners were approaching.

Soon it was bedlam, with the mob yelling abuse or encouragement and the condemned bellowing back. The thieves were cheerfully defiant, jesting with their hecklers and laughing carelessly. The witch looked frightened, though, and the rebels – identifiable by their finer clothes – were white-faced and sullen.

All were unloaded and forced to climb the steps to where the nooses awaited. A chaplain followed, chanting a psalm, but the hangman, unsettled by the unruly throng that pressed noisily around the platform, began to dispatch the thieves before the priest had finished. The onlookers were outraged, and surged forward as a solid, angry mass. The guards drew cutlasses and started beating them back, but not before two of the dangling burglars had been cut down and spirited away by friends, although whether dead or alive was impossible to say.

The man next to Chaloner chuckled his delight at the spectacle. He was a butcher, identifiable by his thick leather apron and the lingering smell of old blood. 'I wish this would happen more often! Hangings have been dull since the Restoration.' He consulted the programme that had been printed for the occasion. 'The three traitors are next.'

He handed the leaflet to Chaloner, who read that the trio had stolen five hundred pounds from the treasury in Taunton for the purposes of funding a rebellion.

'Look!' the butcher crowed. 'They are going to make speeches. This promises to be fun!'

It was a time-honoured tradition that the condemned should have an opportunity to vent in their last moments, and all three pulled reams of notes from their pockets, clearly aiming to make the most of it. Unfortunately for them, the guards were unnerved by what had happened with the thieves and wanted the rebels dead as soon as possible. The executioner agreed, because two were shoved into oblivion before they could say a word. The pages flew from their hands, and Chaloner saw Strange furiously punching the other spectators away so that Quelch could snatch the fluttering sheets from the air. The third insurgent howled at the top of his voice, contorting himself violently to avoid the noose being placed over his head.

'The money was for them – for Strange and Quelch!

169

They promised to buy weapons, but they betrayed us, and I will tell you everything if you let me live. I know secrets, such as the cannon—'

The rest of his sentence was lost as Strange began to pray in a mighty bellow that drowned out all else. Disturbed by the word *cannon*, Chaloner shoved his way forward, but the crowd was too dense and all three prisoners were dead by the time he made any headway. Strange was shouldering his way away from the scaffold, Quelch trailing in his wake as he stuffed the speeches in his pockets. Both stopped when they saw Chaloner.

'What are you doing here?' demanded Quelch.

'The same as thou, of course,' answered Strange, before Chaloner could speak for himself. 'Watching the death of martyrs to the Cause.'

'Is it true?' asked Chaloner. 'Did they steal money for your rebellion?'

'You ask too many questions,' hissed Quelch. 'Desist, or I will slit your throat.'

'Ignore him,' said Strange, when the watchmaker had slouched away. 'He hath an evil-temper – which will see him in hell, because Jesus will not permit such behaviour in the Glorious Design.'

'Did that rebel mention cannon?' asked Chaloner, unsettled enough to be blunt. 'If so, you should let me see them before Easter Day, or I may not be able to—'

'All will be revealed in time,' interrupted Strange serenely. 'Curb thy impatience.'

Grinning wildly, he began to push his way through the crowd again. Chaloner stared after him for a moment, then turned to follow Quelch, but it was the witch's turn to die and the crowd strained forward suddenly, trapping him in a tight press of bodies. Alarmed by the surge, the

170

hangman hurried to complete his grisly task, but the witch began to shriek, terrified, piercing howls that cut through the mob's excited babble. An eerie silence descended.

'Behold, the black clouds of hell,' came another voice, so loud and shrill that it startled a flock of crows, which flapped away from their tree in a panicky flurry. Chaloner glanced up to see that heavy rainclouds had drifted in while the executions had been under way. It was coincidence, but the people around him began to whisper about omens and portents of doom.

'Satan is coming!' screamed the voice again. 'I see him in the sky on a black charger.'

There was instant pandemonium. People began to claw and shove as they struggled to escape. Too many tried to climb over the scaffold, which had not been designed to accommodate such weight, and collapsed with a groan. The agonised cries of the injured did nothing to calm matters, and the guards, seeing the situation was beyond their control, abandoned their duties and fled. It was then that Chaloner saw Eliza Hatton.

She was standing on a cartwheel, one of a number of semi-permanent structures that had been erected to ensure those spectators at the back could be guaranteed a decent view. There was an expression on her cold, beautiful face that was difficult to read, and he wondered whether it had been she doing the yelling. He started to make his way towards her, but by the time he had fought his way across the stream of stampeding people she had gone.

He was about to begin battling his way towards the exit when a scrap of white caught his eye. It was a page from one of the speeches, overlooked when Quelch had grabbed the others. It was trampled, muddy and torn, but still legible. He picked it up, and read that the three 'martyrs' planned to rise from the dead at the Last Millennium, and would repay their executioners by dispensing some judgements of their own. One sentence made his blood run cold though:

O come Glorious Design on Easter Daye, and smite thy enemies with Silver Cannon until the streetes of Olde Lundun runne fulle with the Blacke Bloud of the ungodly.

Was that what the High Holborn Plot entailed? Using cannon on the city? Thurloe was wrong to dismiss their scheme as of no consequence – it promised to be one of the most deadly yet!

Feeling the need for company after the unedifying mêlée at Tyburn, Chaloner aimed for the Thames, to the Folly, or Floating Coffee House. This was a timber shed atop a barge, which was moored by the Somerset Stairs. It was usually anchored midstream, obliging patrons to hire a boat to row them there, but it was being repaired that day and so needed to be tied up at a pier. It had once been a fashionable place, but the river had not been kind to it, and peeling paintwork, rising mildew and the reek of seaweed and sewage meant that modish men had taken their custom elsewhere.

This suited its current patrons, who were mostly sea-officers, for whom the steady rock of waves was a joy rather than a reason to dash for the side. It was the favourite haunt of Captain Lester, whom Chaloner had met the previous autumn. Their friendship had been sealed when Lester, master of the ship that had been wrecked en route to Russia, had insisted on accompanying Chaloner to help him complete his mission for the Earl.

Chaloner climbed aboard and opened the door. There was no heating, so it was bitterly cold, but its atmosphere was relaxed and cordial, and he liked it much more than when it had been frequented by the rakes of Court.

'Tom!' exclaimed Lester in delight. He turned to his companions. 'This is the fellow I was telling you about – the Lord Chancellor's envoy, who risked all to rescue me when I was trapped by falling wreckage on my sinking ship.'

'Hardly,' said Chaloner, disliking the immediate attention the introduction earned. Moreover, he wanted that particular tale kept quiet, lest anyone asked whether the Earl's jewels might not be lying at the bottom of the sea if vital moments had not been spent on saving the captain.

'You are too modest.' Lester took Chaloner's arm and guided him to a place where they could talk undisturbed. 'Have you come to congratulate me on my good fortune? I have just been given *Swiftsure*. We join the Channel Fleet on Monday – word is that the Dutch are planning an invasion, so we must put to sea as soon as possible.'

Chaloner stirred his coffee to mask his dismay. He did not want Lester cut in two by a Dutch cannonball, or drowned, shot or dead of gangrenous wounds. He had known the decision to go to war would mean casualties, but the reality of a friend taking part drove it home with a nasty jab.

'I am happy for you,' he managed to say. 'Is *Swiftsure* a good command?'

173

Lester grinned. 'The best! We shall see action for certain, because Admiral Lawson has the Channel Fleet and he likes a good battle.'

'Lawson,' said Chaloner. 'I need some information about him.'

'An outstanding seaman. He has had the Channel Fleet for years – first for Parliament, and now for the King. He was dismissed at the Restoration, but his men threatened to mutiny unless he was reinstated, so the government was forced to oblige. His enemies were livid, of course.'

'He has enemies?'

'There is no one like him for seamanship, but he is a fool on land. He is probably a Fifth Monarchist, and has the peculiar notion that God has appointed him to smite His foes.'

'How do you know he is a Fifth Monarchist?'

'Sailors gossip, and he has been seen at their meetings. But a man's creed is his own affair, as far as I am concerned, and none of anyone else's business.'

'I beg to differ. Fifth Monarchists are dangerous radicals, so should one really be put in control of a lot of powerful warships?'

'His beliefs will not affect his skill in battle,' argued Lester. 'So what does it matter if they are a little eccentric?'

'Well, there is the fact that his flagship blew up for a start. Perhaps that can be laid at the door of his unorthodox religious convictions.'

'What a terrible thing to say!' cried Lester, loudly enough to make several of his cronies glance towards him. He lowered his voice. 'Three hundred prime seamen died in that incident. It was a terrible tragedy, and we are still reeling from the shock of it.'

'*Incident*,' pounced Chaloner, regarding him intently. 'Not *accident?*'

Lester looked away. 'The official explanation is that someone was preparing cannon-charges using old papers, and there was a mishap. Yet even the most inane fellow knows that gunpowder and naked flames must be kept apart, and it was not a task that would have been delegated to a stupid man, anyway.'

'So what do you think happened?'

Lester's expression was troubled. 'I am not sure, but look at the facts. *London* was sailing up the estuary towards the city for which she was named, where she would have received a rapturous welcome. All hands would have been on deck, either to help shorten sail as she reached narrower waters, or to bask in the glory. No one would have been below.'

'It would only take one man with a candle to do the damage – the purser, perhaps, making an inventory, or a novice not knowing where he should be.'

'We do not allow novices to wander around unsupervised, while I knew the purser – he would have been on deck watching seabirds. Moreover, we always keep powder magazines locked and guarded. The matter reeks, Tom, and I suspect sabotage – although I cannot believe that Lawson's religious views had anything to do with it.'

'The Dutch, then? They are the ones who will benefit.'

'Perhaps. I have been quizzing the survivors, but I have learned nothing as yet.'

'Maybe you will have answers on Wednesday, when she is weighed.' Chaloner thought about Dr Lambe's prediction. 'Unless the attempt fails, of course.'

'It will fail, and I cannot imagine why Lawson, who is the driving force behind the scheme, wants to try.

175

Jeffrey Dare had command of her when she sank, and I hope he never finds out what is planned. He is devastated by what happened, and if he ever learns that they aim to disturb the tomb that *London* has become . . .'

'How did he survive when so many of his crew did not?'

'Because he was at the top of the foremast when the explosion occurred, although he does not consider himself fortunate. No captain likes to live while his ship and crew go down, as I told you when we had our own disaster in the ice recently.'

Night had fallen by the time Chaloner left the Folly. He was walking along the Strand towards home, wondering if Hannah's pickled ling pie would be waiting for him, when a carriage splashed to a halt at his side. It was an unusually fine one, with the crest of the Barber-Surgeons emblazoned on the door.

'You are very elusive,' said Wiseman crossly. 'I have been looking for you all day. Snowflake has something to tell you, and you are to visit the club to hear it. Are you free now?'

'I was about to go home.'

'This will not take long, and Snowflake said it was urgent. Do you like this carriage, by the way? A private conveyance is one of the perks of being Master.'

Wiseman talked the entire way to Hercules' Pillars Alley, mostly about a sudden demand for his services at White Hall. He was pleased and annoyed in equal measure.

'I like the additional work, as it means more money. However, most people want me to prescribe preventatives for various ailments: boils, toothache, canker, plague. But

176

I am a surgeon – I prefer it when they actually *have* those things.'

'You wish ill health on your customers?' asked Chaloner in distaste.

'Of course! A healthy body is of no use to me, and averting trouble means less work in the future, so I am faced with a quandary. Shall I do as they ask, knowing it is cutting my own throat financially, or refuse and risk them taking their custom to another *medicus*?'

'A difficult choice indeed,' murmured Chaloner.

The club looked warm and welcoming with its lamps shining through the gloom of the wet winter evening, but inside the atmosphere was strained – Temperance was putting far too much effort into pretending that all was well when it was clearly not. None of her favourite guests were there, and the few clients who had deigned to appear did not know how to create the air of joyous frivolity for which the place was famous. She came to talk to him, Belle at her heels.

'I was wrong when I said our clients would flock back once you had proved that none of them killed Ferine,' Temperance whispered. She was pale, and some of the brightness had gone from her eyes. 'They still keep their distance.'

'It is as dead as a tomb,' added Belle unhappily. 'Snowflake's stepbrother wrote, asking her to help him sew new stockings, and when she declined to leave in case you came, Maude went instead – something that would have been impossible on a normal night.'

'Where is Snowflake?' asked Chaloner.

'In the stable,' replied Temperance. 'She has a way with horses, and always goes there when she is troubled. You see, her father told her something when he stopped

177

by for a chat earlier, but she refuses to share what he said with anyone but you. She says it is important.'

'Her father did not come to see *her*,' said Belle in disgust. 'He came for a free meal and the chance to hold forth. And he asked for money.'

'He is a perfumer, who lives at Temple Mills in Hackney Marsh,' explained Temperance. 'It is not a very suitable place for that sort of trade, and he is always on the verge of ruin. Are you close to exposing the culprit, Tom? I do not think I can bear many more evenings like this.'

'I have made some progress,' said Chaloner, following her into the yard. 'For example, there are connections linking Ferine to Dr Lambe, who was here that night.'

'He was,' agreed Temperance. 'But he is not the killer, thank God – the Duke would never forgive me if we deprived him of his sorcerer! Fortunately, Dr Lambe has an alibi in me: he was telling my fortune when Ferine died.'

'Are you sure?' Chaloner was disappointed. It would have been an easy solution, and the Earl would have been delighted to learn that his arch-enemy Buckingham had recruited a murderer to his household.

'Quite sure. He did not leave the parlour all evening, and any number of girls will confirm it. He was having too much fun showing off his witchy skills to an admiring audience.' She opened the stable door and unclipped the lamp from the sconce. 'Snowflake? Tom is here at last.'

There was no answer, so Chaloner took the lantern and began to hunt for her in the stalls, wondering if she had grown tired of waiting and had slipped off to do a little moonlighting in a tavern. He was wrong. Snowflake was lying on the floor, her eyes open but unseeing, and it was clear that she had been dead for some time.

Sobbing brokenly, Temperance hurried away to fetch Wiseman, but when Chaloner turned the body over, he did not need a surgeon to tell him that Snowflake had been stabbed. He sat back on his heels and considered what might have happened. Anyone could walk into the yard from the lane, so it would have been easy for an assailant to reach her. Splatters of blood told him where she had been standing when she was attacked – near a large bay gelding, bought solely to impress the club's customers. It was agitated, so he soothed it with gentle words, rubbing its velvety nose.

'If you crooned as lovingly to Hannah, your marriage would be more of a success,' remarked Wiseman, arriving in a flurry of swirling red cloak. His grin faded when he knelt next to Snowflake. 'Damn! She was only a child. Curse the villain who did this vile thing!'

'Yes,' agreed Chaloner soberly.

Wiseman began his examination. 'She was killed with something long and sharp – not a knife, but some other implement. A single blow, expertly delivered. Death would have been all but instant.'

Chaloner searched the stable, but there was nothing in it that matched the description of the murder weapon.

'I should have bought her a horoscope,' wept Temperance. 'Lambe – or better yet, Ferine – would have predicted what was going to happen, and we could have avoided it.'

'I am not sure that is how horoscopes work,' said Chaloner, but Belle was already leading her away to be comforted in the kitchen.

'Lambe would disagree,' said Wiseman. 'He claims that future misfortunes *can* be averted if appropriate precautions are taken – which is why so many courtiers have been after me for prophylactics of late.'

Chaloner raised his eyebrows. 'In other words, he forecasts things that never come to pass?'

'Not entirely, because two people failed to follow his advice and have lived to regret it: Hubbert was punched in an altercation with a servant, while Odowde fell down the Banqueting House stairs and hurt his arm. He screamed most piteously, although there was barely a bruise.'

'Was Lambe nearby when it happened?' asked Chaloner, thinking of sly elbows.

'No, he was with the King, discussing comets. Why?'

'Odowde just fell? No one pushed him?'

Wiseman's expression hardened. 'He was acting the goat, imitating Clarendon's waddle while the Court cackled its amusement. No one was near him – he simply stumbled and fell. I was there and I saw it all.'

Chaloner was perplexed. *Did* Lambe possess an ability to see the future, or had it just been a lucky guess? If Odowde was in the habit of fooling around, then perhaps he had fallen over before, and Lambe's 'prediction' was based on probability. Wiseman cut across his thoughts.

'What are you going to do about Snowflake? Clearly, her murder is connected to Ferine's – someone does not want it solved, and killed her lest she remembered something to help you.'

'Ferine died days ago, and she would have been dispatched long before now if that were the case. She must have been stabbed to prevent her from revealing whatever she had learned from her father – the information she refused to share with anyone but me. However, I doubt a perfumer living in Hackney Marsh knows anything about Ferine.'

Wiseman stared at him. 'Are you suggesting that she knew about a second matter that warranted her being stabbed? That does not sound very likely!'

'No,' agreed Chaloner. 'Are you sure she did not confide in anyone else?'

'Positive.' Wiseman shrugged. 'You will have to visit Temple Mills and speak to her sire. You can take this wicked bay horse and exercise it at the same time.'

'I cannot leave London. I have investigations that—'

'Yes, and one of them is Snowflake,' interrupted Wiseman shortly. 'I would offer to go with you, but the sudden demand for my services at Court means I am too busy.'

Before Chaloner could say that *he* was too busy as well, there was a commotion and Atkinson entered the stable at a run. Maude was gasping at his heels, indicating with an apologetic shrug that she had been unable to stop him. Atkinson faltered when he saw his stepsister's body.

'When Temperance's note arrived, I thought it was a horrible joke. I did not believe . . . But who could have done such a terrible thing?'

'Chaloner will find out,' promised Wiseman; Chaloner shot him a pained glance. 'Her murder will *not* go unpunished.'

'I sat sewing stockings all day,' gulped Atkinson unsteadily, 'while she was stalked by a fiend! How can I live with myself now? She needed me and I failed her.'

'You were not to know,' said Maude kindly, patting his arm. 'Neither was I, or I would not have sat sewing

181

stockings with you. But Tom will catch her killer, never fear.'

Chaloner muttered a few awkward words of sympathy and slipped away, glad to leave the grieving stockinger in Maude's matronly hands. It was cowardly, but his skills lay in other areas, and he decided he *would* do whatever was necessary to bring Snowflake's killer to justice, hopefully without travelling to Hackney Marsh. He had liked Snowflake, and was sorry she was dead.

He considered where best to start. The obvious way forward was to continue monitoring the Fifth Monarchists, given that Snowflake had been one of them. Perhaps she had been eliminated because someone did not want a prostitute on the books when the New Kingdom dawned. He was reluctant to approach the Sanhedrin directly, knowing they would deny all knowledge of the crime, and that would be that. He wondered who else he could ask. Then he remembered Admiral Lawson, who was counted among their number. A discussion with *him* would not go amiss, regardless. He said as much to Wiseman, who had followed him out into Hercules' Pillars Alley.

'That can be arranged. He is my patient, and it is time he was bled again. I am busy, as I said, but not too busy to help with the matter of Snowflake. We shall visit him together now.' Wiseman shot Chaloner a sidelong glance. 'Do you think *he* killed her?'

'Not really, but he might have information to tell me who did. And if that does not work, I will go to Temple Mills.'

'Good. Her father is called Grisley Pate.' Wiseman saw Chaloner's eyebrows go up. 'It is his real name, I

182

assure you. And you had better not refer to her as Snowflake. She was christened Constance, although she was known to her family as Consti.'

'Consti Pate?' mused Chaloner. 'No wonder she changed it to Snowflake.'

He climbed into the Barber-Surgeons' carriage, and they travelled in silence to Duck Lane, where the Admiral lived in a smart brick house. A servant answered the door, and escorted them to a neat parlour where Lawson was entertaining. He had perhaps a dozen guests, none quite comfortable in their fashionable clothes; Chaloner surmised that they were family from the north, making an effort to adapt to strange new London ways.

'Bleed me?' asked Lawson in surprise, when the surgeon announced his intention. 'But you did that last week.' He regarded Chaloner warily. 'And why is he here?'

'The loss of your ship *London* was a nasty shock,' explained Wiseman, ignoring the second question. 'Bleeding will prevent any illness arising from it. After all, we cannot afford to lose you on the brink of war.'

But Lawson was still staring at Chaloner. 'Temperance North's whore-house,' he said, snapping his fingers as memories surfaced. 'I have seen you there twice now.'

Chaloner was perturbed to learn that he had been noticed. Lawson was obviously an observant man, suggesting there was more to the coarse-tongued, cantankerous sailor than met the eye.

'The *club* is an excellent place,' said Wiseman, loyally using the term Temperance preferred. 'You should treat your guests to an evening there.'

'Too expensive,' growled Lawson. 'And they are only family – they do not warrant that sort of outlay. Yet they have been out of sorts since *London* went down. They were aboard her, you see, so I should probably do something to set their humours right. Will you bleed them, too?'

Wiseman's eyes gleamed at the prospect of a larger fee, and Lawson set about jostling his hapless kin into a queue. Naturally enough, they began talking about the disaster.

'It was awful,' said a man who looked enough like Lawson to be a brother. His expression was bleak. 'We would have died, too, had we not been able to swim.'

'And we were on the *right* side of the ship,' added a cousin. 'The explosion was on the left, so we missed the worst of it. Even so, I was blown overboard.'

'We were all fortunate,' said a small, pale woman. 'I was being sick at the time, and it was leaning over the rail that saved me.'

'Did you notice anything odd?' asked Chaloner. 'Did anyone go below decks shortly before the blast? Or did you see someone who should not have been aboard?'

There was a general chorus of denials, while Lawson growled that the King's navy did not allow just anyone to saunter about on its vessels. Crews knew their mates, and strangers were discovered long before they could do any harm.

'People think it is suspicious that we survived when so many sailors did not,' said the cousin. 'But we owe our lives to where we were standing and our ability to float.'

Chaloner nodded, but he thought it odd, too. Had they set the explosion, then retreated to a place where they knew they would be safe? If so, had they acted with or without Lawson's connivance? And why had Lawson not been on *London* himself?

184

'I was busy,' said Lawson, when Chaloner put the question. 'Not that it is any of your affair.'

'What do *you* think happened?'

Lawson shrugged, but his eyes were sly. 'Some daft bugger was playing with naked flames in the powder hold, although Captain Dare assures me that it was locked. We shall find out when she is weighed next Wednesday.'

While Wiseman poked at the Admiral's veins with a blade that was already stained with gore from previous victims, Chaloner took advantage of Lawson's enforced immobility.

'I understand you are a Fifth Monarchist,' he began.

Lawson regarded him narrowly. 'So what? Or are you one of those rogues who dislikes the notion of being ruled by King Jesus? Personally, I relish the thought. Why do you think I have spent so many years smiting His enemies?'

Chaloner's next question was as aggressive as Lawson's last answer. 'What did Jones and Quelch want with you at the club on the night that Ferine was murdered?'

Lawson glared at him. 'Mind your own damn business!'

'Did you know Snowflake?'

'Not in the Biblical sense. She is too skinny, and I like a woman with proper hips, not ones like a cabin boy's. Have you finished, Wiseman? Good. Here is your fee. Good day.'

Chaloner did not like being ousted before he had learned what he needed to know, but he could not force the Admiral to talk to him – at least, not with a dozen kinsmen ready to surge to the rescue if he resorted to rougher methods. Reluctantly, he followed the surgeon outside.

'There are other lines of enquiry to pursue first,' he

185

said, even more determined to learn whether Lawson was connected to Snowflake's death, the Fifth Monarchists' machinations *and* the tragic fate of *London*. 'But if they do not work, I will go to Temple Mills.'

Snowflake's murder had left Chaloner in low spirits and he did not feel like going home, so he began to walk to Chancery Lane. It was raining again, and the mud was more treacherous than ever. He pressed himself against the wall of a house when a dung-wagon lumbered past, flinging up filth as it went.

The Pope's Head was busy because its landlord was selling his ale cheaply so there would not be any left when the lease expired. Sherwin had made the most of the situation, and was slumped in a semi-conscious haze, surrounded by empty pots. Scott and Manning were with him, arguing so fiercely that they did not notice Chaloner until he had been listening for some time.

'. . . a great deal of money,' Manning was whispering. 'You should appreciate that.'

'Oh, I do,' hissed Scott. 'But that is my point. We have a fabulous resource, and we should exploit it to the full. Pellissary will pay far more than the rebels – who I do not trust, anyway.'

'I suppose they are the kind of men to claim that ushering in the Last Millennium should be reward enough,' conceded Manning, his rueful tone telling Chaloner that his devotion to the Cause was rather less powerful than his devotion to lucre. 'However, I gave them my word . . .'

'Well, I did not give them mine,' said Scott. 'And the scheme belongs to me, too. You would not have come this far were it not for me, so I have a say in what

186

happens. Look at how I dealt with John Browne. And I suggest we hear what Pellissary has to offer. He—'

He stopped speaking abruptly when he became aware of Chaloner. Anger flashed in his eyes; fear flared in Manning's.

Chaloner's mind spun with questions. Prynne had mentioned overhearing Scott talking about John Browne, and here was the name again. Chaloner had a feeling that Browne might transpire to be very important – perhaps even the key to understanding what was going on. However, there was a more pressing matter to be pursued first.

'Do you refer to Georges Pellissary, treasurer of the French navy?' he asked mildly. 'You intend to sell your secret to him, instead of my associates at the Talbot?'

Manning gulped, but Scott only smiled. 'We were debating options, like any entrepreneurs worth their salt.'

'I would have thought that your post as Cartographer Royal would preclude you from favouring foreign countries over your own,' said Chaloner.

'France is not an enemy state,' Scott pointed out.

'No, but it is not entirely friendly, either,' countered Chaloner. 'And I have a feeling that you might even deal with the Dutch if the price was right.'

Manning was horrified. 'Of course we would not!'

'You are a fool, Scott,' said Chaloner in disgust when the New Englander made no attempt to deny it. 'You will end up hanged at Tyburn.'

'Not me,' said Scott smugly. 'I have powerful protectors who appreciate my worth.'

'Williamson will not defend you if you treat with Holland,' warned Chaloner.

'Williamson?' squeaked Manning, regarding Scott in

187

alarm. 'The Spymaster? Why should he defend you? Surely you do not know him?'

'I have him in my pocket,' bragged Scott. 'Why do you think our little scheme has been allowed to run? Because he has been promised a percentage – which is another reason why we must secure ourselves the best possible deal. We cannot have *him* disappointed.'

Manning looked as though he might be sick, while Chaloner's heart sank. Williamson did accept bribes, and if Scott was telling the truth – unlikely given his penchant for lies, but still a possibility – the case would be even more difficult to solve.

'I strongly recommend you forget about us, Chaloner,' said Scott, smug in his unassailability. 'Ours is just a small money-making venture, not worth your attention.'

Manning nodded vigorously. 'We are peddling furniture. Good bureaux are almost impossible to come by these days, especially in walnut. Sherwin has devised a way to—'

'It is time he was in bed,' said Scott, bringing a sudden and decisive end to the conversation. He stood, took the slumbering drunk's arm, and hauled him away.

Chaloner stopped Manning before he could follow. 'You are swimming in dangerous waters, and your only chance to avoid the noose is to tell me what is going on. Who is Sherwin? What secret does he hold? And who is Browne?'

But Manning pulled away from him angrily. 'Do not try to browbeat me. Scott said you were not to be trusted, and he was right – there was something wrong with the box of gunpowder you returned to me yesterday – it would not burn and it reeked of rotten eggs. You tampered with it.'

Chaloner was about to put his questions more forcefully when the landlord appeared, six burly patrons at his heels.

'Is anything wrong, Manning?' he asked. 'I do not like to see my regulars harassed, and you appear to be anxious.'

'I am anxious,' said Manning in relief. 'Show this man the door, if you please.'

Chaloner backed away with his hands in the air before they could oblige. The room was too small to allow him to wield his sword effectively, and he doubted he could best them without it. He left frustrated that he still had more questions than answers.

He visited the Swan afterwards, listening outside its door just long enough to hear its customers discussing the witch who had been hanged at Tyburn. They were indignant and bitter, and he was under the impression that some of them had known and admired her. However, there was no sign of Eliza, and when he went in and asked where she was, he was greeted with instant suspicion and a good deal of hostility. He left quickly, deciding to press his luck no further.

His next stop was the Talbot. Strange and Quelch were there with several members of the Sanhedrin, so he insinuated himself into their company, and learned that it was a gathering to honour the three executed men from Taunton.

'I wish *I* had been there,' said a man Chaloner thought was named Tucker – an old sailor with ruddy cheeks and one arm. 'To cheer their first step towards paradise.'

'It was a humbling sight,' declared Quelch piously. 'They died calling on God to avenge them by establishing his Kingdom at Easter. The Last Millennium will certainly come in ten days now.'

'It will, because God hath sent us a sign,' added Strange. 'At Tyburn Field, the skies turned black and Jesus appeared in the clouds. He is impatient for His throne.'

'I heard those clouds were summoned by the witch,' said Tucker doubtfully. 'And that it was the devil who rode across the sky.'

'Rubbish,' said Quelch shortly. 'It was a scene akin to the Crucifixion, and would have awed you all. But let us drink to our success. To the Fifth Monarchy!'

'How can we drink when we do not know what is intended?' asked Tucker, not raising his cup. Neither did a number of others. 'We are the Sanhedrin, yet we are told nothing.'

'What do you need to know, other than that the Kingdom of Christ is imminent?' asked Quelch archly. 'And that He will acknowledge you when he is on His throne in White Hall?'

'But first, thou shalt be awed by mighty explosions.' Strange indicated Chaloner with a nod of his head. 'Our new gunpowder expert will light the heavens with glory.'

'Using silver cannon,' elaborated Chaloner, watching for a reaction as he quoted from the condemned men's speeches. 'And the streets will run red with the blood of unbelievers.'

'*Black* with the blood of unbelievers,' corrected Quelch, regarding Chaloner with an expression the spy could not begin to read. '*Our* blood is red; theirs is black.'

'Speaking of unbelievers, who is this John Browne I keep hearing about?' asked Tucker, bringing hard, challenging eyes to bear on Strange and Quelch. 'Scott says

190

he is no one who can influence our plans, but Manning claims he is a dangerous foe.'

'Scott is right – Browne is not important,' replied Strange, with a feeble attempt at airy. 'Thou needst not worry.'

'But I *am* worried,' pressed Tucker. 'And while we are on the subject of causes for concern, I do not like Atkinson. He thinks too much. But more importantly, the stockings he made for me to wear on Judgement Day shrank in the wash.'

Chaloner almost choked over his ale. He had never heard that given as a reason to distrust a fellow rebel before – and he had heard many odd claims during his years in espionage.

'Perhaps the water was too hot,' suggested Quelch helpfully. 'I lost a lovely pair of drawers to excessive heat last year, and I have learned that hand-temperature yields the best results for wool.'

'Rubbish,' declared Strange. '*Cold* water is best. Anything else maketh the colours run.'

'What do you know of fabrics?' snapped Quelch, nettled by the contradiction. 'You are a mere Baptist pastor, with no practical skills.'

And then an argument was under way, leaving Chaloner thinking that if the Sanhedrin could not agree on how to do their laundry, then how did they expect to run the New Kingdom? However, he could see he was going to learn nothing useful by prolonging his visit, and Quelch, still the best Fifth Monarchist to drag somewhere quiet and interrogate, was clearly going nowhere soon. With a grimace, he supposed he would have to tackle the watchmaker another day. He made his excuses to the plotters, and walked outside.

191

He stopped at Middle Row on his way along High Holborn, and peered through Ursula's window. She was sitting by a fire with a cat on her lap, knitting. He knocked, and was rewarded with a beaming smile as she opened the door. The delicious scent of baking wafted out.

'What a pleasant surprise!' she exclaimed. 'And you are just in time. I have just taken a Double Tart from the oven, and I wager it will be the best thing you have ever tasted.'

'Are you limping?' Chaloner followed her inside, ignoring the voice in his head that told him he should be going home to Hannah.

'I slipped over on my way home from John—from Mr Atkinson's shop. I was helping him make stockings, you see. I have never known such foul mud, and my cat refuses to go out in it.'

'His sister is dead,' said Chaloner bluntly.

Ursula nodded sadly. 'I was in his shop when the message came – not with him, but out at the back pre-paring more silk thread. I heard the commotion and hurried in, but he and Maude had gone. I decided to come home, as Old Ned can finish the stocking order alone now, and I have no wish to intrude on John—Mr Atkinson's private grief.'

They sat in contemplative silence for a while, then Ursula went to fetch the tart from the kitchen. It was a stunning creation – an open case containing apples and a custard of cream, sugar and spices – and Chaloner ate three generous slices while she chatted about the Sanhedrin.

'Mr Jones is prone to chills, so I am knitting him a scarf. And Mr Quelch said his backache eased greatly with the woollen drawers I made.'

192

Chaloner wondered whether it was the pair that had suffered from exposure to hot water. She burbled on, and he learned that Strange was fond of cats, while Jones was only ever happy if he was writing pamphlets. Then she spoke of her sister's dream for a fairer society, where the law would be applied equally to rich and poor, where unjust tithes and taxes would be abolished, and where all debts would be wiped clean.

'My wife would like that,' sighed Chaloner. 'She has amassed quite a few.'

'So has my sister,' said Ursula. 'It is expensive to publish these days, especially tracts that the government does not want people to read.'

Chaloner regarded her curiously. 'Why are you a Fifth Monarchist? Because of her? Or was your husband a millenarian?'

Ursula smiled. 'He has been in his grave these last ten years, and was more interested in fishing than religion. My sister has devoted her life to the Cause, though, and while I do not have her passion, I *can* ensure that our warriors have a decent meal inside them as they fight the good fight.'

Chaloner might have laughed, but the remark had a curious pathos about it. 'What are they planning for Easter Sunday?' he asked, although not with much expectation that she would know. 'I am their gunpowder expert, but I have no idea what they want me to do.'

'Mr Jones will tell us when the time is right,' replied Ursula serenely. 'He learned from the Northern Plot that the more people who know details, the more likely we are to be betrayed. The only person he trusts is Mr Strange.'

'Not Atkinson or Quelch?'

193

She smiled fondly. 'John is a dreamer, not practical at all, while Quelch is opinionated and rather common.' She lowered her voice. 'Between you and me, I cannot help but wonder whether Quelch is all he claims. There is something unsavoury about him, and it would not surprise me to learn that he has done nasty things in the past.'

Chaloner wondered whether she would ask for the drawers back if she ever learned that Quelch was a thief. 'What you are doing is dangerous,' he warned. 'If you are caught . . .'

'I know. But this is a miserable subject, Mr Chaloner, so let us talk of nicer things. Tell me about your wife. I imagine she is a lovely lady, even if she does have debts.'

Chaloner nodded, but could not think of anything else to add.

'Do you have children?' Ursula finished one row of knitting and began another.

He shook his head, never willing to talk about the baby he had lost to plague in Holland.

'A dog, then?' she asked, a little desperately. 'Or a cat?'

'I like birds,' said Chaloner, then felt a little foolish for the admission, feeling he should have professed an admiration for something more manly instead. 'And horses, of course.'

'I find horses rather frightening,' said Ursula, obviously relieved to have squeezed something out of him to take the conversation forward. 'They are so big and unpredictable. And I do not like the way they smell when they are wet. Speaking of wet things, would you like me to sponge that mud from your coat? It will stain if it is left to dry.'

'No, thank you.' Chaloner stood reluctantly. 'I must

194

go home, or my wife will think I am avoiding her pickled ling pie.'

'Pickled ling pie,' mused Ursula. 'There is a dish one does not encounter very often.'

It was encountered far too frequently as far as Chaloner was concerned.

As he was tired, Chaloner took a hackney to Tothill Street, arriving just as a bellman chanted in a gloomy wail that it was ten of the clock and all was well. All was not well in Chaloner's house, however, because instead of darkened windows and silence, it blazed with lights and all the servants were in the grip of frenzied activity.

'Tom! Where have you been?' cried Hannah. She was wearing a close-fitting blue bodice with matching skirts, carefully opened at the front to display the extravagant lace on her petticoat, an outfit he had not seen before. She started to embrace him, but had second thoughts when she saw his filthy coat.

'What is going on?' he asked in alarm.

'We are having a soirée,' she announced gaily. 'I have invited all manner of wealthy and influential people, so be sure to impress them. One may offer you a job.'

'Now?' He gaped at her. 'But it is after ten o'clock!'

'I tried to make them come earlier by offering food cooked with my own hands, but they all said they were busy until after dinner. Jacob? Cut the remains of my ling pie into small pieces and set them on the table. Our guests may still be peckish.'

Chaloner heard Jacob snigger and silenced him with a glare. Inedible though Hannah's baking might be, it was not for servants to mock it.

Hannah was cheerfully oblivious to the interchange.

'I hope you find work soon, Tom, because the vintner is insisting on being paid tomorrow. What a nuisance!'

'He has every right to ask for what he is owed,' said Chaloner curtly. 'And until we are clear of our debts, you should not spend any more money.'

She had the grace to look sheepish. 'Very well, although I organised this evening for your benefit, in the hope that someone will employ you. Will you change before anyone comes? Do not look so sour! I have invited people you like – Will Chiffinch and the Duke.'

Chaloner most certainly did not like those particular men, but the invitations had been sent, so there was nothing he could do except stamp upstairs and grit his teeth while Jacob told him which clothes he should wear. Feeling hot and uncomfortable in heavily beribboned breeches and a shirt with enough lace to supply a small country, he descended in time to greet the first wave of guests.

It was led by Buckingham, who immediately turned the atmosphere raucous. Chaloner was not particularly pleased when Rupert arrived either. The Prince looked around in distaste, as if he considered the house beneath his dignity. When Chaloner asked Hannah in a testy whisper why she had asked him to come, she replied that she had not – Rupert was an interloper. Wondering why the Prince had foisted himself on the gathering when it was obvious that he would rather be elsewhere, Chaloner followed him into the drawing room, aiming to find out. Then he stopped in surprise – Scott was there.

'Your wife invited a whole roomful of people,' Scott explained. 'And I happened to be in it at the time, so I was included. I like visiting the homes of old friends – it tells me so much about them. I imagine an event like this will cost a pretty penny, because the wine is French and there are more candles here than in St Paul's Cathedral.'

'What of it?'

'You are heavily in debt, so perhaps you will accept a small gift to help you over your current financial difficulties. I shall not ask much in return – just a warning if you hear of Manning trying to cheat me. I should be grateful, and so will Williamson.'

'I do not accept bribes.'

'No?' Scott's expression hardened. 'Then how about threats? If you do anything to damage me or my business, you will annoy a lot of powerful men. And remember that I know where you live, while your pretty wife is—'

'You would not risk anything so dangerous,' interrupted Chaloner, his expression so dark and angry that Scott bowed quickly and beat a hasty retreat.

'I heard him mention candles,' came a voice at his side, and Chaloner turned to see that Rupert had been listening. 'You had better explain.'

Chaloner was puzzled by the instruction, but then remembered the conversation in the Privy Gallery, about Rupert inventing ones that did not explode. He was about to see what he could learn from a discussion on the matter when Buckingham jostled into them, spilling wine all over Rupert's exquisite velveteen breeches.

'I am sorry,' said the Duke, surveying the mess with open glee. 'You had better go home and change, because you look as though you have had the kind of mishap that often afflicts men of mature years.'

Rupert scowled, but then saw Scott in the hallway taking his leave of Hannah. He hurried out, pausing only to hiss at Chaloner, 'We shall resume our conversation tomorrow.'

'You have annoyed him!' cried Buckingham in delight. 'Good for you! What did you say?'

'I am not sure,' replied Chaloner, baffled by the Prince's antics.

'Well, if you remember, tell me, because baiting him affords me a good deal of pleasure. He is a dreadful bore at Privy Council meetings – almost as bad as your pompous old Earl.'

'My Earl no longer,' Chaloner reminded him.

Buckingham inclined his head. 'Of course: it slipped my mind.' He smiled a little slyly. 'As you have been gracious enough to invite me here tonight, allow me to include you in a little event I am holding next Friday. It will be an Astrological Soirée.'

'What is an Astrological Soirée?'

'A party where Lambe will show off his unique skills. Incidentally, Hannah tells me that you were asking about Ferine the other day. Why you are interested in him?'

'I am not,' lied Chaloner, wishing Hannah would not talk about his business, especially to the likes of Buckingham. 'Well, no more than anyone else who is intrigued as to why a courtier should be murdered in a brothel.'

'Gossip,' said Buckingham softly. 'You want to be wary of that. It could prove perilous.'

Chapter 7

The following morning dawned wet and grey, and Chaloner stared out of the bedroom window as he gathered his thoughts. He was going to be busy that day, as he had a number of leads to follow and questions to ask. And if they proved unfruitful, he would travel to Hackney Marsh, to ask what Grisley Pate had told his daughter. He wondered how long such a journey would take – it was only a few miles, but the bad weather would slow him down.

First, though, he needed to corner Quelch, and make him talk about the Fifth Monarchists' plans. He would start with a generous supply of ale, and if that did not work, move to less friendly methods of persuasion. Next, he would concentrate on ascertaining the identity of John Browne, after which he would go to the club and try to learn more about Ferine and Snowdrop.

Plying Quelch with drink would require money, so Chaloner went to the store of coins he had secreted behind the skirting-board. He prised it off, then stared in horror when he saw the recess behind was empty. He swallowed hard, dismayed not so much for himself as for the creditors he had intended to pay.

He sat back on his heels. Who had taken it? Hannah, because she knew him better than he thought? One of the servants, who had found it while cleaning? He considered waking Hannah to ask, but then recalled how much she had had to drink at the soirée the previous night. Her morning temper was likely to be toxic if exacerbated by a hangover, and a quarrel would not be productive.

Downstairs, the hall and drawing room were in chaos. The curtains were askew, lumps of ling pie lurked under every piece of furniture, and there was a sour smell of spilled wine and old tobacco. The servants were struggling to put all to rights, and shot him resentful glances as he passed, evidently holding him responsible for the mess.

Absently, he picked up a copy of the latest *Newes* from the floor, but a brief flip through its international summary told him nothing other than that the Pope's nephew was ill. Domestic news revolved around the disease known as the King's Evil – it was generally believed that this condition could be cured by the touch of a monarch, and regular sessions were held in White Hall, so that victims could avail themselves of their King's services. His Majesty, however, had decided to take a break from these arduous duties, so sufferers were warned not to be disappointed if they arrived for an audience and were turned away.

Chaloner was about to put it down when a notice caught his eye. It was near the back, in the section where people advertised wares and services, or offered rewards for the return of stolen property. On occasion, the government used it to circulate descriptions of particularly dangerous felons. The notice was sandwiched between an advertisement for *The Discoverie of Witchcraft* (in sixteen volumes) and a paragraph claiming that Mr Wilcocks of Durham Yard could 'infallibly cure all sorts of gout by Outward Application'.

> Lost or absented: Edward Sherwin, low featured, apple-faced, about 50 years of age. If anyone has knowledge of him, he is to tell Mr Williamson at New Palace Yard, Westminster, and he shall have 10s for his peynes.

Chaloner supposed he would have to ask Williamson why he was interested in Sherwin. The notice said little good about the intelligence services, though – Sherwin was not exactly keeping a low profile and should have been easy to find. Moreover, if Scott *was* working for Williamson, as he had claimed, then why had he not told the Spymaster where Sherwin was?

'Is there anything in there about the new comet?' asked Gram the page conversationally, evidently not of the opinion that respectful deference was part of his job description.

'No,' said Nan the cook-maid before Chaloner could reply. 'And when *The Intelligencer* comes out on Monday, there will be nothing about the devil appearing at Tyburn either. The government would rather we ignored all the strange happenings of late – hauntings, odd deaths, Satan at large . . . The newsbooks always pretend that none of it ever took place.'

'Hauntings?' asked Gram keenly.

'Several buildings in and around High Holborn are infested with spectres,' elaborated Nan. 'Including one where a woman was pushed down the stairs by a hostile faerie. There is also a room in the Antelope where martyrs died, not to mention Hatton House.'

'Hatton House,' mused Gram. 'Eliza Hatton's ghost lives there – when it is not gliding up and down High Holborn. Personally, I shall be glad when the place is demolished. It is sinister, with its ruined popish chapel and empty rooms.'

'Speaking of sinister places, you will not forget the Duke of Buckingham's party at Wallingford House tomorrow, will you, sir?' asked Nan of Chaloner. 'The mistress asked us to remind you about it whenever we met.'

Chaloner frowned. 'He told me it was next Saturday.'

'That is his *Astrological* Soirée,' explained Nan. 'Tomorrow is just a normal one, and the mistress hopes that one of his guests will offer you a job, given that no one came forward last night. Incidentally, a man called here for you yesterday evening.'

'What man?'

'Mr Leving, but Joan refused to let him in.'

'Good.' Chaloner was annoyed that Leving should have visited again after being told not to.

'He said to tell you that a person named Quelch is dead,' Nan went on. She screwed up her face in concentration as she repeated the message verbatim. 'You are to go to the Westminster charnel house at nine o'clock prompt, to inspect the corpse together.'

Outside, the day was so dull that it felt like dusk, and rain fell steadily. Chaloner reached Westminster, and as he was early for his meeting with Leving, he decided to see if Williamson was at his offices in New Palace Yard. He did not enter through the front door, where two

202

uniformed guards stood sentinel, but through a window at the back, which someone had forgotten to lock. It was unlikely that anyone was watching the place, but Chaloner did not want his visit reported to the wrong people.

The Spymaster's domain comprised a large hall on the ground floor, where his clerks and secretaries laboured, and a suite of rooms above for himself. The basement contained a series of grim little cells used for interrogation. The hall was deserted that morning, so Chaloner walked through it unchallenged before running up the stairs to Williamson's lair.

The Spymaster looked as though he had been at his desk all night. He was unshaven, wigless and pasty-faced as he studied a series of maps that lay on the table in front of him.

'I would not put too much faith in those, if I were you,' said Chaloner, watching him jump in alarm at the voice so close to his ear. 'Amsterdam does not lie on the River Rotte, and The Hague is not ten miles inland.'

Williamson glared irritably at him. 'How did you get in? Where are my guards? I hope you have not harmed them. I am short of people as it is.'

He went to the window to see whether his men were still at their posts, and Chaloner noticed, not for the first time, that the room afforded a fine view of the severed heads that were displayed on pikes outside Westminster Hall. These blackened, crow-pecked specimens were barely identifiable as human, yet the government refused to bury them, preferring them to stand as grim reminders of what happened to traitors.

Chaloner heard the faintest of sounds, and moved quickly, so that Williamson's favourite operative – a clerk named Swaddell, whom everyone knew was really an

203

assassin – could not creep up behind him and put a knife to his throat. Swaddell understood exactly why Chaloner had ducked away, and a wry smile flashed across his face. As usual, he was dressed completely in black, with the exception of a spotlessly white falling band. His dark eyes moved restlessly.

'Have you come to report on the Fifth Monarchists?' he asked. 'I would have taken that enquiry myself, but I am too busy with the Dutch war.'

'Or have you come to beg for money because your wife has spent all yours?' remarked Williamson nastily, thus forfeiting any sympathy Chaloner might have felt for him.

'Is John Scott in your employ?' When Williamson nodded cautiously, Chaloner added, 'Then why did *he* not tell you that Sherwin is lodging at the Pope's Head? It should not have been necessary to place a notice in *The Newes*.'

Williamson sighed. 'He did, but we forgot to cancel the newsbook announcement – hardly surprising, when my clerks are stretched so thin. It was not my idea to advertise anyway. Suffice to say that I am juggling the needs of my country with the demands of the powerful.'

'And the hopeful expectations of your purse?' asked Chaloner archly. 'Scott informs me that when he sells Sherwin's secret, you are to have a share of the profit.'

The blood drained from the Spymaster's face, and Chaloner could see that his shock was genuine. 'He said that about me? The bastard! How dare he!'

'He will have an excuse,' said Swaddell disapprovingly. 'He always does. I have never met a more slippery customer, and I wish we were not obliged to use him.'

'We have no choice,' said Williamson tiredly. 'But he will pay for blackening my name, even if it was only to

204

Chaloner, who will, of course, pay no heed to such a slanderous lie.'

Chaloner inclined his head. 'Do you know a man called John Browne?'

Williamson nodded. 'But I cannot elaborate. Suffice to say that Browne made a mistake, and there have been . . . repercussions.'

'He is in Rupert's employ,' pressed Chaloner, recalling the conversation he had overheard in White Hall. 'And Rupert discussed him with Scott. There are connections here that—'

'Yes,' interrupted Williamson. 'But I would not explore them if I were you. It would be inadvisable, to say the least. Concentrate on the Fifth Monarchists.'

Chaloner stifled his exasperation – the visit was transpiring to be a waste of time. 'Very well. Their rebellion will need horses and weapons. Have you detected any mass movements of these things, not just here, but anywhere in the country?'

'No,' replied Williamson. He frowned. 'Is that good or bad?'

'Good, if it means nothing is happening. Bad, if it means the Fifth Monarchists have sufficient influence to keep their activities quiet.'

Williamson rubbed his eyes wearily. 'I am sorry I am forced to keep you in the dark like this, Chaloner. I appreciate it is foolish, but I am under orders.'

'Rupert's,' surmised Chaloner. 'But why is he interested in—'

'I have not heard from Leving in days,' interrupted Williamson, with a glance that said the Prince was not a subject he was able to discuss. 'I assume all is going according to plan?'

'Not really. He is a liability.'

'I imagine so, but he is monitoring other fanatics besides Fifth Monarchists, and I cannot risk alienating him by removing him from the case. I would never have accepted his services under normal circumstances, but I am so desperate for spies that I dared not refuse his offer.'

'We would both be happier if *I* was out there with you,' added Swaddell. 'But I am tied to a desk, trying to make sense of all the information that is flowing in about Holland.'

'Perhaps we should swap,' suggested Chaloner. He was good at analysing intelligence about Holland, and it would be a lot less frustrating than Ferine and the Fifth Monarchists.

'Now there is an idea.' Swaddell brightened. 'Most of these reports are in Dutch, a language I do not speak. I am far better at eliminating . . . at *pursuing* home-grown traitors.'

'Out of the question,' said Williamson briskly. 'Rupert wants Clarendon to bear responsibility for the investigation.' He shot Chaloner a wry glance. 'So you had better succeed, or it will not be you who pays the price.'

'Shame,' sighed Swaddell glumly. 'A Dutch speaker would have been a tremendous asset. Are you sure we cannot afford to hire one?'

'Quite sure,' said Williamson bitterly. 'The Privy Council wants me to probe our enemy's secrets, but insists on cutting my budget. It is a coven of ignorant fools!'

Chaloner said nothing, but thought that Williamson must be fraught indeed to make such an indiscreet remark. The Spymaster flushed when he realised what he had done, and hastened to mask his discomfiture with an attack.

'Do you have anything to report, or did you come to interrogate us because your own enquiries have reached a dead end?'

'I came to tell you that Quelch is dead,' lied Chaloner.

'Christ!' blurted Williamson. 'How?'

'I will know when I see him in the charnel house.' Chaloner tried one last question. 'Will you tell me about Prince Rupert's candles, or is that a secret, too?'

Williamson sighed and rubbed a hand across his face before addressing Swaddell. 'Sometimes I wish I had never left Oxford. I was happy there, you know.'

'But then you would never have met your wife,' said Swaddell kindly. 'And you often say she is the most important thing in your life.'

'Yes, but that was when I had the opportunity to see her. She will not remember who I am by the time I finally have leave to go home.'

'She is unlikely to forget you,' said Chaloner, not altogether pleasantly.

It was not much lighter when Chaloner left Williamson's den, exiting through the back door with Swaddell at his side. The assassin muttered something about meeting a Dutch informant, and slithered away. Chaloner was glad he had gone; he had never trusted Swaddell, with his ready blades and unfathomable black eyes.

He had just reached Old Palace Yard when he spotted two familiar figures, and was surprised to see Sherwin and Scott so soon after discussing them with Williamson. He smiled when he realised someone was tailing them: Manning scuttled between the shadows, so intent on his quarry that he did not notice the amused smirks of the people who saw what he was doing.

207

Chaloner was too far away to hear what Scott said as he pressed a fat purse into Sherwin's hand. Sherwin peered at it, then shoved it in his pocket without a word. Scott flung his arm across Sherwin's shoulders, and whatever he murmured next made the man grin. This was too much for Manning, who hobbled forward. Chaloner also crept closer, using a conveniently parked hay-wagon to keep himself hidden while he listened to what they said.

'There you are,' cried Manning, as though it was a chance encounter. 'Where have you been? I have been looking for you all night, and my chilblains object to being out in the cold.'

Scott beamed brightly, revealing his white teeth. 'I am sorry, Manning, but I did say that we might sample a few taverns in Westminster today. Did you forget?'

Sherwin rolled his eyes at the makings of another spat, and tottered on ahead of them. Manning glared at his partner and spoke in a low, angry voice.

'You are trying to turn him against me. I saw you give him a purse just now.'

'You saw me lend him a handkerchief. No money changed hands.'

Scott lied so plausibly that Manning's offensive faltered. 'I will take him home,' he mumbled. 'He should not be out in broad daylight. What would happen if he ran into Browne?'

Scott fingered his sword. 'I would look after him. But look at us, quarrelling again. It must be because we are both tired. Thank God it is nearly over. On Easter Sunday, we shall celebrate the fruits of our labour – you with the Kingdom of Christ installed, and me with gold.'

'I want gold, too,' Manning reminded him sharply. 'A life of luxury costs, even in paradise.'

'Of course,' said Scott smoothly. 'Shall I accompany you back to the Pope's Head, or can you manage alone?'

He sauntered away without waiting for a reply. Swearing under his breath, Manning turned and limped after Sherwin, where Chaloner could tell that he was asking about the purse he had been given. Sherwin simply shrugged, so the Fifth Monarchist pulled one from his own pocket. It bulged tantalisingly. Sherwin took it without a word of thanks, and began to weave his way up King Street.

Chaloner was about to break cover and waylay them when five ruffians with hard, cruel faces emerged from a nearby lane. Sherwin regarded them with stupid confusion, but Manning understood the danger they were in. He whipped around and tried to run away, but the men caught him with ease and bundled both victims down the alley.

They reached a dingy yard, and Chaloner watched as the pair were ordered to hand over their valuables. Manning obliged with such frantic eagerness to please that the robbers could not take his belongings quickly enough, and some fell on the ground. Then he hauled off his wig and flung it at them before scuttling away as fast as his fat legs would carry him.

'Leave him,' ordered the largest thief when one of his cronies started to follow. 'He gave us everything he got. Help me with this one.'

Frightened by the savage hands that pawed at him, Sherwin began to cry, so Chaloner pried a stone from the ground and lobbed it as hard as he could. It struck the leader, knocking him senseless. His cronies were still gaping their astonishment when Chaloner charged at them with his sword in one hand and dagger in the other.

They took one look and ran, abandoning leader and plunder without so much as a backward glance.

Chaloner collected the dropped treasures, handed them to Sherwin, and then escorted him back to the comforting bustle of King Street. Shaking badly, Sherwin aimed for the nearest tavern, a cosy place named the Axe. Chaloner followed, pleased with the opportunity to corner him alone.

'I know things,' explained Sherwin, tapping his nose when Chaloner asked why Scott and Manning were so keen to keep his good graces. 'About nealing, for example.'

'Kneeling?' Chaloner was nonplussed.

'It means doing things with metal,' explained Sherwin, although Chaloner was none the wiser. 'I am worth a fortune, and Manning and Scott shower me with gifts all the time. Here, have these. They will give me more when I ask, because they can refuse me nothing.'

Chaloner did not want the purses that were thrust into his hand, but Sherwin was insistent, so he accepted. He opened one and was astounded by the number of coins it contained. The second, Manning's, was fuller and heavier, and included a large ruby ring.

'What have you agreed to tell them?' he asked.

'Oh, no,' slurred Sherwin, wagging a finger. 'I cannot have a third man picking my brains. Where is Manning, by the way? Is he still fending off robbers? He suffers cruelly from chilblains, you know. He is always talking about them.'

Chaloner wondered what Scott and Manning thought they were going to glean from Sherwin's pickled brain when the man did not even remember that Manning had abandoned him.

'Who is Browne?' he asked.

Sherwin pursed his lips. 'No one you want to meet, believe me. A desperate villain, dishonest, sly and vicious. Get me a drink, will you?'

'Yes, if you tell me about Browne. Refuse, and I will take you back to those thieves.'

'You will not,' predicted Sherwin confidently. 'I am protected by important and powerful men. You would not dare harm me.'

Chaloner started to say that he cared nothing for important and powerful men, but Sherwin's eyes closed and he started to snore. Chaloner stared at him for a moment, then hauled him into the yard and pushed his head into a trough of cold water. Sherwin cursed and blubbered, but fell asleep again the moment Chaloner released him.

'Do not waste your time,' advised the landlord, who had come to watch. 'He will be no good for at least twelve hours. Take it from me – I know the signs.'

Chaloner persisted anyway, but was eventually forced to concede that the landlord was right. He bundled Sherwin into a hackney carriage and told the driver to take him to the Pope's Head. Doubtless Manning and Scott would be glad to see his safe return.

The Westminster charnel house was an unprepossessing building near the river, sandwiched between a granary and a coal-yard. It did not appear very large from outside, but it was unusually deep, with two handsome parlours at the front and a long hall at the back where the bodies were stored. All was kept fairly clean, and new arrivals were given a place on a scrubbed wooden table and covered with a fresh blanket.

The place was run by a dapper little man named Kersey,

who made a handsome living from dealing with the dead. He gave tours of his domain to ghoulish sightseers and ran a small museum containing some of the more unusual artefacts he had collected through the years – Chaloner was sure that Kersey earned far more than he did. The charnel-house keeper was busy that morning, with both parlours full of bereaved relatives. He looked harried.

'A lot of HMS *London*'s victims are here,' he explained tersely. 'Brought upriver by the tide.'

'You may have more if the ship is successfully weighed next Wednesday,' warned Chaloner.

'She will not be,' predicted Kersey with the confidence of a man familiar with the Thames and its ways. 'The Navy Board is wasting its money. Did you hear what happened to her, by the way? A foolish seaman was using old papers to prepare new charges for her guns, and he accidentally knocked over a candle.'

'I was told that the powder magazine was locked and that all the crew would have been on deck – and would not have used a naked flame in that part of the ship anyway.'

'Perhaps the fellow was drunk, then,' suggested Kersey with a shrug. 'The area around Chatham docks is full of taverns, and *London* was delayed for hours while there was wrangling over her paperwork. I imagine the crew passed the time by swilling ale. Of course, there are rumours that the candle was defective, but that is nonsense, and we should ignore it.'

Uneasily, Chaloner recalled the discussion between Buckingham and Rupert about candles that exploded. Surely Rupert was not responsible? HMS *London*'s loss was a serious blow to Britain's war effort, and for all his faults, the Prince was a patriot.

212

'Are you here for Ferine?' asked Kersey, cutting into Chaloner's disquieting thoughts. 'Wiseman said you are exploring his murder.'

'Actually, I came to see Quelch.'

'Really?' Kersey seemed surprised, but then the door opened and more visitors arrived. He shot Chaloner an apologetic glance. 'I should tend to these folk – it is their first time here. You can either find Quelch yourself or you can wait until I am free. I do not usually allow unsupervised access to my guests, but you are different.'

He hurried away to greet the newcomers, so the spy walked to the mortuary alone. It was a dark, dismal place, as Kersey did not waste money on lights for clients who were beyond caring. Chaloner lit a lamp and looked around rather helplessly. The HMS *London* disaster had filled it to overflowing, and he was not sure where to start.

'Boo!'

Chaloner whipped around in alarm, and his sword was halfway out of its scabbard before he recognised Leving's grinning face.

'That made him jump!' Leving crowed. 'Did you see, Atkinson? He almost hit the roof!'

'I am sorry, Chaloner – we thought you were that keeper fellow, so we hid,' explained Atkinson, standing up sheepishly from behind a table. He was wearing a mourning band around his arm, and his face was white in the flickering lamplight. 'We should not be in here, you see: we were told to wait our turn in the parlour, but I cannot – I need to get back to my shop.'

'Why do you want to see Quelch's body?' asked Chaloner, setting the lamp down so it would not reveal how badly his hands were shaking. Leving had given him a serious start.

213

'Jones sent me,' replied Atkinson. He glanced at Leving. 'I am not sure why *he* is here.'

'Jones sent me, too,' chirruped Leving unconvincingly. 'He said I should do all I can to learn how Quelch died.' He was still grinning like a lunatic, and Chaloner wished Williamson had agreed to lock him away.

'I am glad Snowflake is not in here,' said Atkinson with a shudder. 'She is with Temperance in Hercules' Pillars Alley. I would have taken her to my house, but Temperance thought—'

'Never mind that,' said Leving briskly. 'You are late, Chaloner. We were beginning to think you might not come. Where have you been?'

'With Sherwin,' replied Chaloner, watching for Atkinson's reaction.

The stockinger's jaw tightened. 'I do not trust him. Or his friends Manning and Scott.'

'But Manning is one of us,' said Leving in surprise. 'A Fifth Monarchist.'

'So he claims,' said Atkinson. 'But he is more interested in making money than in ushering in a better world, and I have always been wary of mercenaries.'

'Even so, he is more reliable than Sherwin,' said Chaloner artlessly. 'I hope Jones does not expect me to work with *him* on Easter Sunday.'

'So do I,' agreed Atkinson. 'He is a liability, and we are playing a dangerous game here. I should not like any of our number to be hanged because he does not match up to expectations.'

'What is Sherwin's role in the affair?' asked Chaloner, heartily wishing Leving would contrive to look less avidly interested in the answer.

'I wish I knew,' sighed Atkinson. 'Although I am afraid

it might transpire to be violent, and I have always argued against the use of excessive force.'

'Silver cannon,' said Chaloner. 'They certainly feature in Jones's plan.'

Atkinson raised an eyebrow. '*Silver* cannon? I had not expected to hear flowery language from you – you seem such a practical fellow. However, I hope there will not be artillery of any description, silver or otherwise. But I do not like it in here. Let us complete our business and go.'

With great tenderness, he lifted the blanket that covered the body on the nearest table. Quelch's face was mottled, and vivid marks on his neck showed that he had been strangled. There was blood in his hair from a head-wound: he had been stunned first.

'Who would do such a thing?' asked Chaloner. 'Strange? He and Quelch argued constantly.'

'I doubt Strange would kill a fellow Fifth Monarchist so close to the Day of Judgement,' said Leving. 'Murder stains the soul, you know.'

Chaloner did not bother to point out that Strange might not consider it murder, as fanatics rarely saw their actions in the same light as everyone else.

'Shall I tell you what happened last night?' asked Leving, watching Chaloner inspect the rest of the body for suspicious marks; there were none. 'Quelch failed to arrive for a meeting of the Sanhedrin, so I went to his house to make sure he was all right.'

'Some of the Sanhedrin did gather,' said Atkinson, regarding Leving warily. 'But I was not invited and you are not a member, so how do *you* know Quelch missed it?'

Leving waved an airy hand. 'I happened to be passing, and I saw Jones and a few others assemble. Quelch was

215

not there and I was worried – he is an important part of our plot, after all.'

Atkinson smiled weakly. 'You sound like Ursula – she is concerned about everyone, too.'

'When I arrived at Quelch's house, his neighbours said they had not seen him all day,' Leving went on breezily. 'I made a few enquiries and learned that a body answering his description had been found by the river. I went immediately to tell Jones. And when I had finished with him, I hurried to Chaloner's home . . .'

He trailed off when he remembered that he had been forbidden to go there, but Chaloner was more concerned with why Leving had reported the news to Jones and not the Spymaster. He was about to ask when Atkinson made a dash for the door, after which there came the sound of retching.

'Weak stomach,' grinned Leving. 'And do not berate me for visiting your house again – it was an emergency.'

'Who do you think killed Quelch?' Chaloner spoke urgently, aware that Atkinson might return at any moment.

'God knows. Jones, perhaps, or another of the Sanhedrin. Maybe they suspect that someone is betraying them to Williamson.' Leving chortled softly. 'They will feel proper fools when they find out it is us!'

When Chaloner and Leving left the charnel house, they found Atkinson outside, leaning against a wall with his face an unhealthy shade of green. Chaloner took him to the nearest tavern for a restorative cup of wine, and Leving disappeared on business of his own.

'I am glad he has gone,' said the stockinger weakly. 'I do not like him very much. He is always cheerful and

216

polite, yet there is something unpleasantly slippery about him.'

'He is just nervous about Easter Day,' lied Chaloner. 'I know I am, given that I have no idea what is to happen.'

'I am not sure what Jones wants me to do, either,' said Atkinson gloomily. 'Nor does Ursula. But I suppose all will be revealed in time.'

Chaloner let him talk, prompting him with the occasional question, but it soon became clear that the stockinger knew nothing of import. Then the discussion moved to Snowflake, but Grisley Pate had not visited his stepson when he had been in London, and Atkinson was dismissive of the notion that the old man might have said something that led to her death.

'He lives in the marshes, where nothing ever happens. Moreover, he would never say or do anything to put Snowflake in danger. He liked her. Everyone did. She was a gentle soul, full of life and laughter.'

He described how he had tried to interest her in the hosiery business. However, when he embarked on a description of what was involved, Chaloner was not surprised the vivacious Snowflake had opted for a more lively career. Next Atkinson moved on to Ursula.

'She is my sun and stars,' he said with a sweet smile. 'And I think she likes me, too.'

He regaled Chaloner with an account of her virtues, and described a scheme they intended to promote once the Last Millennium had dawned, which entailed putting the best religious and philosophical books into a public library, so that everyone might have access to them. His eyes shone with the light of his convictions.

'What do you think happened to Quelch?' asked

217

Chaloner, when he eventually managed to steer the conversation around to the conspirators.

Atkinson shrugged. 'I spent all day in my shop, except for a brief foray to the club with Maude to see Snowflake's . . . If anyone accuses me, I can provide alibis to prove my innocence.'

'Why should you think that might be necessary?'

Atkinson looked away. 'I know what the rest of the Sanhedrin think of me – that I am a dull fellow who lacks their fire. They will blame me because I am dispensable, good only for keeping them in free stockings. But perhaps we read too much into Quelch's demise. It might have been a random robbery. It happens, you know.'

Chaloner did know, because he had just witnessed such an attack on Sherwin. Yet it seemed incredible that so dangerous a rebel should come to such a banal end, and he did not believe it.

They parted company eventually, Atkinson to return to his shop, and Chaloner to go to White Hall, where he loitered in the public rooms listening to gossip. Most talk was about either weighing *London* or the devil's appearance at Tyburn, but he also learned that the Dutch had taken another British ship at sea and that Lambe had told the King's fortune, although His Majesty declined to reveal what had been said.

In the evening, restless and dissatisfied, but reluctant to go home and confront Hannah about the missing money, he walked to the Swan, where he lurked in the darkness outside, waiting to see who came and went. His patience paid off eventually: after an hour Eliza arrived. He moved so he could see her through the window, and quickly became aware that he was not the only one watching. So was the man sitting at a table near the door,

218

whose hat and cloak covered all but the tip of his nose. Then the fellow reached out to pick up a newsbook, and Chaloner saw symbols inked on his fingers.

Lambe glanced around furtively, slid a piece of paper inside *The Newes*, and walked out. The moment he had gone, Chaloner grabbed the front door and slammed it twice in quick succession. While the patrons clustered excitedly around it, whispering about angry spirits, Chaloner ran to the back door and grabbed the newsbook. He tweaked out the paper, and was back in his hiding place long before the patrons had returned to their seats. He examined what he had stolen in the dim light from the window. It was blank, and smelled of onions. Writing in onion juice was an old spy trick – the letters were invisible until held near a flame, at which point they went brown. Chaloner slipped it in his pocket to read later.

After a while, Eliza collected a lamp from the landlord, and Chaloner was disconcerted when she left the tavern to glide straight towards him. The hair stood up on the back of his neck as he stared into her ice-blue eyes, and she held the lantern in such a way that it cast eerie shadows on her corpse-white face. It was a disturbing visage, although he cursed himself as a fool for being unsettled by it.

'Do you have the information you promised to bring?' she asked. There was a mocking glint in her eyes, as if she knew he had not.

He forced a smile. 'Tomorrow. May I escort you home? It is late, and Holborn can be dangerous at night.'

'Not for me.'

With that enigmatic remark, she floated away, leaving Chaloner with the uncomfortable sense that something was wrong. The hair on his neck continued to prickle, and he felt that while *she* might be safe, he was not. He forced his unease to the back of his mind and set off after her, intending to follow her home and see what a search of her lair might provide in the way of clues.

Suddenly, a figure emerged from one side, and slammed into him with such force that he stumbled. Hands reached out to steady him, and he slapped away one that fastened around the purses in his pocket. He did not, however, feel the fingers that removed the onion-juice message, and only noticed it was missing when he was halfway home. He cursed under his breath. A clue had been in his possession, and he had lost it! What sort of intelligencer allowed that to happen?

All sensible spies kept boltholes for those times when they needed a refuge, and Chaloner's was in Long Acre, but it was an expense he could no longer justify. With considerable regret he informed the landlord that he would not be renewing the lease. He arranged for the few belongings he kept there – most importantly his best viol – to be sent to Tothill Street, then sat in the chilly garret wishing he had married someone else. It was not just the loss of a sanctuary he resented, but the fact that he would have nowhere for music. Hannah disliked him practising at home, and ignoring her and doing it anyway would negate any enjoyment he might have derived from the exercise.

Suspecting he would thoroughly depress himself if he reflected too long on his lot, he stood, took one last look around and left. He walked to Atkinson's shop, where he waited until the stockinger went to the pantry for ale, then questioned Old Ned and Ursula, who was still helping with the work. Both confirmed that Atkinson had been with one or other of them from the meeting in the Talbot until Temperance's note had arrived informing him about Snowflake's death. The stockinger could certainly be eliminated as a suspect for dispatching Quelch. To be absolutely sure, Chaloner went to Hercules' Pillars Alley to speak to Maude, who was able to say with certainty that Atkinson had been with her and Old Ned in the shop, or with Ursula hunting out more silk in the chamber at the back, for the entire evening.

Afterwards, Chaloner wandered aimlessly along High Holborn, thinking about the plot that was brewing there. Then it started to rain heavily, so he went to Lincoln's Inn, where he sat by the fire in Chamber XIII, grateful both for its warmth and for Thurloe's quiet friendship.

'I hope you are being careful,' said the ex-Spymaster, after Chaloner had furnished him with an account of all that had happened since they had last met. 'Do not squander your life on this Fifth Monarchy nonsense. It is not worth it.'

'Rupert and Williamson would disagree – they think it is *very* important. And there *is* more to it than rebellion, so why will they not tell me? The Prince is an ass, but Williamson should know that I would operate more efficiently with a clear picture of what is going on.'

Thurloe frowned. 'I am concerned by your suggestion that Rupert might have put some kind of exploding candle on *London*. She was Lawson's ship, and they have never seen eye to eye – the Prince despises Lawson's lowly roots and crude manners, while Lawson views Rupert as an arrogant dandy. But to destroy a battleship on the eve of war over a petty quarrel . . .'

'I suspect "candle" is a euphemism for something else. But how do I find out what?'

'If it is a euphemism, then it is probably a weapon. Rupert has certainly devised or improved those in the past. Did you know he is a member of the Royal Society?'

Chaloner nodded. 'Brodrick said he had created some sort of exploding bead.'

'They are called "Prince Rupert's Drops" – an amusing diversion with no real purpose. More seriously, though, he has put his mind to developing better firing mechanisms for heavy artillery, and more potent forms of gunpowder.'

Chaloner glanced at the now-empty coal scuttle. 'Do you think a sample of that was what Jones ordered me to take to Manning?'

'If so, it would explain Rupert's interest in the Fifth Monarchists. And why Williamson does not swoop in and arrest them at once – he and the Prince will want the name of every conspirator involved, to make sure that no one escapes with sensitive military secrets.'

'Or one that is worth a lot of money,' mused Chaloner. 'I heard Williamson tell Rupert that something was more "financial than tactical", although Rupert claimed it might "turn the tide of the war". I think I see a glimmer of sense at last! How can we find out more?'

'Carefully,' advised Thurloe wryly. 'If Rupert and Williamson suspect you know what they have refused to tell, they may take steps to silence you.'

Chaloner mulled over what they had reasoned, gazing idly at the shelf above the hearth. He snapped out of his reverie when he saw two cylindrical objects displayed there.

'What are those?'

'Coining dies,' replied Thurloe. 'The bottom part is called a "pile", while the "trussel" fits over it like a hood. They were once used to make money, but we have special machines to do that now.'

'Ferine gave a set to Snowflake.'

Thurloe shrugged. 'The Lieutenant of the Tower recently found a crate of them in a cellar, and auctioned them off to raise money for the war. Wallis bought me a set as a gift. They are quite worthless, except as an intriguing relic of the past.'

'Ferine told Snowdrop that hers will be make her rich one day.'

'Then he was spinning her a yarn.'

'Perhaps he thought she could set up her own mint.'

'Hardly! The coins produced would be very inferior to the ones milled on a screw-press, and no one would accept them as currency. Shall I show you how the contraption works?'

He set the pile on the table and put a bone button on its top, to represent the silver blank that would once have been used. Then he placed the trussel over it.

'And you hit it with a hammer.' He did not have one, so he used a poker instead. When he pulled the dies apart, the button had been reduced to fragments.

'I see,' said Chaloner drolly. 'Very useful.'

'It would have worked with a *metal* blank,' said Thurloe, a little defensively. 'And then I would have had a coin "minted" in the reign of the last King Henry.'

'So Ferine lied to Snowflake – these would not have made her wealthy. His other gift was a dried toad, which failed to bring her the luck he promised. Perhaps he was not in his right wits. Indeed, he would have to be unhinged to deal with Eliza Hatton – or Alice

223

Fanshaw, as Wiseman believes she is called – because there is something very unsettling about her. The same is true of Lambe, whom I have seen near her twice now.'

'My informants tell me that he is highly regarded at Court, although mostly because he is Buckingham's protégé and so has access to the right circles. His presence there is deeply harmful, though – Londoners do not like the thought of the King and his ministers paying heed to a sorcerer. But never mind this. Who do you think killed Quelch?'

'Strange is the obvious candidate,' replied Chaloner. 'They disliked each other, and quarrelled constantly. Or perhaps Jones did it, to eliminate a source of discord.'

'Jones is certainly ruthless enough to kill for his Cause. What about Atkinson?'

'He has an alibi in Maude, Ursula and Old Ned. I checked it myself.'

Thurloe grimaced. 'Stockingers, farmers, labourers, housewives. I do not blame them for wanting a gentler, fairer society, yet I wager none of them understand what they are doing.'

Chaloner agreed. 'Rupert and Williamson want a list of everyone involved, but they will not have it from me. And they will not have one from Leving either, if I can help it.'

'You will have to give them something, or you will end up in the Tower yourself.'

'I will face that problem when it comes. Has Wallis decoded those papers yet? The ones we copied before I delivered them to Manning?'

'He is busy deciphering missives pertaining to the war, which must take precedence. He will tackle them when

224

he can. The same goes for me – I will work on them when I have a moment.'

Chaloner regarded him curiously. 'What is keeping you so busy?'

'Lincoln's Inn business. There is a complex legal wrangle pertaining to the Pope's Head that is likely to keep its owner – us – tied up for weeks. We are also considering whether to sell some of our land to developers. I have been charged to handle both matters.'

Chaloner frowned, instinct telling him that Thurloe was not being entirely honest. He regarded him in concern, hoping he was not embroiled in something dangerous.

'Property law is complex,' said Thurloe irritably, seeing the look and understanding exactly what his friend was thinking. 'Look at the papers on my desk if you do not believe me.'

The table was indeed piled high with plans and documents, but Chaloner was not so graceless as to take him up on the offer.

'I hope you reject the developers' suggestions,' was all he said. 'If they have their way, we shall have houses from Kensington to Wapping, and from Southwark to Shoreditch.'

'You exaggerate, Tom. The city will never grow larger than it is now. How could it? We are bursting at the seams already.'

Chapter 8

The Tothill Street house was empty when Chaloner arrived home, and there was a scribbled message from Hannah saying she would be home late and that the servants had been given the evening off. Chaloner was not sure whether to be relieved or disappointed that their discussion about the missing hoard would have to wait – relieved because it seemed a waste of his energy to embark on a confontation about so distateful a matter as money, and disappointed because he was angry with her and wanted answers.

He went to the pantry for food, but rejected the exotic treats that were displayed there – stewed peacock, churned cream, orange-peel comfits – stubbornly declining to have anything to do with Hannah's extravagance. He settled for barley-bread and dripping. He carried them to the drawing room, not lighting a fire to save the cost of the fuel, and when he had eaten, took his second-best viol from the cupboard under the stairs and began to play. He only stopped when a door slamming at the back of the house told him that Joan was home.

Hannah returned much later, making sure he woke by putting cold feet on him. He mumbled an objection and eased away, and was just falling back to sleep when a pair of icy hands began to rove across his chest.

'You are very warm,' she murmured.

He retorted that he would not stay that way for long if she insisted on mauling him, and was just dozing off again when she heaved herself close. The chilly fingers came to rest on his stomach, and he could smell wine on her breath.

'I have been to a party,' she whispered. 'To celebrate the twenty-second anniversary of Prince Rupert arriving in England to offer his services to the old king. It was a glittering occasion, and *everyone* was there. Are you asleep, Tom? We can talk in the morning if so.'

'Yes, please,' he mumbled, trying to escape her frigid touch.

'Dr Lambe was there,' she chattered on. With a sigh, he rolled over to face her, suspecting it was nearing dawn anyway. 'He is an eerie fellow, although the Duke admires his skills. He predicted that the devil would appear at Tyburn, you know.'

'Is that so?' Chaloner was thoughtful. He was fairly sure Eliza Hatton had issued the screech that had frightened the spectators into a stampede. Were she and Lambe working together – he making the prediction, and she planting the notion in susceptible minds? And if nature had not contrived to help with rainclouds, would she have found another way to 'prove' him right? Chaloner decided he would have a word with Lambe as soon as he could corner the man alone. And with Eliza, too, if he could catch her.

'He announced it at Court on Thursday morning,'

227

Hannah went on. 'And it came to pass that very afternoon. The Queen says that such people are anathema and should be banished, but it is only a bit of harmless fun.'

'Ferine predicted the future, too,' said Chaloner.

'Yes – he was very good at it. He did a reading for me, and he was right: you *did* come home from Russia before the week was out. Of course, Lambe does more than tell the future – the Duke hired him to help him find the Philosopher's Stone. Rupert scoffs at his talents, though.'

'Why?'

Hannah shrugged. 'The Prince is not a very nice man. He is even rude to the Duke! He has invited us to a party tomorrow, by the way. The Duke, I mean. I would not attend a soirée given by Rupert, not if you paid me.'

Chaloner regarded her askance. 'But you *did* attend a soirée he gave, Hannah – the one you went to tonight, to celebrate the anniversary of his—'

'That was *work*,' interrupted Hannah. 'The Queen was invited, so I had to go, too.'

'Then it is being paid to—'

'Do not quibble. And do not try to change the subject either. I want you there tomorrow, because one of the other guests may offer you a post. All the best people are going.'

'Lambe?' asked Chaloner, thinking it might be a good opportunity to talk to the man.

'Of course. And Rupert, unfortunately. The Duke does not want to invite him – they cannot abide each other – but Rupert is the King's cousin, so he has no choice.'

'Privy Council meetings must be a trial,' mused Chaloner, not liking to imagine the trouble that would accrue when two such arrogantly opinionated individuals were thrust together. It would be even worse when the pompously prim Earl of Clarendon was thrown into the mix, too.

'Admiral Lawson is also going,' Hannah continued, 'although the Duke cannot abide him either. Apparently, Lawson heard it was happening, and told the Duke to expect him at twelve – or a little later if no hackney is available. Huh! The fellow does not even keep a private coach!'

'No,' said Chaloner firmly, sensing what was coming next. 'We cannot afford—'

'We could if you had a job,' Hannah pouted. 'But never mind that now. Meet me in the palace at noon, and we shall *walk* to Wallingford House together. Please do not be late.'

Chaloner sat up, supposing it was as good an opportunity as any to discuss her profligacy. 'These debts,' he began sternly. 'You must curtail your spending before you ruin us.'

'But we are obliged to maintain standards,' protested Hannah. 'And it is hardly my fault that the Dutch war has resulted in heavier taxes.'

'You cannot blame the war!' Chaloner was astounded by the excuse. 'And speaking of money, I left some behind the skirting board, but it has disappeared.'

'I took it,' said Hannah, with a sheepish smile. 'I happened across it one day when I was looking for a dropped button. I needed a new gown, and I knew you would not mind. Lord, I am exhausted! You have kept me talking all night.'

She closed her eyes, and began the deep, measured breathing that told him she was asleep. Chaloner stared down at her, torn between anger and affection. The conversation had left him wide awake, so he rose, dressed and went downstairs. Joan was there.

'The vintner came again yesterday,' she said accusingly. 'And unless you pay his bill within the next week, he is going to alert the bailiffs.'

Chaloner felt the two heavy purses in his pocket, and wondered how many creditors he could satisfy with their contents.

With a heavy step, he went to White Hall, where a few diehard revellers were still enjoying the remains of the wine from Rupert's party. He waylaid several, and asked questions about Ferine, HMS *London*, Lawson, Browne, Lambe and Fifth Monarchists, but they were either too drunk to make sense or they knew nothing of import. When the Earl arrived and began to waddle up the stairs to his offices, Chaloner followed. Clarendon, however, was too busy to talk to him.

'The Dutch ambassador is visiting today,' he said, full of urgent agitation. 'I still hope to negotiate a peace treaty, even if everyone else has given up. And you know what you must do, anyway: thwart the Fifth Monarchists and find Ferine's killer. You do not need further instructions from me, and I do not have time to listen to a report.'

Seeing it was not an auspicious time to ask to be reinstated on the pay-roll before he was arrested for debt, Chaloner went to High Holborn, where he spent an unprofitable morning trying to learn more about the Fifth Monarchists. He met Ursula, who gave him a piece of gingerbread, then accompanied her and Atkinson to Snowflake's funeral in St Dunstan-in-the-West. He shook

230

his head when Temperance raised hopeful eyebrows, asking whether he had solved the murders, and felt guilty when he saw the disappointment in her eyes.

'Please, Tom,' she whispered, clinging to his arm as they stood in the rainswept graveyard together. 'Snowflake needs justice. And the club dies a little more every night. You are my only hope.'

It was noon before the dismal ceremony had finished, so Chaloner took a hackney back to White Hall, where he ran across the Great Court to the Spares Gallery, a chamber so named because unwanted or duplicate pieces of art hung there. It was used as an unofficial common room by minor courtiers, and Hannah was waiting for him when he arrived.

'The Queen is going to Richmond tomorrow,' she said, as they walked towards the gate. 'She wants me to go with her, but I told her I would rather stay here – you have only been home a few days, and it is unfair to expect me to leave you so soon. Besides, the Duke's Astrological Soirée is next week, and I should hate to miss that.'

'I will manage,' said Chaloner, aware that the opportunity to spend money would be considerably reduced in Richmond. He struggled to think of something that would convince her to go. 'The weather will be better there. Drier.'

Hannah ignored that unlikely notion, and continued to talk about Buckingham's unusual party. 'Apparently, Lambe is going to read the future using a bowl of blood and a human femur. I have never seen such a thing, and I confess I am curious.'

The remark gave Chaloner his solution. 'The Catholic Church maintains that all forms of divination are heresy, and the Queen will dismiss you if she finds out.'

231

'She would not! It is all perfectly innocent.'

'It is witchcraft, Hannah. Besides, if you do not go with her to Richmond, you will condemn her to the company of someone who likes her less.'

It was a sly blow: Hannah loved the Queen, and hated the thought of her being miserable.

'But I want to go to the Duke's soirée,' she objected, then added as an afterthought, 'and to stay with you. We have barely spent five minutes together in months.'

'I know, but if word seeps out that Buckingham is meddling with the occult, there will be all manner of trouble. You would lose your post, because the Queen will not condone that sort of thing.'

'No, she will not,' sighed Hannah. 'Damn! It would have been such fun. But you are right: I had better go to Richmond. Are you sure you do not mind being by yourself?'

Chaloner smiled. 'I would rather you were safely away when Lambe starts playing with his bones and blood.'

Hannah smiled back, and stood on tiptoe to kiss him. 'Nothing bad will happen, but the Queen *would* disapprove, and her good opinion is important to me. You can compensate me for the disappointment of missing the Duke's party when I come home by buying me something pretty.' Her expression turned rueful. 'Or perhaps we should just settle for a nice walk together. Then you will not fret about the cost.'

Wallingford House was a gloriously ostentatious mansion that abutted the northern edge of White Hall, a convenient arrangement for a duke who liked to be near the centre of power but not so close that his every move could be monitored by rivals. Hannah marched up to the front door with the confident ease of someone

232

who was a frequent visitor, and addressed the servants by name. They made a fuss of her, and Chaloner wondered waspishly whether it was because she was known for dispensing generous tips.

The Duke was married, but his wife rarely visited London. Consequently, Wallingford House was a manly place, full of heavy statues, paintings of slaughtered animals, and robust furniture. In addition to the usual array of cavernous reception rooms, there was a laboratory and an observatory, both of which were open to visitors that day. When Hannah disappeared to talk to people she knew, Chaloner prowled, looking for someone to question about his investigations, and it was not long before he found himself in the laboratory.

It was a large room with shelves to accommodate the various ingredients needed for the Duke's experiments. The walls were stained and pockmarked, showing that trials did not always go according to plan, and the rank smell attested to the toxic and potent ingredients that were used. He was in luck, because Admiral Lawson and Prince Rupert were there, part of a small group that was listening to Buckingham hold forth about alchemy. Chaloner doubted many understood him – for all his frivolity the Duke was intelligent and his explanations were complex.

'And that is how I shall discover the Philosopher's Stone,' he concluded.

'Give me lead any day,' declared Lawson argumentatively. 'It makes excellent ammunition, whereas gold turns rational men into drooling fools.'

He turned on his heel and stalked out, leaving Buckingham too startled to reply – a rare occurrence, as he was usually a master of the scathing riposte.

'Well, there you have it,' drawled Rupert. 'The great man has spoken. Christ God! And to think that he commands the Channel Fleet. He is unequal to defeating the Dutch, and we shall all be slaughtered in our beds.'

The other courtiers murmured lukewarm agreement, then one asked the Duke whether it was true that Lambe had predicted the current fashion for calling Clarendon's new home 'Dunkirk House'. Rupert echoed Chaloner's opinion – that the tendency had already been there, and the port's current use as a haven for Dutch pirates had done the rest. Buckingham preferred to attribute the practice to his sorcerer, and Chaloner left when they began a sniping debate about it.

Bowls of wine had been provided for guests in the hall outside, and Lawson was standing next to them, drinking his fill. Chaloner went to join him.

'If you have come to tell me to mind my tongue when addressing princes and barons, you can piss off,' the Admiral snarled. 'I am no simpering courtier, and I say what I like.'

'I am sure you do.' Chaloner wondered why Lawson had foisted himself on the gathering when he clearly despised his host, the other guests and even the house. 'I only wanted to wish you luck with the weighing of *London* on Wednesday.'

There was a flicker of something in the pale brown eyes, but Chaloner could not read it. Was it distress? Anger? Unease?

'Half the Court plans to watch,' said Lawson sullenly. 'Ghouls! I am surprised God has not asked me to smite them for their unseemly curiosity.'

'Do you think it will succeed? Lambe has predicted failure.'

'Lambe is a damned warlock! Poor *London* – she was a lovely ship on a bowline. I have transferred my flag to *Swiftsure*, but she is nowhere near *London*'s equal.'

'*Swiftsure?*' Chaloner struggled to conceal his dismay – he did not want Lawson anywhere near Captain Lester. 'Why her?'

'She is a weatherly craft, and will serve my purpose.'

Chaloner sincerely hoped the 'purpose' pertained to fighting the Dutch and not some other, darker agenda. He decided to take the bull by the horns. 'I do not believe *London* sank because someone was careless with a candle. Unless it was a very unusual one.'

Lawson glared at him. 'You can believe what you like – the opinions of landsmen are nothing to me. And you will not regale me with your views again unless you want my sword in your goddam gizzard. Why are you interested, anyway?'

'Everyone is interested. It was a great tragedy, not only for the country, but for the hundreds of families who lost loved ones. Its repercussions will be felt for decades to come.'

Lawson stared at him, his face drained of colour. Then he turned on his heel and stalked away, leaving Chaloner pondering what it was about his words that had struck a chord.

The Admiral left Wallingford House after his conversation with Chaloner. He bawled at the servants to bring him his coat, the tone and volume of his voice more fitting for a quarterdeck in a gale than the company of courtiers. He snatched it when it was brought, and strode out, barking that no, he did *not* require them to summon his coach because private carriages were for idle buggers who could not be bothered to use the legs that God had given them.

'You succeeded where I failed,' came a silky voice, and Chaloner turned to see Rupert at his side. 'I tried to make him feel unwelcome so he would leave, but he merely availed himself of more of Buckingham's refreshments. What did you say to drive him off?'

'I asked about his ship *London*,' replied Chaloner evenly, 'and the possibility that she may have blown up because of an unusual kind of candle. Perhaps one that was rigged to explode.'

Rupert's eyes became twin points of steel. 'Your remit is to infiltrate the Fifth Monarchists. It is not to speculate on matters that do not concern you. If you exceed your orders, you will find yourself in trouble.'

Chaloner fought down his irritation. 'It would be a lot easier if you told me—'

'You have all the information you need. And what are you doing here anyway? No wonder your investigation is taking so long – you spend all your time enjoying yourself.'

Chaloner was not enjoying himself at all, and resented the implication that he was slacking. 'The High Holborn Plot is complicated, and—'

'It is simple,' snapped Rupert. 'There are villains who aim to topple the monarchy and I want to know how. So go and find out before I complain to Clarendon about you.'

He whipped around and flounced away, leaving Chaloner more convinced than ever that the Prince was involved in what had happened to HMS *London*. Unsettled and unhappy, he returned to the main room, where Hannah was on her fourth glass of wine. He watched

236

her from a corner, dismayed to note that the whites of her eyes were yellow, her skin had lost its healthy lustre, and her hair had been crimped so many times into a style it would not take that it was dry and frizzled. She had never been a beauty, but she was spoiling those looks she did have by her fondness for fashion and rakish company. It was a sad realisation, and it depressed him profoundly.

To take his mind off it, he turned his attention to the rest of the guests. At the centre of one knot of admiring people was Scott, resplendent in a handsome new long-coat of wine-red with mother-of-pearl buttons down the front. His lace was as white as his fine, even teeth, and his dark hair was more luxuriant than any wig.

He was talking about his adventures in New Amsterdam, all highly improbable, although his audience cooed appreciatively. Then Chaloner became aware that he was not the only one watching: Williamson and Rupert were also listening intently. Chaloner took a step towards them, intending to ask why – and why Rupert had been following Scott at Hannah's soirée, too – but Williamson indicated with a slight shake of his head that he was to keep his distance. Chaloner complied only because he sensed answers would not be forthcoming anyway.

Also present were Duncombe and Odowde. Duncombe was drinking heavily, a dissipated figure with red-rimmed eyes and a stained coat; Odowde was pale and one arm was in a sling.

'Our friend Hubbert is dead,' reported Duncombe miserably when Chaloner went to exchange greetings with them. 'He had a seizure last night.'

'Lambe said that one of us would follow Ferine,' sighed Odowde. 'We should have listened. I scoffed at his remarks about my arm, and now look at it – broken.'

237

'I thought it was only bruised,' said Chaloner, thinking of Wiseman's account of the incident on the Banqueting House steps.

'Then you thought wrong. Look.'

Odowde moved the bandage to reveal badly swollen fingers. Chaloner was surprised: Wiseman *was* in the habit of downplaying his patients' sufferings, but he did not usually dismiss fractures as of no consequence.

'Lambe is always right,' slurred Duncombe. 'Did you hear about the devil at Tyburn?'

'I was there; Satan was not,' said Chaloner firmly. 'There was nothing but a sudden downpour and a stampede caused by someone yelling nonsense. Indeed, the culprit may have been a friend of Ferine's – Eliza Hatton, who haunts the Holborn taverns.'

Duncombe shuddered. 'Yes, *haunts* is a good word for what she does. I told Ferine there was something odd about her, and I was right. She is dead, you know.'

'Someone has killed her?' asked Chaloner uneasily.

'No, he means she is a walking corpse,' explained Odowde. 'She died forty years ago, and someone has raised her from the grave.'

'Dr Lambe, probably, given that he is a sorcerer,' said Duncombe fearfully.

'Or her name is really Alice Fanshaw, and she is staging a hoax,' said Chaloner practically. 'Because she is no more dead than you are. She—'

He was interrupted by a soft snore: Duncombe had fallen asleep.

Odowde gazed at him. 'He only turned to wine after Ferine died. And Ferine only became superstitious after his wife fell down the stairs. Death can have a very peculiar effect on people.'

238

'It can indeed,' agreed Chaloner drily.

'I told Ferine he was a fool for thinking that Grace was killed by a ghost, but now I am not so sure. Grace drank, but perhaps she did it because their house was infested by evil.'

When someone suggested a game of Blind-Man's Buff, Chaloner left the main parlour, afraid he might be drawn into it. The laboratory was now empty, which allowed him to search it, but all he found were a lot of books about the Philosopher's Stone, and a wide range of expensive, exotic and poisonous substances.

He was about to leave when he saw the corner of a document poking from under a bowl. It was a note, written on a tiny piece of paper that had been rolled at some point, because its corners had curled. It was in an elegant cursive with a flourish to each capital letter – the same as he had seen on the letters that Leving had delivered to Manning:

Your Worke is proceeding soe fast that I doe barely have time to write, and I have much to Reporte. Yet that wich you sent mee has hardly payed my debts and I must aske for more. You will be welle rewarded. I remayne Your Humble Servant Always.

It was Jones who had ordered Leving to take the missives to Manning, so did that mean Jones was in Buckingham's pay? But that made no sense, and the wheedling tenor of the note was not the Fifth Monarchist's style. Chaloner

239

stared at it, but no answers came, so he put it back and climbed the stairs to the observatory.

The King was interested in astronomy, so naturally every fashionable home had a place dedicated to studying the heavens. Indeed, Chaloner suspected it was only a matter of time before Hannah would want one, even though she had no interest in the subject and would never use it. Buckingham's was extravagant, and comprised a chamber constructed to block out light from below. It had white walls, and books about the stars sat in a case against one wall, while cupboards holding scientific instruments were along another. At the far end was a mechanism that allowed part of the ceiling to be opened, along with a telescope.

Lambe was there, scribbling on the walls with a piece of red chalk, his face a mask of intense concentration. Chaloner looked at what had been written, but could make nothing of the complex gamut of symbols and signs.

'Are you sure you should not put all that on a piece of paper?' he asked, watching the sorcerer leap in alarm. 'I cannot imagine the Duke will appreciate his home being defaced.'

'He told me to do it,' said Lambe, recovering quickly and giving one of his suave smiles. 'These are calculations that will help him find the Philosopher's Stone.'

'He is not a fool,' warned Chaloner. 'He will know if you try to trick him.'

Lambe's eyes widened. 'I am no cheat. Everyone at White Hall knows my prophecies are uncannily accurate, which is why they clamour to buy horoscopes from me.'

'Did Hubbert buy one when you predicted that he would die?'

Lambe smiled again. 'No, I imparted that advice free of charge. He should have abstained from anchovies. His stars were not auspicious, and devouring so many gave him a fatal seizure.'

'Then you will not object when the royal surgeons open him up?'

Lambe's calm gaze did not waver. 'I shall welcome it. It will vindicate me once and for all, and even more people will want to hire my skills.'

'Will your friends from the Swan with Two Necks help you meet this demand?'

'The Swan with Two Necks?' asked Lambe with a frown. 'Is that a tavern? I am afraid I am unfamiliar with it. The Duke keeps me very busy, and I have scant time for leisure.'

'I have seen you there.' Chaloner nodded to the ink-marks on the sorcerer's hands. 'They are distinctive, and a cloak will not hide them.'

'You are mistaken,' stated Lambe blandly. 'I do not know the place.'

'Perhaps we should ask Eliza Hatton, then.'

'Do you refer to the woman who was brutally murdered forty years ago? I am a sorcerer, not a necromancer! I do not commune with the dead.'

'Then perhaps you commune with Alice Fanshaw?'

'I have never heard of her,' said Lambe firmly. He peered closely at the spy, then recoiled theatrically. 'Christ God! I have never seen such an aura of danger around a man! You are clearly in need of my services. I shall read your stars, but then you must leave me to my work.'

He grabbed a handle and began to wind, so that the ceiling cranked backwards to reveal the sky. Chaloner was surprised to see that it was dark: he had squandered an entire afternoon at Wallingford House. The night was not clear, but the clouds had thinned, and the occasional star could be seen twinkling through them.

'Oh, dear,' said Lambe, squinting upwards. 'I see nothing good – blood, peril, misery.'

'I place no faith in witchcraft.'

'Then you are a fool.' Lambe seemed to grow taller and broader as he spoke, and his eyes turned peculiarly black. 'The devil has set his sights on your soul. Leave London, before his talons fasten into you and you cannot escape.'

Despite himself Chaloner was unsettled. Lambe's voice had dropped to a hiss, so it echoed eerily. Then the sorcerer moved suddenly, and a small blue flame gleamed at the tips of his fingers. Chaloner knew it was a trick, but the effect was unnerving even so.

'Heed me,' Lambe intoned. 'Now go. Your wife needs you.'

A sound behind him made Chaloner whip around quickly, but there was nothing to see, and when he turned back, Lambe had gone. Chaloner spent a few moments trying to work out how, but the observatory was dark, and the warning made him uneasy on Hannah's behalf. He ran quickly down the stairs and back to the parlour.

Hannah did indeed need him, although he suspected that Lambe had watched her mix wine with some concoction of the Duke's, and had simply guessed that the combination would make her sick. She sat in a dejected huddle as the Blind-Man's Buff raged its raucous progress around her, and smiled gratefully when Chaloner offered to take her home. He deposited her on a chair while he

242

paid a servant to fetch a hackney carriage, and was about to return to her when he saw a shadow in the chamber to his right. It was Buckingham's private office, and Scott was in there alone.

'The Duke does not take kindly to visitors pawing through his personal effects,' he said.

If Scott was shocked or embarrassed at being caught prying, he did not show it. 'I like London,' he declared jauntily. 'And I love being Cartographer Royal. It allows me to attend functions like this. And the one at your house.'

'Do you enjoy watching people drink to excess then? I would have imagined that you had enough of that with Sherwin.'

Scott's smile did not waver. 'Another week should see me finished with him, and I shall be able to concentrate on furnishing His Majesty with maps.'

'A week? Do you mean Easter? I have heard that something deadly is in the offing for then.'

Scott's eyes opened wide. 'Really? Then I hope you have warned Spymaster Williamson.'

Talking to Scott was like trying to catch an eel, thought Chaloner in disgust; the man was far too slippery to pin down. He tried again anyway.

'Who is Sherwin? We both know he is no cabinet maker, and nor does he hail from Dorset.'

'He is no one,' said Scott. 'We have been through this before. You are not—'

'Then why are you and Manning so solicitous of him? What secret does he hold?'

'I have already told you – one pertaining to a personal commercial venture.'

'So John Browne is a merchant, is he?'

'Christ, Chaloner, you play with fire! Back away, or

you will get burned. Powerful men are involved, and one is looking at you this very minute.'

Chaloner had been aware of Rupert's angry gaze for some time. 'He has invented a weapon,' he said quickly, as Scott began to sidle away. 'Is that what this secret entails?'

Scott's shocked expression answered the question more reliably than any words could ever have done. 'Leave well alone, Chaloner – if you want to live.'

He stalked away before Chaloner could stop him, leaving the spy wondering how many more of the Duke's guests were going to threaten him – Lawson, Rupert, Lambe and now Scott. Perversely, it pleased him, because it meant he was making headway. No one would bother if he was looking in the wrong direction.

Chapter 9

The clang of Sunday bells woke Chaloner the following morning, and he stared at the ceiling as worries and questions rattled around his head. The most pressing was the state of his finances, and he reached a decision as he lay there: he would send the domestics to visit their families while Hannah was in Richmond. Running the house was by far his biggest expense, and he did not need six people to see to his needs while she was away.

Seized with enthusiasm, he wrote Hannah a note outlining his plan. When it was finished, he was not sure how to sign it. Sloppy declarations of affection would likely make her suspect he was up to no good, while it seemed absurdly formal to end with 'Your humble servant'. In the end he scribbled something illegible, then made sure it was indecipherable by smudging the ink.

Outside, the streets were busy. People were flocking to church, many going early so that the ceremonies would not interfere with their plans for the rest of the day. Most went willingly, but others were resentful – staying away indicated a dangerous nonconformism, and registers were kept of those who missed without an excuse.

Chaloner was among the resentful ones. He was not a particularly religious man, but unless he wanted to be branded a dissenter, he was obliged to attend Morning Prayer in St Margaret's. Normally, he would have ensured that his name was recorded and then slipped out through the vestry door, but the servants were there, and they were the kind of people to give him away. He fretted and fidgeted through a long sermon on the dangers of divination – presumably a response to the current fad at Court – with increasing impatience.

When it was over, he waylaid Joan and told her that she and the rest of the household would not be needed until Hannah came home. She scowled, Nan burst into tears and the others exchanged sullen glances.

'You are packing us off because you cannot pay our wages,' Joan said accusingly. 'We are to be thrown on the streets after years of faithful service.'

'"Years of faithful service",' repeated Chaloner wonderingly, thinking he had known none of them longer than six months, and not one was what he would have called loyal.

'You will end in debtors' gaol,' wept Nan. 'And it serves you right.'

Chaloner pulled out the smaller of Sherwin's two purses, and slapped it into Joan's hand. 'That should cover what you are owed, and pay some of Hannah's creditors, too.'

'*Your* creditors. The purchases were made in *your* name, as is right in a marriage.' Joan saw Chaloner's angry expression, and prudently hastened to change the subject. 'Leving visited us again last night and said you must meet him at the Talbot at ten o'clock.' Even though she was

246

playing with fire, she could not resist a spiteful smile. 'You will have to run or you will be late.'

Chaloner did indeed have to run, as there were no hackneys available. He arrived, breathless and sweating, just as the clocks were striking the hour, to discover that the Talbot's hall had been hired for another large gathering of Fifth Monarchists. Again, the participants were disguised as lawyers, and again, the real men of law were intensely interested.

Recalling Jones's irritation that he had not donned suitable robes the last time, Chaloner filched a set that had been left unattended near the door. They were too small, but still looked better than the bizarre attire worn by most other conspirators, all of whom seemed to be chatting about feeding chickens, airing beds or paying the milkman. He felt a wave of despair that so many ordinary folk had allowed themselves to become embroiled in such dangerous business.

Leving was waiting. 'You are late,' he said, with one of his vacant grins. 'I was beginning to think I might have to monitor this meeting alone.'

Chaloner scowled at him. 'What did I tell you about sending messages to my home?'

Leving waved a careless hand, leaving Chaloner slightly wrong-footed: he was intimidating when he was angry, as Joan had just seen, yet Leving did not seem bothered in the slightest.

'I have been working on my list of members,' he chirruped merrily. 'I have names for twelve of the Sanhedrin and about twenty of the folk here today. How many have you got?'

Chaloner was unwilling to tell him that he had no intention of compiling such a register, but was spared

247

from inventing an excuse when Manning arrived, his fat, grave face grey and strained. He was limping more heavily than ever.

'Chilblains bothering you?' asked Leving sympathetically.

Manning nodded. 'They are agony. Look.' He slipped a foot from his shoe to reveal a sorely chapped heel. 'And these rough stockings do not help. I wish we were not at war, because then I could have bought some nice soft Dutch ones.'

'Did you retrieve Sherwin after abandoning him to robbers?' asked Chaloner, thinking it was testament to Manning's selfishness that he viewed the conflict in terms of his own comfort.

Manning gulped in alarm. 'I did no such thing! He is quite safe.'

He pushed past Chaloner and entered the hall. Chaloner followed to see upwards of a hundred people there, and could tell by the way some were gazing around that many had not been to the Talbot before – they were different from the last two hundred. His heart sank. Perhaps Jones was right to claim he had ten thousand followers. And perhaps he had chosen Easter Day for his uprising not for its religious significance, but because his supporters would be in the city for Lady Day business.

'Lord!' breathed Leving. 'The only way to find out everyone's name – and remember them for Williamson – will be to ask them as they leave and write them down. Do you think the Sanhedrin would notice?'

Chaloner rubbed his head, wondering yet again whether Leving was in complete control of his faculties. Indeed, he was surprised the man was still alive, and thought Williamson was criminally reckless to use such

248

a buffoon, no matter how desperate for spies he declared himself to be. But there was no time for further reflection, because the dour-faced leaders had arrived. They took their places at the front of the hall, and Jones raised his right hand. Immediately, the Sanhedrin began to chant the oath about secrecy and loyalty, led by Strange in a booming voice that was probably audible on High Holborn. Most of the assembly looked bemused, though, and Jones had to repeat it a phrase at a time, so that they could say it after him. Chaloner was uncomfortably reminded of his wedding vows.

'Horses,' said a baker briskly, when everyone was settled and Jones declared the meeting open. 'Have you hired any yet? Our troops will not be very impressive if they are obliged to race through the streets on foot, and time is getting short now – less than seven days.'

'It is all in hand,' replied Jones smoothly.

'And weapons?' asked Atkinson. He looked troubled. 'I dislike violence, but our enemies will be armed, and we cannot meet muskets and cannon with sticks and garden forks.'

'They are ready, too,' replied Jones. He smiled, but his reptilian eyes stayed cold, which did nothing to relieve the anxieties of the audience. More than a few exchanged worried glances.

'By this time next week, King Jesus will have moved into White Hall,' declared Strange firmly. 'And King Charles will be in the very lowest level of hell.'

'Will he?' asked Ursula unhappily. 'I know he heads a craven government, which bleeds us dry with taxes for debauchery and foreign wars, but I should not like to be responsible for him ending up in hell. He is probably a good man at heart.'

'He is a usurper!' cried Strange angrily. 'And he will not be alone in his fiery pit. There will be plenty of others to share his fate.'

'Good,' said Leving, amiably. 'He will have someone to talk to. Eternity is a very long time, after all.'

The Sanhedrin exchanged startled glances at this remark, although a number of the audience nodded sage agreement. Jones recovered quickly.

'I have written a pamphlet on precisely this subject,' he announced pompously. 'It denounces the Stuart usurper's profligacy, along with his wickedness in arranging firework displays and rebuilding theatres while his poorest subjects struggle to pay the coal tax.'

'Have you?' asked Ursula politely. 'I do not believe I have read it.'

Jones grimaced. 'I cannot afford to publish it yet, so you will have to wait until the Last Millennium. But my musings will make you understand why there is no need to feel sorry for a monarch who places frivolous entertainment before the welfare of his people.'

'I want to know details of the plan,' said the one-armed sailor named Tucker. 'It is all very well saying that King Jesus will appear on Sunday, but what must we do to ensure it exactly?'

'We have been through this,' snapped Jones. 'I shall reveal particulars nearer the time.'

'How much nearer?' pressed Tucker, unfazed by Jones's angry response. 'You will tell me today, or I am leaving the city and you will have to manage without me.'

'Very well,' sighed Jones, when it became clear that most of the assembly felt the same. 'By the end of Easter Day, we shall have seized the Tower, killed the

King, set London alight, established a republic and redistributed all private property. Does that answer your question?'

There was a stunned silence, followed by a clamour of questions and cheers. Jones folded his arms with an air of finality, while Chaloner stared at him, astounded that he thought he could achieve so much in so short a span of time.

'We should execute the government, too,' said Strange, audible only by virtue of having the loudest voice. 'Then they will not make a nuisance of themselves in the Last Millennium.'

'No!' cried Ursula. 'Politicians have just as much right to enjoy the Glorious Design as the rest of us, and some are decent people.'

'But not many,' stated Jones. 'As my pamphlet outlining their sins will demonstrate.'

The debate dragged on until Strange silenced it with an impassioned speech about liberty in place of tyranny and godliness instead of idolatry, concluding with the claim that it was every man's duty to fight against enemies of the truth. It was idealistic claptrap, but it calmed those who thought Jones's plans were overly daring.

Jones ended the meeting with a prayer, after which people filed out, some forgetting to don the disguises they had worn in, and others wrapping their cloaks over their faces in such a bizarre parody of stealth that the lawyers in the Talbot stared in astonishment.

Soon, only the Sanhedrin remained. Atkinson was pale and puffy eyed as he thanked Chaloner for attending Snowflake's funeral. Ursula handed the stockinger a clean handkerchief when he started to weep, and the others

251

stood in awkward silence until he had regained control of himself.

'The meeting went well,' he managed to snuffle eventually. 'Our people are eager for victory.'

'I approve of your aims,' said Tucker to Jones. 'But I think they are too ambitious for a single day. We will never get it all done, especially if we stop for dinner.'

'Then we had better fast,' said Jones frostily. 'In the name of Christ.'

'I do not think we should incinerate the city, though,' put in Ursula, 'but we can certainly redistribute property. This coal tax is killing the poor. Literally.'

'And a republic would be nice,' added Atkinson wistfully. 'It is difficult to have equal rights and justice for all when there are ruling aristocrats around.'

'So who murdered Quelch then?' asked Leving with an appalling lack of subtlety. 'Perhaps it is a traitor – a foul deceiver who has been persuaded to betray his friends.'

Chaloner readied himself to make a dash for the door, sure someone was going to conclude that Leving was the culprit, along with his conveniently available gunpowder expert.

'A traitor?' gulped Tucker. 'Surely not!' Then a worried frown creased his face. 'Yet someone *did* kill Quelch . . .'

'It was not me,' declared Strange, when more than one pair of eyes strayed in his direction.

'His death is a serious blow,' said Tucker in the taut silence that followed. 'Perhaps we should postpone our venture, just to be on the safe side.'

'And how will you explain that to King Jesus?' asked Jones archly. 'We have been preparing the way for months, and He will be disappointed if we falter now.'

'We may have no choice,' said a man whom Chaloner thought was named Venner. 'I am happy to sacrifice my life for the Cause, but I do not want it to be in vain.'

'It will not be in vain,' vowed Strange, eyes blazing. 'It will be for the Supreme Authority.'

'Yet Tucker is right – Quelch's murder is a serious blow,' said Venner. 'I shall feel happier when we know who killed him. Who saw him last?'

'Not I,' replied Strange immediately. 'So thou canst stop eyeing me so accusingly. I have not seen him since we went to the hangings on Thursday.'

'Is that so?' asked Tucker, eyes narrowed. 'Then did I imagine you together in an alehouse on Friday – the night he died? Do not deny it, Strange. You both spoke to me.'

'Oh, yes,' said Strange, flushing red. 'I forgot. Quelch took me to a tavern called Hell, in Old Palace Yard. Hast thou been there? It is not called Hell for nothing. A vile place, and typical of the low kind of establishment that he liked to frequent.'

'Why did you lie, then?' asked Leving baldly. Strange fingered his dagger, and Chaloner wondered whether he should bother to intervene if the burly Fifth Monarchist tried to plunge it into Leving's heart. The investigation would be a lot easier without Leving's bumbling ways threatening to expose them at every turn.

'I did not lie,' said Strange tightly. 'It slipped my mind. What business is it of thine, anyway?'

'Anything to do with this plot is our business,' flashed Venner. 'What did you talk about in this alehouse?'

'Nothing of consequence. The plan. Its shortcomings.'

'What shortcomings?' asked Leving innocently.

'The fact that thou art right – we *do* have a traitor in

253

our midst,' snarled Strange, becoming angry at the inquis-
ition. 'There have been rumours in the coffee houses
about us, which means someone hath broken his sacred
oath. I do not feel safe, and I told Quelch so.'

'Why confide in him?' asked Atkinson. 'I thought you
disliked each other.'

'I was probing him, plying him with ale to see what
he might confess in his cups,' replied Strange tightly. 'But
the devil guarded his tongue and he revealed nothing,
so I do not know who is responsible for sharing our
secrets with the enemies of God. However, when I find
out, I shall slit his gizzard and wrap his innards around
his throat.'

'Lord!' gulped Leving, who could not have looked
more guilty had he tried. 'I am very thirsty. May I buy
anyone an ale?'

Chaloner winced at the transparent attempt to change
the subject, while Leving brandished his purse, an expensive item embroidered with a gold crest. It was not the
sort of thing a common man would own, and told anyone
with eyes that either he had stolen it or he had accepted
payment from a wealthy man. And as accusations of
treachery were being bandied about, he could not have
produced it at a less opportune moment.

'No, thank you,' said Jones coolly. 'However, this talk
of traitors concerns me. I was unaware that anyone had
broken faith with the Almighty by chatting about our
intentions.'

'Perhaps we *should* postpone the uprising,' said Atkinson.
'It would be unethical to risk lives needlessly. Did you
see our followers today, desperate for change and their
faces full of hope? We cannot endanger them without—'

'God will protect them,' interrupted Strange, and

Chaloner saw he was relieved that the discussion had moved away from the murder of Quelch. 'Dost thou not trust Him?'

'Of course,' replied Atkinson. 'Although I confess I am more inspired by the philosophical and moral tenets of our Cause than the religious ones.'

'I shall feel better if I know *how* you plan to seize the Tower, kill the King and all the rest of it,' said Leving, beaming his foolish smile. 'I shall need to buy a new sword if there is to be much fighting, because this one is a bit rusty.'

'All in good time,' said Jones smoothly. 'However, you may certainly expect fireworks.'

'Is that where Chaloner comes in?' pounced Leving. 'He will set explosions?'

Strange narrowed his eyes. 'Thou hast always asked too many questions. Perhaps *thou* art the traitor.' He surged to his feet and shoved his knife towards Leving's throat.

'Stop!' Ursula looked horrified at her first taste of violence. 'No bloodshed. Please!'

Strange released a sharp bark of laughter. 'No bloodshed? What dost thou think will happen when our plan unrolls? Or dost thou believe that London will fall without a blow being struck?'

'Well, yes, actually,' replied Ursula, wide-eyed. 'My sister says everyone will join us when they understand what we aim to do, so this will be a *peaceful* revolution. Now put down your blade, Mr Strange. I do not like you waving it about in such a hostile manner.'

'Neither do I,' whispered Leving.

'Our uprising is too important a matter to leave to chance,' growled Strange, scowling at his victim. 'If thou art innocent, thou wilt rise from the dead in a week, and I shall apologise.'

'Wait,' said Chaloner, supposing he had better do something before a murder was committed in front of him. 'Leving and I have been collecting money for the Cause. He would not have done that if he was betraying you.'

He pulled out the second purse that Sherwin had given him, and dropped it on the table. There was a collective gasp as coins spilled out. It was an impressive hoard, and he wondered how Manning had come by it.

'Where did you get this?' demanded Strange, quickly sheathing his blade so he could reach out and touch it.

'Does it matter?' asked Chaloner, before Leving could say something stupid.

'It is not the Tsar's, is it?' asked Atkinson uneasily.

'How can it be part of the Tsar's treasure when Chaloner and I collected it together?' asked Leving, grinning so idiotically that Chaloner was sure he did not appreciate the danger he was still in. 'What a silly question, Atkinson! I had not taken *you* for an ass.'

'How generous of you both,' said Jones, picking up the large ruby ring and surveying it with a practised eye. 'Thank you.'

Had Leving been remotely reliable, Chaloner would have asked for his help in following the Sanhedrin once the meeting broke up. As it was, he was relieved when Leving said he had other rebels to monitor in a different part of the city. Chaloner watched him saunter away, thinking that if the Fifth Monarchists did not eliminate him, another sect would.

'Thank you for preventing violence,' said Ursula with

a shy smile as she limped up to him. 'Mr Strange so desperately wants us to succeed that he is not always sensible. Likewise Mr Jones, although I am sure he does not really intend to use weapons.'

'Of course he does,' said Chaloner, thinking her a fool for believing that men like Jones and Strange would stay their hands when it came to implementing the Glorious Design. 'There are rumours that silver cannon will play a role.'

Ursula blinked. 'Silver cannon? I did not know there was such a thing. Still, no matter what means are used to bring it about, the uprising will end oppression and injustice. My sister wrote a pamphlet about it, and between you and me, it is better than anything Mr Jones has penned. Shall I look you out a copy? I have hundreds of spares.'

From that remark, Chaloner surmised that no one had wanted to buy it.

'I shall be away from London tomorrow,' he said, thinking it was time to visit Temple Mills and talk to Snowflake's father. Telling Ursula his plans would hopefully ensure that the Sanhedrin was not suspicious when he disappeared.

'Then we shall see you on your return.' She smiled so sweetly that he felt guilty at using her, which was not something that often happened to a man who made his living with lies.

After she had gone, he loitered until Strange and Jones emerged. Atkinson was with them, talking about Mrs Trapnel's *The Cry of a Stone*, which was an account of the visions she had experienced in a multi-day trance during the Commonwealth. Neither was listening, and it was not long before Jones bade him a curt farewell.

Strange did the same, and they left the stockinger staring after them in hurt bewilderment. He shuffled off alone, and Chaloner continued after the other two.

Bells were ringing all across the city to announce more Sunday services, and the bustle meant it was easy for Chaloner to follow his quarry unseen. Jones and Strange walked down Ludgate Hill towards the greasy, foul-smelling Fleet River, then aimed for Thames Street. Eventually, they reached a narrow lane called Garlick Hill, where they entered a pretty little house with ivy trailing attractively over the porch.

Chaloner waited a moment, then approached it. The door was unlocked, so he stepped inside. The house was clean, obsessively neat and sweetly scented with the rose petals that had been left in a bowl on a chest. There was a flight of stairs in front of him, and as he could hear Strange and Jones clattering about in a pantry at the back, he decided to check the rest of the house before attempting to eavesdrop on them. There were two pleasantly furnished bedrooms on the upper floor, both smelling faintly of lavender.

He searched them quickly, but discovered nothing of value – and nothing to indicate that anyone other than Jones or Strange occupied them. He crept back downstairs, and when he heard them chatting in an easy, conversational way together he explored the ground floor, too.

There was a parlour near the stairs, evidently for formal use, because it contained solid furniture and paintings that screamed of staid respectability. There was a harpsichord in one corner, a heavy, stocky item that had been chosen because its paintwork contrasted nicely with the wallpaper – a comparatively new fad from France – and some unusually fine Dutch chairs. On the mantelpiece

258

was a small box of the same powder that Jones had wanted delivered to Manning, suggesting that he had filched a bit before handing it over. There was not enough to do much damage, but it was still not the sort of thing Chaloner would have kept in *his* drawing room.

He stood by the harpsichord as he looked around, and his fingers naturally strayed to the keys. He touched them lightly, but they were oddly stiff. Bemused, he pressed harder and heard a muted twang: something was preventing the strings from sounding. He opened the lid to discover a package. He shoved it in his coat, then crept along the corridor towards the pantry, where he was startled to see a scene of extraordinary domesticity: Jones was chopping vegetables, his clothes protected by the kind of lacy apron that Chaloner's mother used to wear, while Strange knelt at the hearth with a pair of bellows.

'. . . dreadfully expensive,' Strange was saying. 'Thou wouldst not believe the cost of butter. Then I went to the costermonger for peas, until I remembered that thou dost not like them.'

'I do not,' said Jones. 'Would you prefer one onion or two? I recommend two, because Ursula gave us this piece of beef a week ago, and they will help with the flavour.'

'Two it is, then,' replied Strange, more amiable than he was in other company. Once he had the fire blazing to his satisfaction, he sat back on his heels and glanced at Jones. 'I am glad Quelch is gone. He was a liability.'

'It is a pity you were seen quarrelling with him in the Westminster tavern, though. It has made everyone think that you had something to do with his demise.'

'I cannot help the asinine thoughts of fools,' replied Strange shortly. 'But never mind him. How dost thou feel our business is going?'

259

'Not as well as I might have hoped, but I think we shall prevail. The money Chaloner gave us will certainly expedite matters.'

Chaloner grimaced: he had intended to save Leving's life, not give the uprising a financial boost that might see it succeed. He listened a while longer, but heard nothing to help with his enquiries, and when they began comparing recipes for plum jam, he realised he was wasting his time. He left, and went to the nearest coffee house to examine the package.

The Stillyard on Thames Street was a small, dingy place with greasy benches, stained tables and an insalubrious clientele. Chaloner recognised some patrons as belonging to the criminal gang called the Hectors, and had he not been adept at looking after himself, he would have gone elsewhere. As it was, he ignored them and they ignored him, an arrangement that suited everyone.

The package had been wrapped in oiled cloth and tied with so many careful knots that it was clear the contents were important. He cut them quickly, then peeled away layer after layer of protective covering until he reached two reports, one in Dutch and the other in French. Both had identical diagrams of a cannon, along with notes that gave technical details of its making. He peered at the words in the yellow light of a lamp that was too far away to be helpful. However, it was not long before he began to understand their significance.

Most artillery was made of brass, as it was one of few materials that could withstand the powerful forces generated by hurling missiles over long distances, yet the documents in his hand gave details of cannon that could be made of iron. This was innovative, as iron normally became too hot and blew up. He recalled the argument

260

he had overheard between Rupert and Lawson in the club, when they had debated which metal was better. Rupert had argued for iron, and the documents Chaloner held described a process whereby guns could be made with it. The invention was attributed to 'PR' and references to Court and the Royal Society made it perfectly clear that this was Prince Rupert. Chaloner and Thurloe had been half right: the Prince had devised not a new weapon, but a new way to manufacture them.

So this was how Rupert used his creative talents, thought Chaloner, as a number of answers snapped clear in his mind. He studied the reports more closely. In both French and Dutch were phrases that could be translated as 'turned and annealed', terms he had heard Rupert throw at Lawson. And when Buckingham had asked whether Rupert had devised a 'candle' that was less prone to explode, he had actually been asking after the Prince's experiments with iron guns.

Chaloner pondered the implications of what Rupert had done. Iron was lighter than brass, so would be easier to transport. It was also cheaper. The invention would be worth a fortune – more than a fortune, because it would give one fighting force an advantage over another, and no price could be put on that. If the Dutch knew the secret, and the documents Chaloner had found said they either did or were about to, it might affect the outcome of the war.

So why did Jones and Strange have the reports? Were they going to sell them and use the proceeds to fund their rebellion? Were Rupert's guns the 'silver cannon' mentioned in the speech of the three rebels who had been hanged at Tyburn? Did Jones intend to turn these weapons on London?

Regardless of the answers, it explained why Rupert was keen for the High Holborn Plot to be crushed – and crushed so completely that not one of its members would be left free to talk. It was not an uprising he feared so much as someone making off with his secret. And *that* was why Rupert had been following Scott, both at Hannah's party and Buckingham's – Scott was not a Fifth Monarchist, but Manning was, and the pair of them were partners.

At last, Chaloner felt as though he was in a position to move forward with his enquiries.

Acting on impulse, Chaloner went to Middle Row. He knew Jones had not confided in Ursula – she would not have been *his* first choice of a co-conspirator either – but perhaps she had overheard something that would make sense now that he understood what was involved. She took a long time to answer the door, and when she did, her hair was rumpled and her face flushed.

'It is only Mr Chaloner,' she called over her shoulder. 'He must have smelled the soup we are about to eat. My broths are famous all over London, so it is to be expected.'

She was speaking to Atkinson, who emerged shyly from the parlour.

'I came to bring her some yarn,' the stockinger said, although Chaloner could tell from the cosy layout of the rugs between the fire and the virginals that neither soup nor thread had featured in what they had been doing.

'You must eat with us,' gabbled Ursula, blushing scarlet when she realised where Chaloner was looking. 'I shall bring bowls, while John tidies up the mess my neighbour's children made of the mats when they visited earlier.'

Chaloner followed Atkinson into the parlour, where

the stockinger hastily toed the offending items into a less incriminating arrangement.

'Do not tell Jones,' begged Atkinson, when he saw Chaloner was not deceived by their explanations. 'He already thinks I only joined the Fifth Monarchists because of her, and if he learns that we have become close . . . well, he will assume I do not care about the Cause.'

'And do you?' asked Chaloner.

'Oh, yes! I should very much like to live in a just and ethical republic, where all men and women are equal, and where everyone is gainfully employed. I think I shall ask her to marry me on Easter Sunday, once all this has come to pass.'

Ursula arrived with the soup at that point, sparing Chaloner the need to comment. She served it with fresh bread and generous slices of cheese, simple but wholesome fare that was a world away from pickled ling pie and orange-rind comfits.

'Do you like it?' Ursula asked pointedly. Both men had been too busy eating to pay her the compliments she considered her due.

They hastened to oblige, although the fact that they had not immediately sung her praises meant it was a while before she was satisfied. Chaloner let Atkinson do most of the talking, feeling the stockinger needed the practice if he was going to spend the rest of his life with her.

'Why did Clarendon really dismiss you?' Ursula asked of Chaloner, when Atkinson eventually stuttered into silence, his store of flattery spent. 'Because I do not believe you mislaid the Tsar's treasure. That would have been careless, and you do not strike me as a silly man.'

Chaloner hoped the rest of the Sanhedrin did not

share her scepticism, and wished again that the Earl had devised a better excuse for their 'falling out'.

'The ship chartered to take me to Russia sank,' he explained. 'And the hold containing the jewels flooded before I could reach them.'

'Heavens!' breathed Atkinson, agog. 'Did you know that the philosophers Aristippos and Zeno were shipwrecked? I taught myself Greek in order to read great masters like them. And Latin, of course. Have you studied Cicero? His *De Legibus* states that the law should promote good and forbid evil – a simple tenet, but one that our judicial system seems to have overlooked.'

'All will be set right at the Last Millennium,' said Ursula soothingly.

Chaloner seized the opportunity to put the questions he had come to ask. 'Do you think Jones is so eager to see it installed that he will make a pact with the Dutch? Or the French?'

'Of course not!' exclaimed Ursula, shocked. 'We are at war with the Dutch. And the French are not particularly nice either.'

'Quite,' agreed Atkinson. 'It would be terribly wrong. Besides, we shall be a lot more stable after our uprising than we are now, so the Dutch will gain nothing from helping us.'

'You may not believe it, but Mr Jones is a very gentle man at heart,' said Ursula. She was right: Chaloner did not believe it. 'He wept when I sang "Flow my Tears" by Dowland.'

The investigation flew from Chaloner's mind at the mention of one of his favourite pieces. 'Will you sing it for us?'

She regarded him uncertainly. 'What, now?'

Chaloner nodded, and as it was a song that was meant to be accompanied, he went to the virginals and played the opening chords. The viol was his first love, but he was perfectly proficient with several other instruments, too. Smiling, Ursula began to sing, and although her voice was not the best he had ever heard, it was perfectly creditable and her diction was excellent. Atkinson was full of praise, of course.

'Wonderful!' he cried, when they had finished. 'I would ask for a little Palestrina, but he is best performed in multiple parts. How about Gibbons instead? You take the virginals again, Chaloner, while Ursula and I warble a duet.'

Never one to refuse an opportunity for music, Chaloner obliged, and although he was aware that time was passing, he played on anyway. It was Ursula who eventually indicated that she had had enough, although he could have continued much longer.

'Thank you,' she said with a smile. 'I have not enjoyed singing so much since my sister visited last year. She plays the virginals, too, although not as well as you.'

'I am glad she is not here,' said Atkinson. He shrugged at Ursula's surprise. 'Our rebellion would not please her. It is too mysterious, and she would dislike the way Jones declines to tell us what is happening. I know he is worried about betrayal, but he should trust his Sanhedrin.'

The remark allowed Chaloner to ask a number of questions about the Fifth Monarchists and the possibility that Jones had acquired the secret of Rupert's iron guns, but it did not take him long to ascertain that Ursula and Atkinson knew even less than he did. The names of the Sanhedrin they confided were probably aliases, and neither could tell him why Jones and Quelch had been to speak to Admiral Lawson at Temperance's club.

'I hope they have not invited *him* to join in,' said Atkinson. 'I know he professes to be one of us, but he is more interested in smiting God's enemies than in establishing an equitable society.'

'And it is odd that all his sailors died when HMS *London* blew up, yet his family survived,' added Ursula. 'What are the chances of that happening? I do not believe that all his kin can swim and all his sailors cannot. I am not accusing him of anything untoward, you understand, but my mind is uneasy.'

So was Chaloner's, although he doubted putting questions to Lawson again would be any more successful than it had been the last time he had tried. A sudden clamour from the street made Ursula wince.

'The Fleece tavern,' she explained. 'It attracts some terribly noisy patrons.'

'Speaking of taverns, have you ever been to the Swan with Two Necks?' asked Chaloner, supposing he might as well see whether they knew anything about the peculiar business that took place nearby.

'No,' said Atkinson stiffly. 'It is the haunt of very dubious people. Necromancers, no less.'

'Necromancers?'

'Witches who commune with the dead. One was hanged at Tyburn on Thursday, and the devil came along and saved her.'

'Moreover, a woman named Eliza Hatton frequents the Swan,' added Ursula with pursed lips, 'but she has been dead these last forty years. A necromancer raised her up to walk among us, but her hands are like ice, and she is deathly pale because there is no blood in her veins.'

Eliza's hands *were* cold, thought Chaloner, remembering their touch when she had grabbed one of his own.

Then he recalled that Wiseman was treating her for some medical condition that caused an unnatural chilling of the extremities, and could only suppose she was putting her affliction to good use by allowing such rumours to circulate about her – people might be more inclined to buy her witchy services if they thought she was special.

'I have met her,' he said. 'She is not dead.'

'But that just demonstrates the skill of the necromancers,' said Ursula sagely. 'They can make even the most decayed of corpses look fresh. And if you do not believe me, visit her tomb in St Andrew's Church. Her painting is above it – that will prove I am right.'

The clocks were striking eight as Chaloner left Middle Row. His mind was full of answers and questions in equal measure, and he wanted to discuss them with someone he trusted. He headed for Lincoln's Inn, but Thurloe was out and the porter said he was not expected back until the following day. Disappointed, he took a hackney to Clarendon House, supposing he had better report to the Earl. It was very dark along Piccadilly, with no moon and unusually heavy clouds.

'There you are at last!' cried Kipps in relief. 'The Earl expected you at six, and is vexed to have been kept waiting so long. So watch your tongue – even a hint of insolence tonight might see you clapped in irons.'

He had bundled Chaloner into My Lord's Lobby before Chaloner could tell him that he had no idea what he was talking about. He had certainly received no summons, and would not have been pleased if he had, given that he and the Earl were supposed to be estranged. The door closed behind him with a snap, so he made his way across the vast expanse of Turkey carpet to where a monstrous

267

fire burned in the hearth. The Earl was not alone, as 'Mr Smith' and 'Mr Lee' were visiting him again.

'About time,' said the Earl crossly. 'We were beginning to think you were not coming.'

'I hope you have something to tell us,' growled Rupert, who was sprawled opposite, dirty boots leaving indelible marks on an exquisite silk rug that would have cost Chaloner a month's salary. 'I should not like to think that we have been kicking our heels here for nothing.'

'The Earl sent his letter to your house this afternoon,' said Williamson coolly. 'Asking you to meet us here at six. *Six*, not eight.'

Chaloner looked at them. Williamson and Rupert were angry, and the Earl had never liked him very much. Kipps was right: incautious replies would indeed be unwise. 'My apologies, sirs. I have been out all day, monitoring Fifth Monarchists. I did not receive the—'

'Then let us hope you have something useful to report,' interrupted Rupert curtly.

Aiming to appease, Chaloner provided a detailed account of the rebels' meetings, along with Jones's bald declaration that Easter Sunday would see the King assassinated, the Tower seized and London put to the torch. However, when Rupert demanded the names of the Sanhedrin, Chaloner provided several fictitious ones among the likes of Jones, Strange and Tucker, unwilling to sacrifice misguided fools like Atkinson and Ursula until he knew how far they were prepared to go in their efforts to usher in a better society. He saved the best part until last.

'And they have learned about a new kind of weapon,' he said, presenting the reports he had found to the Earl. 'Which I believe they intend to sell overseas – if they have not done so already.'

'What?' Rupert leapt up to snatch the documents from Clarendon's hand. He scanned them quickly. 'French and what seems to be Dutch. Where did you get these?'

'From Jones's house in Garlick Row,' replied Chaloner. 'Hidden in a harpsichord.'

Rupert was white, although whether from rage or horror was difficult to say. Williamson was impassive, and the Earl looked confused – clearly he had not been told about the guns.

'You speak French and Dutch,' said Rupert, brandishing the papers in Chaloner's face. 'So tell me, have you read these?'

'Of course,' replied Chaloner. 'Or I would not have known they were important.'

'He makes a valid point,' said Williamson quickly, as Rupert girded himself up for a tantrum.

'What do they say?' asked the Earl curiously.

'They are designs for a new kind of cannon,' replied Chaloner, speaking over Rupert, who began to claim they were nothing. He forged on, suspecting he would be safer once the matter was in the open. 'Iron ones that have been "turned and annealed". They will be cheaper, lighter and safer than brass.'

He glanced at the Prince, wondering whether he would have the decency to confess that the invention was his, and that his chief interest in the matter was fiscal.

'How interesting,' said Williamson in the silence that followed.

'I have done what you asked and learned the Fifth Monarchist's plans,' said Chaloner, when no one added anything else. 'Nothing will be gained from letting them progress further, so I suggest you arrest the leaders without delay.'

269

And spare ten thousand farmers, tradesmen and labourers from showing their hands, he thought. Men and women who wanted no more than reasonable taxes and a fair legal system.

'No,' said Rupert, and Chaloner saw a flicker of annoyance in Williamson's eyes at the presumption – such decisions were the Spymaster's to make. 'We want to snare the entire movement, not just a few officers.'

'Why?' challenged Chaloner. 'The foot-soldiers are nothing, and will slip back into oblivion once the ringleaders have gone. They will be no trouble.'

'I disagree – they have tasted treason, which is a heady cup,' argued Rupert. 'They can never be trusted again, and we must purge the country of the lot of them. We will arrest no one yet, but let the matter run its course and strike nearer the time. You will continue to earn their trust, and produce a list of every man, woman and child who dares to move against us.'

'But—' began Chaloner.

'Do as I tell you,' snapped Rupert. 'And say nothing about these documents to anyone. Do I make myself clear?' Then he hesitated, uncertain for the first time. 'Have you heard anyone talk about Hackney Marsh or Temple Mills during your enquiries?'

Chaloner was tempted to remind him that Snowflake hailed from there, and that Rupert had discussed the place with her at the club, claiming to know her father. When Snowflake had first mentioned the conversation, Chaloner had assumed that Rupert had lied, to inveigle himself into her good graces. Now the mystery had thickened and Snowflake was dead, he suspected it had been the truth. He regarded the Prince narrowly, thinking that if Rupert had been complicit in her

270

murder, he would pay the price, member of the royal family or no.

'Yes,' he replied carefully. 'A young woman I know came from there. She was friends with Ferine and was stabbed three days ago. I plan to ride there tomorrow to visit her family.'

'Do not go,' ordered Rupert. 'You have more important matters to attend here.'

He stalked out, taking the reports with him. The Earl, disconcerted by the Prince's sour temper, went to the table to pour himself more wine. Williamson took the opportunity to whisper to Chaloner when his host's back was turned.

'He is right. Any malcontent escaping this purge will race to join another revolt at the first opportunity. We cannot afford to be merciful to people who seek to destabilise our country.'

'Yet their demands are not unreasonable,' Chaloner muttered back. 'And arresting them will win the sympathy of the entire nation. Then there really *will* be trouble.'

A short while later, Chaloner walked down Clarendon House's drive, weary now and ready for bed. It was still raining, a light, airy drizzle carried by a gusting breeze. His hackney had gone, so he resigned himself to walk, no pleasant task in the wet and pitch dark.

He had not taken many steps along Piccadilly before the sound of someone skidding warned him that he was not alone. He reached for his sword, but too late: someone crashed into him, knocking him from his feet, although he could tell by the way his assailant staggered that it had not been intentional. He struggled to his knees, but was hit a second time from behind.

271

There followed a desperate struggle. As he flailed with his sword, Chaloner sometimes glimpsed the shadowy outlines of his assailants, but it was too dark to count them, so he had no idea how many he was fighting. The dense blackness worked to his advantage, though: it meant his attackers struck each other more often than him.

Yet he was losing ground even so. There were too many opponents, and each time he fell or was knocked down, it was harder to rise. He lunged with his blade, only to meet empty air, which made him stumble. A unlucky punch completed the rest, and he went down again, this time falling a good deal farther than he should have done. With alarm, he realised he was slithering into one of the great ditches that ran along the edge of the road.

He reached the bottom, and immediately began to scramble upwards, disliking the notion of being trapped in such a place, but it was difficult to gain his footing. Then he heard a punch and a grunt. The fight was still in progress, as his assailants had yet to discover that he was no longer there.

It was his chance to escape. Paddling silently through icy, calf-deep water, he headed away from the skirmish. When he felt he had put enough distance between him and his attackers, he clambered out. He listened intently, but the only sounds were the patter of rain and the whisper of wind in the trees. He waited until he was sure he had not been followed, then cut across the open fields towards Tothill Street. It was a muddy, miserable journey, but he arrived eventually, letting himself in through a window at the back lest someone was watching the house from the road.

Inside, the place felt cold and abandoned, and Joan had placed sheets over the furniture, stopped the clocks and set mouse-traps in every corner. He washed in the dark, unwilling to light a candle lest it was seen.

Feeling better in a clean shirt and an old woollen jacket, he raided the pantry for food. Not surprisingly, nothing perishable had been left, but there were several bottles of pears and a jar of pickled eggs – ones that had been prepared by Joan, rather than Hannah, and so were edible. He washed them down with the dregs of some wine he found in the cellar, and went to bed.

Chapter 10

Chaloner slept poorly that night, starting awake at every creak and groan. In the end, he gave up, and sat staring out of the window. It was roughly two hours before dawn and the day was Monday, which meant he had less than a week to learn what Jones was plotting and stop it. He began to make plans.

Rupert's question about Temple Mills told him that he needed to travel there immediately, not only to speak to Snowflake's father, but also to determine why the Prince had forbidden him to go, although he thought he already knew the answer to that.

He shaved quickly, then donned clothes that were respectable enough for visiting bereaved parents and suitable for riding – a doublet with flared skirts for warmth, a laced shirt and breeches for elegance, sturdy boots, and an oiled overcoat with a felted hat. He slipped out the house via the window, but his wits were sluggish from lack of sleep and he felt the need for a dose of Farr's medicinal coffee. He walked briskly to Fleet Street, arriving so early that Farr was still in his nightclothes, yawning and snuffling as he stoked up the fire and set water to boil.

'There is a message for you,' Farr said, handing over a scrap of paper that had been ripped from the bottom of a newsbook. 'A nice naval gentleman left it.'

It was from Captain Lester, and urged Chaloner to visit his lodgings by White Friars' Stairs as soon as possible, no matter what the hour. Chaloner set off at a run, coffee forgotten. He arrived to find lights blazing and the house thronged with people. Lester was in the parlour, dressed in sea-going clothes and surrounded by a seething horde of sailors, victuallers and port officials.

'Tom!' Lester gestured that everyone was to leave the room, and it was testament to his natural authority that they went quickly and quietly. 'Your house was closed up, so I was reduced to leaving a note at the Rainbow. *Swiftsure* sails with the tide, so I am frantically busy, but there is someone I want you to meet before I go.'

'Who?' asked Chaloner curiously.

'Jeffrey Dare, who had command of *London* when she went down. He rents the rooms on the top floor. Did you know that the ghouls at Court will start travelling east today, to watch her being weighed? They hope to see corpses, no doubt.'

Chaloner followed him upstairs, where a bandage-swathed man lay in a bed, his eyes full of haunted horror. Lester laid a hand in quiet sympathy on his shoulder as he addressed the spy.

'The tale about candles igniting old cartridge papers is a nonsense. Something else happened on *London*, and we want you to discover what.'

'I was in the crosstrees.' Dare began speaking before Chaloner could point out that he had no authority to investigate shipwrecks. 'Do you know where they are?'

Chaloner had spent enough time travelling by sea to know they were near the top of a mast, and their purpose was to stop it swaying too far from side to side. 'Yes, but—'

Dare cut across him. 'I was watching for shoals – the Thames Estuary is famous for them and I did not want to run her aground. Then there was a loud crack from starboard, followed by an explosion. We were going to take on more powder at Queenhithe, so the starboard hold was empty – it was the *larboard* magazine that ignited.'

'You see?' said Lester. 'I told you it was sabotage, and Dare's testimony proves it.'

Chaloner thought it proved nothing of the kind. 'You were looking ahead when the blast occurred,' he said gently to Dare. 'Not to starboard *or* larboard. And everything must have happened very fast . . .'

'It did,' admitted the captain. '*London* sank in minutes. But I know what I heard, and we heeled so violently to starboard that our mainmast sprung.'

'Let me explain it in lubberly terms,' said Lester, when Chaloner looked blank. 'Dare heard a crash on the *right* side of the ship before the explosion, but the powder was stored on the *left*. And the ship heeled to the *right* after the blast.'

'I understood that much,' said Chaloner. 'But what does it mean?'

'Obviously, that whatever set off the blast had nothing to do with the magazine,' said Lester impatiently. 'Which was locked anyway, so no one could have been in there.'

'Then perhaps a cannon exploded,' suggested Chaloner, still not quite sure what their 'evidence' showed. 'I understand there were eighty of them.'

276

'They were housed,' said Dare. 'And the crew were either manning the sails or on deck. No one was with the guns.'

'How can you be sure?' asked Chaloner. 'There were more than three hundred people onboard, and you cannot verify the whereabouts of them all.'

'Three hundred and twenty-seven,' supplied Dare promptly. 'And I *can*, actually. I sailed with that particular crew for more than a decade, and I knew them. None would have been meddling with a gun when we were sailing up the estuary. That leaves the visitors – the Admiral's kin. And they were all on the quarterdeck.'

'We cannot have civilians roaming unsupervised around warships,' explained Lester. 'They were all where they could be seen, with the chaplain minding them.'

'The chaplain survived, too,' said Dare with a bleak smile. 'He visited me yesterday, and said he could account for all his charges. Ergo, there was no sabotage by crew *or* visitors.'

'Then what?' asked Chaloner. 'A device rigged to explode with a fuse?'

'Impossible,' said Lester. 'It would have been noticed – fuses stink. And our sailors *know* guns and ammunition anyway – anything suspicious would have been reported immediately.'

'Then what *do* you think happened?' asked Chaloner, becoming exasperated.

'If we knew, we would not be asking you to find out,' said Lester shortly. He turned to Dare. 'Tell him what happened, Jeffrey. Start at the beginning.'

Dare nodded feebly. 'We had been in the Royal Dockyard at Chatham for a refit, and should have left on the dawn tide, but there was a delay – some papers were not in order, and it took an age to resolve. I was champing at the bit all morning.'

Lester jabbed Chaloner in the ribs, prompting him to ask questions. Chaloner obliged only out of compassion for the man who lay picking miserably at the bedcovers. 'What happened during that time? Were there any unexpected visitors or last-minute deliveries?'

Dare shook his head. 'We were closed to everyone and everything except two chests for the Admiral. Commissioner Pett, who runs the shipyard, told me they contained Lawson's viols.'

'I doubt Lawson plays the viol,' said Chaloner, unable to imagine any musical instrument in the hands of such a crude, unsophisticated man. Except perhaps a drum.

'They were massively heavy,' Dare went on. 'The viols were metal, you see, so they would not lose their tone in the damp sea air.'

'There is no such thing as a metal viol,' said Chaloner, adding 'thank God' in his mind.

'I imagine it was wine,' said Lester. 'Sailors like a drink, and Lawson is no exception.'

'Have you asked him about it?' asked Chaloner of Dare.

'God, no!' exclaimed the captain. 'I would not presume! He would demand my resignation, and I like being in the navy.'

'Then is it possible that the explosion originated in one of these chests?'

Dare frowned. 'I suppose so, but they were locked. As was the spirit store, where we put them.'

'Where was the spirit store?'

'Amidships. As I said, sailors like a drink, and will do anything to get one, so that room is guarded day and night – I ordered the chests stored there to prevent some nosy tar from poking around in the Admiral's personal property.' Dare's expression turned troubled. 'But I cannot get it out of my head that Lawson has some odd friends. Fifth Monarchists . . .'

'I suppose they might have been to blame,' acknowledged Lester. 'However, *he* will have had nothing to do with it. He would never harm his crew.'

Chaloner hoped Lester's faith was not misplaced, and that the 'fireworks' predicted for Easter Day would not entail the Admiral turning the Channel Fleet against the city.

'Will you look into it, Tom?' asked Lester. 'I would do it myself, but I sail in a few minutes, and I may not return. It would give me great peace of mind if you were to oblige.'

Put like that, Chaloner could hardly refuse.

Chaloner accompanied Lester to the quay, where *Swiftsure* was already casting off her moorings. There was no sign of Lawson, and enquiries revealed that the Admiral had decided to hoist his flag on *James* instead. Chaloner was relieved beyond measure. He watched *Swiftsure* ease away from the quay, angry that a good man like Lester was about to risk his life because the selfish hedonists on the Privy Council wanted to steal Dutch trading routes.

He walked to Temperance's club, to borrow a horse for the journey to Temple Mills. It was still before dawn, a time when the place was usually in full swing, but it was silent that morning. Temperance and Maude were in the parlour drinking coffee, neither able to adjust to the earlier opportunity to sleep. Chaloner shook his head when they offered him some: it was so thick that the sugar they added sat on the surface, unable to sink or dissolve.

'Is it too strong for you?' Maude always teased him about his aversion to her brews.

'No, I am afraid for my teeth,' he said, then wished he had kept quiet when she and Temperance smiled and he saw that both had fewer fangs than he remembered.

'There are not many men who can take it,' said Maude comfortably, as though she had achieved something worthwhile. 'My first husband had one sip and died on the spot.'

'Then Tom cannot have any,' said Temperance soberly. 'We need him alive to solve these murders, because business will not return to normal until he does.' She came to fasten the top button on his coat, and began to lecture him. 'Remember: Snowflake's father is Grisley Pate and he is a perfumer. And do not forget that he knew her as Consti.'

'Have you learned anything useful since we last met?' asked Chaloner hopefully. 'About Ferine or Snowflake? You must have been asking questions and listening to rumours.'

'How can we, when no one comes?' asked Temperance bitterly. Then her expression softened. 'Although Buckingham has promised to bring a few friends soon.'

'And his sorcerer,' added Maude. 'He thinks Dr Lambe's presence might attract a few more customers – people like having their fortunes told.'

'Be careful,' warned Chaloner. 'Such activities are—'

'Dear Tom,' said Temperance fondly. 'Always so respectable. However, I doubt Lambe's antics will come close to competing with some of the entertainment we have staged here in the past.'

280

Chaloner was intrigued. 'Why? What have you—'

Maude interrupted him. 'Speaking of wild entertainments, the King is going to watch the ship *London* being raised. He made the announcement yesterday, so most of the Court has decided to go as well. Many will leave today, as the wet weather will make travelling difficult, and Prittlewell is a journey of some forty miles.'

'Then you had better go now, Tom,' said Temperance briskly. 'You do not want to get stuck behind all those lumbering coaches.'

'You must ride Lady,' said Maude, before Chaloner could explain that they would be taking different roads. 'Our new bay horse. She will be the fastest. Here is some money for your expenses. No, do not refuse, or we shall be vexed.'

Chaloner was glad of the funds, given that his own reserves were spent. He saddled Lady, sorry the animal had owners who did not know enough about horses to tell that 'she' was a gelding. He was just leading him into the yard when he saw Wiseman sneaking in through the back gate. The surgeon was wearing a black cloak over his scarlet robes, holding part of it over his face like the arch-villain of children's stories.

'What in God's name are you doing?' asked Chaloner.

'Visiting Temperance incognito,' explained Wiseman in a hoarse whisper. 'I am obliged to be more discreet now that I am Master of the Company of Barber-Surgeons.'

'I would have thought your post as Surgeon to the King would demand discretion, yet you have never felt obliged to practise it before.'

'His Majesty is very liberal; my medical colleagues are not. Incidentally, I saw a letter on Williamson's desk an hour ago.'

Chaloner raised his eyebrows. 'You read the private correspondence of spymasters?'

'Not as a rule, but this one caught my eye because it looked to have been written in blood, although a closer inspection revealed that it was only red ink. It was from someone who has infiltrated the Fifth Monarchists and signs himself as Trojan Horse – hardly original. I did not recognise the writing, although it was not yours and not Will Leving's.'

'How do you know Leving?' asked Chaloner, hoping the man's status as 'turned' was not common knowledge.

'Williamson thinks he is insane and asked me to examine him. Some of the tests I performed necessitated writing. He has a very distinctive hand.'

'And is Leving insane?' asked Chaloner, supposing he should have guessed that Williamson would have a third agent in place. Obviously, a madman and a former Parliamentarian spy would not be deemed sufficient for so important a matter.

'Oh, yes, quite unhinged. Anyway, this letter said that Easter Day may be marked with some major explosions, and I thought you should know. And while I am blabbing secrets, I should also mention that there has been another death connected to Ferine.'

Chaloner nodded. 'Hubbert. I heard. I do not suppose you examined him, did you?'

'I did, but there was no evidence of foul play. However, his demise was predicted, and not even my superior skills can detect every poison.'

'What are you saying? That he was fed a toxin?'

'I have no grounds for making such a claim. I merely point out that Lambe foretold that Hubbert would die, and die Hubbert did – which is damned convenient for Lambe. I do not like him, even if he is the Court's current darling.'

Chaloner recalled the conversation he had had with Lambe, when the sorcerer had smugly declared that he would welcome a surgeon investigating Hubbert. Was it because Wiseman was not the only one who knew that some poisons were undetectable?

'You look tired,' he said, changing the subject. 'Have you had a hard night?'

Wiseman nodded. 'First, several clients were after me for remedies recommended by Lambe, and then Williamson called me to the Westminster charnel house to examine the body of a rebel. He did not have the courtesy to remain there while I worked, which is why I had to visit his office afterwards – to tell him my findings.'

Chaloner did not blame the Spymaster for not wanting to watch what Wiseman did; he disliked it himself. 'Did this dead rebel have a name?'

'A Fifth Monarchist called Nat Strange.'

'Damn!' breathed Chaloner. 'He was my main suspect for killing Quelch.'

'You mean the other insurgent? Williamson asked me to look at him, too. He was stunned with a blow to the head and then strangled. But not by Strange, whose hands would have been far too large to make the marks on Quelch's neck. You will have to revise your theory about that particular solution.'

'How did Strange die?'

'Stabbed,' replied Wiseman. 'A violent end for a violent man.'

Chaloner thought about the ambush outside Clarendon House the previous night. Had Strange been among the attackers, and been killed by a wild blow in the dark, when no one had been able to see what was what?

Chaloner rode past St Paul's, then followed a complex series of turns that took him to the Shoreditch road. He had intended to use the time to think about his investigations, but his attention was taken by Lady, who was delighted to be out and itched to gallop. He was an evil-tempered brute, and Chaloner wondered what had possessed Temperance to buy him.

It was a miserable day for riding, and the volume of traffic using the London roads had turned them into rivers of rutted mud. Sometimes the track was contained between rows of houses, sodden and drab in the unrelenting drizzle, but elsewhere it had expanded ever wider as horsemen, pedestrians and drivers had attempted to find a less boggy route. Chaloner lost count of the carts and carriages that were stuck, some abandoned, some guarded by disgruntled owners, and others in the process of being levered free.

The mud was as foul as any he had seen, and Lady made heavy weather of it. In the end, Chaloner abandoned the road and set off across the countryside. It was easier riding, but he was obliged to fight his way through hedges and jump swollen streams. The hours ticked away fast, and it was afternoon before he reached Hackney Marsh, a low-lying region of sedge, bog and alder interspersed with the occasional farm, windmill or hamlet. Curlews wheeled overhead, and the land smelled of wet vegetation and stagnant water. It was a clean scent, though, and a pleasant change to the rank stench of London.

Temple Mills was a tiny village centred around an

284

ancient watermill that straddled the River Lea. A new mill had been raised a short distance from the first, and it throbbed with the hum and hiss of industry. Unusually for such structures, it was surrounded by a wooden palisade, as if the owner was afraid of being burgled, although Chaloner could not imagine that thieves were much of a problem in such a remote and desolate place.

He dismounted and entered a dingy inn to ask after Snowflake's father. The landlord pointed out a modest but well-maintained house at the end of what passed for the high street. As the inn had a stable, Chaloner left Lady there, shrugging apologetically at the alarmed expressions of the grooms who would have to tend the creature.

He knocked on Pate's door and was answered by a man in his sixties on an accompanying waft of something sweet. Pate was a perfumer, he recalled, although Hackney Marsh seemed an odd place to base such an enterprise. No wonder Snowflake had said the business was on the brink of failure – it was unlikely to attract much passing trade. Then, for the first time, it occurred to him that the family may not have heard about her death, and he might have to break the news himself.

'I have come about Snow—I mean Consti,' he began, suddenly uneasy.

'My stepdaughter,' said Pate, beaming. 'The second child of my fifth wife. Or was it the first of my sixth? I cannot recall now. I am on my ninth, you see, so it is difficult to keep track. Unfortunately, they do not seem to last very long, and I am always having to replace them.'

Chaloner took a deep breath to blurt, 'I am sorry to tell you that Consti is dead.'

'Is she?' asked Pate, with more disapproval than distress. 'I told her she would come to a bad end if she followed a career in strumpetry. What took her? A pox?'

'She was murdered.'

'By a client, I suppose,' said Pate grimly. 'That club is nice, as far as whore-houses go, but it still attracts scoundrels – rich ones, perhaps, but scoundrels nonetheless. Do you work there?'

'No. I am not pretty enough.'

As soon as the words were out, Chaloner wished he could retract them: flippancy was hardly the best way to win the man's good graces. Pate stared at him for a moment, then threw back his head and laughed heartily, slapping his thighs and declaring it the finest joke he had heard since the parson's nose had been savaged by his pet turkey.

'Come in, come in,' he managed to gasp eventually. 'You must repeat that witty nugget to my children. They all love a joke.'

Alarmed, Chaloner tried to back away, but Pate seized his arm and hauled him to a spacious parlour, bawling for his family. Immediately, people of all shapes and sizes began to assemble, forming neat ranks with the small ones at the front and the taller ones behind. They ranged from a man who was well into his eighties to a babe in arms. All guffawed appreciatively when Pate repeated the 'joke', and only when the last chortle had died away were introductions made.

'These are my children and stepchildren,' Pate explained. He gestured to the elderly gentleman. 'Henry here has twenty years on me, but that is what happens when one weds an older woman.' Then he smiled fondly at a girl who could not have been more than eighteen.

286

'And this is wife number nine, who came with two young-sters from a previous marriage.'

Chaloner tried to imagine the worldly Snowflake in the homely parlour, but the image would not come – she had travelled too far beyond her origins. However, he could certainly envisage Atkinson there, perhaps bouncing one of the toddlers on his knee, or laughing in his affable way.

'Consti is dead,' announced Pate baldly. 'Are any of you her siblings?'

There was a rumble to say none of them were, and someone added helpfully that Consti's sister had died at the same time as their mother Martha, of marsh fever, some years before.

'Martha!' breathed Pate, lust gleaming in his eyes. 'She of the flaxen hair. Now there was a fine lass. Perhaps it is as well that she is in her grave, because she would have wept and wailed at the news we have had today. And I do not hold with weeping and wailing.'

There was a muted mutter to say that the 'children' did not hold with it, either.

'Does John know?' asked Pate of Chaloner. 'John Atkinson, I mean, another of my stepsons. He is a dear, sweet fellow who did his best to keep her decent. He will be devastated when he hears, so *you* must tell him, because I could not bring myself to do it. You will be well rewarded, though – he is a lovely man, and your life will improve on making his acquaintance.'

The chorus of agreement almost deafened Chaloner. When he could make himself heard, he started to ask his questions.

'You told Snow—Consti something when you last visited, but she died before she could pass it on. I need to know what it was, because it may help me catch her killer.'

'Did I?' Pate was startled. 'Lord! I have no idea what it might have been. It was days ago, and I have seen a lot of people since then. I know we talked about the village, and she was keen to hear about the animals. She loved animals, especially horses.'

Chaloner sat forward. 'Would you mind thinking carefully, sir? It is important.'

'Heavens!' breathed Pate. 'I only went to see her because I had spent all my money on ambergris, and I wanted something to eat. That Temperance may be a whoremonger, but she always treats me very kindly, and her cook bakes lovely pies.'

The family murmured to say that this was true.

'Please,' pressed Chaloner. 'Anything you can remember would help.'

Pate frowned in thought, and even the baby seemed to be holding its breath as everyone waited. The silence stretched on and on, broken only by the distant rattle of the mill.

'Damn!' said Pate, shaking his head. 'It will not come! I do not recall what else we said to each other, except her reminding me to warm a little porridge for the chickens on cold mornings. I do, and our hens are very appreciative.'

It was a moment of pathos for Chaloner, learning that the jaded prostitute had been concerned for the family birds. He stood, feeling he had wasted a day for nothing – a glance out of the window told him it would be dark soon.

'Surely you are not thinking of riding back to London now?' cried Pate. 'You will ruin your horse – assuming he does not ruin you by taking a tumble. Stay here and leave in the morning.'

A growl of consensus from the family said that this was certainly the best option. Chaloner declined, but they were insistent, and that evening was one of the most bizarre he could ever recall spending. First ale was provided, although he and Pate were the only ones to partake, the others looking on anxiously, then smiling when the brew was complimented. Next it was cakes, and finally stew. Chaloner was unused to eating in front of an audience, and wondered how the King could bear it – watching His Majesty dine was one of the Court's most popular pastimes.

Pate did most of the talking, holding forth on subjects as diverse as cooking, sport, philosophy and agriculture. Each time he made a statement, his family would murmur deferential agreement. At first, Chaloner assumed it was because no one wanted to risk being disinherited, or that Pate was a bully who ruled with a rod of iron, but there was no evidence to support either notion, and the reverence they afforded their patriarch was obviously inspired by genuine affection.

'That new mill is a nuisance,' said Pate, after providing Chaloner with an exhaustive account of the hamlet's history, right from its first mention in a document dating to the thirteenth century. 'It clunks and clatters all night.'

'Grinding corn?' asked Chaloner, aware that he was expected to prompt the speaker.

'Corn?' cried Pate. 'Here in the marshes?' There was a gale of unrestrained laughter from the family, which he joined in, wiping the tears from his eyes. 'You are a wit, and I am glad Consti knew you. You must have kept her laughing from morning to night. Or should I say from night to morning, bearing in mind her chosen profession?'

Amusement exploded yet again, and Chaloner began to wish he was riding home to London, because even sleeping under a hedge would be better than the Pates and their odd sense of humour. When the merriment had finally died away, Pate resumed his diatribe on the mill.

'It makes buttons, not flour,' he said. 'A prodigious amount of them, given the hours it works. It is never still, from one sunrise to the next. I never use them, of course. Call me a Puritan if you will, but there is nothing wrong with good honest laces.'

There followed a detailed vilification of buttons and why they must surely delight the devil. Chaloner's mind wandered to ways he might escape, and he had just decided to use checking on Lady as an excuse when Pate's sudden yell made him and the entire family start in alarm.

'I remember now! I discussed the *mill* with Consti! I told her about the delivery of an enormous wheel. We have no idea what it might be for, but she said "I must tell Tom". Those were her exact words. She meant you, do you see?'

Chaloner blinked. Why had she thought he would be interested in that? 'Did she say anything else?'

'No,' replied Pate. 'But I recall the conversation quite clearly now I have had a chance to reflect. It was my report of the wheel that intrigued her.'

When Pate decided it was time to sleep, the house became a flurry of activity, and straw mattresses appeared from nowhere. They covered every inch of the floor, and the residents lay down wherever there was space, while Pate and his latest wife had the luxury of a private room upstairs. Chaloner was allocated a spot in the parlour, along with a dozen others of both sexes. Exhausted, he fell asleep immediately, but he did not stay that way for long. His roommates snorted, shuffled, scratched and whispered, and when two people began a series of sloppy kisses in the corner, he gave up trying to doze and went outside.

He sat on the doorstep. It had stopped raining, although the air was damp and cold. A dog whined farther down the street, while Pate's latest child was grizzling somewhere at the back of the house. Pate himself was snoring gustily, vying for dominance with the stentorian grunts emanating from three burly sons who had bedded down in the kitchen.

As Chaloner pondered Snowflake and the wheel, it occurred to him that he might understand why she had wanted to tell him about it if he actually saw the thing. The small hours of the morning was not a time he would normally have visited such a place, but the mill was ablaze with lights, and a rhythmic thumping emanated from within. The workers were busy with their buttons, but might spare a few moments to talk to him.

He stood and walked to the end of the street, where the building was huddled on the river bank. The wooden wall that surrounded it was taller than he had first supposed – too high to see over. He located the gate, intending to knock, but it was unusually sturdy, and through a gap in the wood he could see guards patrolling with dogs.

He watched thoughtfully. These were precautions far in excess of what was needed for button-making, so clearly something else was being manufactured. And the mill's taut security confirmed what he had suspected for some time now. He backed away from the gate and walked around the fence until he found a spot where it was possible to climb over. He straddled the top, and looked around.

The mill comprised a large yard protected by the palisade on three sides and the river on the fourth. There were six buildings in the compound – the mill itself, which was larger than any he had ever seen, and five sturdy sheds. It did not take him long to note that the guards followed specific routes, which they repeated at set intervals. He waited until they were all farthest away from him, then jumped down and padded towards the mill.

It had been built with very thick wood, presumably to mute some of the racket produced by the machinery, and its only door – large enough to accommodate a sizeable wagon – was secured from the inside by a bar. He put his eye to a crack, but although he could see a number of men labouring there, he could not tell what they were doing.

He stepped back and considered. He could probably jiggle the bar out of the door from where he stood, but then he would be seen by the workmen – and it was clearly not a place that welcomed visitors. Then he saw that someone had been considerate enough to site the building next to a large oak with spreading boughs, presumably to shield some of the structure from sight.

He climbed quickly, then crawled along a branch until he was over the roof. He let himself drop, and immediately began to slide – rain had rendered it slick and it was steeply pitched. But he regained his footing and scrambled towards a flue, hoping the noise of the mill's machinery would mask the din he felt he was making.

Working fast, he prised off the vent's slats with his dagger, but unfortunately, when he had finished, all he could see were ceiling beams. He swore under his breath when he realised he was going to have to climb inside.

It was a tight squeeze, but he managed eventually, and was rewarded with a clear view of the interior. It was brightly lit, both by lamps and by the furnace that was going full blast. About a dozen men were labouring, some dealing with the oven, and others manhandling moulds with thick levers. He nodded to himself. It was what he had expected: here was Prince Rupert's gun-making factory, sited deep in the marshes to keep it from prying eyes. Except, of course, that the secret was out, as the reports in Jones's harpsichord attested.

There was an enormous wheel at the far end, and it did not take him long to understand what was meant by 'turning' a gun, while the furnace allowed them to be 'annealed'. And *that* was the connection Snowflake had made: she had linked her father's remarks with things Rupert must have said when they had discussed the Hackney Marsh together. It had nothing to do with Ferine – it was a young girl realising that something serious was afoot and deciding to confide in a man whom she knew worked for a member of the government.

Of course, Rupert had every reason to want the venture kept quiet. Building the mill and purchasing raw materials would represent a major financial outlay, and the fewer people who knew about the operation, the more secure his investment would be. And Williamson? Chaloner imagined he was eager to keep the weapon from hostile hands of any description, but especially Dutch ones.

So was this why Snowflake had been killed? To prevent Chaloner from making the connection between Rupert, Temple Mills and the 'silver cannon' that the Fifth Monarchists might use to usher in the Last Millennium? If so, it had failed, and Chaloner determined to do all he could to ensure that her killer faced justice, no matter who he transpired to be.

He focused his attention on the activity below. The men worked with practised, efficient movements, and spoke rarely, although one was clearly in charge. He was a large, thickset fellow with a single eyebrow in a dark slash across his face. His demeanour was one of unsmiling competence.

'Hey, Browne,' called one of the workmen to him. 'This one is ready.'

More answers snapped clear in Chaloner's mind. Here was the mysterious John Browne, whom Sherwin had called a 'desperate villain, dishonest, sly and vicious'; whose name Prynne had overheard mentioned in discussions between high-ranking people; whom Williamson had castigated to Rupert for being careless; and whom Scott claimed to have 'managed'.

He watched Browne walk towards the man who had hailed him, light-footed for a fellow his size, and begin to slather a barrel with grease. As he worked, Browne revealed hands and forearms that were marred by a mass of small burns, some old and some fresh. They were identical to the ones Chaloner had seen on Sherwin.

And then Chaloner understood exactly why Sherwin was so confident of his worth – he had worked in the mill and knew how to make iron cannon. He was a

294

drunk, so Browne had dismissed him, after which he had fallen into Manning's greedy hands. Then along had come Scott, who had conned Manning into a partnership. Scott had taken Sherwin to the club in an effort to impress him, where Snowflake had heard him mutter about something being 'turned'. Chaloner had assumed he had meant a person, but Sherwin had been talking about guns.

But why had Sherwin been allowed to walk away from the foundry to hawk the secret? Chaloner could only suppose that he had disappeared before Rupert could stop him. Then why had he not been arrested when he had arrived in London? The answer to that was obvious, too: Williamson's spies – including Scott, if he was telling the truth – had found him too long after his escape, and now it was a case of learning to whom he might have talked, so that they could be silenced as well.

Questions and answers whirling in his mind in equal measure, Chaloner was about to leave when there was a clatter of hoofs outside. He could not see the horse from his position on the beam, but within moments, its rider was standing almost directly beneath him.

It was Admiral Lawson.

Chaloner was exasperated. He thought he had had the makings of a solution at last, but the Admiral's appearance threw him into confusion again. Why was Lawson there when he had made his disdain for iron cannon abundantly clear? Yet Browne did not seem surprised to see him, and Chaloner could tell by the Admiral's easy familiarity with the place and its employees that it was not his first visit. He and Browne began to talk, but the background noise meant Chaloner could only hear snatches of their discussion.

'. . . been generous,' Lawson was saying. 'You promised to hurry.'

'I will,' snapped Browne. 'Gun and powder will be ready in . . .'

'Time is of the essence,' Lawson snapped back. 'There is not . . .'

They moved away at that point, and Chaloner heard no more. Moving with infinite caution, he climbed back through the vent and across the roof. He scrambled down the tree, and because he was near and the door was open, he took a moment to inspect one of the sheds.

A number of guns were there, standing in neat rows. Their muzzles were enormous – presumably the turning and annealing allowed for a much bigger bore. He was impressed. If they worked, they were certainly something that should be kept from the enemy – he hated to think of such monsters in the hands of a capable Dutch gun crew.

There were several casks nearby, and one had been broached. Chaloner raised the lid to see it was full of the same fine powder that he had delivered to Manning and that Jones kept on his mantelpiece. Clearly, the new guns preferred a different kind of ammunition.

A yell broke into his thoughts, and he turned to see someone running towards him, stabbing an accusing finger. Immediately, workmen poured from the mill, and so did Lawson. Chaloner pulled his hat low against recognition and began to sprint towards the fence. But it was too far, and he knew he would not make it, especially when the guards appeared. Their dogs worried him most: they were straining at their leashes, snarling and barking. He changed direction, zigzagging until the workmen were

296

between him and the hounds. Then he resumed his dash for the palisade.

The guards released their animals but, as Chaloner had hoped with his manoeuvre, the beasts were confused, and sprang for the workmen instead. There were screams, a yelp and a lot of panicky swearing. Chaloner gained the wall, and scaled it quickly, landing clumsily on the other side. But the chase was not over. As he ran, urgent shouts and the eager baying of dogs told him that he was being tracked. He stumbled towards the river, knowing that water was his only chance of losing them.

The howling grew closer: the dogs had picked up his scent. A quick glance behind saw the first of the animals hurtling towards him. Gritting his teeth against the cold, he waded into the icy flow, while the hound raced down the bank, yipping its triumph. His pursuers homed in on the sound, and so did Lawson. One guard held a lamp, and he raised it, pointing at the same time.

'There he is!'

Lawson had a handgun. He took aim and fired, and Chaloner heard the bullet zip into the water at his side. Furious at missing, the Admiral pulled a second weapon from his belt. Chaloner had only one option: he took a deep breath and plunged beneath the surface.

Chapter 11

The River Lea was normally a gentle, meandering stream, favoured by herons and dabbling ducks, but that night it was a treacherous torrent fed by the recent rains. Chaloner was swept along at a furious rate, which allowed him to escape Lawson's pistols, but that made him wonder whether he might drown instead. It took all his strength just to keep his head above the surface, and trying to swim for the shore was impossible.

Just when he thought he could fight it no longer, the current lessened: he had been cast up in a pool. He paddled to the edge and struggled up the bank, which was not easy when his limbs ached with cold and exhaustion, but he managed eventually and lay gasping at the top, listening for sounds of pursuit. All he could hear was the hiss and gurgle of fast-flowing water.

When he had recovered enough to stand, he staggered away from the river, moving blindly in the pitch dark. He tripped over furrows and ruts with no notion of direction or how much distance he had travelled. Then he saw the mill lights in the distance.

It was enough to give him his bearings, and he was relieved beyond measure to learn that he was on the right side of the river for going home – he would not have enjoyed a trek to the nearest bridge, which might be miles away, while swimming across the torrent would have been impossible. He shivered violently as he went, and his misery intensified when it started to rain. It could not make him wetter, drenched as he was, but it sucked away any warmth he had managed to generate by trotting. He pressed on, aiming to collect Lady and start back to London immediately, but he was just passing Pate's house when the perfumer himself stepped out. Chaloner braced himself as Pate peered at him. He did not want to knock the man senseless, but he would if the alternative was being exposed.

Pate started to chuckle. 'We should have warned you that the latrine is a long way from the house. And now it is pouring with rain, and you are soaked!'

'Yes,' said Chaloner tightly. 'I am.'

'You had better come and sit by the fire then,' said Pate, still chortling. 'And you shall have a cup of hot brandywine, too. It is expensive, but you have provided us with such an unending stream of amusement that we should repay you somehow.'

Chaloner knew he should leave Temple Mills, but the thought of a fire and a warming drink drew him after Pate into the house. Telling himself that he could always skewer the perfumer and escape through a window if there was trouble, he followed him into the kitchen.

Three of Pate's sons, solid, steady, grey-haired fellows in their forties, helped him wring out his clothes and set them to dry on a rack, tittering at the notion of their guest's sodden foray to the public conveniences. Pate poured generous slugs of what he claimed was brandy-wine, but that tasted foul and was almost certainly illegal. It gradually restored the warmth to Chaloner's body, though, and eased his temper, too, so he was even able to smile when Pate said 'latrine' and all four men dissolved into more paroxysms of laughter.

'James here thinks we should build one in the garden,' said Pate, once he had his mirth under control. 'But I am not sure it would have enough use to warrant the cost.'

'How many people live here?' asked Chaloner, suspecting it would never be empty.

Pate began to list them, but Chaloner lost count at thirty. When Pate started to hold forth about latrines he had known, Chaloner steered the conversation around to Rupert.

'Yes, I did meet him once,' replied the perfumer. 'He was riding a white mare with black socks, and I asked whether he would like to buy some scent. He was bundled up in his cloak and hat, but Consti had talked about his horse so often that I recognised it at once.'

'Why did he come?' asked Chaloner, wondering what lie the Prince had told to explain his presence in such a bleak part of the world.

'He wanted to buy some buttons for his mistress. Then he purchased my biggest and most expensive bottle of lavender oil in exchange for me keeping his mission quiet. I have kept my end of the bargain, but it was weeks ago, so I doubt the surprise will be ruined by me chatting to you now.'

'Do many people visit the mill?'

'No one does, except the fellows who deliver the raw materials. Their wagons are great lumbering things, and if Mr Browne had not shown me the buttons, I would have assumed they were making something else entirely. He gave me some. Look.'

Chaloner was presented with a handful of shiny metal discs, which Pate said he could keep, as he himself had no truck with fancy devices. Absently, Chaloner put them in his pocket.

'Did a man named Edward Sherwin work here?'

'Yes – a sot, who kept escaping to drink in the tavern. Browne got rid of him in the end. I heard them arguing, and Sherwin was so angry that he could barely form the words to curse.'

'How are the finished goods exported? You mention raw materials delivered . . .'

'They put them on barges and send them down the Lea to the Thames. They can go anywhere from there.'

They could, thought Chaloner, including the great dockyards at Chatham or Wapping, ready to be installed on the navy's warships. Or were the finished guns intended for another destination entirely – France, perhaps, or the United Provinces of the Netherlands?

'Speaking of the Thames, did you hear about *London*, the ship that exploded near Prittlewell?' Pate chatted on. 'Well, James was there when it happened. He was collecting ambergris from the coast. We use ambergris as a fixative in perfume making, you see, and—'

'What did you see, James?' interrupted Chaloner.

'It is not what he *saw* that was significant, but what he *heard*,' said Pate, before his son could reply for himself. 'He was in a local tavern the night before the blast, where some men were talking. It was not an accident with a candle, as has been put about – it was done deliberately.'

'By whom?' asked Chaloner, his pulse quickening.

'By villains,' replied Pate, unhelpfully. 'Decent men do not blow up ships, especially the ones we need for defeating the Dutch at sea.'

'Can you describe these villains?' asked Chaloner of James.

Again, it was Pate who replied. 'One was small, dark and malevolent; one had a scar on his face; and the last was yellow-haired and kept talking about King Jesus. They whispered, but James has inherited my sharp ears, and heard most of what they muttered.'

'What did they say?' asked Chaloner, his thoughts in turmoil. 'Exactly.'

Pate must have heard the urgency in his voice because he indicated that James was to answer for himself. James obliged in a voice that was uncannily like his sire's. 'They said that blowing up the ship would be a "fine outrage for the Cause". Those were their precise words. They left then, and were nowhere on shore when she exploded the next day.'

'How do you know?'

James looked troubled. 'Because they had unsettled me, so I looked for them. Our stepbrother John often talks about fanatics, and I had a feeling that these were three such rogues.'

So Jones and Strange had been responsible for what had happened to HMS *London*, while the third man was almost certainly Scarface Roberts. Had they used one of Rupert's guns and the unusually fine powder to carry out their monstrous act? And if so, then had Roberts died because the new invention was

302

unpredictable and dangerous to use? Chaloner knew he would have to find out quickly, before any were deployed on Easter Day.

It rained steadily for what remained of the night, but the weather brightened at dawn, even showing patches of blue among the grey. Chaloner had quizzed Pate and his family further about HMS *London*, the mill and Rupert, so that by the time it was light enough to leave, he had answers to a number of questions and a clear view of what to do next.

He still had far too many questions, though. Why had Lawson been at the factory, when he had expressed reservations about iron cannon and obviously thought little of Rupert's inventive talents? Why had Jones, Strange and Roberts destroyed his flagship? It was most certainly not 'a fine outrage for the Cause' and would turn people against the Fifth Monarchists if the truth ever came out.

Although he could not have said why, Chaloner felt that the best way forward was to concentrate on HMS *London*. She was due to be weighed the following day, and while it would not be easy to cover more than thirty miles on muddy, flooded roads, he intended to try. Of course, if he was wrong, there would be hell to pay. Rupert would be furious with him for leaving the conspirators unmonitored, and so would Williamson. Temperance would also be vexed, because it was time spent away from the murders of Ferine and Snowflake. However, it might help to fulfil his promise to Lester, and that was as important to him as anything else.

Lady was in a feisty mood, and Chaloner was hard-pressed to prevent him from bolting. He let him have

303

his head once they were clear of the village, but the track was too rutted and uneven for speed, so he was forced to rein in. After that, conditions worsened, and he was obliged to dismount. Twice, he lost the road, and wasted valuable time trying to find it again. In all, it was a strained, miserable, exhausting day, and by dusk, both horse and man were thoroughly fed up with each other. He continued on foot once the daylight had gone, letting the moon light their way. He camped in the open eventually, but it was far too cold to sleep, and he was on the road again long before the stars began to fade the following morning, Lady trailing sulkily behind him.

Eventually, he saw lights in the distance. Scenting clean stables and warm mash, Lady began to dance towards them. They had reached Prittlewell at last. Unfortunately, it was not where they needed to be.

'You want the hamlet we call South-End for the raising of *London*,' said a smugly gleeful farmer who was feeding his cows. He pointed. 'Two miles in that direction.'

With a sigh, Chaloner mounted up, at which point Lady tried to rid himself of the unwelcome burden by bucking. Chaloner was too experienced a rider to be thrown, but it was tiresome nonetheless, and it became even more of annoyance when the road began to fill with other travellers. He recognised the crests on several coaches, along with a number of horsemen – London's idle rich, come to watch the spectacle of a shattered ship rising from the deep.

He listened to snippets of conversation as he rode. Dr Lambe had evidently reread the stars, and was now predicting that the venture would be a success,

Item(s) Borrowed

Branch: Cults Library

Date: 31/07/2019   Time: 2:37 PM

ID: 63356000281030

ITEM(S)   DUE DATE

Murder on High Holborn.............. 28 Aug 2019
30000000108654

The girl who takes an eye for an eye. 28 Aug 2019
30000000217554

Your current loan(s): 2
Your current reservation(s): 0
Your current active request(s): 0

Please retain this receipt and return items on or before
the due date

Thank you for using Aberdeen City Libraries.

https://www.aberdeencity.gov.uk/services/libraries
and-archives

Tel 03000 200293 or 01224 652500

although only as long as certain precautions were taken. However, no one had managed to learn what these might be, other than that one involved doing something to a snail in moonlight – something no one at Court had attempted. Lambe was clever, thought Chaloner. If his forecast proved wrong, he could simply say that the conditions he had stipulated had not been followed.

'He prophesised something about Buckingham, too,' Chaloner overheard the silly Lady Muskerry tell Mrs Chiffinch as their coach jolted along. 'That he will suffer a misfortune on Friday.'

'Good Friday,' murmured Mrs Chiffinch. 'The day of the Duke's Astrological Soirée. I am not surprised – it is an evil, godless business, and only fools will attend.'

'I am going,' said Lady Muskerry brightly.

'You do surprise me, dear,' replied Mrs Chiffinch blandly.

There was other gossip, too. Ferine's killer was still at large; Rupert's unpredictable temper was earning him much dislike; Williamson had asked the Privy Council for more money to spend on spies, but his request was unlikely to be granted; Lady Day was transpiring to be a nuisance because of an usually large influx of visitors; and everyone was looking forward to the firework display, although there was some concern that the current Green Man might prove unequal to the task of setting them off – the Master of Ordnance might be the best qualified man available, but that did not mean he would actually be any good at it.

There were, however, no rumours about the Fifth Monarchy rebellion that was to be staged in four days' time, which Chaloner thought remarkable given the number of people involved. Was the oath they swore responsible for the blanket of secrecy? Regardless, he found himself sorry that their expectations for a more decent society were unlikely to be realised, and that Sunday night would almost certainly see the King still debauching himself in White Hall.

South-End was not much of a place – a few rows of fishing cottages and three rough inns. There was also a chapel, currently used to house HMS *London*'s dead, which continued to wash up each day. Chaloner imagined it was usually a sleepy hamlet with nothing to disturb it but the occasional storm. That day there was a merry bustle, not just with visitors, but from canny locals who aimed to capitalise on the arrival of a lot of bulging purses.

Stalls had been set up outside almost every house, selling freshly baked bread, pies, griddled fish and cakes. Others had broached barrels of ale, while small boys darted everywhere, fetching refreshments and selling their older sisters to anyone who wanted a different form of entertainment. A surprisingly large number of courtiers did.

Chaloner made for the biggest tavern, as those fishermen who were not engaged in the brisk commerce outside were there, telling eager listeners what had happened when they had gathered on the beach to watch *London* sail past. He left Lady with a gaggle of enterprising youths who were operating a horse-minding service, and walked inside.

'She blew up! Bang!' one halfwit was braying. He was a huge, moon-faced creature with massive hands and the guileless grin of a child. 'Boom!'

'Now, Peter,' said a fisherman whose pipe was so firmly clamped between his teeth that it looked as if it would only be removed by surgery. 'Go and feed the chickens, there's a good lad.'

Beaming merrily, Peter went to do as he was told, while the courtiers turned back to the story-tellers. Chaloner eased forward, recognising a number of people in the audience, including Rupert, Buckingham and Lambe. The fishermen resumed their tale, ending with the firm prediction that the engineers would not succeed in weighing *London*.

'That is not what this sorcerer says,' interjected Rupert, gesturing to Lambe in a way that was not entirely pleasant. 'He did a number of nasty things with skulls, snails and tobacco leaves last night, and calculated that HMS *London* would be afloat by mid-morning.'

'But only if the engineers follow my precise instructions,' cautioned Lambe immediately. 'If they vary in a single detail, the endeavour will fail.'

'Speaking of precautions, when will you tell me how to avoid the calamity that will befall me on Good Friday?' asked Buckingham. 'I should not like to be a spectacle at my own soirée.'

'If you do, it will be God's vengeance on you for coming here,' declared Rupert haughtily. 'The Almighty does not like ghouls.'

'No?' asked Buckingham archly. 'And you are different how, exactly?'

'I am here in the spirit of scientific enquiry, as a member of the Royal Society,' replied Rupert loftily. 'I did not come because I yearn to see bloated bodies bobbing about.'

'I am a member of the Royal Society, too,' Buckingham reminded him. 'Invited to join for my experiments with the Philosopher's Stone.'

307

'Invited because you offered to pay a higher subscription,' countered Rupert nastily. 'You are not in the same league as me.'

'No, you are in a league of your own,' said Buckingham ambiguously, and promptly turned back to the head fisherman. 'I missed the beginning of your tale. Start again.'

'You are right to listen to Mr Westcliff,' said the taverner approvingly. 'You can't tell him nothing about these waters and ships. His opinion is worth having.' He shot Lambe a look that indicated he thought the same could not be said of everyone.

Westcliff obliged. 'I recognised the ship *London* immediately, so I called everyone outside, and we all stood along the beach to cheer her on her way. Then there was a crack followed by a great billow of smoke, and she listed to one side. A moment later, we heard the blast.'

'Caused by fools trying to wrap new powder in old cartridge papers,' scoffed Rupert. 'The navy could learn a lot from the army regarding ordnance.'

'Bilge,' spat Westcliff, not at all awed by the lofty company around him, and so unafraid to speak his mind. He either did not see or did not care about Rupert's shock at being so bluntly contradicted. '*London*'s crew would not have been doing that in the estuary.'

'It was gas,' stated Buckingham with considerable authority. 'From when the sailors used the lower decks as a latrine while she was in dry dock. We all know what happens when latrine fumes ignite. A sailor went below with a lamp, and . . .' He spread his hands.

'We shall miss the fun if we loiter in here,' said Rupert,

308

dismissing the Duke's theory by ignoring it. He finished his drink and stood. 'Who is coming with me?'

No one volunteered, so he left on his own, although the tavern emptied moments later when Buckingham posed the same question. Chaloner spent a few moments pressing Westcliff for additional information, then walked to the beach himself, aware that the halfwit was trailing him.

'A cannon in a boat,' Peter chanted, performing a series of clumsy skips. 'And a boat in a cannon. Bang! Boom!'

The shore was a gently sloping shelf of sandy mud, kissed by ripples from the estuary. It was littered with flotsam, mostly wood that Chaloner assumed had comprised the stricken ship, along with a smattering of the kind of debris that cluttered any beach downstream of a major city: rags, coal, bones and unidentifiable sludge, all mixed with mounds of seaweed and broken fishing nets. Gulls wheeled overhead, and there was a sharp tang of salt in the air.

A number of boats had been hauled up, and opportunistic villagers were selling seats in their lee, so that visitors could sit out of the wind. Most had been snapped up, as the weather had turned dull and cloudy with a brisk wind, and not much was happening with HMS *London*. A flotilla of small craft bobbed a little way offshore, cables and ropes forming a complex net between them, but the men operating them were sitting down. Chaloner looked at the spectators on the beach.

First and most colourful were the courtiers, who flitted here and there in their finery, concentrating on being seen by the right people. Next were the eccentrically clad gentlemen of the Royal Society, who huddled together deep in debate. Third were engineers from the Navy Board, who were directing the operation. And last were the industrious locals, bustling busily as they homed in on the opportunity to profit from the occasion.

Suddenly, there was movement on one of the boats, and winches began to wind. There was a murmur of excited anticipation onshore as something broke the surface, and everyone strained forward to see. Lambe's expression turned smug. The object hung a foot above the water, spinning slowly and trailing seaweed. It was one of *London*'s cannon.

'They have to retrieve those first,' explained Rupert importantly. 'Because otherwise their weight will make it impossible to lift the rest of the ship. It was I who realised this, and the engineers are acting on my advice.'

Chaloner imagined the Navy Board knew perfectly well how to weigh a ship, and did not need Rupert to tell them. Buckingham did a very accurate impression of the Prince's strutting walk behind his back, which had his cronies spluttering with malicious laughter. When Rupert whipped around to see what was happening, Buckingham was looking innocently at the sky.

'I hope the engineers remembered not to point at the moon last night,' said Lambe. 'That always brings bad luck. However, I saw seven jackdaws this morning, which is a *good* omen.'

Daylight did the sorcerer no favours. It lent the designs on his neck and hands a tawdry, homemade appearance, while his patterned coat appeared shabby. Even his height worked against him, making him look lanky rather than imposing. Chaloner regarded him in distaste, thinking he was definitely a man who benefited from the shadows.

The men on the boats lapsed into inactivity again, so the courtiers began to chatter among themselves. Lambe's eyes narrowed suddenly, and when Chaloner followed the sorcerer's gaze, he saw it was fixed on Odowde, who was standing with a group of minor courtiers. Lambe stalked towards him and pulled him away so they could talk undisturbed. Odowde nodded hastily to whatever was said, and sighed his relief when the sorcerer strode away.

'He is a sinister devil,' said Chaloner, making Odowde jump by speaking close behind him. 'You might do well to avoid his company.'

'I might do well to avoid yours, too,' said Odowde, putting a hand to his heart and closing his eyes. 'You made me leap out of my skin, sneaking up on me like that. However, you are right about Lambe. He *is* a sinister devil, and I wish he had never come to Court.'

'He predicted you would hurt your arm, but I know he did not push you, as he was with the King at the time. So what did he do? Pay you to stumble?'

'What are you talking about?' demanded Odowde in alarm. 'I never—'

'I imagined you agreed to "fall" and wear a bandage,' Chaloner forged on. 'But Surgeon Wiseman was there, and he declared the injury insignificant. That did not suit Lambe, despite the fuss you made. He wanted something serious enough to convince his detractors.'

'*I* am a detractor,' gulped Odowde, but his words sounded mechanical and carried no conviction. 'Or I was. I changed my mind when I saw his power—'

'Wiseman may be insensitive, but he does not refer to

311

broken bones as "barely a bruise".' Chaloner looked pointedly at Odowde's blue and swollen fingers. 'Ergo, that happened *after* your tumble down the Banqueting House steps.'

'No!' breathed Odowde, although his frightened eyes told the truth. 'I never . . .'

'You are Lambe's accomplice,' surmised Chaloner. 'Like Ferine, Hubbert and Duncombe. But why did you and Duncombe persist with the arrangement after Hubbert died? I understand you dismissing Ferine's fate as happenstance, but you must have been suspicious when a second of your number died. And it is obvious what is going on: Lambe no longer needs you, and is eliminating the nuisance you have all become.'

'No!' cried Odowde, distraught. 'Wiseman found no evidence of foul play. Hubbert passed away because Lambe said he would. Lambe is a powerful man. Powerful and evil.'

'And ruthless,' added Chaloner, not without sympathy. 'Did Lambe hurt you himself, or did another of his minions oblige?'

Odowde hung his head, and what little fight he had left drained out of him. 'He gave me a potion to numb the pain, then hit me with a cudgel. But his brew did not work, and it was agony. He said he would break the other one if I told anyone about it.'

'Why did you agree to it? For money?'

Odowde swallowed hard. 'Courtiers are paid a pittance, yet we are expected to spend a fortune on clothes, jewellery, suitable transport . . . just ask Hannah. So yes, I leapt at the chance to make some easy cash. So did Ferine, Hubbert and Duncombe, but now all three are dead . . .'

312

'*Duncombe* is dead?' Chaloner wondered if he had misheard.

'He had a seizure, just like Hubbert. Lambe says I will have one, too, unless I do as I am told.'

'Poison,' surmised Chaloner. 'One that is undetectable.'

Odowde was near to tears. 'Yes, but no one will ever prove it. Perhaps he will do the same to me once I have outlived my usefulness. And Buckingham.'

'Lambe will not harm Buckingham – the man who pays him and takes him to Court.'

'He will not be paid and taken to Court when he fails to deliver the Philosopher's Stone,' flashed Odowde. 'Which he cannot do, because it does not exist. He has already "predicted" bad luck for Friday: he is preparing to strike, and will use the Duke's death to further his reputation as a great seer.'

'No one will hire Lambe if he predicts premature ends for all his customers,' Chaloner pointed out, not unreasonably.

'Of course they will, if he also tells them how to avoid such mishaps, which he has been doing for everyone else – although the poor Duke still awaits instructions. But I can say no more and you should forget this discussion or it will be *you* suffering a fatal seizure.'

He hurried away, leaving Chaloner staring after him thoughtfully. It was a nasty business, and he decided that when everyone was back in the city, he would expose Lambe as a vicious charlatan. But he had more urgent matters to attend that day, and with a sigh, he turned his attention back to the beach.

Out on the water, the rescued cannon had been winched on to a pontoon, and there was another hiatus while it was carefully secured. For the first time, it began to occur to the spectators that nothing was going to happen in a hurry – and certainly nothing dramatic. Moreover, the King had not made good on his promise to come. Some folk were already drifting back to their carriages, and there was a general atmosphere of anticlimax.

Among those who lingered was Spymaster Williamson. He perched on the rim of a wreck, gazing across the grey water at nothing in particular. He was not alone for long: John Scott approached and sat next to him. Curious to hear what they had to say to each other, Chaloner eased forward, and was torn between disgust and satisfaction when he was able to crouch behind the hulk and listen to every word.

'How much longer?' Williamson was demanding irritably. 'The Prince is beside himself with worry, and he is becoming difficult to control. Meanwhile, this uprising is scheduled for four days' time, and we must have answers before then or—'

'I will not let you down,' interjected Scott smoothly. 'You can trust me.'

'Can I?' asked Williamson coldly. 'Why, when I have it on good authority that the maps you sold me at such great expense are wildly inaccurate?'

'Then your "authority" is wrong!' Scott sounded hurt. 'My drawings are used by governments and military commanders all over the world, and no one has complained before. I am Cartographer Royal, you know.'

'Do not spin your yarns to me,' snapped Williamson angrily. 'Preparing a few charts does not make you Cartographer Royal. And the King would certainly not appoint one who put the River Rotte in Amsterdam and

314

The Hague ten miles inland. God only knows what other mistakes are—'

'Those will be the copyist's fault,' stated Scott firmly. 'But to show good faith, I shall correct them personally, at no extra cost.'

'At no extra cost?' exploded Williamson in open-mouthed disbelief. 'I did not pay for works of fiction, and your offer to make amends is too late anyway – duplicates have been distributed to the navy. What you have done is tantamount to treason.'

'Treason?' cried Scott. 'How can you say such a thing when I came to England – at great personal expense and inconvenience – to tell the King how to oust the Hollanders from New Amsterdam? You *know* I am loyal, and I resent your words extremely.'

Not for the first time, Chaloner marvelled at Scott's talent for deception, because his offended tirade took the wind out of Williamson's sails.

'Make your report,' the Spymaster said stiffly. 'Information has been far too sparse in this business and it is time that was rectified.'

'There have been some developments,' obliged Scott, indignation still in his voice. 'However, I might be persuaded to spend more of my time working on your behalf if you were a little more generous with . . . Ah, that will do nicely. I shall send you my testimony as soon as I can.'

'As soon as you can?' echoed Williamson incredulously. 'What about the "developments" you just mentioned? And the list of names you promised?'

'Both coming along splendidly, thank you for asking. However, names are no good alone, so I also intend to present you with details of the villains' homes,

315

meeting places and known associates. But these things take time.'

'We do not have time,' snapped Williamson.

Scott bowed jauntily. 'Then I had better be about my business.'

Chaloner heard crunching footsteps as the New Englander sauntered away, and grinned when he also heard a medley of very colourful curses; Williamson did not often lose control, but he certainly indulged himself that morning. Chaloner was about to emerge from his hiding place when he heard someone else approaching. He ducked down again.

'I received your report, *Trojan Horse*.' Williamson placed sardonic emphasis on the codename. 'Although I recommend you use black ink next time. Red is overly dramatic, and I am sure it caught Wiseman's eye. Not that it would have told him much. You did not specify what *manner* of explosions are planned for Easter.'

'Because I do not know,' came a voice that Chaloner recognised, but that he had so little expected to hear that it took him a moment to place. 'I need more time.'

'Does no one appreciate the urgency of the situation?' muttered Williamson. 'Then what about the list of rebels? How are you proceeding with that?'

'I have roughly a third of the names,' replied Atkinson. Peering through a hole in the wood Chaloner saw the scholarly face creased in worry. 'I shall work on the others, but it is not easy. Everyone is suspicious of everyone else, especially after the deaths of Strange and Quelch.'

'What of Chaloner? Have you told him you are working for me yet?'

'No. He will be wary of such a claim, and unlikely to believe me.'

Atkinson was right: he was the last man Chaloner would have suspected of betraying his fellows. The spy was not sure whether to be relieved or angry – relieved because the gentle stockinger was not a rebel after all, but angry because Atkinson was hopelessly out of his depth and should not have been swimming in such deadly waters.

Williamson scowled. 'You must. You will be more effective working together. I would tell him myself, but I have no idea where to find him. He seems to have closed up his house.'

'Very well,' said Atkinson unhappily. 'But do not worry about Easter Day. Jones is leaving everything so late that he will almost certainly not be ready.'

'Do not worry?' breathed Williamson disbelievingly. 'What a stupid thing to say!'

Eager for answers, but unwilling to tackle Atkinson where they might be seen, Chaloner trailed the stockinger to the chapel. It reeked of decay and seaweed, and not surprisingly the Court had given it a wide berth. Chaloner watched him weave through the shrouded forms to the altar, where a woman knelt. It was Ursula, who stood to favour her lover with a very passionate kiss.

'We should go home,' Atkinson said, when he could draw breath again. 'I have spoken to Williamson, but he is a—Chaloner! Good God! You startled me!'

'It is not what you think,' said Ursula, hastily straightening her clothes. 'We were praying together for the souls of these poor dead men. But what are you doing here?'

'Reporting to Williamson,' lied Chaloner. He looked hard at Atkinson. 'The same as you.'

'You know?' Atkinson closed his eyes. 'Thank God! I

317

abhor deception, but I did not know how to tell you that I . . . Ursula wanted to offer her services, too, but I thought it wise to keep her out of Williamson's clutches.'

So did Chaloner. 'What drove you to take such a path?'

Atkinson's expression was pained. 'I thought we would stage a *bloodless* revolution, with dialogue in place of violence, but the Sanhedrin have made it perfectly clear that they will kill and maim without distinction. My conscience will not allow that.'

'They have been buying arms and horses, in readiness for pitched battle,' added Ursula.

'But they have not,' said Chaloner. 'There has not been so much as a whisper about it, and it is not the sort of thing you can keep quiet.'

'Oh.' Atkinson frowned. 'Then how will Jones achieve what he has promised? He cannot seize the Tower, kill the King, establish a republic and redistribute property without some show of force. People will just laugh at him.'

'I think he intends to use a new kind of cannon against the city,' explained Chaloner. 'One that Manning's friend Sherwin knows how to make.'

'I see,' said Atkinson grimly. 'No wonder Jones has not seen fit to share the details of his plan with the Sanhedrin – he is afraid even they will baulk at such an outrage.'

'So you have heard nothing about it?' Both shook their heads, and Chaloner struggled to mask his frustration. 'Why did you come here? Surely not just to report to Williamson?'

'I do that by writing to his office,' replied Atkinson. He smiled impishly. 'In red ink, although he has just asked me to use a different colour, which will not be nearly as satisfying.'

318

'And we came because we thought Jones might try to harm the King here,' added Ursula soberly. 'We were going to save him. But His Majesty has stayed in London, so now we must race home and hope that nothing dire has happened in our absence.'

'Have you caught Snowflake's killer yet?' Atkinson looked pleadingly at Chaloner, the brief spark of mischief fading when he remembered his dead kinswoman.

Chaloner shook his head, sorry to see the stockinger's disappointment. 'But I have made some progress.'

'Then travel home in our carriage and tell us about it,' invited Ursula. 'We shall have the best part of two days to chat – the roads are dreadful.'

'I cannot spare that much time,' said Chaloner apologetically. 'I need to ride.'

'Then I shall hire a horse and ride with you,' determined Atkinson. 'No, you cannot come, dearest. You are still lame from your tumble. You will slow us down.'

'I will not!' declared Ursula indignantly, although they all knew that she would be unequal to the kind of journey Chaloner had just made. Even if she had not been limping, the fashionable clothes she wore would hamper her movements.

Atkinson smiled as he rested an affectionate hand on her arm and hastened to distract her. 'Give Chaloner his present, love. You have been carrying it around for days, and it will not be worth having if it spends much longer in your reticule.'

'Oh, yes.' Ursula rummaged in the little bag she carried on her wrist. 'We made you some stockings, because yours are so shabby that we decided you needed new ones. Pay special attention to the decorations around the knees. It is John's own design.'

319

Chaloner took them with genuine appreciation, although it seemed odd to accept hose in a chapel filled with corpses. Yet the High Holborn Plot had been a peculiar mix of the unnervingly deadly and the touchingly mundane from the start, and he was growing used to it.

'Put them on,' instructed Atkinson. 'I take my trade seriously, and I have never sold anyone a pair that does not fit.'

'Not now.' Chaloner pointed to his filthy boots and breeches. 'It would ruin them.'

'As soon as you get home then,' said Ursula. 'Ready for Easter Day, when all this will be over, and we shall join together to praise God for delivering us from evil.'

'I met your stepfather yesterday, Atkinson,' said Chaloner, changing the subject because he was afraid Ursula would ask him about his own beliefs and he did not want to be exposed as impious.

'Grisley?' Atkinson's face lit up. 'A fascinating man! I could listen to him for hours. But why did you meet him? Surely, you were not in Temple Mills?'

'Yes – to tell him about Snowflake,' explained Chaloner.

'That was kind. They were not close, but he would want to know, and so would the rest of the family. But we can talk about this as we ride. Come, we should not waste time.'

'Go in the carriage with Ursula,' ordered Chaloner. With any luck, the courtiers' carriages would have churned the road into a worse state than ever, and neither would reach London in time for the rebellion. Atkinson looked set to argue, so he added a lie. 'You cannot let her travel alone. There are rumours of robbers.'

As he had predicted, the stockinger was appalled by

the notion that his beloved might be in danger if he was not there to protect her. 'Very well,' he said unhappily. 'But before you go, take a few moments to interview a villager named Seth. I think he might be a Fifth Monarchist, and may have information to share.'

Chaloner watched them hurry to the place where coaches were waiting, then turned back towards the village, where he tracked Seth to the smallest and meanest of the three taverns. However, while Seth was indeed a Fifth Monarchist, he was also one who believed that his role in the Kingdom of Christ would be to supply the newly risen dead with gloves. He knew nothing of import, and Chaloner was about to leave when the door opened and Lawson walked in.

The Admiral, exhausted, mud-splattered and wet, was guarded by four sailors with cutlasses. Clearly, he was taking no chances on the long, isolated track between Temple Mills and the coast.

'Is this whole damned village dry?' he bellowed irritably. 'Where is Prittlewell's famous ale? And not in some piddling cup either. I am God's agent on Earth, and I want a *jug*.'

The taverner hastened to oblige, and when the Admiral was settled by the fire with a veritable bucket in his hands, Chaloner sat on the bench next to him and sidled close. Lawson's indignation at the liberty turned into a furious glare.

'What do you want?'

'Metal viols?' asked Chaloner softly, hoping the Admiral would not know that *he* was the one who had invaded the mill. 'I have never heard of such a thing.'

'What?'

'The two chests that were loaded on HMS *London*

321

shortly before she sailed from Chatham. They were for you, and they contained metal viols.'

'What of it?' snarled Lawson. 'A man's sea-chests are his own affair, and it is not for you to ask what he puts in them. Who are you, anyway? You are everywhere I look these days – in the club, helping Surgeon Wiseman, hobnobbing with Rupert and Buckingham . . .'

'Speaking of Rupert, I imagine he will be interested to know that you visit his gun-making factory at Temple Mills. And that you—'

Lawson whipped a gun from his belt, pointed it at Chaloner and squeezed the trigger. It happened so fast that Chaloner did not have time to duck and would certainly have been dead had the powder not been as sodden as its owner. Lawson reached for another dag, while his sailors fumbled for their cutlasses. Chaloner dived for the door, and it was fortunate that he was fast on his feet because the shot missed him by a fraction.

Lawson's violent reaction to his questions told Chaloner that the Admiral certainly warranted further investigation. However, it could not be done in Prittlewell when the man was armed, guarded and dangerous. Moreover, Atkinson and Ursula were right to be concerned about what Jones might be doing in their absence. It was time to return to the city.

He was on his way to collect Lady when he saw the halfwit Peter. The boy had fallen foul of a party of young courtiers, who had taken his hat and were tossing it to one another like bullies in a schoolyard, laughing as he lumbered clumsily from side to side, wailing his distress. Chaloner snatched it from the air and glowered at the lad's tormentors until they slunk away. He handed it over, and received a wan smile in return.

'A cannon in a boat,' Peter sniffed miserably. 'Bang! Boom!'

'Eighty of them,' said Chaloner, looking across the water to where the engineers were sitting in their boats again, smoking. No wonder the spectators were bored.

'One,' said Peter, suddenly intent. 'I can count to ten, and there was *one*. One cannon in a *little* boat. I know where they hid it. Do you want to see?'

He grabbed Chaloner's hand, and although the spy could have pulled free, he was loath to do anything that might hurt the boy. Besides, Peter's remarks had puzzled him, and he had learned from past experiences not to dismiss the testimony of simple people.

Peter moved with quiet purpose, surprisingly agile. Once away from the village, the only sounds were the gentle lap of waves, the cry of gulls and the soft hiss of wind across the sand. Eventually, Peter jigged left along a path that led to the salt marshes. He stopped triumphantly by a mound of dried grass, and began to pull it away, singing softly to himself. It did not take him long to expose the wreck of a boat. It had been adapted to form a makeshift shore-battery, and metal rings showed where a gun had been attached.

'A cannon,' said Peter, pointing. 'A big silver cannon.'

Wheel tracks indicated where the piece had been brought in by cart and ferried away again, while discarded wadding, powder-stains and other marks suggested that it had been used within the last few weeks. Chaloner's thoughts whirled.

Before the blast, Captain Dare claimed to have heard a crack on *London*'s starboard side, which would have

323

been the one nearest the shore on which Chaloner now stood. Could a gun have been used against her – had the 'crack' been the sound of it discharging and hitting the ship, after which she had exploded? Peter's 'bang' and 'boom' also indicated that there had been two distinct sounds. It did not seem possible that someone could sink one of His Majesty's warships with a single shot – and there could not have been more, or Dare and Peter would have heard – yet it seemed that was what had happened.

'Did you see it fire?' Chaloner asked of Peter, who was sitting in the grass, humming to himself.

Peter nodded. 'One gun. One bang. Bang! Boom!'

'Did you see the men who used it?'

Peter nodded again. 'A big one with yellow hair, a little one with dark hair, and one with a scarred face. They talked about Jesus, but Gentle Jesus would not like them.'

Chaloner was inclined to agree. He searched the boat thoroughly, but all he found was a scrap of paper with a shopping list on one side and notes for an anti-Court pamphlet on the other. The writing was spiky and all but illegible.

'Would you like to see one of the men?' asked Peter suddenly.

Chaloner nodded, then recoiled when Peter pulled away more grass to reveal a body. It had suffered from the ravages of gulls and crabs, but there was enough left to deduce two things: first, that there had been a scar on his face, and second, that he had been shot in the chest.

'Scarface Roberts,' murmured Chaloner. 'Not blown up experimenting with a stolen batch of Rupert's dangerous new gunpowder, but killed by a pistol.'

'Yes,' said Peter, nodding earnestly. 'The yellow one shot him. Bang!'

'Why?' asked Chaloner, confused.

'To keep it secret,' replied Peter earnestly. 'The scarred one promised never to speak, but the yellow one didn't believe him. He shot him dead. He would shoot me, too, if he saw me.'

'Yes, he would,' agreed Chaloner. 'And someone still might, so you should not tell anyone else what you have found.'

Peter nodded soberly. Chaloner looked back at the body, his stomach churning. Jones, Strange and Roberts had destroyed one of His Majesty's finest warships, and sent three hundred souls to a watery grave. If they had managed that with such ease, what was being planned for Easter Day?

Chapter 12

Although he knew he should do what Atkinson had suggested and return to the city with all possible speed, Chaloner felt he was close to a solution with HMS *London*. He recalled Dare saying that she had been delayed by paperwork in Chatham, during which the 'metal viols' had been taken aboard. The fact that Lawson had drawn a gun rather than reveal what was in the chests made Chaloner determined to find out more about them.

He stared at the distant smudge on the horizon that represented the Kent coast. The Royal Dockyard could not be more than twenty miles away as the crow flew – across the estuary and up the winding Medway. The wind was in the right direction, and a fast, well-handled vessel should be able to manage it by dusk. Then it would be an easy ride from the shipyard back to the city, because that particular road was used by navy officials, and was kept in better repair than the one to Prittlewell.

He walked back along the beach, where the spectators had given up on seeing anything interesting and were leaving in droves, allowing village life to return to normal. A few boys still clamoured to run errands, while women offered ridiculously low prices for their last few pies. Chaloner bought one on his way back from collecting Lady, and ate it as he approached the line of fishing boats. He was in luck: several were preparing to put to sea.

Not surprisingly, none were bound for Chatham, but Westcliff agreed to make a diversion for half the money in Temperance's purse. It took the other half before he agreed to carry Lady as well, although he would not help with the loading, and said he would tip the beast over-board if it misbehaved and put the ketch in danger. Lady seemed to understand the threat, and confined his ill nature to an equine scowl.

It was not an easy journey. There was a heavy swell coming in from the North Sea, and the boat had a shallow draught, so rolled abominably. It began to rain, too, and the sails seemed to funnel gouts of water to wherever Chaloner happened to be sitting. He gave up trying to stay dry, and stood in the bows watching the coast grow steadily closer.

Eventually they were across the estuary, and into the calmer waters of the Medway. Westcliff peered ahead in the dull afternoon light, cutting a zigzagging course to miss sandbanks and shallows. Then they were in a deep channel, skirting low, flat islands that were home to huge colonies of raucous birds. It was almost dark by the time he steered the little craft towards a pier, where Chaloner and Lady were unloaded with almost indecent haste, lest the port authorities should see and demand a landing fee.

Chaloner tethered Lady to a bollard, confident that the gelding was far too mean to tempt thieves, and began to trawl the waterside taverns. Most were rough, and it was not easy to encourage people to talk when he had no money to buy ale. Eventually, he sold Lady's saddle. Matters improved thereafter, although it was still nearing eleven by the time he was directed to a small, sooty-haired man with bad skin. His name was Norris.

'HMS *London*,' the fellow said, sipping the ale Chaloner set in front of him. 'Yes, I remember her. She was due to sail on the morning tide, but Commissioner Pett delayed her with paperwork. It was all nonsense, of course. He could have let her go when the captain asked, but he refused.'

'Why?'

Norris shrugged. 'The ways of commissioners are beyond the likes of me, although there will have been money involved – Pett will do nothing unless he is well rewarded. He does not share his good fortune, though. He paid me a pittance to carry the Admiral's chests aboard.'

'I understand they were heavy.'

'Like lead. Not that Pett gave me and my mates extra for our labours.'

'What was in them?'

'Musical instruments, apparently, but the captain laughed when I told him, so I imagine it was something else.'

'Brandywine, perhaps? Or rum?'

'They were too heavy for that.' Norris spoke with such conviction that Chaloner was sure he knew what he was talking about. 'I thought it odd that Lawson should want them put on here, though. Why not send them to the city, where he was to board himself?'

'Do you think they had anything to do with the explosion?'

Norris shook his head. 'It was not gunpowder that was in them – the balance would have been different. Maybe it was money – coins. But you should be asking Commissioner Pett all this, not me. Come. I will show you his house.'

While they walked, he confided that the Pett family had had control of the shipyard for generations, clawing power and influence through a range of sly and dishonest dealings. Their home was a lavish affair, a gem of glory in an area that was otherwise functional and dirty. Through one of its windows, Chaloner saw Pett sitting at dinner, despite the lateness of the hour, with a woman who was obviously his daughter. Pett was an ugly, moustachioed man with untrustworthy brown eyes, and his daughter looked much the same. She wore a pearl necklace of such length that half of it was submerged in her soup.

Knowing that no deceitful official liked answering questions, and that if he knocked on the door and asked for an audience he would be refused, Chaloner broke in, padding along a hallway that was full of fine furniture, much of it French and very new. There was a range of expensive clocks, none of them showing the same time, and their clangs, tings and gongs rang out in a constant medley of noise. They disguised any sound he might have made as he tiptoed towards the dining room and opened the door.

'I am not here to harm you,' he said, locking it behind him and making a sign to warn them against howling for help. 'I just want to talk.'

'I know nothing about that shipment of lead sheathing,' squeaked Pett, frightened. 'If it has gone missing, it has nothing to do with me.'

329

'The ship *London*,' said Chaloner. 'I have been charged to find out what happened to her.'

Pett gulped. 'A terrible tragedy. We had fitted her with a new timber hull, a taller foremast and eighty brass cannon. I am told the guns may be retrieved, but Lawson is mad if he thinks she can be weighed. He was going to try today – him and the Navy Board engineers.'

'What do you think happened to her?'

Pett swallowed hard. 'Well, perhaps some of the cartridges we supplied were a bit old, but that should not have caused her to explode. If you ask me – and I *do* know ships – I would say that a cannonball crashed through her amidships, igniting the powder magazine. Although obviously that cannot have happened – the Dutch have not invaded yet.'

'Tell me about the two chests that were carried aboard. What was in them?'

'Admiral Lawson told everyone it was musical instruments, but he confided the truth to me: it was soil from his estate in Yorkshire.'

'What?' That was not an answer Chaloner had expected.

'To make him feel at home,' explained Pett. 'And he said it is useful for scattering across the decks before a battle, to soak up the blood.'

'You believed him?'

'Of course. Blood *is* a nuisance during a skirmish, as it makes the decks slippery. Seamen losing their footing can mean the difference between success and victory at sea.'

'I meant why would he go to the trouble and expense of bringing dirt onboard?'

330

Pett shrugged. 'Admirals are peculiar men, and Lawson is odder than most.'

'Why did you delay *London*'s sailing?'

Pett licked dry lips. 'I did not delay it – there was paperwork to be completed. Captain Dare had neglected to obtain certain permits, and his departure was postponed because of it.'

Chaloner rested his hand on the hilt of his sword. 'The truth, Pett.'

'All right, I was paid,' bleated the Commissioner, cringing away. 'A substantial sum, as it happens. But what else was I supposed to do?'

'Refuse the bribe and warn Captain Dare that something was amiss?' suggested Chaloner coolly. 'It is what a decent man would have done.'

Pett released a startled burst of laughter. 'You do not refuse a bribe! It would not be right!'

Chaloner blinked. 'And allowing the destruction of one of His Majesty's warships is?'

Pett shook his head in vigorous denial, but Chaloner could see that the notion was not new to him – he had asked himself the same question. 'You cannot prove the delay had anything to do with that,' he blustered. 'It—'

'I think I can. And unless you tell me everything about whoever paid you, I will make sure the King knows it. You will be executed as a traitor, and your family will never live down the disgrace.'

Pett opened his mouth to plead his innocence again, but something in Chaloner's angry demeanour warned him against it. He sagged in defeat. 'The fellow wore a hooded cloak, so I did not see his face, but I do not believe I have met him before. I wish I could describe him to you, but I cannot.'

331

'There is one other thing, Father.' The woman spoke for the first time. 'He said you were the kind of man who would prosper in New York, and he sold you a lovely map of the place.'

John Scott, thought Chaloner sourly.

Chaloner felt he now had more than enough information to prove the Fifth Monarchists – and Scott – were involved in the sinking of *London*. He left Pett's house quickly, melting into the shadows when he heard the Commissioner bellowing for his servants to rouse themselves and hunt for the dangerous felon that had broken in and menaced him with a sword.

It was too dark to begin the journey home that night, and it would be self-defeating to risk Lady needlessly, especially as he would be riding bareback, so Chaloner found a hedge on a quiet farm and crawled beneath it, wrapped in his coat. He did not think he would sleep, given that it was cold and his mind raced with questions, but he started awake some hours later when a cart trundled past. Dawn was still some way off, but there was enough light for him to lead Lady along the road and knock four or five miles off the journey.

After, he rode hard through the brown, rainswept countryside, feeling time slipping inexorably away from him. It was Maundy Thursday, his third day away from the city, and the Fifth Monarchists' uprising would start in less than seventy-two hours. Would the arrest of the ringleaders be enough to stop it?

He rested Lady at noon, and continued again until a grey-yellow haze on the horizon told him that he was nearing London. Slowly, the silence of the countryside gave way to the distant thunder of wheeled vehicles, the clank of machinery and the hubbub of the markets. He fancied he could smell the great city, too, mostly the acrid stench of coal fires, but also the earthier aroma from the laystalls – deep trenches where dung and other rubbish was dumped – that formed a reeking halo around the outskirts. Traffic was heavier as well, and he chafed at the decreased pace.

It was almost dark by the time he crossed the Fleet River on Holborn, and it was then that he saw Eliza Hatton. Her face gleamed palely under her hood, and her cloak billowed as she glided along, attracting more than one uneasy glance from passers-by. As she drew level with Chaloner, she stared at him, an unearthly glower that made the hair stand up on the back of his neck.

He pulled himself together irritably. He was cold, wet and tired, but that was no reason to let his imagination run away with him. He rode on, but as he was passing St Andrew's, he recalled Ursula's challenge, issued days ago, to look at the painting of Eliza Hatton above what was alleged to be her tomb. He dismounted and walked towards the church.

The door was open, ready to receive the faithful who wanted to keep vigil in preparation for Good Friday. It did not take him long to find the Hatton tomb – a large Elizabethan monstrosity picked out in red and gold. A man and a woman had been carved under a garish canopy, he wearing a massive neck-ruff and she with a child's body and pathologically proportioned hands. Their faces were stylised, and might have been anyone. A painting had been hung above the memorial, but the church was too dark for Chaloner to see it.

He fetched a lamp from the back of the church and

held it up. It illuminated the portrait perfectly, and he gaped at it in astonishment. It *was* Eliza Hatton! Alone in the dark building, with shadows leaping eerily all around him, a small voice at the back of his mind asked whether the woman who inhabited Holborn might indeed be a spectre.

Then his common sense returned to him. Eliza was probably a descendant of the lady in the painting, as she had told him, and that was why they looked so disconcertingly similar. And even if she was Alice Fanshaw, as Wiseman believed, much could be achieved with face-paints, wigs and carefully selected clothing.

He felt, rather than saw, someone behind him, and whipped around to see Eliza standing there. She was wearing the same long, dark cloak as the woman in the picture, and had an identical half-smile. A chill air seemed to emanate from her and the lantern went out. He reminded himself firmly that St Andrew's was a draughty building, and that the icy wind had nothing to do with the breath of the grave. The breeze grew stronger, so he abandoned the lamp and stepped forward, but Eliza had gone.

'Wait!' he called. 'I need to talk to you.'

There was no reply, but the cold current became chillier still as he groped his way forward. He followed it to a door, which was ajar, and pushed it open to see it led to the cemetery. His stomach did an unpleasant flip when he saw her among the graves, illuminated by the lantern she was holding. A low mist rose from the ground, which served to give her a distinctly other-worldly appearance. He started to walk towards her, but voices made him turn. A family was approaching, taking a short-cut through the churchyard as they aimed for Holborn.

'It is the ghost!' screeched one of the children, stabbing a chubby finger. 'Look!'

Eliza turned very slowly to look at him, and the smile she gave was so chillingly evil that even Chaloner was unnerved. With terrified wails, the adults grabbed their brats and raced away. Chaloner looked back to where Eliza had been standing, only to see she had disappeared again. He closed his eyes and listened: his eyes might play tricks, but his ears would not. Yet there were no footsteps or muffled curses as Eliza made her way across uneven ground in the dark. There was nothing but silence – an eerie one given that bustling Holborn lay so close.

Something lay on the ground near where she had been standing, and he stooped to pick it up. It was a piece of paper covered with the same symbols as were inked on Lambe's neck and hands, and that the sorcerer had drawn on the walls of Buckingham's observatory. Chaloner began a systematic search of the area, but Eliza had vanished into the night.

Wearily, he rode to the club, where he rubbed Lady down and settled him in a clean, dry stall. Then he prepared a warm mash of oats, and stayed with him while he ate, talking in a low, soft voice. The gelding had endured two long, hard journeys and an unpleasant jaunt across an estuary, so he deserved a little consideration.

'Lord!' breathed Temperance, when Chaloner walked into her parlour some time later. Maude was there, too, and they were drinking and smoking. 'What have you been doing?'

He glanced down at himself. His clothes were thick with splattered mud, and badly rumpled from hours spent in the saddle and sleeping under hedges. He flopped into a chair, and smiled gratefully when Maude brought him mulled wine and a slice of venison pastry.

'Have you discovered who murdered Ferine and Snowdrop?' asked Temperance. She tried to keep the tremor of anxiety from her voice, but did not succeed.

'I believe so,' he replied. 'Although I still have questions about—'

'Thank God!' she breathed. 'Who is it?'

'It would be better not to say until he is in custody.'

He expected her to insist on an answer, but she only nodded, and he saw what a strain the whole affair had been on her, draining her of the strength to argue.

'There are tales now about Ferine's wife,' said Maude. 'That he murdered her, which is why he shut up his High Holborn house. Now her ghost haunts it.'

'Superstitious nonsense,' said Chaloner dismissively. 'Perhaps Ferine did push her down the stairs, but there is no such thing as ghosts.'

He fully believed what he said. His quiet time with Lady had allowed him to analyse the incident in St Andrew's churchyard, and he was fairly sure he understood what had happened. The same was true of Hatton House and Ferine's home. None had anything to do with the supernatural – there was a human hand at work, and he knew exactly to whom it belonged.

Maude inclined her head, although he could see she did not believe him. 'You were gone a long time. I suppose you were caught in the floods, like the rest of Court. We have heard such tales of abandoned coaches, highwaymen, nasty accidents . . .'

Chaloner frowned. 'What floods?'

'The ones north of Canvey Island,' explained Temperance. 'It has rained so much that the roads are

336

virtually impassable. Only those courtiers on horseback have been able to return, while those in carriages have to be dug out every few miles. The King says he is glad he stayed home.'

'And it was all for nothing, apparently,' added Maude. 'They were promised the spectacular sight of a drowned ship rising from the deep, and all they got was mud, rain and tedium.'

'They should have come here instead,' said Temperance in a feeble attempt at jollity, while Chaloner thought it no wonder that people were disillusioned if they had gone to Prittlewell with that sort of expectation. 'We offer fine entertainment without the need to be cold, wet or inconvenienced.'

'We have bad news, though,' sighed Maude. 'Duncombe is dead. Of a seizure, apparently, but he was another of our patrons, and people are beginning to say we are cursed. They will say it even more if that prediction of Lambe's comes true, and Buckingham does die tomorrow.'

Chaloner frowned. 'Buckingham will die? I thought he was just to suffer some bad luck.'

'That is what the Duke believes, but Lambe told Brodrick the real truth, and Brodrick told me,' explained Temperance. 'Buckingham will die tomorrow – Good Friday.'

'What a pity,' said Chaloner flatly. 'His country will miss him.'

'He is a friend to the club,' said Temperance sharply. 'And a friend to Hannah. Can you imagine how devastated she will be if he passes away? You will have to save him.'

'I imagine you would rather I caught Snowflake's killer.'

Temperance regarded him balefully. 'No, I would rather you did both.'

It was too late to do anything that night, so Chaloner accepted the offer of a bed in Hercules' Pillars Alley. There were plenty of spare rooms now there were no clients, and Temperance had even sent some of the girls to visit their families, so as to avoid having hordes of them sitting around doing nothing but eat, drink and quarrel.

As he had not been in a proper bed since Sunday – and that had been after the ambush outside Clarendon House, which had rendered him too unsettled for restful repose – Chaloner fell into a deep, dreamless sleep the moment his head touched the pillow. He woke an hour before dawn the following morning, Good Friday, refreshed and ready to tackle whatever the city's murderers and rebellious fanatics threw at him.

He felt even better when he discovered hot water available for washing and shaving, and that Maude had thought to lay out clean clothes for him – ones that had been abandoned by clients, it was true, but carefully laundered and pressed. He would have liked to wear his new stockings, but they were blue and the breeches were green, so he put them in his pocket instead, along with the buttons Grisley Pate had given him.

He left the club before anyone was awake, listing in his mind all that needed to be done that day. Most pressing was to visit Atkinson and Ursula, to see if they had learned anything new while he had been in Chatham. He also had to find out Jones's plans, and warn Buckingham to be on his guard.

He walked briskly to Middle Row, but a quick prowl inside Ursula's house told him that no one had been there for several days. He supposed the coach carrying her and Atkinson was caught in the floods, and was torn between relief that they were away from trouble, and alarm because even their amateur help would have been better than none.

He went to Garlick Hill next. Despite the early hour, the streets were busy, as more people poured into the city for Lady Day, now less than twenty-four hours away. Tradesmen were opening their stalls sooner than usual to catch more business, and the atmosphere was one of excited anticipation. Worriedly, Chaloner realised that he would never know if an uprising was in the offing, because he could not distinguish between eager Fifth Monarchists and folk who had come for legitimate business.

Lamps were lit at Jones's house, just visible beneath shutters that were still closed against the night, and there was a black wreath on the door to indicate a house in mourning. Chaloner was surprised – he had not imagined Jones to be a sentimental man, even if Strange had been a friend.

He drilled with his dagger until he had made a hole in the soft, rotten wood of a window frame that had spent too many years battered by rain, and was rewarded by the sight of Jones serving breakfast ale to Leving, Manning and some of the Sanhedrin. He was using silver goblets on a matching tray, and his clothes were protected from accidental spillages by the incongruously lacy apron. Leving was chattering like a monkey, while Manning was glowering at someone on the other side of the table. It was Scott, who leaned back in his chair with his feet on the table. They did not stay there long: Jones fixed him with a look of extraordinary malevolence, and the chair came to rest on all four legs with a thump.

Chaloner could only suppose that Scott had bludgeoned Manning into inviting him to the Fifth Monarchists' meeting, but what would the New Englander do with what he learned? Tell Williamson? Use the information to extort more money from whoever wanted to buy the secret of Rupert's cannon? Or was he a secret Fifth Monarchist himself, and had played the Spymaster for a fool? Regardless, Chaloner knew his presence there spelled trouble for everyone concerned.

Then the door opened, and Atkinson and Ursula stumbled in, travel-stained, rumpled and grey with exhaustion. Ursula was limping badly, and both were nervous, causing Jones to regard them sharply. Chaloner winced – they were going to give themselves away with their guilty faces!

He was on the verge of joining the party, simply to divert attention away from them, when Scott began to speak. Chaloner could not hear everything, but he caught enough to know that it was a résumé of Sherwin's work with the cannon. Manning's face was dark and angry as he listened – Scott was revealing details that had not been shared with him first.

When Scott had finished, others stood to make their reports. Chaloner cringed when he saw Leving surreptitiously making notes under the table and Atkinson frowning in his effort to memorise as much as possible. And none of the news was worth the risks they were taking – one man said a printer had offered to publish Jones's pamphlets free of charge if the Last Millennium did dawn on Sunday, while a tailor named Glasse had bought a quantity of red velvet, lest the stuff in White Hall should transpire to be below par.

'I wish Strange could see it,' he concluded softly. 'He would have been impressed.'

'His killer will not escape unpunished,' said Jones in a low yet harsh voice. 'I shall see to that.'

'You need not trouble yourself,' said the one-armed soldier named Tucker. 'King Jesus will take care of that sort of thing on Sunday.'

'Of course,' said Jones shortly, making it obvious that he intended to exact his own revenge anyway. The remark made Chaloner wonder yet again about the strength of Jones's commitment to the Fifth Monarchists and their beliefs.

Scott patted Jones's shoulder sympathetically, and Jones stood abruptly, although whether because he feared he might weep or to escape Scott's unwelcome touch was difficult to say. He raised his right hand, and the conspirators chanted their oath, after which he began to collect the empty goblets. The meeting was over, and it was the sign for his guests to leave.

Ursula and Atkinson were first out, and Chaloner trailed them to Thames Street, glad the rest of the conspirators were lingering to chat outside Jones's house, thus giving him the opportunity to waylay the couple unseen by the others.

'We have spent the last two days lurching from one morass to another,' said Atkinson, his voice hoarse with tiredness. 'What a waste of time! And now Scott and Manning report that they *do* have special artillery to use on Sunday – you were right. What should we do about it?'

'Tell Williamson,' replied Chaloner promptly.

'We asked how the guns were to be used, but Jones would only say that there will be fireworks,' said Ursula unhappily. 'And he asked where you were, because he will need your expertise soon.'

Chaloner rubbed his chin thoughtfully. It was difficult to move heavy weapons without being noticed, and while the odd gun might have been slipped into London unseen, it would take a whole battery to defeat the Tower, take over White Hall and set the city afire. Moreover, Jones would need more than one gunpowder expert to realise his plans. Try as he might, Chaloner could make no sense of it all.

'It was Scarface Roberts who destroyed the ship *London*,' he said, deciding to be open with them. 'On the orders of Jones and Strange. The evidence is indisputable. Tell Williamson that, too.'

'Oh, God!' groaned Atkinson. 'And now Jones wants you to blow up something else! But what? Not White Hall, because King Jesus will want to live there. St Paul's, perhaps?'

'No,' said Ursula. 'I imagine God would like that preserved, too. It must be the Tower. Jones did say he was going to seize it.'

Chaloner made a decision. 'It is time Jones shared his ideas with his gunpowder expert. Now – today. I am tired of being fobbed off with promises of future revelations. If he wants my services, then he is going to have to confide in me. The threat of walking out should work, because I doubt he will find a replacement at this late stage.'

'Then be careful,' warned Atkinson. 'It occurs to me that *he* might have murdered Strange and Quelch. I have no idea why he would slaughter his own followers, but there is much I do not understand about this business.'

342

'Strange was more than a follower – they were friends.'
Ursula sounded shocked. 'They lived together.'

'Even friends can disagree,' said Atkinson. 'And to argue with Jones might well be fatal.'

Chaloner hurried back towards Garlick Hill, ducking into an alley as a gaggle of the Sanhedrin passed. They were braying about the Last Millennium and what they planned to do when they were invested with unlimited power. Chaloner recalled what Thurloe had called them: spiritually arrogant, humourless, vociferous fanatics. The ex-Spymaster had coined them perfectly.

Behind them, Manning and Scott were engrossed in another conversation. When Manning stopped walking and leaned against a wall to ease the pain of his chilblains, Chaloner crept behind a stationary hackney carriage so he could listen to what was being said. Scott paced impatiently while he waited for Manning to recover.

'. . . will cheat us,' he was hissing. 'We cannot trust them.'

'I agree,' said Manning. 'And I have decided that I do not like the sound of their Glorious Design. To hell with gainful employment and equal distribution of wealth! I want lots of money for myself, so I can live in indolent luxury for the rest of my life.'

'Then put your trust in me,' urged Scott. 'I have contacts.'

'Like Georges Pellissary of the French navy?' asked Manning archly. 'I found a letter from him in your rooms, which read as though you have started negotiations with him. You should not have done, not without my consent. And for God's sake do not approach the Dutch, or we will both swing at Tyburn.'

343

'I have *negotiated* with no one,' said Scott smoothly. 'Just made a few enquiries about prices. You know I would never do anything without consulting you. We are partners.'

Manning started to walk again, but Chaloner decided there was no harm in letting the pair know that their discussion had been overheard. 'It is treason to sell weapons to foreign governments,' he said, stepping out in front of them. 'French *or* Dutch.'

'As if we would,' said Scott, recovering quickly and filling his voice with hurt reproach. 'We are patriotic men, and I am Cartographer Royal.'

Manning was less adept at hiding his terror. 'I paid Ferine a fortune to predict whether I should persist with this venture,' he gulped. 'He should have warned me that it might turn deadly.'

'It has done nothing of the kind,' said Scott firmly. 'Now go and make sure Sherwin is still safely in the Pope's Head. I will join you there shortly.'

'Why?' asked Manning, all suspicious alarm. 'What are you going to do?'

'Have a word with Chaloner here, to ensure that he knows it is unwise to cross us,' replied Scott. 'Then I shall investigate other buyers – ones who will pay us what we deserve.'

Chaloner would not have believed him for an instant, but Manning promptly scurried away, openly relieved to be away from a conversation that carried threats of treason. Or perhaps it was the prospect of more money that had convinced him.

'Williamson will not protect you if you sell Rupert's secret,' warned Chaloner. 'Be it to overseas powers or home-grown lunatics.'

'What a low opinion you have of me,' chided Scott. 'I thought we were friends.'

'No friend of mine would bribe Commissioner Pett to delay HMS *London*'s sailing, thus allowing Strange and Jones to murder three hundred British sailors.'

For the first time, Scott's composure slipped. 'I did nothing of the kind! Besides, Pett is an infamous liar, and no one will believe a word he says.'

'Regardless, I would not like to be in your shoes when Williamson—'

'Williamson trusts me,' snapped Scott. 'And you would do well to remember it.'

'So are you saying that you were not in Chatham when *London* sailed? If Williamson sends his agents to ask questions, they will find no one who saw you there?'

'I did not say I was not there,' hedged Scott. His eyes were cold and hard, but there was a sheen of sweat on his brow. 'I said Pett is a liar. Doubtless he delayed *London* for reasons of his own. Everyone knows he is corrupt, and will do anything for money.'

He had a point: Pett had virtually admitted as much himself. Yet Chaloner had believed Pett, and he did not believe Scott.

'You have sold inaccurate maps to the navy, you have conspired to destroy one of His Majesty's warships, and you are attempting to sell military secrets to hostile foreign powers,' he said harshly. 'Even Williamson will not be able to save you from—'

'You are treading a dangerous path, Chaloner,' hissed Scott. 'You understand nothing, and you would be wise to stay away from this business if you want to live.'

He turned on his heel and stalked away. Chaloner could have stopped him, but he decided it was not worth the bother. He was about to resume his walk to Jones's house when he spotted Leving, who was sauntering along humming to himself. The turncoat beamed merrily when Chaloner intercepted him, and laughed when he was hauled out of sight behind the hackney carriage.

'Lord, Chaloner, you do enjoy the dramatic! Where have you been these last few days? I was beginning to think the Oldenberg Conspirators had murdered you for infiltrating them.'

'Who?' asked Chaloner in confusion.

Leving looked blank for a moment, then chuckled. 'I mean the Fifth Monarchists. I am monitoring so many rebellious factions that it is difficult to keep track of them all. But you and I are working together to foil Jones, Quelch and Strange. I remember now.'

'Quelch and Strange are dead,' said Chaloner, recalling that Wiseman had declared Leving insane. He was becoming increasingly convinced that the surgeon was right.

'I know,' declared Leving, a little defensively. 'I saw them in the charnel house at Chelsey.'

'Christ!' muttered Chaloner. 'Tell me what you have learned since Monday.'

'Well, the government is refusing to lift the coal tax, the Pope's nephew has a nasty cold, and the Dutch fleet is travelling to—'

'About the Fifth Monarchists,' interrupted Chaloner impatiently.

Leving frowned, tapping his lips with a forefinger as he considered. 'My list of conspirators now comprises almost seventy people – schoolmasters, housewives, haberdashers, tailors and cooks. A very deadly horde. Some of them even invited me into their homes and gave me bread,

346

cheese and ale when I went to check their addresses. Fanatics, you see.'

'They are not fanatics,' snapped Chaloner. 'And you had better be sure of their guilt before you pass that list to Williamson. If they hang because of it, their blood will be on your hands.'

'Better than my blood on theirs,' quipped Leving airily. 'But why do you defend them? Have you joined them in their lunatic opinions? Shall I include *your* name on my register?'

'You must have learned more than names in all this time?' pressed Chaloner. 'Surely *some* of these folk discussed their plans with you?'

'Of course,' replied Leving happily. 'They aim to kill the King, seize the Tower, burn the city, establish a republic and redistribute property. I thought you were there when Jones made the announcement.'

'Go to Williamson,' ordered Chaloner curtly. 'Do not give him your list, but tell him all that you have learned. I am sure he will be grateful.'

And if the Spymaster was worth his salt, he would see that Leving had lost what little reason he had left, and would incarcerate him before he did any harm.

Sure that tackling Jones directly would not work, Chaloner set about following him, hoping he would learn something from where the rebel went and whom he met. Carefully locking his house behind him, Jones visited the grubby Stillyard Coffee House on Thames Street, where he read the newsbooks, sipping the heady brew with every appearance of relish. Then he went to St Paul's Cathedral, where he sat for a long time with his head bowed. At first, Chaloner thought he was asleep, but then he saw his lips moving: Jones was praying. Or talking to himself.

After an age, during which Chaloner fretted about the passing time, Jones rose and sauntered west. He ambled along Fleet Street, stopping to watch a juggler, although he was the only one who did not toss the man a coin, and then turned north, towards the market in Covent Garden, which had opened early to accommodate the increased business from Lady Day visitors.

When Jones pulled what appeared to be a list of groceries from his pocket, Chaloner decided he had had enough – he was not about to trail after the man while he did his shopping. He marched up to Jones, grabbed him by the collar, and hauled him behind one of the stalls, so they could talk undisturbed.

'Oh,' said Jones, pulling away from him and brushing himself down. 'It is you. I was wondering when you would deign to put in an appearance. Where have you been?'

'Away,' replied Chaloner shortly. 'But it is Friday, and if you want me to be ready for Easter morning, you had better let me know what is expected. I do not like to be rushed.'

'And I do not like to be manhandled.' Jones's eyes were gimlet hard. 'Yet you are right: it is time you knew what was happening. Come to the Pope's Head at midnight, and all will be revealed.'

'I would rather know now.'

'Then I am sorry,' said Jones, trying to push past him. 'The Cause is more important than its component parts, and you will just have to wait.'

'I want answers to some questions, or you can find yourself another gunpowder expert,' snapped Chaloner,

348

moving to block his way. 'Which will not be easy at this late hour.'

Jones gave an irritable sigh. 'Very well, ask. However, I warn you now, if your questions jeopardise the Glorious Design, I shall decline to reply.'

'Who killed Strange and Quelch?'

Jones folded his arms. 'I should like to know that myself. I was fond of Strange in particular, and nothing would give me greater pleasure than to see the culprit dead – if not by my hand, then by another's.'

Chaloner had no idea whether to believe him – or even whether this was a subtle way of inviting Chaloner to dispatch the culprit himself – but he could see that Jones would not be persuaded to say more. He moved to another matter.

'What was in the letters you gave Leving for Manning last Tuesday?'

Jones frowned. 'You mean the coded missives that I asked *you* to deliver to the White Hind, along with that box of powder? I tried to follow you, to ensure you did as you were told, but you slunk into the Fleet Rookery and I lost you.'

'No, earlier than that,' said Chaloner. 'Before we met.'

Jones's scowl deepened. 'I gave Leving no letters for Manning. Why would I? Leving is barely sane, and I have more reliable messengers at my disposal.'

Chaloner regarded him sceptically.

'I can prove it,' said Jones testily. 'Either you can ask Manning and *he* will tell you the truth, or you can think about the writing on the package that Leving allegedly delivered. Here is mine. It is quite distinctive, as any of my friends will tell you.'

He waved his grocery list to reveal an ugly, spiky scrawl

349

that Chaloner recognised at once from the scrap of paper he had retrieved from the makeshift battery in Prittlewell. It was as different as it was possible to be from the documents that Leving had passed to Manning, which had been in an elegant cursive with ornate capital letters. He was about to ask more when there was a sound behind him. He turned to see three members of the Sanhedrin, all armed with guns.

'No, Glasse,' said Jones quietly, putting out his hand when the tailor took aim. 'We need him for our fireworks. Let him go.'

'Are you sure?' asked Glasse suspiciously.

Jones nodded and favoured Chaloner with one of his cold smiles. 'Do not forget – midnight tonight at the Pope's Head.'

Chapter 13

Chaloner left Covent Garden even more convinced that blood would be spilled in two days. Even if the farmers and housewives saw sense, the Sanhedrin was poised to cause trouble, and he hated the notion of Rupert's cannon in their hands. He dashed off a note to Williamson, warning him that the High Holborn Plot might involve artillery – it was true that Atkinson was doing the same, but there was no harm in telling him twice – but he had a bad feeling that the Spymaster and Rupert would be more interested in protecting the secret than in preventing an atrocity. Worried and unhappy, he went to the one place where he knew he could rely on sound, reliable counsel.

He arrived at Chamber XIII to find the ex-Spymaster surrounded by paper, charts and coded messages. Thurloe looked tired, but stood to take Chaloner's arm and draw him towards the fire. Chaloner disengaged himself and picked up one of the maps. It was of the Dutch coast.

Thurloe took it from him and placed it face down on the table. 'You are one of few men I allow in here while I am working, but only because I trust your discretion. Please do not make me question it.'

'I hope you are not placing too much faith in *that* chart,' said Chaloner tartly. 'It contains significant errors, and on no account should it be used for military or tactical purposes.'

Thurloe frowned. 'You are mistaken. I am told the source is very reliable.'

'Only if you consider Scott reliable. I discussed the United Provinces with him a few days ago, and he said he had never been there. I imagine he was telling the truth for once, which means he cannot possibly have taken those coastal soundings. He probably made them up.'

'How do you know that map is from Scott?' asked Thurloe uneasily.

'Because he drew one for Sherwin in the Pope's Head, and I recognise his style. His work is pretty and contains a wealth of information, but you will never know which parts are accurate and which are imagination.'

Thurloe was aghast. 'But these have been passed to our navy! Why would Scott do such a terrible thing? To wound us in the war? As a quick way to make money?'

'Both, probably.'

'Heaven help our poor sailors!' Thurloe indicated the documents on his table. 'All this came from a single source, and it is so extensive and complex that Williamson asked me to evaluate it for him – he should hire a professional really, but he cannot afford one, and my services are free. Are you saying that the *lot* must be treated with caution?'

Chaloner nodded. 'Scott has been negotiating to sell the French a new kind of gun, and may well have been doing the same with the Dutch. He cannot be trusted.'

Thurloe gestured impatiently for him to elaborate, so Chaloner outlined all he had learned about Rupert's

352

cannon, Temple Mills, HMS *London*, Ferine, Scott, Sherwin, Manning and the Fifth Monarchists. When he had finished, Thurloe gazed at the papers on his table.

'Scott's misinformation will hamper our fleet considerably. Do you think he was paid to provide our government with bad intelligence?'

'Perhaps. Is there anything there about the Fifth Monarchists and their plans for Easter Day?'

'Not a word. And my informants have heard nothing either, which means an uprising is very unlikely. Williamson is a fool to waste your time with it.'

'I disagree. Jones *is* planning something serious for Sunday. He says he will seize the Tower, kill the King, burn London, establish the Kingdom of Christ and redistribute property.'

Thurloe regarded him lugubriously. 'All in a day?'

'His followers certainly think so. I tried to ask him how, but some of his Sanhedrin arrived to cut the conversation short – after I had wasted hours watching him drink coffee, read newsbooks, marvel at the antics of a juggler and stroll to Covent Garden.'

'Then I suggest there is no rebellion,' said Thurloe promptly. 'If there were, he would be busy making late-minute preparations.'

'Not if everything is already in place.'

'And how likely is that? Moreover, there have been no mass movements of troops, horses or weapons or I would have heard about it. Nothing will happen, so you might as well arrest this foolish little cabal before they make a nuisance of themselves.'

'They sank *London* and have the secret of Rupert's iron cannon – with special powder to fire them,' argued Chaloner. 'They are more than a nuisance.'

353

'Even if Rupert *has* found a way to substitute iron for brass, the weapon will require extensive testing before it is safe to use. It poses no immediate danger. And the sinking of *London* was a despicable act that should be punished accordingly. My advice is to clap Jones and his Sanhedrin in the Tower as quickly as you can.'

'I will suggest it to Williamson, although Rupert seems to be in charge, and he wants to delay until he can be sure of snaring everyone who might have the slightest inkling of his secret. All the troops and most of the Sanhedrin have no idea that these weapons are available, of course, but Rupert does not believe me.'

'Rupert was never a very good strategist,' said Thurloe disdainfully. 'As you should know from Naseby – it was thanks to him that the Royalists lost. I hope you do not intend to go to the Pope's Head tonight, by the way – I imagine Jones intends to kill you there. It will be empty, because the taverner's lease runs out today.'

'Oh, yes,' said Chaloner. 'I had forgotten.'

Thurloe glanced at the clock on the windowsill. 'I would talk longer, but I have to go to Wapping on Lincoln's Inn business, and I really should write to warn Williamson about this flawed intelligence before I leave. However, I have something to give you first.'

He went to the desk and removed a letter from a hidden compartment. 'From Wallis,' he explained. 'He has deciphered the papers that you took from Jones's harpsichord.'

Chaloner read the translations quickly. The first document was a draft agreement between Quelch and Manning about purchasing the secret of Rupert's guns; there was no mention of Scott – Manning had cut him out. The second was a list of questions about the metal used to make them. And the third contained advice about how Manning might spirit Sherwin out of the country after Easter, recommending the United Provinces as a suitable refuge. Wallis had returned the originals as well, and Chaloner immediately recognised the spiky hand of the last two messages.

'Hah! Jones does not believe the New Kingdom will dawn on Sunday, or he would not be telling Manning to make for the coast the day after. And this list of questions is odd. Why does he seem more interested in the iron than in the process to "turn and anneal"?'

'I suggest you ask him when he is in custody,' said Thurloe briskly. 'And now if there is nothing else, I really must be about my own business. Listen! The clocks are striking three already.'

'Buckingham's Astrological Soirée will start soon,' said Chaloner absently, still thinking about the documents. 'I am glad Hannah will not be there, especially if the Duke is to die today.'

Thurloe stared at him. 'What?'

'Lambe predicted it,' Chaloner explained. 'Partly to enhance his standing at Court when it comes true, and partly so he will not have to produce the Philosopher's Stone – which he has been paid to do.'

Thurloe was horrified. 'Then you must thwart this vile deed!'

'Clarendon will not thank me for that. The Duke is his fiercest opponent, and I imagine he will be delighted to be rid of him.'

Thurloe fixed him with a steely glare. 'I do not like Buckingham either, but I cannot condone his murder. You must prevent it.'

Chaloner disagreed. 'Hannah told me that Lambe aims to use bowls of blood and a human femur to divine the future. I cannot attend that sort of occasion – the Earl would never rehire me if he thought I dabbled in witchery. Besides, I do not have time. I must thwart Jones and the—'

'There will *be* no rebellion,' said Thurloe irritably. 'How many more times must I say it?'

'They have Rupert's cannon. For all we know, they may be the most deadly weapons ever invented, and Jones is about to point them at the city.'

'Then convince Williamson to act. Regardless, you must save Buckingham.'

'Send him a letter,' suggested Chaloner.

'And if it goes astray, or he does not read it? Here is a new wig and a respectable coat. We cannot have you refused admission for looking shabby.'

Chaloner was disgusted with what he had been charged to do when he felt the matter of Jones was far more pressing. Yet as he sat in a hackney carriage bound for Wallingford House he supposed he might turn the situation to his advantage. He knew enough to confront Lambe with his crimes, and Buckingham might have invited other suspects he could interrogate, too.

The light was fading as he alighted, but the building was unusually dark because all the window shutters had been closed to prevent anyone from seeing what was happening within. There was also an unpleasant smell.

'Burning potions, sir,' explained the footman who answered the door; Chaloner recalled that his name was George. 'The kind that witches like. Dr Lambe says they are always used at gatherings of this nature.'

'Have you heard the rumour that your master will . . . suffer a mishap tonight?'

356

George nodded unhappily. 'But Dr Lambe hopes to avert the calamity with powerful spells. However, he says that *someone* will perish today, and that is a certainty.'

'Will he be using human bones and bowls of blood for these spells?' asked Chaloner uneasily.

George shuddered. 'Very possibly, although I have seen him meddle with far worse. Do you know the way to the observatory, sir? That is where tonight's party is being held.'

Chaloner climbed the stairs to the top of the house, where he discovered that Lambe had been at the walls again, because there was barely an inch that had not been daubed with symbols. Some were in chalk, but the sorcerer had clearly decided that this was not sufficiently dramatic, so the rest had been painted in blood. Chaloner sincerely hoped it had come from a butcher.

He tried to decipher what had been written, but could make no sense of it – the Latin and Greek were garbled, while the mathematical symbols were meaningless as far as he could tell. Several words were Dutch, but they meant nothing either, and he suspected Lambe had just scribbled down whatever rubbish had entered his head.

A number of wealthy and influential courtiers stood around in excited anticipation, although not as many as Chaloner would have expected, and he could only suppose that some were still stuck on the Prittlewell road. All were close friends of the Duke, which meant they were the Earl's sworn enemies, and Chaloner felt acutely uncomfortable as he moved among them. Fortunately, his 'dismissal' meant he was now tolerated, and although he would never be part of their circle, at least no one was overtly hostile.

'You should be hunting Fifth Monarchists,' hissed an

357

angry voice. 'And where have you been these last few days? Clarendon says you have not reported to him in an age.'

Chaloner was startled to see Rupert there, given the antagonism between him and the host. And the Prince was not the only surprise guest: Admiral Lawson had been invited, too, and was already flushed with drink.

'I have some answers,' replied Chaloner carefully. 'But—'

Rupert stretched out an imperious hand. 'Good. Now give me the register of members you were charged to compile. And tell me their precise plans so I can catch them red-handed.'

'Midnight,' said Chaloner, declining to reveal that he had not prepared a list and was not going to. 'I will know their precise plans at midnight.'

Rupert scowled. 'Then I shall expect you to come and tell me immediately.'

He turned on his heel and stalked away. Chaloner watched him go, thinking it was no surprise that the Prince was unpopular, even among courtiers, who were generally an unpleasant crowd. Turning, he saw Buckingham talking to the silly Lady Muskerry near the window, and supposed it was as good a time as any to warn him of the threat to his life.

'You are in danger,' he said bluntly, but as the Duke was unlikely to believe that Lambe was the culprit, he settled for, 'Unscrupulous fraudsters are predicting the deaths of certain people, and killing them to "prove" it. You will be their next victim.'

Buckingham regarded him with dislike. 'You think *I* will fall prey to swindlers? That I am so stupid I cannot see through such schemes?'

'It does not matter what I think.' Chaloner struggled for patience: he had better things to do than argue with Buckingham. 'But it *does* matter that you might be hurt. Hannah would never forgive me if I did not warn you.'

Buckingham smiled smugly. 'I can look after myself, thank you.'

Lady Muskerry simpered adoringly at him. 'So bold! So brave!'

'Lambe has explained how to avoid the misfortune he prophesised, and I have followed his advice to the letter,' Buckingham went on. 'I am quite safe. However, *you* will not be if you spoil my party with foolish alarms.'

He strutted away, all imperious disdain, and Chaloner was tempted to leave him to his fate, feeling the country would be well shot of him, but he had spoken the truth when he had said that Hannah would never forgive him if something happened that could have been prevented. More importantly, neither would Thurloe.

He stood in the shadows by a window, and listened to anyone who spoke within earshot. Most talk revolved around the fact that the journey to Prittlewell had been a waste of good carousing time, but there was also a lot of laughter about the fact that everyone now called Clarendon's mansion Dunkirk House – Lambe's 'prediction' had come true. A few people worried about the city's resentment over the coal tax, but far more were interested in the possibility that Buckingham might unveil the Philosopher's Stone that evening.

'The Philosopher's Stone!' sneered Lawson. 'It is a lot of nonsense if you ask me.'

'But no one *has* asked you,' said Buckingham. His eyes gleamed with spiteful triumph, and Chaloner was suddenly suspicious. Why had Lawson and Rupert – and

Chaloner himself for that matter – been invited to the soirée when the host so obviously detested them? He determined to stay alert for trouble and keep well away from any experiments. He eased farther into the shadows, lest Lawson tried to shoot him again.

'Why did *you* grace us with your presence tonight?' asked Rupert, regarding the Admiral with aloof disdain. 'Do you not have common sailors to gossip with?'

Lawson eyed him with equal contempt. 'There is a rumour that Buckingham will die today, and I should hate to miss that.'

He and Buckingham began a sniping argument, peppered with caustic asides from Rupert that did nothing to soothe ragged tempers, and the longer Chaloner watched, the more he was certain that something sly had indeed been arranged. The Duke was taut with barely suppressed excitement, and Chaloner became increasingly convinced that if someone did meet an unfortunate end that night, it would not be Buckingham, but one of his guests.

For a long time, the soirée was just like any other that Chaloner had attended over the years. There was plenty of wine, too few snacks, and the conversation was spiteful and shallow. Eventually, there was a low, eerie moan that caused an instant hush. It was followed by a clash of cymbals that made everyone jump, and Buckingham smirked when Lawson spilled claret over himself. Suddenly, there was a puff of red smoke, and Lambe appeared, wearing a garish gown covered in crescent moons. It was cheap and theatrical, and the spectators were unimpressed.

'I have seen better from penny actors on High Holborn,' brayed Lawson.

'We would not know,' drawled Buckingham. '*We* do not frequent such places.'

Lambe ignored them both, and began to perform a series of old but clever tricks. Astutely, he involved his audience, and soon won them around with a combination of sleight of hand and sharp humour. Chaloner declined to be seduced, though, and so did Lawson. The Admiral yawned artificially to convey his boredom, then left the observatory and walked down the stairs to an antechamber, where more drinks had been set out. Chaloner followed.

'You again!' exclaimed Lawson, reaching for the dag in his belt.

Chaloner showed him the knife he held. 'It will be in your heart long before you can draw,' he said softly. 'I strongly advise you not to try.'

Lawson glowered, but let his hand drop to his side. They were alone, because the servants had abandoned their stations to watch Lambe, and were in a spellbound semicircle around the door at the top of the stairs. No one could see what was happening below.

'You would not be threatening me if my pistol had behaved yesterday,' Lawson growled. Slowly and with deliberate contempt, he turned away and poured himself a cup of wine.

'No,' acknowledged Chaloner. 'Why did you react so violently to such a simple question?'

'None of your damn business. And you may as well sheath your blade, because we both know you will not kill God's beloved, especially in front of witnesses.'

'What witnesses? No one is looking this way, and a knife is silent. Unlike you, I have more sense than to blast at my victims with firearms.'

361

'It is not a mistake I shall make again,' vowed Lawson. 'What do you want from me?'

'The truth about your visit to Rupert's gun factory on Tuesday night. I know you bribed Browne to sell you powder and cannon. What will you do? Sell them to the Dutch?'

Lawson whipped around to gape at him, astonishment taking the place of angry defiance. 'Sell them to the Dutch? What do you take me for?'

'A man whose flagship was blown up after two heavy chests were taken aboard,' replied Chaloner coldly. 'Chests containing "metal viols". However, we both know they held nothing of the kind, and that your hapless crew paid the price.'

The blood drained from Lawson's face. 'Christ God! Is that what you think? That I would harm my own men? I do not know what happened to my ship, but I swear on my soul that when I find out who was responsible, I will rip the bastard to pieces with my bare hands.'

'Yes, yes,' said Chaloner, although the Admiral's conviction made him wonder whether the conclusions he had drawn were correct. 'Yet it is curious that your family survived while—'

'They survived because of where they were standing and because they could swim,' snarled Lawson. 'We have already been through this. Who are you, anyway?'

'Someone who has quite a tale to report to Williamson,' replied Chaloner tartly.

Relief flooded the Admiral's blunt face. 'You are one of his agents? Thank God! I thought you were another bloody fanatic. Or worse, one of those conniving courtiers. By all means report our discussion to the Spymaster. It is time he knew what is happening on his watch.'

'By "what is happening" do you refer to the Last Millennium, which is apparently scheduled for Sunday? You Fifth Monarchists think nothing will matter after that, and you doubtless believe that your three hundred mariners will rise from their graves to stand with—'

'Stuff and nonsense! And I am *not* a Fifth Monarchist. An officer of mine – who joined the sect after losing an arm at the Battle of Marston Moor – said they would tell me about Rupert's guns if I pledged myself to their Cause. And as Rupert refused to oblige, I had no choice. There will be a Last Millennium, of course, but I doubt it will be on Sunday.'

'Not Henry Tucker?' asked Chaloner, thinking of the one-handed sailor on the Sanhedrin.

Lawson nodded. 'A decent fellow who wants a society bound by God's laws, not ones invented by the bloody fools on the Privy Council. A noble dream, if an impractical one. He introduced me to Jones and Quelch. Do you know them?'

'Oh, yes.'

'They procrastinated for so long that I thought I was going to have to find another way to get the secret, but then they appeared at Temperance's club one evening and offered to open negotiations.'

'The night Ferine was killed?' asked Chaloner pointedly.

'No, no – a month before that. On the night of the murder, they came to ask if I was interested in helping them install the Kingdom of Christ. I told them I was too busy.'

'So you paid them for Rupert's secret?'

'Do you think me witless? Of course not! I strung the bastards along until I learned that *they* intended to purchase it from a pair of villains named Manning and Scott, thus making a profit for themselves. So I cut out the middlemen and applied directly to the masters.'

'You bought it from Manning and Scott?'

'No. They are scum, and I would never trust them to provide me with accurate technical information. What I bought from them – or rather from Scott, as Manning was unwell on the day, apparently – was the location of Rupert's factory. I visited it and reached an arrangement with John Browne. He sold me two guns and some powder, which I intended to test at sea.'

'And that was what was delivered to HMS *London* in the two chests?' asked Chaloner, not surprised to learn that Scott had cheated Manning.

'Yes. Unfortunately, they were lost before I could so much as look at them, so I was obliged to visit Temple Mills on Tuesday to buy replacements. Was it you we chased into the river?'

Chaloner ignored the question. 'If Browne did what you claim, then he is no better than Sherwin – whom he dismissed for revealing secrets while in his cups. He is a hypocrite.'

'Every man has his price.' Lawson drank the wine and poured himself some more.

Chaloner was confused. 'Why go to such trouble? I thought you despised iron guns.'

'I do, but Rupert claims he has overcome their failings, and we need every advantage we can get if we are to win this Dutch war – it is my duty to find out whether his boast is true. But he refused to show them to me, because he wants to patent the invention and make himself lots of money. Patriotism comes second to personal gain with that rogue, you see.'

'He is not the only one,' muttered Chaloner, thinking of Browne, Manning, Scott and Sherwin. 'Why did you come here tonight? You cannot enjoy this sort of company.'

'Too damn right! However, I take every opportunity I can to be in Rupert's company – to needle him, in the hope that he will let something slip.' Lawson blanched suddenly as a thought occurred to him. 'Bloody hell! Do you think he or the Fifth Monarchists learned that I had circumvented them, and they destroyed my flagship in revenge?'

'Not Rupert, but Jones and his cronies. Browne probably told them. You had no difficulty in suborning him, which means others will not either.'

Lawson's face was grey. 'So *London*'s fate was my fault? Christ God! I knew something odd had happened on her, given my family's descriptions of the disaster and Captain Dare's insistence that the powder magazine was secure . . .'

'Is that why you ordered her weighed?' Chaloner put his knife away. 'Not to raise her from the riverbed, which as a sailor you know is impossible, but to allow your engineers to dive down to her hull and find the truth? Let me guess what they discovered: a cannonball hole in her side. I assume the shot hit the chest holding the powder?'

'They could not tell.' Lawson was still coming to terms with what they had reasoned, and the brash confidence had gone from him. 'But it may have been a contributing factor to her loss.'

'A *contributing* factor? What do you mean?'

'I mean she would not have foundered if those thieving, corrupt bastards at the shipyard had not skimped on repairs, disguising rotten timbers with lead sheathing. The ball punched right through her to the larboard powder magazine, where the resulting explosion ripped out her bottom.' Lawson's expression was bleak. 'Did the missile come from one of Rupert's guns?'

'I believe so. A wrecked boat was used as a makeshift shore-battery. I saw it and the body of the man whose expertise was used to fire it.'

Lawson's eyebrows flew up. 'It killed its operator? The design is flawed?'

'He was shot by his accomplices.' Chaloner stared at the Admiral, and made up his mind. He needed help if he was to bring Jones and his helpmeets to justice, and he could tell that Lawson's shock at the revelations was genuine – they were on the same side. Briefly, he told him all he had learned at Prittlewell and Chatham.

'I am going to Williamson right now,' determined Lawson, coldly angry when Chaloner had finished. 'And I will be at the Pope's Head at midnight – with reinforcements. Those bastards will pay for what they did to my sailors. Pay with their damned lives!'

Chaloner wanted to go with him, but dared not leave Wallingford House as long as Buckingham was in danger. Cursing the Duke for his foolish obstinacy, he returned to the observatory, where Lambe was in the process of muttering incantations and flinging around compounds that created great billows of coloured smoke and foul smells. When Lady Muskerry coughed, he fixed her with such a baleful glare that she went purple trying not to do it again.

As the sorcerer worked, he seemed to grow taller, broader and more imposing. His voice took on a low, sinister timbre,

366

and Chaloner was sure he had attached some device to his throat, because the sounds that emerged were barely human. For the first time, Chaloner noticed that Odowde was in the audience, pale and shaking.

'When will you produce the Philosopher's Stone?' asked Buckingham, becoming tired of the pyrotechnic display and hinting that it was time to move on.

'Soon,' promised Lambe. 'But it comes with a price.'

Chaloner was sure it did, although the eager, almost manic expression on Buckingham's face said it was one he would be willing to pay.

'A life,' Lambe went on. 'A sacrifice, as it were.'

'No!' wailed Odowde, so shrilly that everyone jumped. His eyes flicked towards Lambe, seeking approval, and Chaloner was disgusted that the courtier had persisted with the association after his confession at Prittlewell. The guests started a second time when the door slammed and seemed to lock of its own accord. Several ran towards it and began to haul on the handle.

'You asked the Dark Master to come this evening,' Lambe boomed in a sepulchral voice. 'And he is waiting. You must all stand in a circle around me. Anyone outside the ring will die.'

There was a concerted rush to comply, although Chaloner held back. He had seen a servant lurking at the top of the stairs, and knew perfectly well who had manipulated the door. Buckingham's smirk said he was also in on the deception, and was thoroughly enjoying his cronies' discomfiture. Then there was the biggest puff of smoke yet, and someone appeared to be rising through the floor. It was cleverly done, as the small recess in which the figure had been crouching was so cunningly disguised as to be all but invisible.

A bright flicker of light made everyone blink, and the person used the opportunity to stand up, so that by the time the audience's vision had cleared, she was standing tall and ethereal. Her face was white even by her standards, and her sapphire eyes glowed like blue flames.

'It is Eliza Hatton's ghost!' shrieked another servant whom Chaloner suspected had been well paid for his performance. 'I have seen her tomb in St Andrew's church, and there have been rumours that she has risen from the grave.'

Eliza made a gesture with her hand, and there was a dull thump followed by a brilliant flash. Judging from her briefly startled expression, it was rather in excess of what she had expected, and the courtiers at the front of the circle fell back with cries of shock.

'I cannot see,' wept Lady Muskerry in distress. 'That wretched sprite has blinded me.'

'The Dark Master did it,' declared Lambe quickly. 'You summoned him, and you must bear the consequences. No one can control what he does, not even a great wizard like me.'

'Now just a moment,' said Buckingham, uneasy for the first time. 'You said nothing about blinding my guests or summoning *actual* dark masters . . .'

'You want the Philosopher's Stone.' Lambe's hand went to his neck and his voice became funereal again. 'And you shall have it. But the Dark Master wants a sacrifice.'

'A sacrifice,' echoed Eliza, speaking for the first time, her voice every bit as deep and sinister as the sorcerer's. Unsettled by it, some courtiers eased towards the door again.

'Be still,' Lambe ordered sharply. 'Or you will be torn

to pieces by demonic claws. I predicted that someone would die tonight, and someone will. The Dark Master expects it.'

'This is nonsense,' declared Rupert irritably. He addressed Buckingham. 'I have had enough of this unchristian prattle. Let me out. I am leaving.'

'Will it be you, then?' asked Lambe, pointing at him with a long, inky finger. 'Shall we exchange *your* life for the Philosopher's Stone?'

'Not unless you want to hang for treason,' Rupert's eyes flashed haughtily. 'I am the King's cousin.'

Lambe gave him a look that could only be described as malignant before turning to Buckingham. 'Choose another, My Lord. The Dark Master awaits with ready talons.'

'Lawson,' replied Buckingham, although the grin he gave was sickly, and Chaloner saw he was unnerved by the intensity of Lambe's performance. 'Unfortunately, he seems to have left, so we shall forget about the sacrifice, and move on to—'

'Someone else then,' pressed Lambe. 'There *will* be a death tonight. I have predicted it.'

The guests began to murmur fearfully, while Chaloner watched the servants, identifying those he thought were in on the act. It was not difficult, because they were overplaying their role, squealing too loudly and rolling their eyes in a manner that would have been amusing had he not had the distinct sense that something very nasty was about to happen.

'Him,' said Lambe, pointing at Chaloner. 'The Dark Master will take *him*.'

Chaloner was not surprised to be singled out, given that there had been no luck with Rupert and Lawson.

Buckingham started to object, evidently realising for the first time that his sorcerer was not in jest, but Eliza fixed him with an icy gaze and the words died in his throat.

'But the Dark Master wants a servant first, to whet his appetite,' Lambe went on. He pointed at a small man with sly eyes and oily hair. 'He will suffice.'

Chaloner decided the charade had gone on quite long enough. He stepped forward and addressed Lambe in a calm, reasonable voice, aiming to soothe the frightened spectators. 'Now why choose him? Would it be because you know him from the Swan with Two Necks? I imagine he is new to the Duke's staff, perhaps even hired just for tonight.'

'He arrived this evening,' blurted George the footman shakily. 'How did you know?'

'Because his uniform does not fit, and the odd bulges you see under his coat are almost certainly bags of animal blood,' explained Chaloner. 'They are used in the theatre, and when he is "sacrificed" he will doubtless put on a splendid display of gore.'

Alarmed, the 'servant' began to back away, but Chaloner grabbed him by the collar and shook him hard. Several fat pouches dropped to the floor, and there were cries of revulsion when Chaloner stamped on one, causing it to burst in a crimson gout. While the audience muttered its indignation at the deception, Chaloner shoved one in his pocket, to be presented as evidence later should the others happen to disappear.

'He is nothing to do with us,' declared Lambe, swirling his cloak and deepening his voice again to regain control. 'The Dark Master has no need for tawdry tricks, and he grows impatient for his sacrifice.' He started to point at Chaloner, but evidently decided the spy might prove

370

too problematical, so his finger swivelled to Odowde instead. 'Him.'

Odowde backed away, white with genuine terror as Eliza glided towards him. Chaloner stepped between them, and her eyes glittered with rage when she realised he was going to spoil her performance. She swung around to address the Duke's guests.

'The Dark Master grows restless and angry with these foolish delays. Bring these two men to me, and the rest of you will be spared the consequences of his wrath.'

Chaloner drew his sword when several spectators looked as though they might take her up on the offer. When they faltered, Eliza began to sway, and as she did, mist seeped from her clothes. It was another trick, but in the dimly lit observatory, it was decidedly unsettling. She began to moan.

'Stop it,' ordered Rupert irritably. 'Open the door, Buckingham. I am going home.'

'You may leave when we have finished,' growled Lambe. He turned to Buckingham, his voice softly coaxing. 'Do you want the Philosopher's Stone, My Lord? It will be yours if you let me do my work. You are so close to victory. Do not allow the sceptics to spoil it.'

He knew how to manipulate his master, because Buckingham nodded eagerly. 'You are right – I have invested a good deal of time, money and energy in these experiments, and no one here will begrudge me a few more minutes. Put up your sword, Chaloner. No one will hurt you – this Dark Master can have someone else instead.'

Afraid they might be chosen, more of his guests edged towards the door, and Lambe and Eliza exchanged a silent signal. She began to writhe, drawing attention away

371

from Lambe while he reached inside his cloak and drew something out. It was a small glass ball, which he lobbed, doing so in such a way as to make it seem as though he had conjured it from thin air.

The ball hit the floor near Chaloner, where it exploded to release a lot of pungent yellow smoke. Lambe threw another, forcing the spy to scramble away or risk being set alight. Then Eliza appeared to levitate, and there was a loud roaring, uncannily like thunder. Courtiers screamed, and only Buckingham stood fast, hands clenched together as if willing Lambe to continue. Chaloner fought his way through the chaos towards Rupert.

'These are just tricks,' he shouted. 'Their helpmeets are outside, hammering on sheets of metal, and I am sure you will find that Eliza Hatton is connected to the ceiling by a wire. If you help me regain control of this mêlée, I will prove it.'

Rupert did not need to be told twice. He whipped out a pistol and shot Lambe dead.

The gunfire was louder than any sound the hoaxers had made, and the observatory suddenly went quiet. Guests and servants stopped babbling, Odowde stopped whimpering and Eliza stopped chanting. The silence was absolute.

'That is not quite what I had in mind,' said Chaloner, the first to find his voice.

'Damn you, Rupert!' cried Buckingham, pale and stunned. 'The Philosopher's Stone!'

'Well, he did say his Dark Master wanted a sacrifice,' said Rupert, unrepentant. He drew a second weapon and glowered at Eliza. 'And do not think *you* will go

372

unpunished for your role in this unsavoury affair, madam. You will rot in Newgate, and so will your damned accomplices.'

Eliza's face turned slowly from shock to fury. She gave a nod, and her helpmeets, unwilling to surrender after Rupert's threat, darted towards a chest. Pulling scarves over their mouths and noses, they began to lob more glass balls, so that the observatory filled with a dense, multicoloured smoke that was difficult to breathe. The guests started to choke and gag.

'The rogues must have raided the Lady Day firework display,' coughed Rupert, eyes streaming. 'Damn these fumes! I cannot see who to shoot.'

He raised his gun anyway, and Chaloner batted it down, aware that it was pointing in Buckingham's direction, although whether by design or accident was difficult to tell. At that point, Eliza used the powerful voice she had employed at Tyburn to chant curses. The guests were more interested in breathing, however, and when she saw she was being ignored, she pulled a crucifix from her robes and did something to make it burst into flames. Unfortunately for her, it quickly became too hot to hold, and she hurled it away with a yelp of pain.

'Madam, desist!' rasped the Duke, racing to douse it before it set his books alight. 'There is no point in persisting now Lambe is dead. It is over.'

'Nothing is over,' howled Eliza. She lifted her hand to her throat, and her voice slid down an octave. 'The Dark Master is angry about the death of Lambe. He wants revenge in—'

'Stop!' ordered Buckingham. 'Tonight was meant to be a bit of harmless fun, culminating in me getting the

Philosopher's Stone. No one was supposed to die. Now cease that ghastly cursing before I lose patience.'

There was a moment when Chaloner thought she would comply, but a glance at Rupert's vengeful face seemed to strengthen her resolve to trick her way out of the predicament. She nodded to her assistants, and the barrage of missiles intensified, as did the violence of her incantations. The courtiers nearest her backed away in alarm, gasping for air. Then she began to rise towards the ceiling again, hands outstretched as she called for the Dark Master. Chaloner dived at her, and when Rupert did likewise, the wire snapped and all three fell to the floor.

Eliza spat, hissed and scratched, and it was not easy to subdue her, especially when her friends raced to her rescue. Rupert's rapier made short work of several, flailing with such brutal efficiency that Chaloner was sickened.

Even then she did not give up. She frothed at the mouth, screaming that the devil would take anyone who touched her. Rupert eyed her dispassionately for a moment, then slapped her. She gaped at him in astonishment. Before he could do it again, Chaloner shoved her in a chair, where he quickly bound her hands and feet. Her shock at being so roughly treated did not last long. She opened her mouth to howl again, so he gagged her. As he worked, he called to the footman.

'Open the windows to disperse the fumes. And turn up the lamps so we can see.'

George hastened to obey, and the flood of light revealed Buckingham's observatory to be sadly stained and singed. The panic eased once the audience could breathe again, and there were even some sheepish grins. Lady Muskerry was still unsettled, though.

374

'Let me out!' she sobbed. 'I do not want to stay in here.'

'I cannot – I do not have the key.' Buckingham looked at his servants, who were lining the surviving imposters up against a wall, but they shook their heads, so he knelt and jabbed at the lock with a knife. He did so with more vigour than competence, and Chaloner felt a surge of tension. He had no idea of the time, but he could not miss his meeting in the Pope's Head. Yet he could hardly demonstrate his skill with locks in front of so many of the Earl's enemies. To take his mind off his agitation, he turned to Odowde, who was slumped on a stool, his face ashen.

'You owe the Duke and his guests an explanation.'

'Who does?' Buckingham twisted around to see who Chaloner was talking to. 'Odowde? I do not recall inviting you tonight.'

'It was not my idea to come,' whispered Odowde miserably. 'Lambe made me.'

'Made you?' echoed Rupert with the cold disdain of one who had never been 'made' to do anything in his life. 'How? Come on, man, speak. We do not have all night.'

From the inept way that Buckingham was poking the lock, Chaloner had a bad feeling they might. Then he noticed that Eliza's glittering blue gaze was fixed on Odowde, who was obviously terrified by it. He stepped between them, blocking her line of sight with his body. A stifled scream of rage filtered through the gag.

'Start with the murders,' he prompted Odowde. 'The first being Grace Ferine's. Eliza and Lambe arranged for her to "fall" down the stairs, then persuaded her grieving husband to abandon conventional religion for witchery. They convinced him that his house was haunted—'

'But it *is* haunted,' gulped Lady Muskerry. 'Ghosts are rife in High Holborn. Ask anyone.'

'Tricks,' said Chaloner. 'With wires, hidey-holes and mirrors – much as happened here tonight. They met Ferine in the Swan with Two Necks, and encouraged him to spread his beliefs at Court. People began to pay a fortune for Lambe's predictions—'

There was an immediate uproar as people demanded to know whether they had been cheated.

'I assume they then killed Ferine?' Rupert's question rose above the babble, as his voice was louder than anyone else's.

'Yes, because he began to produce his own horoscopes,' explained Chaloner. 'He was good at it, better than Lambe, so it was unwanted competition.'

'*You* went to the Swan and offered to take Ferine's place,' said Odowde, spite in his eyes as he addressed Chaloner. 'I saw you. You were going to gather inform- ation from courtiers who wanted their fortunes told. You are part of this deception, too.'

'What is this?' asked Rupert, eyes narrowed.

'I went to find out what Ferine had embroiled himself in,' explained Chaloner, recalling the confused conversa- tion in which he had tried to discover what it was that Eliza sold. 'I do not know what methods *he* employed to predict the future, but I suspect that Lambe and Eliza used witchcraft.'

'That is illegal,' whispered Lady Muskerry, all wide-eyed shock. 'She could hang for that.'

Eliza had managed to spit out the gag. 'Lambe calcu- lated *your* horoscope, Chaloner,' she hissed, full of angry malice. 'Your future involves smoke, explosions and blood, and death will surround you. He foresaw

376

something else, too – a terrible plague that will ravage London and leave *thousands* dead.'

Chaloner ignored her. 'They murdered Hubbert and Duncombe next. They—'

'No, they didn't,' interrupted Lady Muskerry. 'Those two died because it was predicted. Ask Mr Wiseman – he found nothing amiss.'

'A large dose of mandrake and poppy juice leaves no trace,' said Chaloner, recalling how Eliza had secured some from the unwitting surgeon. 'They died purely to give credence to Lambe's so-called prophecies.'

'Did you throw yourself down the Banqueting Hall stairs for the same reason?' asked Rupert, regarding Odowde contemptuously. 'I saw it happen, and I thought it looked bogus.'

Odowde looked as though he might deny it, but a glance at Rupert's stony, unforgiving face saw his courage wilt, and he nodded miserably. 'Lambe forced me to.'

'Forced you!' sneered Eliza. 'You did it willingly – for money.'

'And *you* gave money to this scoundrel,' said Rupert to Buckingham, prodding Lambe's corpse with his toe. He smirked. 'I hope you are not too seriously out of pocket.'

Buckingham eyed him coolly. 'He helped me move forward in my quest, so it was worth the expense. However, I wish you had not shot him. It was quite unnecessary.'

'He was going to kill us,' stated Rupert. 'And anyone who says otherwise is a fool – as are you, for believing the Philosopher's Stone exists in the first place. Even if it did, the likes of Lambe would know nothing about it.

And if you cannot get that damned door open, stand aside and let someone else have a go.'

Chaloner was so anxious about the passing time that he was on the verge of offering to tackle the lock himself, but the Prince had other ideas. He took his pistol and fired it at the mechanism. When that did not work, he reloaded and did it again. The door swung open, and there was a muted cheer from the courtiers. Lady Muskerry was first out, although she paused to favour Buckingham with a coy smile.

'Thank you for an entertaining evening, My Lord. It is not one I shall forget in a hurry, and I hope you will hold another soirée soon. Life at White Hall can be so very *dull*, and it was fun to experience something a little different.'

Others voiced similar sentiments as they filed past, and Chaloner listened in disbelief. Perhaps the Fifth Monarchists were right to want the Court disbanded and sane men installed in their place.

Chapter 14

When the guests had gone, Chaloner sent George to fetch the palace guards, so that Eliza, Odowde and their helpmeets could be taken into custody. Eliza was safely tied to the chair, while the others stood in a line along the wall, sullen and frightened. Chaloner dared not leave Buckingham and the remaining servants to watch them until George returned in case they broke loose. Chafing at yet more wasted time, he prepared to wait, sword drawn against any attempts to escape. Buckingham slumped on a bench and gazed at Eliza, his face a mixture of resignation and anger.

'So it was all a lie,' he said heavily. 'You and Lambe conspired to make a fool of me. Was he even the son of my father's sorcerer-physician?'

Cunning glinted in Eliza's icy eyes. 'I know nothing about him or his business.' She nodded towards her cronies. 'We were only hired for this evening, and none of us had ever met Lambe before. We can prove it. Ask around – you will not find a single person who saw us together.'

'I did,' put in Chaloner. 'Twice, in the Swan with Two

Necks. *And* there was the time in St Andrew's Churchyard when you "disappeared". I found a piece of paper covered with the symbols he liked to draw – he was helping you with your vanishing tricks and he dropped it by mistake.'

Eliza regarded him coldly. 'Then it will be your word against mine.'

'However, you usually communicated via notes hidden in newsbooks,' Chaloner went on. 'I saw him leave you one once.'

She grinned in sudden triumph. 'And do you actually *have* one of these alleged missives?'

As it was obvious that she knew he did not, Chaloner could only assume that she or one of her cronies had pickpocketed him outside the Swan.

'As I said, it is your word against mine,' she said smugly when he made no reply. She could not resist a further gloat. 'And even if you do happen across one of these so-called messages, you will find nothing written on it.'

'And that proves my case,' pounced Chaloner. 'The letters were penned in onion juice, which is invisible until heated. You would not have known the notes appear to be blank unless you had received them.'

'What did you mean when you said she "disappeared" in the churchyard?' asked Buckingham, while Eliza gave Chaloner a look of such hatred that he struggled not to recoil.

'She did it to reinforce the notion that something supernatural was happening,' Chaloner explained. 'But it was all artifice. She used cleverly concealed devices in Hatton House, Ferine's home and the graveyard, and was aided in her tricks by Lambe and patrons from the

380

Swan. I imagine it was they who made the beam drop in Hatton House's chapel when I was there.'

'I wish it had crushed him,' he heard one man mutter venomously.

Chaloner tensed when there was a ripple of agreement from the others, anticipating trouble, but nothing happened. They were all waiting for someone else to make the first move, and he was glad that Eliza was fastened to the chair, knowing she was certainly bold enough to lead the way. She was struggling to free herself, although she would not succeed: he had tied the knots too well.

'These are serious crimes,' said Buckingham sternly. 'Defrauding the King's friends, deceit, murder . . .'

'Not murder,' said Eliza quickly. 'Not us. That was Lambe.'

But Chaloner knew otherwise. 'Lambe did not kill Ferine – he had an alibi in Temperance.'

'I hope you are not suggesting that one of us did it,' said Eliza coldly.

Her helpmeets growled their own denials, and Chaloner saw them gaining strength from her bravado. Except Odowde, who was hunched in silent misery.

'I said from the start that Ferine was murdered by someone familiar with the club,' said Chaloner, aiming to puncture their growing defiance before it became a problem. 'It—'

'Then we are all exonerated,' Eliza interrupted victoriously. 'Obviously, *we* have never been to such a place. It caters to wealthy men, a criterion none of us meet.'

'You knew it through Lambe, who was a frequent visitor. You climbed the ivy to the storeroom window – your antics tonight prove that you are agile – and you

381

emptied the wine in the room that Ferine was to use. You hid behind a curtain until Snowflake went to fetch more, and the moment he was alone, you went in and smothered him.'

Eliza directed her reply to Buckingham. 'How could I, a weak woman, do such a thing?'

'How strong do you need to be to sit on a drunken man and hold a pillow over his face?' asked Chaloner archly. 'And you are not weak anyway – your acrobatics keep you fit.'

'He is deluded,' said Eliza, still speaking to Buckingham. 'But Lambe is not the only one who knows about the Philosopher's Stone, My Lord. Let us go, and I will help you to—'

'Odowde.' Chaloner addressed the courtier quickly when he saw the spark of hope in the Duke's eyes; Eliza had correctly identified the one way that might see her free, her crimes conveniently forgotten. 'Tell the truth, or you will bear the blame for all that has happened.'

'She *did* kill Ferine,' obliged Odowde dejectedly. 'She also pushed Grace down the stairs, and gave Hubbert and Duncombe poisoned wine, all with Lambe's connivance.'

'Liar!' snarled Eliza angrily. 'You will say anything to save your own neck.'

'I will swear any oath you like,' said Odowde to the Duke. 'They *made* me follow orders – they are ruthless bullies and I was powerless against them. But I was beginning to fight back. I had no intention of showering Prince Rupert with that bucket of excrement up in the ceiling *or* of stabbing Chaloner.'

'Did you not?' asked the Duke mildly, causing Chaloner to glance sharply at him.

382

'So that is why you invited me,' came a voice from the door. Rupert had not left Wallingford House, and had been listening to the entire discussion. 'Now I understand.'

Chaloner did not think he would ever be pleased to see the Prince, but he found himself relieved as Rupert strutted in with his customary arrogance. The prisoners might overpower him while the Duke looked the other way in return for help with his ambitions, but they would not best him and Rupert together.

'I tried to warn the Admiral, too,' bleated Odowde. 'But he would not listen. If he is killed, you cannot say it is my fault. I did all I could to save him.'

'Save him from what?' asked Chaloner in alarm, speaking over Eliza's immediate denials.

'The robbers who will attack him tonight. Lambe was going to predict it . . .'

'Another so-called prophecy come true,' said Rupert in disgust. 'How could you allow these villains to deceive you, Buckingham? I thought you had more sense.'

Buckingham stood with a rueful sigh. He was no fool, and knew Eliza was never going to be in a position to help with his experiments now that the Prince was there. Slowly and deliberately, he turned his back on her.

'I was blinded by my desire to discover the Philosopher's Stone,' he said, although with no hint of remorse. 'Single-minded dedication is an occupational hazard for intelligent men like me – we are driven by our zeal to expand the frontiers of knowledge, and we fail to see the evil around us. Ah! Here is George with the guards. Good! Take these villains out of my sight.'

Eliza did not go quietly, and the guards grew visibly uneasy when she began to curse. Sighing irritably, Rupert snatched the scarf from her neck and wrapped it around her entire head, not only gagging her, but hiding her blazing eyes, too. As he did so, a small wooden box fell to the floor – the device that had allowed her to alter her voice. He stared at it for a moment, then crushed it under his heel before stalking away, indicating with an imperious flick of his fingers that Chaloner was to follow.

Outside, it was late and very dark. It was also unusually quiet: Good Friday was a sombre, serious occasion, and even the jaunty Lady Day visitors seemed content to have an early night.

'It is almost midnight,' said the Prince curtly. 'You said you would have answers by then.'

'In the Pope's Head,' said Chaloner. 'But first I must warn Lawson.'

'Then I shall come with you,' determined Rupert. 'Not on foot, though. We shall travel in my private coach, like gentlemen.'

Chaloner did not want Rupert with him, but was not in a position to refuse an offer of help. He sat in silence as they rattled along, wishing it was Thurloe at his side, or even Williamson. He hated the idea of being supported by Rupert's over-ready pistols.

The Prince ordered his driver to take them to Westminster, in the hope that the Admiral would still be with Williamson. However, they were rattling along the Strand when Chaloner saw a cluster of people standing around several bodies. He leapt out of the coach before it had stopped, ignoring Rupert's yell that respectable men waited for the steps to be lowered first.

Chaloner inspected the bodies quickly, and soon found Lawson, his hair matted with blood. It had started to congeal, suggesting the attack had occurred soon after the Admiral had left Wallingford House. He peered more closely at the white face, then reached out to shake Lawson's shoulder. The eyes fluttered open, drawing gasps of astonishment from the onlookers.

'I thought he was dead,' breathed one. 'He certainly looks it.'

'The villains came at me out of the blue,' whispered the Admiral, when he saw it was Chaloner who crouched next to him. 'But I gave a good account of myself. God was with me – He always is when I smite His enemies.'

'Help is coming,' said Chaloner, hearing Rupert issue orders for a surgeon to be fetched.

Lawson waved an impatient hand. 'So go – thwart the villains at the Pope's Head. But do not expect help from Williamson. I was attacked before I could warn him.'

'Prince Rupert is with me.'

Lawson pulled a disagreeable face. 'He is better than nothing, I suppose. Go – hurry. Midnight is almost on us, and I want the bastards who sank my flagship to swing.'

Chaloner ran back to the coach and climbed in. Rupert rapped on the roof, and they were off again. They made good time, hurtling through the empty streets as if the devil himself were on their tail. As they lurched along, the Prince began a vicious diatribe about rogues who invited a man to their homes with the sole intention of embarrassing him with slyly concealed buckets.

'Better that than what was planned for Lawson,' said Chaloner tartly.

'Nonsense! I would have been a laughing stock for the rest of my life – a slow death, compared to the Admiral's brisk end. But Buckingham did himself a grave disservice with his foul pails today – no one will ever invite him anywhere ever again.'

Chaloner was far from certain of that, given what he had heard Lady Muskerry and others murmur as they had left. The Court was ever eager for novel entertainment.

'Doubtless Lambe ordered Eliza to stab Snowflake, too,' the Prince went on. He smiled nastily. 'Buckingham let a vicious brute into his household, and I shall never let him forget it.'

But Chaloner knew that Eliza had not murdered Snowflake. He shot the Prince a sidelong glance: Snowflake had died because she had guessed the secret of the gun factory at Temple Mills, and her killer was still at large.

They reached the Pope's Head, but all was in darkness. Chaloner was about to embark on a cautious and discreet surveillance when Rupert marched up to the front door and hammered imperiously. Chaloner winced: the man was going to get them both killed.

'No one is here.' Rupert turned to him accusingly. 'How will you have answers from an empty tavern?'

'The landlord has been evicted, but Jones said it was . . . Where are you going?'

'To tell Williamson that it is high time he did what he is being paid for,' snapped Rupert. 'I want that list of Fifth Monarchists, and I want it *now*. He has had plenty of time to compile it, and if he cannot oblige me, he can start looking for a new appointment.'

Chaloner watched him go with a sense of helplessness. While he had not wanted the Prince's company, it was still unnerving to be left alone to tackle what might transpire to be a very deadly plot. Perhaps he should just go home. After all, it was Rupert's fault that there was a secret to steal, and Williamson's fault that the Sanhedrin were not under lock and key already. But then he thought about Snowflake and HMS *London*, and his resolve returned. He would see justice done for her and Captain Dare's three hundred sailors.

He studied the tavern. It did not look as though it was about to be used for a meeting of rebels. He found a window with a loose shutter, and was through it in a trice. Once inside, he lit a candle. Most of the furniture was gone, although a few chairs and the odd table remained, too battered or ancient to warrant the effort of moving. A number of jugs lay on the floor, broken, dented or stained, which added to the feeling of recent abandonment. A bellman on Fleet Street called that it was midnight.

Perhaps Jones had sent him to the empty tavern to keep him out of the way while part of the plot swung into action. Or maybe Thurloe was right, and ambushers were lying in wait in the seemingly deserted building. As he considered the various possibilities, Chaloner became aware that there was a light in one of the rooms in the back. He drew his dagger and crept towards it.

A fire glowed in the hearth and a lantern hung from the ceiling. There was only one occupant: Sherwin was slumped on a bench, his chin on his chest. There was a half-finished jug of ale in front of him, and a bottle of claret on the mantelpiece, presumably for later.

Chaloner listened carefully, but there was nothing to say that anyone else was in the building. Determined to have answers once and for all, Chaloner grabbed Sherwin's shoulder and shook it, but Sherwin slipped to

387

one side, and he saw the man would never answer questions again.

He was dead.

Moving quickly, Chaloner searched the body and discovered two letters. Both offered vast rewards for Sherwin's expertise. One bore a seal that Chaloner recognised from his spying days: Georges Pellissary of the French navy. The other was unsigned, but had quirks of grammar that told him it had been written by a Dutchman. If he had not been so tense, Chaloner might have laughed at the knowledge that Sherwin had gone behind Scott and Manning's backs.

'What have you done!'

Chaloner whipped around to see Scott and Manning standing in the doorway, both holding guns – he had been so engrossed in Sherwin's letters that he had not heard them approach. He swore under his breath. He did not have time for complex explanations.

'He was dead when I arrived.' It sounded lame even to his ears.

Manning glared accusingly at Scott. 'You said Sherwin would be safe here, with a bottle and no one to bother him.'

'I thought he would,' said Scott tightly. He nodded towards Chaloner. 'Search him.'

Sensing that Scott would not scruple to shoot, Chaloner stood still while Manning removed every last item from his personal arsenal. They, along with the contents of his pockets, were tossed on the table next to Sherwin's belongings.

'How did you kill poor Sherwin?' asked Scott coldly. 'Poison?'

'It must have been,' said Manning, opening the packet containing the stockings that Ursula had made for Chaloner, and whistling his appreciation at their quality. Then he sat on the bench, pulled off his own hose and donned the new ones. 'Lovely! They will make a big difference to my chilblains.'

'I did not kill him,' said Chaloner. 'But I cannot stay to debate it. There is a plot afoot to—'

'You are not going anywhere,' snapped Scott. 'You have deprived me . . . *us* of a fortune by dispatching Sherwin, and I aim to make you pay.'

'Too right,' growled Manning. 'Ouch! There are still pins in these things!'

Chaloner appealed to Scott. 'You will not be Cartographer Royal if Jones succeeds on Sunday, and—'

'Shut up,' snarled Scott. 'I need to think.'

He leaned against the doorframe, scowling. Manning picked up Sherwin's ale, sniffed it cautiously and put it down again, wiping his hands on his breeches as he muttered about toxins. Then his eye lit on the bottle on the mantelpiece.

'If you think Sherwin was poisoned, should you be drinking that?' asked Chaloner, watching him take a long, deep swallow.

'The bottle was sealed.' Manning took another swig in churlish defiance. 'Besides, I imagine you put the poison in his ale. It was his favourite, after all.'

Chaloner turned back to Scott. 'You know we share a master, so let me go. I must warn him that an atrocity is in the making.'

'It is very hot in here,' muttered Manning, wiping his forehead. 'Don't you think?'

Ignoring Chaloner's appeal, Scott came to a decision.

'We shall visit your home, and see what you have in the way of valuables. The place is closed up, there are no servants to challenge us.'

'I do not feel well,' said Manning, sudden alarm in his voice. 'My innards . . .'

'It is your imagination,' said Scott dismissively. He returned to the subject that interested him more. 'We can still sell Sherwin's secret, of course. I know most of the particulars died with him, but we can always make them up.'

'Neither the French nor the Dutch are easily deceived,' warned Chaloner.

'I own no Dutch connections,' said Scott. 'However, I have very good ones in France, while Williamson is putty in my hands. Two interested parties should drive up the price nicely.'

'I feel sick.' Manning sat heavily on the bench. 'Really, I do.'

'The club,' said Chaloner, as something became clear about Scott. 'When I went once, you were playing cards with Lawson, Rupert and Lambe. Lambe was irrelevant, but you and the other two were playing a curious game – and not lanterloo either.'

Scott smirked. 'Then what was it?'

'Lawson was watching Rupert, hoping to learn something about his iron artillery; Rupert was watching you, because he does not trust you; and you were watching Lawson, to ensure he did not tell Rupert that you had shared with him the location of the gun factory.'

'Rupert would have killed me had Lawson blathered,' said Scott with a shrug. 'I tried very hard not to fleece him at cards, lest he spoke up out of spite, but he was more interested in monitoring the Prince, and I could not help myself.'

'You are in trouble,' said Chaloner. The New Englander was not the only one who could lie, and it was high time Scott had a taste of his own medicine. 'You bribed Commissioner Pett to delay HMS *London* until she could be blown up. Williamson wants answers, and so do the others I told about it.'

Scott's composure slipped. 'Who?' he demanded.

'More people than you can silence. And Pett will not protect you. He gave you up almost eagerly. Why did you do it? For money?'

Scott shrugged again. 'A bag of gold in exchange for having a word with Pett. How could I refuse?'

'A bag of gold from whom?'

'Someone who will kill me if I betray him, so I decline to say. Open the cellar, Manning.'

One hand to his stomach, Manning staggered to the middle of the floor, where he kicked aside a rug to reveal a trapdoor with a metal ring. He tugged it open, and Chaloner's heart sank when he saw what had been exposed: it looked like a dungeon.

He braced himself to resist when Scott came towards him, but Scott had his own way of subduing awkward customers. He drew a knife and stabbed at Chaloner, jumping back with an angry curse when blood spurted across his fine white stockings.

Chapter 15

Chaloner was as startled as Scott when blood gushed through his coat and sprayed in a wide and impressive arc: he had pressed too hard on the bladder he had taken from Wallingford House, and learned too late that there was a skill to using them that he had not appreciated.

'Damn!' cried Scott, gazing down at his ruined hose. His expression hardened as he levelled the gun. Step by step, he forced Chaloner backwards until they were at the edge of the hole, then made a darting move. It was a feint, but it caught Chaloner off balance just long enough for Manning to give him the shove that sent him tumbling down into the cellar.

He lay stunned, dimly aware of an argument taking place above his head, after which something landed heavily beside him. There was a pause, then another thud followed by a crack. He forced himself to open his eyes. The cellar was pitch black, and he realised the last sound had been the trapdoor slamming closed. He experienced a moment of panic, but forced it down. There was no time for it. He struggled to his knees.

'I am dying,' came a soft whisper. 'I should not have touched that claret.'

It was Manning, breathing in a shallow, unhealthy way. Chaloner clambered to his feet and made his way towards the voice, but tripped over another body en route.

'Sherwin – Scott threw him in here after me.' Manning laughed bitterly. 'You will keep company with the corpses of your victims until you die yourself.'

'We shall shout for help,' said Chaloner firmly. 'Someone will hear.'

'Not so. The taverner is evicted, and a legal wrangle will keep this place empty for weeks. There will be no rescue for you.'

'Then I will climb out and—'

'How? The trapdoor is impossible to open from the inside.'

It was not what Chaloner wanted to hear, and he set about exploring their prison to prove Manning wrong. The chamber was roughly ten feet square, and empty except for a barrel. He rolled it under the faint rectangle of light that was just visible above, clambered on top of it, and heaved with all his might. The trapdoor did not budge.

'Jones warned that Scott would turn against me,' came Manning's voice again. 'But I thought I could control him, fool that I am. Oh, Lord! I cannot move my legs!'

'Maybe Jones killed Sherwin,' said Chaloner, more to himself than Manning. 'To ensure he passes his secret to no one else.'

'Jones was never here. He had forgotten the place was closing today, and when I reminded him, he changed his meeting to the Talbot.'

Panic was gnawing at Chaloner. Being locked in an

underground cell was bad enough, but the prospect was far worse with corpses. 'Tell me about Sherwin,' he ordered, to take his mind off it. 'I know he worked in Rupert's gun factory and was dismissed for drunkenness.'

'I was going to sell him to Jones . . .'

'Sell *him*?'

'Have you ever made a clay pot? The principle is simple, but it takes years of practice to produce a good one. It is the same with guns. You could follow a set of instructions to the letter, but your cannon would never work, because you need *know-how*. And Sherwin had it. Not only could he turn and anneal to perfection, but he was skilled at creating exactly the right balance of metals.'

'No wonder he was so sure of his worth.'

'Oh, yes! But there is a secret that Rupert is even more keen to keep quiet: namely that his guns are very expensive to manufacture.'

Chaloner frowned. 'I thought the main appeal was that they are cheaper than brass.'

Manning laughed hollowly. 'Everyone does, but they take months to construct and need all manner of pricey equipment. According to Sherwin, they cost three times more than their brass equivalents. But Rupert thinks they are marvellous, which has convinced people that they must be worth having. It is a lie.'

'Why did you choose to deal with Jones?' Chaloner was not sure what to think.

'I knew him through the Fifth Monarchists, and I am not exactly awash with contacts who want to purchase artillery.' Manning's voice turned bitter. 'I only joined for Ursula's cakes. And Jones lost interest once I sold him the recipe for gunmetal, almost as if he had what he really wanted. Maybe that is why he started sending Leving to deal with me, instead of coming himself.'

'You must have sold him a cannon as well,' said Chaloner, thinking of HMS *London's* sorry fate.

'He borrowed the one that Sherwin stole from Temple Mills – said he wanted to test it. He brought it back very dirty.'

'With sand and marsh mud, I suppose.'

'Yes,' said Manning in surprise. 'How did you know?'

Time passed slowly. Chaloner slumped in a corner, listening to Manning's laboured breathing and the distant chants of bellmen, who ambled along Fleet Street calling the time. He clenched his fists in an agony of frustration, wishing he was anywhere but trapped uselessly underground. Then the bellmen's voices were replaced by the rumble of traffic as the day began – heavier than usual, because it was Lady Day and carts, carriages and horses were pouring into the city at a tremendous rate. He sat up sharply when he heard footsteps on the floor above.

With nothing to lose, he yelled at the top of his voice, and was rewarded moments later by the sound of the trapdoor being unbolted. Light flooded into the cellar, making him squint. Leving peered down at him.

'Where are Jones and the Sanhedrin?' Chaloner demanded, hearing Leving draw breath to ask what was likely to be the first of many questions. He did not have time for them.

'Well, they held a meeting at the Talbot last night, but it was just more empty promises and hot air. Then they all went home. Why?'

Chaloner climbed on the barrel and gripped the edge of the hole. 'We must find them.'

Leving prised his fingers off the rim, 'Not so fast. I do not want to be on Williamson's side if the Divine Authority *does* appear tomorrow, so I intend to wait and see what happens. And that means I would rather you stayed down there.'

Chaloner glared at him. 'What will happen is that Williamson will kill you. He is not very gentle with those who offer to work for him and then renege.'

When he tried a second time to haul himself out, Leving trod on his hands. 'But he will not know, will he? You are hardly in a position to tell him. And I have to think of myself.'

The selfish admission made something click clear in Chaloner's mind. 'Jones claimed he never gave you letters for Manning. He was telling the truth – you have been dealing with Manning behind his back. No wonder you refused to let me open them! You pretended to be shocked by the notion, but the reality was that you did not want me to know they were from you.'

'I have to make ends meet,' shrugged Leving. 'Williamson does not pay me very well.'

'*I* will pay you,' offered Manning in a hoarse whisper. 'Help me, and I will give you Rupert's secret. I do not care that you deceived me by pretending to be Jones . . .'

Leving considered for a moment, then grabbed the empty claret bottle and lobbed it into the cellar. Chaloner ducked, and whether by design or accident, it struck Manning's head. Leving giggled in a way that suggested Wiseman's diagnosis was right: he was unhinged.

'Now all I have to do is kill Scott, and Sherwin will

be mine,' said Leving in an oddly sing-song voice. 'Where is he, by the way?'

Chaloner knew he would never escape if Leving learned that Sherwin was dead. 'Let me out, and I will take you to him.'

'No. Tell me where he is, or I will shoot you.'

He pulled a gun from his pocket, and as he did so, a piece of paper fluttered out. Instinctively, Chaloner caught it. It was only a note reminding Leving to visit his tailor later that afternoon, but the spy stared at it in horror.

'Is this your writing?'

'Yes,' acknowledged Leving cautiously. 'Why?'

'You pen distinctive capital letters, and I have seen them twice now: once on the packet you delivered to Manning the day we met, but more tellingly in a note sent to Wallingford House, which said you had much to report and begged for more money. Williamson is not your only master: you are in Buckingham's pay, too!'

Leving scowled. 'That is none of your concern. Now where is Sherwin?'

'I should have guessed in the Talbot,' Chaloner went on, 'when I noticed that your purse was embroidered with a crest – Buckingham's crest. *He* hired you to learn Sherwin's secret.'

Leving waggled the gun in a way that made Chaloner flinch. 'Why would he do that?'

'Because he and Rupert hate each other, and he probably wants the venture to fail.'

Leving grinned suddenly. 'You are quite right, of course. But I *much* prefer Buckingham to Williamson. He is more generous and does not threaten me with execution every time we meet.'

397

'You really are insane,' said Chaloner wonderingly. 'You spy on Fifth Monarchists, meddle in spats between powerful barons, and deceive a dangerous spymaster.'

Yes,' chuckled Leving. 'And no one has suspected a thing. I have also infiltrated five other sets of rebels. I am invincible! You, however, are not.'

He took aim with the gun, and Chaloner gazed up at him steadily, unwilling to demean himself by looking away.

'Well, well, well,' came a soft voice that made Leving jump. The dag went off, showering Chaloner with splinters from the wooden edge of the hatch. 'So you are the rogue who has been betraying us.'

Chaloner saw Leving's eyes go wide with astonishment as Jones stalked towards him, while his own heart sank. How would he defeat the Fifth Monarchists now? Jones nodded an order, and two of his Sanhedrin hurried forward to seize Leving's arms. Then he leaned down and offered Chaloner his hand. Warily, Chaloner took it, and was hauled upwards.

'You misunderstood whatever you heard,' declared Leving, as Chaloner scrambled clear of the hole and backed away from everyone. 'I am no traitor.'

'We followed you here,' hissed Jones, softly sibilant. 'We heard almost everything you said. And we arrived just in time. You murdered Manning, but we managed to save our gunpowder expert.'

'Nonsense!' cried Leving. 'I only dropped in to see whether the landlord had left anything worth salvaging. I had no idea Chaloner and Manning were here until I heard them yelling.'

'I wondered why Chaloner did not attend our meeting last night,' Jones went on coolly. 'You not only failed to inform him of the change of venue, but you imprisoned him in that cellar—'

'Guilty as charged,' flashed Leving. 'And do you know why? Because *he* is the traitor. I did the Cause a considerable favour by shutting him away.'

Jones eyed him with rank disdain. 'I should have known that you were too stupid to escape from gaol after the Northern Plot collapsed. You had help – Williamson's help.'

'No,' shouted Leving. 'I have never met the Spymaster. Chaloner, on the other hand, plays the viol for him three times a week. They are close friends.'

'Your lying tongue betrays you,' said Jones in distaste. 'Williamson hates music and he does not have friends.'

'Perhaps that bit was untrue,' admitted Leving. 'But Chaloner *is* a traitor. He never lost the Tsar's jewels, and he is still in Clarendon's employ. I agreed to work for Williamson just to expose him for you. And look! He is covered in blood – it must be Sherwin's.'

'There is no reason to think any harm has befallen Sherwin,' said Jones. 'But Chaloner is limping, so I hope you have not hurt him. We shall need his expertise today.'

'What for?' asked Chaloner, trying to disguise his alarm.

'To prepare for the Last Millennium,' replied Jones calmly. It sounded like a threat.

'Listen to me,' said Leving, more annoyed than alarmed by his situation. 'Buckingham has more money than sense, and I can get you on his payroll. He will shell out handsomely for information, and you can tell him whatever you like. It is what I have been doing – feeding him lies. I am on *your* side.'

Jones listened with an icy contempt that would have

399

silenced any normal man, although Leving gabbled on. Chaloner collected his weapons from the table. He was as taut as a bowstring, expecting to be attacked at any moment, but no one took any notice as he buckled his sword around his waist and slid his daggers into their various sheaths.

'I wondered from the start whether you were the traitor,' said Jones, finally cutting through Leving's self-serving tirade. 'But I could not believe that any spymaster would stoop to using such a dimwit.'

'There is no need to be rude,' said Leving stiffly. 'And if you suspect me, then you must also suspect the gunpowder expert that *I* introduced to your fold.'

'I might, but in an act of ineptitude typical of you, you actually managed to recruit one who is perfect for our needs. But enough chatter.' Jones turned to his cronies. 'Toss him in the cellar and let us be about more important business.'

Leving struggled hard, but his captors were strong, and it was not long before he disappeared into the hole.

'Wait!' he shrieked, as Jones started to close the trap-door. 'Sherwin is down here. Chaloner is a killer, and you are not safe with him. Look! I can show you the corpse.'

His vindictive howls went from shrill to muffled as the panel dropped into place. Jones rubbed his hands together and turned to his followers, his reptile-eyes bright. Something akin to excitement lit his dark face.

'Our time draws nigh. Are you ready, Chaloner?'

'Ready for what?' asked Chaloner, full of apprehension.

'Why, for the fireworks, of course.'

Chaloner was hopelessly confused as he followed Jones and the Sanhedrin out on to Chancery Lane, and was

400

horrified to see it was nearing noon – he had lost hours in the cellar. The streets were full of revellers: farmers, labourers, housewives, tradesmen, widows and shop-keepers. Were they Fifth Monarchists, pouring into the city to bring about the Last Millennium, or visitors come to pay their Lady Day dues?

For the first time in an age, the sun was shining and it promised to be a fine day. The change in weather affected everyone, and the atmosphere was relaxed and gay. Even the grim fanatics of the Sanhedrin seemed happy, and Chaloner heard one mutter that it was a favourable omen from God, a sign that their venture would succeed.

'Wear this,' said Jones, removing his cloak and handing it to Chaloner. 'You cannot wander around London drenched in blood. People will think you are an insurgent.'

He gave a low, creaking chortle, although Chaloner did not think there was much to laugh about. They reached High Holborn, and Jones led the way to Ursula's house. She was expecting them, because she opened the door before Jones had finished knocking and ushered him inside. She smiled wanly at Chaloner, then stood back as the others filed past her.

The rest of the Sanhedrin, plus a large number of folk who had attended meetings in the Talbot – the more serious ones, who had gone to foment unrest rather than to chat to friends and eat free cakes – were already there, and the little house was bursting at the seams. As usual, it was fragrant with the scent of baking, and the newcomers immediately began to shoulder their way through the throng towards a table that was loaded with biscuits.

'Please do not drop crumbs on the floor,' called Ursula after them, for once failing to inform them that her wares were the best they would ever taste. 'Use plates.'

Chaloner was stunned by the banality of it all – rebels being cautioned not to make a mess before they loosed their madness on London. It was like being in the depths of some bizarre nightmare, and he was not sure that anyone would believe him if he were ever in a position to relate the tale later. He unfastened the cloak – Ursula had fires going, and the press of people was making him uncomfortably hot.

'Blood!' cried Ursula, regarding the red blots in horror. 'Do you need a surgeon?'

'It is not his own,' explained Jones. 'It is not Leving's either, more is the pity.'

'Leving's?' echoed Ursula, but then evidently decided that she did not want to know, because she fixed her attention on Chaloner's clothes. 'Give them to me before they stain permanently.'

'You need to change anyway,' said Jones, passing Chaloner brown breeches and a buff jerkin with striped sleeves. It was the uniform of the palace guard. 'This is what you must wear today.'

Chaloner did not want to remove his clothes while Fifth Monarchists were packed so tightly around him, feeling it would put him at a distinct disadvantage. He indicated the stairs. 'May I?'

'Surely you are not shy?' smirked Jones.

'My wife would not appreciate me undressing in front of other ladies,' said Chaloner. It was lame, but he could hardly tell the truth.

Amusement flashed in Jones's eyes. 'Do not be long then. We move in a few moments.'

Chaloner ran up the steps and went to the window,

aiming to climb through it and dash directly to Williamson, but it had not been opened in years and was stuck fast. He would have to find another way to escape the rebels' clutches. He threw off his stained clothes, pulled on the uniform, and was about to leave when he saw a bundle on the bed, wrapped in a lacy apron.

'Chaloner!' shouted Jones impatiently. 'Hurry up!'

Chaloner unravelled the apron to reveal a stout wooden box. There was no time to pick the lock, so he broke it with the hilt of his dagger. He flipped open the lid, and saw a number of objects inside, all wrapped in cloth pouches. He unfastened one, and stared in mystification.

It was a coining die, and he had seen two just like it recently – Ferine had given Snowflake one, while the other had been on Thurloe's mantelpiece. The ex-Spymaster had said they were an amusing curiosity, items sold from the Tower to raise money for the war. He had smashed a perfectly serviceable button demonstrating its use.

Puzzled, Chaloner grabbed another bag. It was full of silver discs, akin to the buttons that Grisley Pate had given him in Temple Mills. He retrieved them from the pocket of his abandoned coat and compared them. As far as he could tell they were identical.

But there was no time for speculation, because he could hear footsteps on the stairs, even over the noisy gusto of fanatics enjoying their food. He closed and rewrapped the box, and was just fastening his jerkin when Jones walked in. The rebel regarded him oddly, and Chaloner knew he suspected that something was amiss.

'Are you ready?' was all Jones said. 'It is time.'

*

Chaloner was in a turmoil of confusion as the coach carrying him, Ursula, Jones and three of the Sanhedrin rattled towards White Hall. The rest of the gathering were in hackney carriages bound for other destinations.

'Where is Atkinson?' he asked.

'In position,' replied Jones shortly. 'How familiar are you with the Privy Garden?'

'Not very,' lied Chaloner. 'Why?'

Jones smiled humourlessly. 'Come, now, there is no need for false modesty. Clarendon's offices overlook it, so you must have seen it hundreds of times.'

Cornered, Chaloner shrugged. '*Seen* it, yes, but retainers are not encouraged to stroll there. All I know is that it is a large open space with rose beds, hedges and a fountain in the middle.'

'And what of its borders?'

As it was relatively easy to gain access to the palace, Chaloner suspected that Jones already knew what it looked like, and that he would betray no secrets if he described it. 'High walls on two sides, and buildings along the others.'

'Do you know the gardeners' quarters?'

Chaloner wondered where the conversation was going. 'A single room in the south-west corner that is used for storing their tools.'

Jones smiled. 'Atkinson is waiting for us there.'

'Surely, we should seize the Tower first,' said Chaloner, stomach churning. The Fifth Monarchists were better prepared than he had expected – that particular part of White Hall was generally overlooked by the palace guards, and it would be simple for the rebels to take up station there. And once they had a foothold . . .

404

'Not before we have dealt with the King,' replied Jones, eyes glittering. 'Lord! Look at these crowds! Anyone would think the Last Millennium was at hand.'

With that enigmatic remark, he fell silent. Chaloner tried to make him talk, but Ursula indicated that he should desist with an urgent shake of her head, and he knew she was right. He could not afford to rouse Jones's suspicions with a welter of questions now, especially with three of the Sanhedrin watching him with cold faces – and two of them had handguns.

Agitated, he pondered the significance of the Privy Garden. The weather was fine, so the King would almost certainly enjoy an open-air event of some sort there that day, and the firework display was scheduled for the evening. Did Jones intend to turn the silver cannon on His Majesty and his courtiers? If so, it would plunge the country into anarchy for certain.

It had to be stopped, but how? The Sanhedrin alone numbered thirty determined individuals, and there had been another twenty disciples in Ursula's house – not to mention the ten thousand who were waiting for the call to arms. How was Chaloner to defeat them when his only allies were an idealistic stockinger and a frightened widow? His sole hope was that Rupert had spurred Williamson into action. But the Prince was more interested in protecting his cannon, and the chances were that his report would be skewed to that end alone. With a sinking heart, Chaloner realised that there would be no help from the Spymaster's troops.

As the coach rattled closer to White Hall, he began to formulate wild plans. He had a sword and three knives. Could he kill or maim Jones in the hope that the rebellion would falter without its leader? But the other three members of the Sanhedrin watched him unblinkingly, and fingers tightened on triggers when he moved his hand from the armrest to his lap. They would kill him before he could draw a weapon, and then nothing would stand between Jones and his objective.

Then could he jump out of the coach and dash to Williamson? Outside, the press of Lady Day visitors was so great that the driver had to rein in or risk trampling them. Casually, Chaloner rested his fingers on the window, preparing to undo the catch, but Jones leaned forward and knocked them down.

'Did your mother never teach you to keep your hands inside moving vehicles? We cannot afford an accident now. How would you perform your duties?'

They arrived at White Hall, where Chaloner was appalled to learn that security had been thrown to the wind because it was a holiday – the palace guards were evidently of the opinion that assassins and rebels would not be so ungentlemanly as to strike at such a time. Chaloner's uniform ensured that he and Jones's party strolled through the Great Court without a second glance from the soldiers on duty. He tried to signal that all was not well, but their attention was on a woman who was asking directions, and none noticed his urgent gesture.

The palace thronged with people, some handsomely dressed, but many in rough clothes that indicated they were servants or tradesmen. Or Fifth Monarchists, thought Chaloner, looking at the unfamiliar faces and desperately trying to determine whether they were fanatics. He was too agitated for rational judgement, and found himself suspecting everyone.

'You will not identify them,' whispered Ursula, reading

him rather too well. 'They all look perfectly normal. Like you and me.'

She was right, and Chaloner's despair deepened.

Jones led the way across the Great Court and through the short corridor that led to the Privy Garden. A party was in progress there, and the entire expanse teemed with courtiers and high-ranking officials. Musicians played, and servants moved through the knots of people with cups of wine on silver platters. Some guests had already had too much to drink, and the atmosphere was raucous. Chaloner regarded them in dismay. With half of them intoxicated, any atrocity was likely to result in even greater carnage, because they would not be able to move fast enough to escape.

Jones aimed unerringly for the gardeners' room. He looked around quickly, then opened a door and ushered his followers inside. It was a dark, low-ceilinged, dusty chamber full of tools, plant pots and neatly stacked pieces of wood. There was a faint smell that was instantly recognisable to Chaloner. It was gunpowder.

He glanced around quickly, but could see no cannon or anything that might be used as one. There was, however, a large number of small, squat barrels, of the kind that were used to transport explosives. So was that their plan, to blow up this room in the expectation that the King and his ministers would perish in the blast? But the Privy Garden was a huge open space, and explosions worked better in confined ones. Was it possible that the rebels were so badly informed that they did not know this?

'There you are,' came a voice from the gloom, and Atkinson emerged holding a hoe. He lowered it sheepishly. 'Where have you been? You are late, and I have been worried.'

407

Jones beckoned, and everyone followed him through the room to a door at the far end, which also led to the garden. It was ajar, and through it Chaloner saw the trench that Kipps had complained about so bitterly some days before. It had been empty then; now it was full of packages, all covered in tarpaulin and with fuses trailing from them.

'Light them, Chaloner,' ordered Jones. He gave an odd salute. 'You will almost certainly be caught or killed, so we shall not meet again. Wait five minutes for the rest of us to reach our designated posts and then begin. God be with you.'

'Wait,' snapped Chaloner, as the conspirators started to move away. 'How can I light them when I do not know the size or the precise location of all the charges?'

Jones raised his eyebrows. 'You are a gunpowder expert – that should not be a problem.'

'But—'

'Think about the Cause,' said Jones smoothly, 'and how pleased the Supreme Authority will be with your role in it.'

'He will not be pleased with murder,' argued Chaloner.

'Murder?' echoed Jones, eyebrows raised archly. 'These are fireworks, not bombs.'

Chaloner frowned in confusion. 'Fireworks?'

Jones pointed to the trench. 'Surely you can tell the difference?'

Chaloner could not, but was reluctant to say so. 'I do not understand,' he said helplessly.

Jones's smile was bland. 'White Hall plans to celebrate Lady Day with fireworks, as you have no doubt heard. Igniting them is a skilled business – any amateur attempting it is likely to blow himself up. However, Leving assured us that it is well within your capabilities. So off you go.'

Chaloner looked at the packages again, and saw that names were visible on some: White Candles, Catherine Wheels, Red Rockets. Then he stole a glance at the little barrels. The lids were off a few, and he could see they were empty – it had been the fireworks that had been transported in them, not gunpowder.

'But why light them now?' he asked, more baffled than ever. 'It is daytime and no one will see them properly.'

'No,' agreed Jones. 'Which is the point: it will emphasise the wastefulness of Court. Fireworks are obscenely expensive, and people will object to such a shocking squandering of money if the things are set off at a point when they cannot be appreciated. Folk will be filled with righteous anger, and will cry out against this decadent regime.'

Chaloner shook his head in incomprehension. 'You said you were going to kill the King.'

'The *people* will kill the King when they witness his profligacy,' said Jones, eyes glittering. 'After all, it is Lady Day, and London is full of visitors from all over the country. It is the perfect opportunity to expose His Majesty as a greedy spendthrift who cares nothing for his subjects.'

'Does this mean you are *not* going to seize the Tower, set the city on fire and establish a republic?' asked Chaloner, bewildered. 'Your supporters will be disappointed. So will Jesus.'

'That is not your concern.' Jones reached into his pocket and withdrew a pamphlet, obviously aiming to read from it. As he did so, several silver discs fell out. Chaloner stared at them as they tinkled on the floor,

409

thinking about what he had found in Ursula's house, plus what snippets he had learned about the new gunmetal that Rupert had devised.

'I understand now,' he said. 'This is not about rebellion, it is about making money. Literally.'

Chapter 16

There was silence in the room after Chaloner made his announcement. Ursula and Atkinson gaped their disbelief, while the three members of the Sanhedrin stood silent and impassive – the revelation was no surprise to them. Then a chorus of laughter wafted from the garden, along with the strains of a melody by Lawes. It was one of Chaloner's favourites, but he did not hear it. All his attention was fixed on Jones.

'What are you talking about?' asked Ursula eventually. 'Making money?'

'Jones is no Fifth Monarchist,' said Chaloner, recalling all the times that he had questioned the man's dedication to the Cause. 'He is just a common criminal.'

'How dare you!' cried Jones angrily. 'Now light the—'

'There will be no rebellion,' said Chaloner. 'Jones was lying about seizing the Tower and all the rest of it – a fabrication on the spur of the moment when people demanded to know his plans. He never intended to revolt. How could he, when no one has bought arms or horses?'

'Are you sure?' whispered Atkinson, stunned.

'Yes. Three men from Taunton stole money to fund

411

such purchases, but it was almost certainly spent on learning about Rupert's cannon. Jones sent Strange and Quelch to watch their executions, to ensure nothing incriminating was said in their final speeches.'

Jones heaved an irritable sigh, but did not seem unduly alarmed by Chaloner's revelations. 'So what? The truth does not matter now.'

Atkinson gazed at him. 'You do not deny it?'

Jones shrugged. 'As I said, it does not matter now. Light the fireworks, Chaloner, so we can all be about our business. Refuse, and these two die.'

He nodded to his cronies. One was the tailor, Glasse, who shoved Atkinson and Ursula against the wall. He had a pair of handguns in his belt, and so did one of the others, although neither drew them. Chaloner knew why: discharging firearms in a palace was not recommended, as it would attract unwanted attention. He wondered how he could turn their caution to his advantage.

'You will kill them anyway,' he said, declining to budge. 'You cannot let them live, knowing they will tell Williamson what you—'

'On the contrary, they can tell him what they like,' interrupted Jones. 'I do not care what he, the King or the Court know about me and my plans. The point is that the *people* will see fireworks set off in daylight, and they will take exception to the waste – especially when they read the pamphlet I have written on the matter.' He waved it.

Ursula found her voice at last. 'But what about the Last Millennium?'

'It will come,' replied Jones. 'Just not tomorrow.'

'I do not understand,' she whispered. 'You made speeches, wrote tracts . . . although not ones that have been published, of course.'

412

'But they will be,' declared Jones, and suddenly his eyes were blazing. 'And *that* is when this revolution will come to pass. It will be because of *my* writing and *my* ideas.'

'And my sister's,' interposed Ursula. 'She is—'

'No!' stated Jones vehemently. 'She is a dangerous lunatic, like all Fifth Monarchists, and there will be no room for those in *my* republic.' He turned to Chaloner. 'I assume the spies sent to infiltrate the movement have a complete list of its members now?'

'What spies?' gulped Ursula, shooting an uneasy glance at her lover.

Jones sneered. 'You thought you were so clever, but I knew exactly what you were doing. The same with Scott and Chaloner, although I admit that Leving's treachery came as a surprise.'

'What makes you think that I—' began Chaloner.

'Because of the purse you donated to the Cause. It was not yours to give. It was *mine* – money *I* paid Manning for the formula of Rupert's gunmetal. The fee included a ruby ring, which I recognised at once. The fact that you parted with a small fortune so readily told me that you are in the pay of someone powerful and generous – namely Williamson.'

Chaloner might have smiled at the notion that he was so well paid that 'small fortunes' were nothing to him, but he was too disgusted with himself. Handing over a readily identifiable object had been stupid, and he should have known better. Bitterly, he recalled Jones's odd willingness to trust him, and the way he had prevented Quelch from causing him harm. He had been used.

'If you knew I was a spy, why did you not stop me?' he asked sullenly.

413

'Because you were doing exactly what I wanted – working against these foolish fanatics. And if your list of names is incomplete, you will find a full one in my lodgings.' Jones smirked. 'Have you decoded the documents I gave you for Manning? I know you will have made copies.'

'So that is why they were in cipher,' said Chaloner. 'If you had written them normally, he would have read them and thrown them away. But you wanted him to keep them, so they would incriminate him when you betrayed him. And he has kept them, of course – being a greedy man, he would never destroy anything that might work to his advantage.'

Jones inclined his head. 'The code I used was a complex one, to keep him busy. Did it defeat you, too? Do not worry if so. I have left plenty more damning documents for you to "discover".'

'One letter told Manning how to leave Britain,' recalled Chaloner. 'It proves that you do not believe the Last Millennium is at hand, or escape would be irrelevant. And you recommended the United Provinces as a refuge.'

'Why should that matter?' asked Atkinson hoarsely. His face was pale, and he was clearly appalled by what he was hearing.

'Because he is in their pay,' replied Chaloner coldly. 'The fine Dutch chairs in his house represent part of the reward he has accepted for Sherwin's secret – a far richer one than he gave Manning. He has negotiated with the French, too, as the papers in his harpsichord attest.'

'You took them, did you? I might have known. But pleasant though it is to review my brilliance, we must make haste. Light the fireworks, Chaloner.'

'Wait!' cried Ursula. 'You cannot betray our members to Williamson! He will execute them, and they are only

414

folk who would rather have Jesus in White Hall than a debauched King.'

'They are lunatics,' declared Jones. 'Thank God my association with them is at an end!'

'But why?' breathed Atkinson, shocked. 'Is Chaloner right to say it is for money?'

'*Making* money,' corrected Chaloner. 'Manning said Jones wanted the formula for gunmetal, and lost interest once he had it. The truth is that Jones never cared about the cannon – he wanted Rupert's iron to manufacture *coins*.' He prodded one of the 'buttons' with his foot. 'From these.'

'But how?' Atkinson was wide-eyed with shock. 'You cannot just establish a mint and start churning the stuff out. It requires special machinery.'

'It does now,' said Chaloner. 'But coins used to be made with dies, and the Tower has recently sold a batch of them. Jones has left some in Ursula's house, knowing he will not be able to return to his own home after today—'

'I bought three,' interrupted Jones smugly. 'Rupert's iron makes *excellent* shillings.'

'No one will accept them,' warned Chaloner. 'They will look too different.'

'Will they?' Jones tossed him one. It was old, worn and dirty grease obscured parts of the inscription; Chaloner had no idea if it was real. 'You see? Rupert's metal makes money that looks and feels exactly like the real thing, especially when rubbed with a bit of grime.'

'But you are not a greedy man!' whispered Ursula, stunned. 'Not the author of *Mene Tekel*.'

'No,' agreed Jones, and suddenly his bragging manner became earnest. 'But the Northern Plot taught me that

415

outright rebellion is not the way to achieve my objectives. So-called disciples make promises they fail to keep, and the thing stutters to a standstill after a few heady days.'

'So what will you do instead?' asked Ursula in a small voice.

'Two things. First, I shall mint enough money to flood the country with my pamphlets. Your sister might be able to publish what she likes, but *I* cannot – the presses are too expensive.'

'And second?' asked Chaloner.

Jones smiled. 'Money begets money, as any rich man will tell you. These coins, along with payments from the French and the Dutch – the reports you found were copies: the originals have already been sold – and the five hundred pounds from Taunton will make for a tidy sum.'

'You plan to keep it for yourself?'

'Some, perhaps. But the lion's share will go towards funding a *proper* rebellion, with horses, weapons and professional troops. There will be no more amateur bungling for me, and this despotic regime will crumble when I appear with an army at my heels.'

'You are a hypocrite,' said Ursula, tearful in her anger. 'You claim to oppose oppression and tyranny, yet you blew up a ship carrying three hundred sailors.'

'That was to show the world that Fifth Monarchists are dangerous fanatics who must be eliminated,' explained Jones impatiently. 'We cannot have a perfect society with the likes of them roving around.'

'But no one knows they were responsible.' Chaloner wondered how Jones could not see that he was a dangerous fanatic himself.

'They will when I write a tract about it.'

Chaloner thought about what James Pate had

416

overheard Jones say the night before HMS *London* had been destroyed: that 'it was a fine outrage for the Cause'. The words made sense now he understood what Jones aimed to achieve from the atrocity.

'No,' cried Ursula. 'I am not listening to any more of this. You are a nasty, wicked man!'

She shoved past Glasse and ran at Jones, who turned his back on her contemptuously. But she had a blade, and his eyes went wide in astonishment as it sliced into him. His mouth opened and closed several times in mute disbelief before he collapsed to the floor.

There was a fraction of a moment when no one moved, but then Chaloner gathered his wits, and managed to do so more quickly than Glasse and his friends. He punched the tailor, knocking him senseless, and was whipping around to deal with the other two when Atkinson sprang into action. The stockinger also had a knife, and tears of rage sprung from his eyes as he flailed wildly with it. Chaloner was taken aback by the ferocity of the assault, but there was no time to ponder.

'Quickly,' he said. 'We must stop the Sanhedrin from—'

'Stay where you are,' ordered Ursula.

Chaloner frowned in surprise at the harsh tone of her voice. 'What—'

'I said stay where you are,' she snapped, and he gaped his disbelief when he saw the weapon she held. It was a knitting needle that had been sharpened to a vicious point.

'Oh, no!' he breathed. '*You* stabbed Snowflake! Wiseman said the weapon was no knife, but something long and—'

417

'I have an alibi.' Ursula removed the guns from Glasse's belt and Chaloner was too stunned by his realisation to stop her. 'I was sewing stockings with John, Old Ned and Maude in his shop.'

'*They* sewed stockings.' Chaloner was still gazing at her. 'You went to a back room for silk, where no one knew whether you stayed or not. Maude *assumed* you were there – and I believed you when you told your tale – but you slipped out. You left the shop to kill Snowflake, and did not bother going back again. I visited you in your home later.'

He had a sudden vision of watching her knit by the fire. Had she used the murder weapon then, plying it in front of him and safe in the belief that he would never guess the truth? He turned to the stockinger for support, and was horrified when he saw that Ursula was not the only one who had grabbed weapons from the felled Sanhedrin. Atkinson had a pair of handguns, too.

'We did what had to be done.' Atkinson's voice was low. 'I was more sorry than I can say.'

'Snowflake loved you,' said Chaloner accusingly. 'How could you?'

'But she never loved the Cause,' said Ursula quietly. 'Indeed, she was going to tell you everything, and urge you to stop us. And do you know why? Because she finally tumbled to the fact that there will be no place for her vile club in the Kingdom of Christ. She wanted to save it by thwarting the coming of the Last Millennium!'

'So you stabbed her while she was petting Lady,' said Chaloner, still struggling to come to terms with what they had done. 'It agitated him, and he injured you when you tried to calm him – you told me yourself that you do not like horses. And that is why you have been

418

limping ever since. You did not slip in mud on High Holborn.'

'We would not be having this discussion if you had killed him when I suggested,' said Ursula crossly to Atkinson. 'I told you he would be a problem.'

'You arranged the attack outside Clarendon's mansion,' surmised Chaloner. 'To prevent me from going to Temple Mills and learning what Snowflake had wanted to tell me – namely that Rupert had invented iron cannon. You feared the resulting fuss might deprive the Cause of them.'

'I thought we had succeeded,' sighed Atkinson. 'I was astonished to see you in Prittlewell.'

'So you suggested we ride back to London together, aiming to try again. When I declined, you sent me to listen to that deranged Fifth Monarchist in the tavern, to delay me until you could arrange an ambush. But I took a boat to Chatham instead. Did you wait long?'

'Not really,' replied Ursula coolly. 'And we had another plan in play anyway.'

'The stockings.' Chaloner was disconcerted to learn how hard they had tried to make an end of him. 'It was not Sherwin's claret that killed Manning, but the pins in the hose. They must have been dipped in poison.'

'We should have insisted that you don them at once,' said Ursula venomously.

'Why *did* you go to Prittlewell?' asked Chaloner. 'Not to save the King.'

'To witness his death,' said Ursula coldly. 'We were sure Jones would not pass up such an opportunity to strike – but he did not even attempt an assassination, and you have just helped us to understand why.' She turned to Atkinson. 'It is just you and me now, dearest.

419

All the traitors have gone, and we shall stand together to welcome in the Last Millennium.'

Chaloner groaned. 'So you are real Fifth Monarchists? Williamson recruited a—'

'I volunteered to serve the Spymaster,' said Atkinson, 'as a way to learn what he was doing. He was so relieved by my offer that he trusted me instantly, and told me all about you.'

Chaloner had trusted Atkinson, too, although with hindsight he supposed he should have been suspicious of the stockinger's failure to confide that he was in the Spymaster's pay from the start. But the situation had gone quite far enough, and he could spend no more time talking.

'Jones has sent the most fervent members of your sect to cause trouble elsewhere,' he said urgently. 'He aims to have them caught red-handed, to give the government an excuse for bloody reprisals. If you want to save them, come with me to—'

He stopped speaking when Ursula took a gun in both hands and levelled it at him. 'I am sorry, but we are close to victory now, and no one can be allowed to interfere. My sister was quite clear on that point – she had a vision about the Kingdom of Christ, you see.'

'I doubt there will be a place in it for killers,' warned Chaloner. 'Or for those who stand by and do nothing while atrocities are committed. Please! You know I am right. Help me to—'

'All *our* crimes will be forgiven,' said Atkinson earnestly. 'Unlike yours. I cannot imagine a greater sin than betraying one's friends. And so many of our so-called confederates have been doing it – you, Leving, Manning, Scott, Jones and his friends here, Strange, Quelch . . .'

420

'*Quelch* berayed you?' Chaloner was bemused for a moment, but then he understood. 'He had a criminal past. I suppose Williamson found out, and threatened to expose him unless he agreed to spy. The fact that *you* know what he was doing probably means you are his killers. I thought Strange was the culprit, but Wiseman said that Quelch had been strangled by smaller fingers . . .'

Atkinson looked down at his hands. 'It had to be done.'

'It troubled you, though,' Chaloner went on. Disgusted, he realised that he should have been more sceptical of Atkinson's alibi for the time of Quelch's death – Maude and Old Ned while they sewed stockings, but Ursula while he was in the back room. She had killed Snowflake and he had strangled Quelch, both sneaking out while Maude and Old Ned laboured away with their needles and thread on Atkinson's behalf. 'When you saw Quelch's body in the charnel house, it shocked you into vomiting.'

'A foolish weakness, for which I am ashamed.'

'And Strange?' Chaloner glanced at Ursula. 'He was stabbed, like Snowflake.'

'He started to make enquiries to prove his innocence, and discovered that *I* had been with Quelch the night he died,' said Atkinson. 'She acted to protect me.'

Chaloner turned to more urgent business. 'Your fellow Fifth Monarchists are in grave danger. You *must* help me stop what Jones has set in motion before . . .'

He faltered as both Atkinson and Ursula took aim. Neither could miss at such short range, and if he died, so would hundreds more, rounded up and executed when the rebellion failed and Rupert discovered the list of names in Jones's home. He used the only weapon he had left.

'Would you kill a man without letting him make peace with God?' he asked softly.

421

They exchanged a glance, and the guns wavered. Chaloner made as if to kneel, then hurled himself through the open door and into the fireworks trench. There was a sharp report, and he was sure he felt the shot zip past his face. It was followed by an explosion, after which something whooshed into the sky amid a spray of scarlet flames – the bullet had ignited a Red Rocket. Was this what Lambe had had in mind when he had forecast smoke, explosions and blood?

He scrambled to his feet and ran, clambering frantically over the canvas-covered packages. There was a second crack, and this time it was a Catherine Wheel that exploded. He cringed as he was doused in a cascade of silver sparks. Afraid they might set him alight, he threw himself out of the trench, hoping the smoke would conceal him from sight. His hopes were dashed when a third shot cracked into the ground at his feet.

'Hey!' came a loud, indignant voice. 'Someone is shooting at a palace guard.'

'No!' shouted Chaloner, as several courtiers hurried towards him with drawn swords, drunk enough to imagine that blades were a match for firearms. 'Stay back!'

But the Catherine Wheel was making too much noise, and they kept coming. With a surge of horror, he saw Wiseman join them. Then a fourth shot rang out, causing them to scatter in alarm. Four bullets – by Chaloner's calculation, it was time for Ursula and Atkinson to reload. He raced back to the storeroom, aiming to be there before they could do it. Dagger in hand, he flung open the door, only to find the place empty.

'What was that about?' demanded Rupert, making him jump by speaking close behind him. Unlike the other guests, he carried a no-nonsense handgun, which he began to load with deftly practised movements. 'Who are they, and what do they mean by spoiling the King's fireworks?'

'Fanatics,' replied Chaloner shortly. 'Did you speak to Williamson? Tell him what—'

'Are they on the list you promised to give me today?' The Prince rammed the shot home with a vigorous jab, clearly not in the mood for answering questions.

'Oh, yes. They are by far the most dangerous Fifth Monarchists still alive.'

'Then get after them while I fetch help.' Rupert shoved the primed dag into Chaloner's hand. 'Take my gun – you will not defeat them with a knife. They will be aiming for the river. Hurry!'

Chaloner set off at a run. He reached the water gate, and opened it warily. Rupert was right – Atkinson and Ursula were indeed intending to escape on the Thames. They had a boat, and Atkinson was manoeuvring it into the water. Chaloner started to run towards them, but Ursula had managed to reload with impressive speed. He flung himself sideways as she fired at him, hearing the bullet ricochet off the stones where he had been standing.

Atkinson jumped into the little craft and turned to help Ursula. Then he grabbed the oars while she aimed at Chaloner a second time. From his prone position, Chaloner fired Rupert's dag, but his faith in the Prince's competence with firearms was misplaced: it had been poorly primed, and the missile it spat out was ineffective. Ursula's was not, though, and it snapped into the mud just inches from his face. He leapt to his feet and ran

423

again, hoping she had not had time to reload the other two guns as well.

In his panic, Atkinson could not make the oars bite, which allowed Chaloner time to plunge into the water and wade after them. Silt sucked at his legs, slowing him down, while Ursula screamed at the stockinger to row, struggling to prime another gun at the same time. Atkinson twisted the paddles into a more effective hold, and suddenly the boat was on the move. Chaloner strained forward with every fibre of his being, and managed to grasp the stern.

Atkinson heaved for all he was worth when he felt his speed checked, tugging Chaloner off balance. Chaloner fought to regain his footing, and had just succeeded when Ursula started to batter him with the gun, hammering at the hands that were preventing their escape. Chaloner let go with one, and caught the flailing weapon with the other.

But Ursula still had her needle, and her eyes flashed with fury as she swiped at him. Fortunately, the leather jerkin saved him from serious harm.

'You will be the first to see hell when the Kingdom of Christ comes!' she raved. 'You are a traitor to the Cause, and I will stand with Jesus to denounce you.'

'Stop!' Chaloner urged. 'It is over. Give up and—'

With a shriek of rage, she stabbed at his head, her face unrecognisable as belonging to the woman who liked knitting and baking. He jerked backwards, still clutching her other hand, and the abrupt movement tugged her out of the boat.

Atkinson released a wail of anguish when she disappeared beneath the surface. Abandoning the oars, he scrambled towards her and managed to grab one of her legs. Meanwhile, Chaloner had an arm, but there was

424

something wrong: she was limp, and blood washed around her.

'She is hurt,' Chaloner shouted. 'Let her go. I will help her.'

'She spoke the truth!' Atkinson howled, tugging on her leg as hard as he could. 'All corrupt and evil men will perish and only the righteous will—'

'You are keeping her head under the water,' yelled Chaloner. 'Stop! She is drowning!'

'You let go!' Atkinson screeched. 'You let go.'

Chaloner did, but so suddenly that the stockinger fell back with a crash, Ursula flying out of the river to land top of him. The boat shot forward, and Chaloner struggled after it again.

'No!' cried Atkinson, his face twisted with distress as he held his beloved. The deadly needle was embedded in her chest. He rocked back and forth, sobbing. Then, with chilling abruptness, his expression went from grief to rage.

Chaloner released the boat and tried to move away, but it was too late. Blind with fury, the stockinger leapt off the boat and fastened his hands around Chaloner's neck. Chaloner went under. He forced himself upwards, but could not take a breath, because Atkinson's hands gripped him too tightly. This was the man who had throttled the massive Strange, Chaloner thought distantly, hearing wild shrieks about a perfect society before he was forced under again, his world nothing but dirty brown bubbles.

He drew the knife in his belt and lashed out, but Atkinson was impervious to pain, and the killing hold did not ease so much as a fraction. The weapon slipped from his fingers as darkness clawed at the edges of his vision. Brown water turned black, and the roaring in his ears faded.

Then the pressure around his throat eased, and he felt

himself being pulled towards the shore. He opened his eyes to see the sky bright above him. Someone was pounding on his chest, hard enough to hurt. His first breath made him choke, and it was some time before he had recovered sufficiently to take stock of his surroundings. Wiseman sat with him until his breathing returned to normal, then patted his shoulder in an awkward but sincere gesture of friendship before wandering away.

'You should have shot them,' said Spymaster Williamson, coming to loom. 'Rupert told me you had a gun.'

'Not one that worked,' rasped Chaloner. 'Atkinson?'

'He was dead when Wiseman pulled him off you – dead with his hands fixed around your neck.' Williamson shuddered. 'It is not a sight I shall forget very quickly, I can tell you! But what of the plot? What else will they do today? Or tomorrow?'

'There is no plot,' said Chaloner tiredly. 'There never was – at least not one that will amount to much. A few misguided lunatics might stage an assault the Tower, and I imagine there will be a fire or two, but nothing serious.'

Williamson sighed his relief. 'Then all that remains is for you to provide me with a complete list of these insurgents, and we shall do the rest. But tomorrow will suffice, no matter what Rupert says. He is distracted, anyway, because there is plague in the city.'

Chaloner stared at him. 'Plague? Lambe's prediction came true?'

'It would seem so. Two or three houses are already sealed up. God save us all.'

Epilogue

The steady rain of the past two weeks seemed to have blown over, and Easter Day dawned bright and clear. The sun shone gently in a sky that was flecked with white fluffy clouds, and the sound of birdsong had taken the place of dripping, gushing, trickling and gurgling. The gardens at Lincoln's Inn smelled of damp earth and spring blossom as Chaloner strolled around them with Thurloe at his side.

'I hear Temperance's club is back in favour,' said Thurloe. 'Last night, it was so packed that some guests were turned away. Apparently, Buckingham persuaded the King to visit, and where His Majesty goes, the rest of the Court follows. I imagine it will survive now that His Majesty has graced it with his presence.'

'Yes,' agreed Chaloner with a satisfied smile. 'It will.'

Thurloe shot him a sidelong glance. 'You play a dangerous game, Tom. Bullying a man like Buckingham to do what you want is hardly wise. He is unlikely to forget it.'

'I did not bully him. I merely pointed out that his sorcerer was ultimately responsible for Ferine's murder, so he should at least try to put matters right for Temperance.'

'Well, it worked. I could hear them carousing from here!'

Chaloner was thinking about Lambe. 'The Court has already forgotten that Paul and Grace Ferine, Hubbert and Duncombe were murdered to give credence to that sorcerer's so-called prophecies. All they talk about is the plague, and how he predicted that it would come.'

Thurloe shuddered. 'So far, the sickness has been confined to a few houses. Pray God that it stays that way.'

'Buckingham really does believe in the Philosopher's Stone, you know,' said Chaloner, reluctant to dwell on what was happening in the crowded tenements not far from where they walked. 'How can he be so gullible?'

'People have hankered after it for centuries. And he is intelligent, has money to buy costly ingredients, and is prepared to dabble in dangerous waters. He thinks these factors confer an advantage that was denied other seekers, so that he will succeed where they have failed.'

Chaloner yawned. He had slept badly the previous night, waking several times to imagine himself being drowned by determined hands. Hannah had not helped by arriving home from Richmond in the small hours, and seizing him in an enthusiastic hug before he was fully awake. It was fortunate that there had been no weapons to hand or he might now be a widower.

'So many lies and betrayals,' he said. 'I do not think I met an honest person in the entire affair. Lawson transpired to be on the right side in the end, but even he lied to the Fifth Monarchists in order to acquire Rupert's guns, and he was quite happy to cheat Jones and Quelch by dealing directly with Scott.'

'He will live, by the way. He claims it is because God

428

needs him to smite the Dutch on His behalf. Regardless of the reason, he will soon be at sea to command the Channel Fleet.'

'And Scott was another liar,' Chaloner went on. 'Perhaps the most accomplished one I have ever met. He was never Cartographer Royal, and I seriously doubt he told the King anything that enabled Britain to take New Amsterdam from the Dutch.'

'He has disappeared, and the suspicion is that he will run to Georges Pellissary. I told Williamson to let him go. Jones has already sold those reports, and I doubt Scott can tell Pellissary anything he does not already know. Besides, it is in our interests that foreign governments are keen to probe the matter now.'

'It is?'

Thurloe nodded. 'As Manning told you, Rupert's secret is worthless without an experienced man to direct operations, and they will waste time and money trying to produce their own iron guns. It will be years before they realise they will never do it.'

Chaloner thought about Manning's admission that Rupert's cannon were more costly than brass ones, and wondered what Scott would do when the French found out. Then he grimaced. Scott would slither out of trouble, just as he always did.

'He is a slippery devil,' he said aloud.

Thurloe agreed. 'So is Leving, who tells anyone who will listen that everything he did was on Buckingham's orders. The Duke denies it, of course, but Rupert believes Leving, and there are deep divisions on the Privy Council. Your Earl is pleased – it has driven Rupert into *his* camp.'

'And there is another injustice,' said Chaloner sourly. 'Rupert shot Lambe in cold blood, but the King has

429

declared the case closed. The Fifth Monarchists are right to rail against a legal system that lets a prince murder an unarmed man without so much as a reprimand.'

'Hush,' said Thurloe mildly. 'It is not for us to question His Majesty's decisions. Incidentally, Wiseman was right about Eliza. Her real name *was* Alice Fanshaw.'

Chaloner nodded. 'I went to Hatton House this morning, and found the panel that allowed her to disappear in the chapel. It was well hidden, but I took a torch. I am sure there are similar devices in Ferine's home and St Andrew's churchyard. She is just a woman with a passing resemblance to an ancient painting and an ability to scare people out of their wits.'

'Probably. She will not do it again, though – she killed herself in prison last night.'

'That is very convenient,' said Chaloner suspiciously. 'Are you sure?'

'Williamson is,' replied Thurloe flatly. 'He found her body himself.'

The bells of St Dunstan-in-the-West began to ring, a joyous sound announcing Easter Day. They joined the dozens of other peals across the city, although they failed to raise Chaloner's spirits. He felt soiled by the entire affair.

'I was correct in my assessment of the Fifth Monarchists,' said Thurloe eventually. 'There was no rebellion, and my description of them as worms who think they can thresh mountains was apt.'

'I disagree. Most are decent folk who want fair laws and gainful employment. I do not blame them for thinking that the Kingdom of Christ is preferable to what we have now – a society governed by rogues like Buckingham, Rupert and Williamson.'

430

'If they were truly decent, they would not have been contemplating rebellion,' said Thurloe tartly. 'Your "decent folk" have a nasty edge, and perhaps Jones was right to highlight the menace they pose.'

'By having them blamed for sinking HMS *London*, an act of which they were innocent?'

'Nat Strange and Scarface Roberts were not innocent. They carried out the atrocity.'

'But Jones's list will see housewives, millers, labourers and farmers charged with treason,' argued Chaloner. 'That is grossly unfair.'

'Well, no one will ever see it, so do not concern yourself unduly.'

Chaloner regarded him warily. 'You seem very sure.'

'I am sure. One of my old spies was charged with searching Jones's house, and that particular document is currently in my chambers. I shall work on it later, and substitute Fifth Monarchy names with some of London's nastier felons. That will keep Williamson busy and purge our streets at the same time.'

'Lord!' muttered Chaloner. 'Do you think it will work?'

Thurloe nodded, and moved to another subject. 'I cannot say I am sorry Jones is dead. So many people died on his account, just because he wanted to bring about a "perfect" society on his terms – one where we would have been inundated with his own lunatic discourses.'

'His egotistical machinations caused the deaths of three hundred sailors, Strange, Quelch, Snowflake, Scarface Roberts, Manning, half the Sanhedrin, Atkinson, Ursula, Sherwin . . .'

'Actually, Wiseman says Sherwin died of natural causes, if a pickled liver can be deemed natural. He just slipped

431

away over his ale, and it was unfortunate that you happened to be the one to discover his body.'

The bells stopped for the ringers to catch their breath, and instead came the sound of Thurloe's fellow benchers singing hymns in Lincoln's Inn's chapel. They bellowed gustily about the Resurrection, and Chaloner's thoughts returned again to the Fifth Monarchists.

'I half wish the Last Millennium had come today,' he said. 'It is something of an anticlimax to find everything the same.'

'Religious sentiments, Thomas?' asked Thurloe mildly. 'That is unlike you.'

'Maybe I am just tired of people trying to kill me – Lambe, Eliza, Lawson, Ursula, Atkinson, Scott, Manning, Leving, Rupert—'

'Rupert?' echoed Thurloe, startled. 'I sincerely doubt he would bother with you.'

'He gave me a gun that did not work and sent me off to tackle Atkinson and Ursula alone.'

'Guns are unpredictable, Tom, as you often say yourself. It was unfortunate that his failed to go off when you needed it, but I doubt it was deliberate.'

'Of course it was deliberate! He is a soldier, and should know how to load a gun properly. He wanted me dead because I know about his cannon. If Wiseman had not been on hand, he would have let me drown.'

'But you were laying hold of Ursula and Atkinson for him – two people who were a lot more dangerous than you could ever be.'

'The palace guards would have picked them off – they were sitting ducks on the river. But Rupert hoped I would die in the struggle, too, and thus draw a line under the whole affair.'

'Perhaps you are right – it sounds like his thinking. Clarendon would have been livid, though. Has he reinstated you yet?'

Chaloner nodded unhappily. 'Although people now wonder why I have been so suddenly forgiven, and there is a rumour that I blackmailed him into taking me back.'

Thurloe smiled. 'Such a reputation will do you no harm at White Hall. But the Earl usually finds you some overseas errand once you have been home a week or two, and by the time you return folk will have forgotten all about the Tsar's jewels.'

'Unfortunately, he wants me to stay here this time,' said Chaloner gloomily. 'Which is awkward, as I need not only to avoid Rupert, but some of Hannah's creditors – at least until we have some money to pay them what they are owed.'

'Then I have a solution. One of Cromwell's sons is experiencing some difficulties deep in the Fens, and he is dear to me for his father's sake. You are the only one I trust to help him.'

Chaloner brightened. 'When do I leave?'

Leving was not particularly concerned to find himself in the Tower. He was a useful commodity, and powerful men would soon hire his services again. And if not, he would buy his freedom by producing a register of every Fifth Monarchist in the country.

Of course, it would be bulked up with names that should not be there, like Scott and Chaloner, who had never professed any support for the millenarians. But it would serve them right to be arrested and executed with the rest of them. After all, how dare Scott make off with the secret of Rupert's guns? And how dare Chaloner

433

take the credit for defeating Ursula and Atkinson? He, Leving, had been the one monitoring them, and although he had not guessed they were double-crossing the Spymaster, that was beside the point.

He sipped the excellent claret that Buckingham had sent to sweeten his time in prison, and smiled. The Duke would not allow his faithful servant to languish too long in a dismal cell, and the wine was proof of it.

He walked to the bed and lay down, suddenly weary. He took the wine with him, and had another gulp. It really was very good, and he was aware of a pleasant lethargy creeping over him. He would repay *all* his enemies with that list, and the slate would be wiped clean.

As he lay there, staring at the ceiling, he became aware that his legs felt oddly heavy, and they ached. He tried to turn over, but did not have the strength, What was the matter with him? Was he ill? Then a horrifying thought occurred to him. What if Buckingham did not want to continue their alliance, and had put something in the bottle to bring it to an end? But surely the Duke would not harm a loyal servant? Leving was still wondering as he slipped slowly into death.

Historical Note

It would have been impossible for Charles II to return to his throne in 1660 and expect to be universally accepted. Hence Joseph Williamson, who ran the country's intelligence network, was constantly alert for trouble. And there was plenty of it, particularly in the early years of the Restoration. One such plot occurred in the north in 1663, and caused something of a stir because it involved such a large number of people. Among them were a stockinger named John Atkinson, a Fifth Monarchist named Nathaniel Strange, and Roger Jones, alleged author of an infamous underground pamphlet entitled *Mene Tekel, or the Downfall of Tyranny*.

Prompt action saw the Northern Plot foiled, and many of its perpetrators were arrested. One was William Leving, and Williamson was quick to take advantage of the situation by making him an offer he couldn't refuse. Leving gratefully accepted Williamson's terms, and was allowed to 'escape' to track down and trap those rebels who had managed to evade custody. He travelled to London, where he fell in with Atkinson (who did indeed have a kinsman named Grisley Pate), eventually betraying him to Williamson. There is evidence to suggest that Atkinson was also 'turned' but played false, accepting the traitor's penny with no real intention of harming his Cause.

Leving turned to highway robbery in 1665, but was no better at this than he was at rebellion. He was arrested and taken to York, where he wrote a plaintive letter to Williamson begging for help. Williamson responded by transferring him to Newgate, where it is likely that they brokered another agreement, because he was suddenly sent back to York to testify in the trial of Jones and Atkinson. He was poisoned in his cell before he could do it.

Leving's murder has never been solved. Some historians believe that Atkinson was responsible. Others have highlighted a peculiar relationship between Leving and Buckingham, and suggest that the Duke was the villain, aiming to prevent details of their association from being made public. Either is possible, but unless more evidence comes to light, the mystery will remain.

The Fifth Monarchists saw the execution of Charles I as the first step in ridding Britain of earthly rulers, to clear the way for 'King Jesus'. Needless to say their expectations were dashed when Charles II was crowned, and they staged a rebellion in 1661, known as the Venner Uprising. A number of leaders were executed or arrested, forcing the movement underground, where it limped along for a few more years before sliding into obscurity. It was probably never very large, and Thurloe did indeed describe its members as 'worms who thought they could thresh mountains'. It was largely London-based, but its leaders claimed a national following some ten thousand strong.

Active members in the 1660s included Strange, who was a Baptist pastor described by contemporaries as 'a rash and heady person'; a watchmaker named Richard Quelch; Timothy Roberts; Thomas Glasse; Henry Tucker; John Venner; and Sarah Trapnel, a visionary who was imprisoned for her beliefs and writings. She had a sister named Ursula Adman, who was arrested in 1669 for holding Fifth Monarchy meetings in her house. Roberts and Strange died in 1665, and Tucker was executed in 1666. They proposed that the Kingdom of Christ should be ruled by a Sanhedrin (comprising themselves, naturally), and a plot in 1665 really did aim to kill the King, seize the Tower, ignite London, establish a republic and redistribute all private property.

Hatton Garden was the scene of several bloody incidents involving the persecution of Catholics, and a strange legend grew up around Elizabeth Hatton, wife to the nephew of the man who built Hatton House. She was alleged to have been torn to pieces in a place that came to be called Bleeding Heart Alley. As with many such tales, it evolved from an aggregation of incidents and people, including one Alice Fanshaw, who married into the Hatton family and was suspected of making pacts with the devil. Elizabeth died quite peacefully in 1646.

Other incidents in *Murder on High Holborn* have also been taken from actual events. Three men were hanged for stealing five hundred pounds from the treasury in Taunton for the purposes of rebellion, while Buckingham's father did have a sorcerer-physician named Dr Lambe, who was torn to pieces by an angry mob in 1628.

Paul Ferine and John Duncombe were Grooms of the Robes in 1660, but neither held the post for long,

Duncombe leaving after only ten days. Thomas Odowde and Richard Hubbert were courtiers, and both died in 1665. Peter Pett was Commissioner of the Royal Dockyard at Chatham, and was said to be corrupt; Samuel Pepys's diary is full of contemptuous references to him. Richard Wiseman, Surgeon to the King, was appointed Master of the Company of Barber-Surgeons in 1665.

John Scott was one of the seventeenth century's more colourful characters. An inveterate liar and opportunist, he was involved in many schemes to make himself rich, most of which failed. He claimed to have been transported to New Amsterdam for cutting the girdles of Parliamentarian war horses. He returned to England in the 1660s, offering his services as a mapmaker, and styled himself Cartographer Royal; his American wife Dorothea promptly divorced him for desertion.

It was on this visit that he fell into company with Edward Manning, described in reports as 'fat and grave'. Manning had met Edward Sherwin, a disaffected engineer from Prince Rupert's Temple Mills gun factory (where John Browne was a foreman), and the three of them decided to sell the secret of Rupert's cannon to the highest bidder.

We cannot be sure exactly what Rupert had designed, only that it involved 'turning and annealing' iron in such a way as to give it all the advantages of brass. The Prince fancied himself as an inventor, and had already worked on improvements to other weapons, as well as a particular kind of exploding glass – 'Prince Rupert's Drops'. The method of making the guns was kept in strictest secrecy, but they were probably expensive to make and never did make him rich, although he did patent his metal and the process of making artillery with it.

Various shenanigans followed as Scott, Manning and Sherwin flirted with Georges Pellissary, treasurer of the French navy, all trying to cheat and double-cross each other. The upshot was that the French spent a large sum of money to pay for a prototype, but it never materialised and the project fizzled out – although not before Manning and Scott had decided that the gunmetal would do rather nicely for making counterfeit coins.

Manning and Sherwin fade into oblivion at this point, but Scott went on to other adventures. He was the man largely responsible for the arrest of Samuel Pepys in 1679. The accusations were malicious nonsense on Scott's part, and an investigation by Pepys proved it. Scott was never punished for his perfidy, though; he slipped away to the Caribbean where he became Speaker of the Montserrat Assembly and died in 1704.

War with the United Provinces of the Netherlands was officially declared on 22 February 1665. Thus when HMS *London* exploded on 7 March 1665, it was regarded as a significant setback. Pepys wrote in his diary that three hundred people were killed, with only twenty-four surviving the blast.

She had been travelling up the Thames to collect Sir John Lawson (actually a Vice-Admiral rather than an Admiral), who was to take her to join the Channel Fleet, and a number of his relations were on board. The cause of the explosion was unknown, although as a man-of-war, she would have been carrying gunpowder. One theory is that a sailor was careless with a candle. However, she has recently been the subject of a marine excavation, and if she survives the attentions of unscrupulous treasure hunters, perhaps we shall have answers at last.

Lawson was a 'tarpaulin', a man who had grown up

with the sea and knew its ways. He was a lively character, whose rough tongue, low birth and lack of formal education led many to underestimate him. He was not a skilled politician, and recklessly consorted with fanatical sects like Fifth Monarchists. Various strokes of luck in his early career led him to assume that God approved of what he was doing, although his good fortune abandoned him at the Battle of Lowestoft in June 1665. He was wounded in the knee, and died shortly thereafter of gangrene.